Creatures

ON DISPLAY

Creatures

ON DISPLAY

– A NOVEL –

WM. STAGE

FLOPPINFISH PUBLISHING CO. LTD.

SAINT LOUIS

floppinfish
PUBLISHING COMPANY, LTD

Floppinfish Publishing Company Ltd.
Post Office Box 4932
St. Louis, Missouri 63108

Library of Congress Control Number 2014921393

Stage, Wm. [1951-]
Creatures On Display
–fiction
1. United States–Public Health–Sexually Transmitted Disease–HIV/AIDS early cases

ISBN 978-0-692-34807-9

Certain passages in Malloy's punitive essay were taken from "Venereal
Disease and the Great" by A. Dickson Wright, published by
the British Journal of Venereal Diseases, 1971. Wright, in turn, cited
numerous erudite sources.

Printed in the United States of America
Set in Adobe Jenson Pro
First Edition

floppinfish
PUBLISHING COMPANY, LTD

To Rich Knaup, Dean Mason, Karen O' Rourke, Harold Rasmussen, Arnold Ellis, Jack Stubbs, Mark Long, Joe Moore, O.C. Williams, and the other investigators of the St. Louis STD Clinic back in the day, who, like Sisyphus of old, tried like hell to push that boulder up a hill. Some days, it actually budged.

floppinfish
PUBLISHING COMPANY, LTD

CAST OF CHARACTERS

THE CLINIC

Shaun Malloy – Epidemiologist - Public Health Officer
Arnold Redmond – Epidemiologist - Public Health Officer
Betsy Parrish – Epidemiologist - Public Health Officer
Derald "Tut" Tutweiler – Epidemiologist - Public Health Officer
Martha Warrick – Epidemiologist - Public Health Officer
Leo Schuler – Epidemiologist - Public Health Officer
Karl Benda – Epi Supervisor
Joe Sargent – Chief of Epidemiology STD Clinic
Mike Wassermann – Lab Technician
Mohammed Shafi MD – Medical Chief, STD Clinic
Prudence Calder MD – Health Commissioner

MAN 2 MAN CONTINGENT

Bryson "Trey" Vonderhaar III – Entrepreneur and Founder Man 2 Man
Freddie DuCoin – Personal Assistant to Trey Vonderhaar
Brock Silber MD – Private physician
Drew Conger – Sexual mercenary
F. Laughton Dunaway – Legal Counsel to Trey Vonderhaar

THE REST

Mark Walter – Mayoral Aide and ally of Trey Vonderhaar
Sgt. Joe McBride – Beat Cop, Lafayette Square
Teri Kincaid – Bail Bondsman, Malloy's best friend
Timothy "Timba" Clarkson – Parking Lot Attendant
Sheila Noonan – Malloy's landlord
Darius - Homeless newspaper seller
Urban Lehrer – Investigative reporter

Creatures

ON DISPLAY

INTRODUCTION

THE EARLY 1980S was an experiment in pushing limits, a time when the most outrageous behavior was almost commonplace, a time when virtually every one under thirty-five seemed to be asking—demanding—where's mine?

To be sure, it was a time quite unlike today, where technology plays huge in daily activities. There were no cell phones—smart or dumb—no cable TV, no Facebook, no Internet at all because computers hadn't been introduced. There were no Big Brother electronic eyes at major intersections, doling out $100 tickets, and no GPS devices to guide us to our destinations. People actually worked on their own cars, wrote letters to each other, and loaded cameras with film.

But it was a time of sexual freedom. Not since the final days of the Roman Empire had there been such licentiousness. The Stonewall Riots of 1969 emboldened gays to point their erections every which way, while straights on the make had the pill, the ace in the hole of sexual liberation. Herpes, chlamydia and a few other "minor STDs" were around, but weren't commonly considered, weren't a factor in the one-night stand equation. The social revolutions of the sixties freed young people from silly agonizing over the morality of sleeping around. So they slept around. A lot.

Epidemiology, the cornerstone of public health, was done largely the way it had been done since the late nineteenth century. In the field of venereology, the procedure was to interview the positives for gonorrhea and syphilis, elicit names of sexual contacts, round up those contacts, get them tested and treated, interview those positives and start the whole thing over again. The STD epidemiologist was nothing less than a medical detective, knocking on doors, canvassing tenements, bath houses, taverns. Asking questions, expecting to be lied to. Patience and perseverance were their greatest attributes; assertiveness was not far behind. Still, one had to think on one's feet and those feet had better be pointed in the right direction.

It was a job like no other. And it wasn't so much the job that they liked, these intrepid soldiers on the front lines of public health, it was *the work*.

OCTOBER, 1981

AT A QUARTER to eight on a warm Tuesday evening, two men walked in to a smut store in downtown St. Louis. One was a public health officer, an epidemiologist named Shaun Malloy. The other was Malloy's reluctant accomplice. A pale and nervous young man, Paul Brand had recently been diagnosed with a case of primary syphilis. Since the only contacts Brand could name were anonymous patrons of the smut stores he frequented, Malloy told him in no uncertain terms that they would have to visit these locations where he, Brand, would point them out.

"You mean like undercover?" Brand asked.

Malloy regarded Brand's pinched face with its upturned nostrils and a fresh batch of pimples erupting on the left cheek. The kid couldn't have been more than nineteen. "Yeah, a secret mission," he assured. "No one knows that we're together. You point them out, I'll do the rest. How many do you think there are?"

Brand rolled his eyes dramatically. "Maybe three on a good night. Then I'd get bored with it and head for the diner. That kind of thing builds up an appetite."

"That kind of thing" was sex, fast and furtive. Liaisons were made among the racks of books and magazines, though the actual encounters occurred in the boxy confines of movie stalls, dim and unattended. Brand was an active player, that is, he preferred to give rather than receive. He was not averse to anal sex, which is almost certainly how he caught syphilis, but his forté was giving head. In fact, he bragged to Malloy that he was a blowjob artist in demand throughout the city. "They'll be weavin' and wobblin' after I'm done with them," he proudly claimed. Tracking down his many contacts was going to be a full time job for Malloy.

The Peppermint Lounge on Washington was the first place. Malloy had his blood kit tucked away in a small backpack. He would have to find a discreet place to draw blood, that is, if the contact could be talked into giving a blood sample He had done this many times, drawing blood in laundromats, department store restrooms, back seats of cars, and he was damn good at it.

They browsed separately, Malloy looking to Brand each time a new one walked in, the signal being a tug on the earlobe. Brand was not making eye contact with Malloy, making Malloy wonder whether Brand would really deliver when the time came. There were three others present, but none prompting the telling signal.

Malloy found a copy of *Juggs* that wasn't sealed in plastic and he began thumbing through. There were some jugs all right, gazongas the size of party balloons. He was partway into a feature titled "Busty Wilson, Strip Star Mom, and Her Stripper Daughter, Holly" when he heard the clerk call out, "Hey, you with the backpack. You reading or buying? This ain't no library." A minute later, Malloy brushed past Brand and whispered "Follow me."

They went downstairs to the movie booths. The room was illuminated by Christmas tree bulbs, small and multi-colored, giving it a fake, cheery ambiance. The lighting, however, couldn't cloak the smell, the musk of a thousand men with a hint of freshly applied Pine-Sol. There were eight booths in two rows. The booths were spaced about six feet apart, each with operating instructions printed near the curtained walk-in: PUT A QUARTER IN THE SLOT TO WATCH A MOVIE—CLEAN UP AFTER YOURSELF. From a corner booth came the whirring sound of a movie in progress. The sound stopped and they heard muffled dialogue, some movement, jostling per-haps, and then two men emerged. Malloy looked to Brand and saw that he was looking at the floor. The guys shuffled past them, one silent and cir-cumspect, the other snickering about something. Like that, they were gone.

"Well?" said Malloy.

"No, not them." said Brand.

"How do you know? You never even glanced at them."

"I did look, but you were looking, too. You didn't see me look. If it'd been one of them, I would have pulled my earlobe ... I forget, which earlobe am I supposed to pull?"

"It doesn't matter, just let me know." Malloy was flustered. He wished he were a couple miles away, in McDowell's Public House, working on a pint of Guinness. He shook his head at Brand, held out open palms. "Look, I'm sorry. I know this isn't easy for you, but keep in mind you're doing a public service here. Hey, why don't you show me how the encounter works."

Brand merely stared at him, puzzled.

"The connection, the hook-up."

A switch flipped in Brand's stunted brain. "Oh. Well, the way it usually works is one guy will give another 'the eye' and go into a booth. The second guy will follow."

Malloy waited for more. It didn't arrive. "Yeah, then what?" he prompted.

Now it was Brand's turn to be short. "They get it on, what d'you think?"

"Oh, silly me. I was thinking maybe some chit-chat beforehand: 'Hi, I'm Randy. This is my first time so please be gentle.' Something like that."

Brand guffawed. "That might happen, but mostly it's about two guys getting off. They're just using each other. They don't really give a shit about the other one's personal life. Five-ten minutes after they walk in, they walk out and probably never see each other again."

Malloy gazed around, his mouth twisting into a kind of grimace. "Yeah, I can see that Cupid skips over this place."

"Probably so," agreed Brand. Then he fidgeted a bit, like a shy kid at a dance, and said, "Anyone ever tell you that you look like Robert Redford?"

"The Sundance Kid? Yeah, I guess I've heard that."

"Well, it's true," affirmed Brand, "only you're even handsomer—is that a word?" Then he got a look on his face, something approximating a leer. He looked to Malloy, said, "So you want a blowjob? I mean, while we're down here waiting."

That caught Malloy off guard. His first impulse was to cuff the little weasel, but he realized he should've seen it coming. It was to be expected from a guy like Brand, always on the lookout for a quickie. Maybe he should be flattered instead of annoyed.

"I can think of several good reasons why that's a bad idea," he told him, "but the most compelling is that doing something like that would be incredibly unprofessional."

"That's interesting, the main reason you don't want a liplock on your joint is because it'd be unprofessional. Why isn't the number one reason because straight guys frown on sex with other guys? I think you're one of them latents, afraid to admit you're gay or at least bi."

"You're barking up the wrong tree, man."

Brand shrugged; he'd called him out and it felt good. "Whatever. But you don't know what you're missing."

"You'll be missing a few teeth if you don't behave." Malloy wagged his head in amazement. "Besides, you better not be doing that stuff for a while. You might still be contagious."

"What do I care if I give it to someone else. Whoever gave it to me didn't much care, did he?"

Nothing shaking, they walked down Washington past the hat factories and the late night diners to the Downtown Bookstore. As they approached they discussed the plan, which was the same as it had been at the Peppermint. Enter separately, browse far enough apart so as not to seem familiar yet close enough to be able to send a signal when the time came. If a contact happened to be in the place already, Brand would simply leave and wait outside. Malloy would follow a few minutes later and Brand would indicate the contact by describing his features and clothing.

Then they were in, the sex addict and the epidemiologist. Malloy stationed himself between the sex toys and the hetero porn mags. This might take a while, he knew, and he began to peruse the inventory. Like before, the magazines were encased in plastic, but even with the genitals of the men and women obscured by red censor tags, it didn't take much to imagine what was going on.

He migrated to the paperback section at the far wall in the rear of the store. So many suggestive titles, an art in and of itself. He passed up *Young And Hung, Dog Show Girl, Mom's Eager Beavers, Leather Brutes*, and finally settled on *The Cockmaster* by Rod Strong. It was about a guy who was born with an extra-large penis, and because of it winds up in all sorts of predicaments.

Malloy read on—here, at least, the clerk didn't scold the customers— and marveled at the exploits of the Cockmaster. His sexual partners, both men and women, saw it as great sport, bringing him to climax. Jokingly, they compared his erection to a ripe zucchini, a bowling pin, an enormous toadstool. They asked if he could tie it in a knot. They toyed with it, throttled it, talked to it as if it were something apart from the man who owned it.

Before Malloy knew it he found himself with a boner. A sharp-eyed

customer noticed and fell upon him like an owl on a vole. He sidled up to
Malloy, whispered, "Would you like to go downstairs and see a movie?" The
guy was terrible to behold—skinny, shiny, and eager to please.

"What's playing?" inquired Malloy, feigning slight interest.

"I don't know. We could find out."

"Why don't you go ahead and start without me. I want to finish this
book."

The guy lifted one eyebrow, a sign of hope. "Maybe later then?"

"Yeah, much later," said Malloy. "Like 1994."

Malloy saw hurt on the guy's face, his lips quivering. "You don't have to
be mean," he spluttered and turned away.

Malloy scanned the store for Brand and saw him off in a corner by
himself. He seemed a little nervous and Malloy supposed he was, too. This
situation had never been covered in epi school, and he wondered how it
would go down if they did spot a contact. What if he was hostile? Would
he willingly provide his name? Would he allow Malloy to take his blood?

Malloy returned to the Cockmaster. Something sad about the guy, Malloy decided. Sure, he commanded all the sex he wanted, but the pleasure
was hollow. Men and women desired him solely because of his prodigious
member. He moved in a society where everyone took advantage of everyone else and, as a result, his personality was vain and self-centered. The one
woman he had ever loved could not take him full brunt; she complained his
thing stretched her out or gave her a tummy ache. She wound up leaving
him for a guy with an average-sized penis. Understandably, the Cockmaster
felt that Nature had played a cruel joke on him.

Almost an hour had passed and things were at a lull when a strange bird
strolled in. White guy, slacks, sport shirt, glasses, thinning hair, looked like
a young Woody Allen. Malloy knew he was a catch when he went over to
Brand and patted him on the ass. As Woody left Brand to pat someone
else on the ass, Brand looked to Malloy and gave an exaggerated yank of
the ear lobe. Then the guy was at the checkout, talking to the clerk, a hulking black man decked out like a pimp, complete with a bright, red feather
sticking out of the band of his stylin' Homburg. Malloy watched him get
change and walk through a swinging door to the movie booths in the back.
Now Malloy had to decide whether to follow him or wait until he left and
approach him outside.

Impatience won out. Malloy went for it, walking up just as the guy disappeared into a booth. He waited. A minute later the fellow emerged, shaking his head and chuckling at something. He noticed Malloy as he was about to enter a second booth. He winked and thrust his pelvis at Malloy, who took it as an invitation. Malloy took a breath and followed him in.

Before anything else, there was the smell. A commingling of sex, excrement, and amyl nitrate—poppers—assaulted the olfactory. There was a movie in progress: two nude men, slick with oil, were rolling around on a tile floor, getting acquainted. A vixen in Frederick's of Hollywood lingerie stood over them, looking bored, methodically cracking a bullwhip on their bare asses. The cinema's pallid flicker illuminated the patron's face.

All Malloy could manage was "Hi."

"Hello yourself," said Woody, exposing a set of bad teeth. "Uh, I don't have a lot of time. How do you like it?"

He went to stroke Malloy's cheek and Malloy drew back. "I don't like it any which way," he asserted firmly. "I'm here to tell you that you've been exposed to an infectious disease."

"What! Who the hell are you?"

Oops. Malloy realized that he'd forgotten to show his credentials. He unzipped his jacket and brandished his CDC-issued picture ID fastened to a lanyard around his neck. "Shaun Malloy, VD Control," he said matter-of-factly. The guy recoiled as if stung by a hornet. Later, when Malloy looked back on this, it was easy to see where he went wrong. That line, stolen from *Dragnet*, was too intimidating. Coming on like Joe Friday only caused paranoia; the guy must have thought Malloy was going to take him downtown and book him.

Woody stepped back, as far as he could in the cramped space, then kicked the plywood wall with all his might. "I can't believe this," he seethed. "I can't fucking believe you have the nerve to follow me in here and accuse me of carrying a disease. What makes you think I've got something anyway?"

"Just calm down," Malloy tried in a soothing tone. "There's been an outbreak of syphilis in this bookstore. You've been identified as a person who's been in contact with someone who has the disease. And let me tell you, it's very serious. It can cause paralysis, mental degradation, and even death. At the very least I'll need your name and a blood sample." Malloy patted his backpack. "I've got the blood kit right here with me and, yes, it is necessary."

"Necessary? Hah! What you're doing isn't even legal!" He shoved past

Malloy and stormed out.

When Malloy got back on the floor he saw Woody at the counter, talking loudly and indignantly to the big man at the register. "Health Department's here. Did you know that? This guy here"—indicating Malloy as he walked up—"this guy here comes into my booth claiming I've got some disease, wants to take my blood like some vampire!"

Big Man regarded Malloy with contempt. "That right?"

"It's true," Malloy affirmed. "I'm with City Health—Intervention Services—and your customer here has been fingered as someone who's been exposed to a serious disease."

"*Shee-it!*" Big Man roared like a bull moose, rounding the counter and advancing with clenched fists. Malloy's ticker palpitated as the goon loomed over him, shouting in his face like a drill instructor. "You don' know who he is and I don' know who the fuck you is, but you come in my store with some shit like this, you talk to me first." He stooped down so he was eyeball to eyeball with Malloy. Then, low and menacing, "Got that, motherfucker?"

Malloy could smell the fried chicken on the man's breath and it reminded him of Fat's Chicken Shack back home, in Kokomo. "I don't answer to motherfucker," he told him calmly. "Name's Shaun, and yeah, you're right, I should have run this by you. Next time, promise." He looked around the store for Brand, who apparently had flown the coop. Not only that, but at this very moment Woody was heading for the door.

Malloy sidestepped Big Man and went after him, but Big Man grabbed his jacket, held him fast. "Whoa, you ain't goin' nowhere 'til you show some credentials. I wants to know who you is."

Without a tussle, Big Man took the ID card, still around Malloy's neck. He scrutinized it thoroughly, reading aloud the issuing authority in a tone of skepticism. He made a big deal out of comparing the picture of the person on the laminated card to the man standing before him. Finished, he dropped it back onto Malloy's chest. By now it was too late to catch Brand's contact, all that waiting for nothing.

Now it was Malloy's turn to froth. "This is serious, interfering with the duties of a health officer. That guy may pose a legitimate threat to the community and you just let him escape. The health commissioner won't like this—no, not at all."

Big Man snorted derisively.

"Go ahead, laugh," said Malloy, "but we know exactly what goes on in here. Disease. What kinds and how much. You don't think we could shut this place down? It's already been discussed, brother. I report to my supervisor, he speaks to the health commissioner who makes a recommendation to Chief Kinealy who in turn tells the vice squad to pay you a little visit, and before you can spit it's over. The place is boarded up and suddenly you've got bail to make, possibly a court battle after that. Think about it. Is one customer worth all that? I know he's a regular here. If I were you I'd tell me right now where I can find him."

Big Man seemed unimpressed with Malloy's speech. "Don't nobody threaten me in my own store. You do what you want, but there's the door. Don't come back."

Malloy, exasperated, started to leave, but then turned and tried one final tack. "Pretty please?"

Big Man looked him square in the eye for what seemed like a minute. "Try the Oasis on Broadway and Market," he said at last.

Malloy went straight to the place, a nightclub, and found Woody there bussing tables. Seeing Malloy negotiate his way around tables like a skier on a slalom course, the busboy dropped his towel and started to bolt. But Malloy was quick, cutting him off as he made for the exit. Malloy lunged, caught him by the back of his collar, spun him round, and said, "Now, where were we?"

Woody's eyes went wide with terror. For a moment he struggled in Malloy's grip, then he gulped, blinked, and yelled, "*Help!*"

Joe Sargent had just finished watching *Magnum P.I.* It was a good one with Tom Selleck chasing a criminal into a volcano—a dormant one, of course. Still, it was dark in that volcano and the bad guy actually had the drop on old Magnum, but his shot missed and Magnum saw his chance. They threw punches for at least a minute until Magnum clocked him with a roundhouse. Now the stolen jewels would be returned. End of story. Even though Magnum amused Joe with his wisecracks, he liked *Hawaii Five-O* better and wished it were still on the air. Steve McGarrett was the bomb.

Joe went into the kitchen and made himself a bowl of saltine crackers with warmed up milk. His ulcer. He did this every night before bed to soothe the fiery beast, and it worked pretty well. It was a bitch having an ulcer. He was chewing contentedly when the phone rang.

He answered the phone at home in the same business-like way he did at work: "Joe Sargent here." Pronouncing it Sar-*gent*.

The voice on the other end seemed tentative, unsure. "Uh, yes, this is Cal Portnoy, manager at the Oasis? We're a club downtown. Yeah, I'm sorry to bother you like this, but we got a man here claims he's an epidermist ..."

Joe heard Malloy in the background. "Epidemiologist! A VD investigator—get it straight!"

"Yeah," said Portnoy, "and even though he's got some ID, you can't be too sure. There's a lot of fakes going around, you know? Anyway, he said give you a call, that you're his boss and you'd vouch for him."

"Why are you calling to begin with?" asked Joe. "What's he done that you need to call me at home on a week night?"

"Oh. It's preposterous. He barged in here and attacked one of our employees and now he's saying this employee has a disease ..."

Again, Malloy piped up, apparently shouting so Joe could hear. "*Exposed*. I said exposed to a disease, that's all."

The manager continued. "Now he wants this employee's blood, good Lord! He's got like a, well, it looks like a shaving kit that you buy at Famous-Barr—black, folding flaps on top, a bunch of syringes inside."

"Right, that's a blood kit, and the man holding it is Shaun Malloy, a trained epidemiologist, a public health officer. And yes, he's on the job. I sent him down there to investigate a case of ... sorry, I can't divulge the exact nature of the disease, but it's rampant and nearly out of control and I need you to give him all the cooperation in your power. For now, we'll need this employee's name, address, and like Mr. Malloy said, a blood sample."

"Maybe I should phone the police," the manager said somewhat dubiously.

"That's up to you," said Joe, "but you probably have a crowd about now and you certainly don't want them wondering what the police are doing in your place. If I were you I'd just provide the two of them with a private area that has a table and let Mr. Malloy do his work. It'll take a few minutes and then he'll be out of your hair."

"I don't know ..."

"Meantime, could you put him on?"

The club manager gave the phone to Malloy. "Keep it short."

"Hey Joe, what's shakin'?"

"Listen, Shaun, you tell this guy that he needs to come to the clinic tomorrow, and that if he fails to show we know where to find him. And any bloods you have from tonight? Get them to your place and in the fridge pronto. I'll see you in the morning."

"Yeah, Joe, it's a date."

"And no stopping off at the bar, hear?"

"What're you, a mind reader?"

Joe Sargent went back to his ulcer treatment. The saltines had spent too long in the warm milk, becoming soggy. He took a spoonful anyway, not really liking it. Suddenly, the thought of Shaun Malloy chasing syphilitics on a nice evening in downtown St. Louis wormed its way into his skull. That guy is all right, he thought, grudgingly. For a Yankee.

TWO

SHAUN MALLOY WALKED INTO WORK around nine-thirty. Those who worked evenings got to come in late. Walking up, he took in the Missouri Theater Building at 634 North Grand, a solid, traditional ten-story edifice in Midtown, built with American know-how just after World War One. As a transplant to St. Louis, he appreciated the location of his office, in the cultural heart of the city. Next door, to the north, Powell Symphony Hall; to the opposite direction, The Fox Theater, built in 1929, and once the jewel of St. Louis but now shuttered and forlorn. Another block to the south, a Woolworth's, and on that same corner, an imposing erection, a bone-white art deco skyscraper, the Continental Life Building, a.k.a. the Superman Building, because it looked like the one George Reeves launched himself from at the beginning of every episode. It, too, was vacant. A little beyond that, across busy Lindell Boulevard, was the main campus of Saint Louis University.

Except for a few private physicians, the suites and floors of the Missouri Theater Building were devoted to health department business. The City Laboratory was on the ground floor; TB was on the fifth; Immunization was on the fourth; Environmental Health including Lead Control on the third. The STD Clinic occupied all of the second. Malloy chose the stairs over the elevator.

He popped his head into the waiting room to see how busy they were. It looked like a classroom with chairs lined up in rows front to back, public service posters on the walls, an American flag depending from a wooden standard in the corner. Capacity was sixty; right now there were maybe twenty and they were a lively bunch, chatting, laughing, like being here was all a big joke. Which, to some, it was. As usual, Malloy walked over to the check-in station and said hello to Danielle, the first person to see the visitors as they made the transition from citizen to patient.

She was framed in an open window, face down, involved with some form. He rapped on the side of her perch. "Hey there, good morning."

She looked up, smiled. "The verdict's still out on that."

"Just rattling your cage. Nice crowd you got here. Anything interesting?"

Danielle would know. She did the preliminary intake, handing out the six-by-nine cards for patients to complete prior to seeing a clinician.

"I don't know about interesting," she said, "but this one's worth a chuckle." She picked through the stack and found the one she wanted. On the form to be filled out ONE SIDE ONLY were several boxed-off areas; one of them said REASON WHY YOU ARE HERE. In the box was written "privacy hurts".

"I'll bet it does," said Malloy. "Throbbing, tingling, burning."

"Like ouch," said Danielle.

There were three sections to the L-shaped STD clinic: clerical, also known as "the henhouse," on the other side of the waiting room behind Danielle; clinical, down at the end of the south hall, the entrance accessed from the waiting room; and epi or investigative, which was down at the end of the longer east hall. The interview rooms and offices of epi supervisor, Karl Benda, and chief of epidemiology, Joe Sargent, were spaced on both sides of the hallway. Malloy headed to the epi room, hoping that Karl or Joe wouldn't have their doors open so that he wouldn't be hailed and asked to recount the events of the previous evening. Later.

Malloy walked in the epi room, an open space with desks, said hello to any or all. Arnold looked up, grinned, helloed back. Betsy, on the phone, signaled hello. Tut, busy stringing paper clips together, grunted something unintelligible. The rest were either in the field or doing interviews. The way it worked, the investigators were expected to stay in the clinic half a day, answering random calls from a concerned public, following up on contacts who said they'd already been treated or promised to get treated, writing up field activity, and interviewing patients seen that day who turned up infected with gonorrhea or syphilis. The other half of the day, and it alternated between morning and afternoon, was spent out in the field, driving around in their own cars all over the city, knocking on doors, seeking contacts in their neighborhoods and hangouts. There were eight investigators, and it was a rule that at least half of them be in the clinic at any given time. Malloy cherished his field time.

Just as he pulled his chair up to his desk, the intercom beckoned: "There's a call on twenty-six for an investigator."

He punched the blinking button. "Malloy here, may I help you?"

"Are you a doctor?" said a hopeful voice.

"No ma'am, just an expert on venereal disease. What can I do for you?"

"Well, it's probably nothing," she began haltingly, "but I got some new teeth and I went down on somebody last night."

"You got new teeth and you went down. What's the connection?"

"I got sores all over my mouth today. I want to know whether it's from giving a BJ or if it's from the new teeth."

He launched into a ready explanation, "Okay, it's not gonorrhea. That doesn't cause sores. It's not syphilis since that takes longer than a day to develop symptoms. Might be herpes, who knows? Why don't you come into our clinic and we'll check you out at no cost. Then at least you can rule out a venereal problem."

"Oh, I could never do that," her tone changing abruptly. "I'd be too embarrassed. All those people would know why I'm there."

"Lady, all those people are here for the same reason as you. This is 1981. There's no longer any shame about having VD. It happens to the nicest people. We get people from all walks of life—pimps and preachers, hodcarriers, secretaries, teachers. Even celebrities." Malloy was referring to Terry Fallon, lead singer for Wet Kiss, a band which had had several hits on the pop charts years ago. Fallon was now living off his laurels by being a notorious rake about town and a regular at the clinic, not wanting to spend his hoarded royalties on private physicians.

"That may be true," she said, "but even so I could never. I might see somebody I know."

"Suit yourself, ma'am. I hope your mouth heals up."

Malloy looked across his desk to Arnold Redmond, sitting seven feet away. They had started work on the same day three years ago, and their desks had butted up, facing each other, ever since. Arnold looked a lot like Cassius Clay before he became Mohammed Ali.

"Some of the calls we get," said Malloy, pretending to pull his hair out.

"People want diagnoses over the phone, they want medication brought to their houses. They call to report suspicious lesions on family members, even neighbors."

"Pets, too," added Arnold. "'Is that a syphilitic chancre on my bowser or is it mange?' Give me a break. Now everyone wants to know about herpes. It's the disease *du jour.* 'Are you sure there's no cure? I heard about some kind of ointment they're giving in Canada.' Thank god we don't do epidemiology on that."

"Remember when Donahue had that STD guy on, researcher from Johns Hopkins, said we're entering a scary new era of venereal disease? Lethal forms, impervious to treatment."

"What I remember about that," said Arnold, "is we were flooded with calls for the next week."

"That's just it. Every pronouncement on venereal disease, legitimate or bogus, believable or not, funnels through this office."

"Fruit loops," Arnold concluded. "How'd it go last night?"

"Well, my dedication to the job almost got me punched out by a cashier-bouncer in a dirty bookstore. King Kong in a Superfly get-up. The guy let my contact escape but I caught up with him, took his blood in a nightclub. Sometimes I wonder who's crazier, me or some of these nutjobs I'm after."

"They screw and we pursue," offered Arnold.

"Hey, I like that. But what they don't know is that I'll do almost anything to bring them in, see that they get their meds."

"Right on," said Arnold. "You're like one of those Canadian Mounties, always get your man. Or at least you give it a damn good try."

"That's me," said Malloy with a mock salute. "Dudley Do-Right at your service."

Karl Benda walked in the epi room. He was snappily dressed as usual. Pleated khakis and wingtips, perfect break at the cuffs, blue pinstripe button-down collar, forest green vest with yellow paisley tie. "Attention please. I just gave my Toastmasters general-ed spiel to two positives, both GC, both guys, and they're in the conference room, waiting for their one-on-one. Who's up?"

GC was the abbreviation for gonorrhea as in *gonococci,* the causative agent. Betsy, still on a call, held up an index finger: give me a minute here. Arnold volunteered to take one and Malloy the other.

Karl looked over at Tut, intently twirling a No. 2 pencil. "Tutweiler, when's the last time you did an interview?"

Tut started to answer and it came out as hemming and hawing.

Benda cocked his head, cupped his hand behind an ear. "What's that you say? You can't recall? Well, now is the perfect time to brush up on your interview technique. Get in there, sir. Educate, motivate, elicit contacts. That's the name of the game. So, Tutweiler and Malloy it is. Grab your forms, notepads, and writing tools, and off you go."

"The clap you have today could have belonged to practically anyone at some time or another. Lee Harvey Oswald or Raquel Welch may have had it. Once upon a time, it may have belonged to Jesse James. Going further back, it may have come from Napoleon or Cleopatra or even old Adam himself. This nasty germ inside you is there because you screwed somebody who had it in their body. Up until now this germ has never been stopped. It's passed through hundreds of thousands of people only to end up in your body and today we knocked it out with antibiotics. Listen carefully, you can hear the death cries of those last remaining germs."

This was what Malloy told the OP—original patient—a grizzled character sitting before him in the interview room. He took Malloy seriously and cocked his head downward, eyes closed, concentrating. Seconds passed and he looked up, disappointed. "I don't hear nothin'," he said.

Malloy sized him up. White guy, mid-sixties maybe, tufts of fine hair sprouting from his ears, a nose too big for his face, and watery blue eyes set deep in their sockets. He definitely had not aged gracefully. He mentioned that he had lived in Arkansas most of his life and had moved to St. Louis only a few years back. He had a pickup truck and he advertised for light hauling and tree removal. Even before he began his contact elicitation, Malloy sensed that this guy was going to tell him a prostitute story. His precognition was in fine form this day.

"You're not gonna believe this," the patient drawled, "but I picked this up on the Stroll the other day."

"You're right," Malloy shot back. "I don't believe it. You're only the third guy today who's told me that bullshit story. You think I'm that gullible? C'mon, you can do better than that."

The old guy seemed offended. He insisted it wasn't a story, but the truth.

Malloy looked the geezer in his rheumy eyes, a mistake, since it caused his own eyes to water. "I'll need a detailed description of her then."

The OP got a wistful look, probably reliving the wonderful time with his paramour-for-hire. "She was purty as a speckled pup," he said, dreamily.

"Oh, well, that's going to help me find her. C'mon, man, I need a name and a physical description."

Every bit of information attained was like prying rusty nails from a board, but finally Malloy had a workable description. Name: Brenda. Caucasian, 22 to 26 years of age, approximately five foot six, pudgy, stringy blond hair with dark roots, the name "Ricky" tattooed on her right butt cheek (but you had to pay $20 to see that). Stands at Newstead and Olive, not far from the health department, an intersection considered by local boulevardiers as *The* Most Likely Place To Find Trouble. She flagged him down, he stopped, they negotiated, and then went to a nearby house to do their thing.

By this time Malloy half-believed the old man, but she wasn't the only one.

"All right, that wasn't so hard, was it? Now, who else?"

"No one, she was it."

"Untrue," snapped Malloy. "That wasn't a chance encounter. You were there looking to get laid. You knew where to go because you'd been there before. You called it the Stroll, and only johns like you call it the Stroll. So c'mon, there was Brenda and before her?"

"Nope. There mighta been Brenda twice, two different times, but the others on that corner? Black girls." He shuddered. "Not my thing, nosirree."

Malloy continued to press him for another ten minutes until they were ready to wring each other's necks. The guy was steadfast in his story and Malloy had to be content with one contact, Brenda Unk—surname un-known—that he would probably never find. In parting, he opened a drawer on his side of the table, pulled out some condoms and gave the guy a batch. "You know what to do with these," he said. "Use one every time and you won't be back here."

The old man grinned, for the first time loosening up. "One? Hell, I'll be double-wrappin' it. This clap is just the worst! I don't know what stings more, that feelin' when you piss or the shot I just got to cure the dang thing."

THREE

TELEPHONE POLES SNAPPED LIKE TOOTHPICKS. That's a cliché, the "snapped like toothpicks" part, but sometimes the phrase has become clichéd simply because there's no better simile. Snapped like hockey sticks doesn't really work and neither does snapped like celery stalks. Why were the telephone poles on I-65 South through central Indiana, down to Indianapolis and then to Terre Haute and beyond, snapped like toothpicks? From the accumulated weight of ice on the lines. The precipitate had fallen as rain and almost immediately turned to ice or near-ice, which stuck to the lines and as more icy rain fell it, too, stuck to the lines until such mass formed that it strained the otherwise sturdy poles, causing their spars to, well, snap. It had to be pretty unusual because Malloy had done a lot of driving in all kinds of weather and he had never seen this.

He had left Kokomo for St. Louis on this Easter Sunday, 1978, during a terrible ice storm that had cars slipping and sliding all over the interstate. And if you did make it through the sinister patches of black ice there was the real possibility you would run out of gas, for three out of four service stations were closed because of the weather.

He had been hired by the Centers for Disease Control, a job that he would start tomorrow. Until a few days ago he had been driving an ambulance in Kokomo, a job that was interesting and fun while he was an Army medic in Germany but not fun at all driving for a private ambulance outfit. Too many pissant rules, felt like he was walking on eggshells.

He'd seen the flier on the bulletin board at a hospital, calling for recruitment of public health officers to work in various health departments all over the country. The qualifications were not daunting. A clean record validated by the local police department and a college degree in virtually any discipline. Malloy had it covered. His felony for assault and battery at age seventeen had been expunged under the Youthful Offender Act. And he had a bachelor's degree, major in anthropology, from IU-Bloomington, thanks to the GI Bill. The initial interview had taken place in a state office building in Indianapolis. He made it past that and a month later he was called to Chicago for a second interview at CDC's regional office. He left that interview with a pat on the back and the promise that they would call him with an answer in a few weeks and, if he was on board, he would then learn the location of his first assignment. He knew it would be a large metro area and he had fun imaging where he might land. New Orleans or

San Francisco or Seattle, he hoped. He definitely did not want the East Coast; too crowded, and he found the accents annoying. A Midwestern city never entered his mind. The call came on a weekday morning as he was rushing out the door.

"St. Louis," he repeated to the human resources suit on the other end of the line, sitting in an office cubicle in Atlanta. "Great! I've never been there, but I like their beer."

What an astounding transition from Kokomo to St. Louis, two cities only 325 miles apart but, oh, what a difference that distance made. It was a sad reality that Kokomo held no decent jobs for anyone with more than an associate degree, had no night life to speak of, and seemed to sap the drive out of people. Leaving Kokomo was nothing less than an emancipation from the stodgy, narrow-minded Evangelical culture prevalent in north-central Indiana.

There was so much to like about St. Louis. The architecture, for one. Large, stately, lavishly-ornamented buildings, which knocked him out at first sight, and everything built of brick, red brick, which he found quite attractive. Second, the place was old, and he liked old even when the plaster in his $200-a-month apartment fell into his bowl of cereal. Also, there were taverns on every corner and he was doing his best to try them all.

Another big plus was the police presence. In Kokomo, you could not so much as ride around with your pals, cruising the hamburger joints, having a few brewskis, without getting pulled over and manhandled by John Law. Conversely, to be stopped in St. Louis, one would need to be speeding the wrong way down a one-way street, tossing empties out the window, brandishing a handgun and taking pot shots at lawn ornaments. So there it was. The police in St. Louis had much bigger fish to fry.

But he had to get there first. For twelve hours that Easter Sunday it was touch-and-go, driving by feel, never knowing if he would see the famous Gateway Arch looming on the horizon or become stranded in Skunk Holler, Illinois. Here and there he witnessed poor slobs slogging out of culverts, their cars out of commission, yet no help could he offer. His little Datsun B210 was jam-packed with all that he owned. There wasn't an inch of room for a rider. Included in that jumbled mix was The List.

He had started it six years before, when he was twenty-one, and it was pretty straightforward as lists go, just the name, location and time of the sex act. A typical entry might read: "Lydia Borowitz, Gun Lake, Summer

1975." Sometimes it was a one-nighter and he couldn't recall the name, e.g. "Nurse from Kansas City, Hotel Boulderado, Fall, 1976." With prostitutes he'd had during his tour in Germany, it was even sketchier: "Gap-toothed brunette in Innsbruck while en route to 'religious retreat' at Garmisch, January 1972." If he'd had a break with a lover, he would duly note that: "Sue Brandhorst, all over Kokomo and surrounding areas, 1973-74, and again at Larry's cottage, Summer, 1975."

He did not rate them on sexual performance. He did not put stars next to their names to indicate favorites. He did not draw little frown faces beside their names to indicate that he wished he'd stayed away. Although Pam, who gave him the clap in college, he did place an exclamation point next to her. No, he never thought of his list as an exercise in egotism or a record of sexual conquests, or at least that's what he told himself. He simply wanted to remember these lovers, and sometimes all that's needed is a name to prompt the memory in full. With only a name, it can all come back in detail, the sensory experience of sex. The fumbling with the brassiere, the electric excitement of first seeing her in the buff, the awkward pre-coital fondling of the genitals, the sight of breasts jouncing as you pound her on the edge of the bed, drool running down her chin, even her words intimately whispered during the height of passion: "God, I can't believe you already came!"

Frankly, Malloy's list was rather paltry as of that Easter Sunday, consisting of less than fifteen names, going back to the very first entry, that of his high school sweetheart: "Mary Pat Ryan, Founder's Cemetery, high school graduation night, June, 1969." He did not know it yet, but his new home would become a carnal boomtown, a city as rife with romantic possibility as Paris. For, once he got settled in and was able to get out and explore, he noticed something that gave him a charge. Pretty girls everywhere he looked. They dressed nicely and carried themselves well and, if that weren't enough, they were friendly. Which was not to say promiscuous, like they'd put out on the first date. Second date, maybe; first date, no. Over time, the entries on The List would increase prodigiously, many of them one-timers, sampled like so many cheeses on a platter.

FOUR

MONDAY MORNING nine o'clock sharp the entire epi section had to be present in the conference room for Chalk Talk, a congress wherein each investigator would present some particularly challenging case and the others would chime in. Group problem-solving. Standing before a large green chalkboard, the investigator would lay out the case, detailing actions taken, obstacles encountered, and the game plan as it stood. Game plan was right, for the convoluted diagrams produced on that chalkboard—lines with arrows pointing to circles containing code letters and numbers, everything intertwined—bore a strong resemblance to certain plays that a football coach might propose to his players.

Like any specialized discipline, STD epidemiology has its codes. To use a solar system analogy, the original patient (OP) is the sun. His contacts are solar flares shooting out from the sun; contacts are high priority.

Beyond contacts there are suspects (S) and associates (A). Only infected persons may name suspects, whereas uninfected persons may name associates. Suspects might be considered as planets in this solar system, although they could become suns.

Associates are as moons around the planets, perhaps someone the investigator believes is a contact to the OP. A roommate or someone from the social circle, but a person the OP has not actually named. In that instance the investigator named the associate, but associates are also named by persons tangential to the case. For example, syphilis patient Roland (OP) names Tristan as a contact. Tristan comes in for testing, is negative for syphilis but is treated anyway. Upon interview, Tristan names Hermione (A) as a possible sex partner to Roland. Now the investigator must follow up with Hermione as well.

Gays, in additon to any other ciphers, had their own peculiar designation: C4. In the epidemiology universe, C4s are comets and meteors that suddenly, fleetingly light up the night sky, leaving onlookers to ponder the capriciousness of the cosmos.

The meeting got underway as soon as Joe Sargent walked in with his coffee and donuts and legal pad for taking notes. Joe was a big man with a hair-trigger temper—large and in charge, the inside joke—liable to go off on some investigator for the smallest failing.

Joe and Karl Benda, both CDC lifers, ran the epi section. The company commander and his colonel. Of the eight investigators, four were City of St.

Louis hires, one was a state worker, and three—Leo Schuler, Pam Grady, and Shaun Malloy—were entry level CDC Health Program Reps. This was the arrangement in virtually every metro health department, professionally-trained personnel "on loan" from CDC, overseeing every relevant aspect of epidemiologic activity and channeling reports to higher authorities. And CDC, being a national clearinghouse for future top-notch medical detectives, decreed that all recruits except doctors mark time in STD.

If you had good reports, you could expect to move to other divisions that had nothing to do with venereal disease, possibly even land a long-term assignment with a built-in element of adventure. Joe, for instance, had worked in India for two years on the final eradication of cholera. Under this system, all of the CDC hires hailed from somewhere else— Joe from Boaz, Alabama; Karl from Charleston, South Carolina; Leo from Spokane; Pam from Omaha; Shaun from Kokomo—and they could expect to work an assignment from two to four years before they were transferred to somewhere else.

Betsy Parrish, a city employee, went first. She had spent the last two weeks working on the Truck Stop Hooker, a case in which an enterprising woman had set up shop in the parking lot of the Flying J on I-55 South. While her van was rocking and rolling, she had managed to pass gonorrhea to at least thirty-four drivers and counting.

"This was a remarkable case," Betsy told them, "in that no less than seven health departments in three states were involved and the degree of cooperation was laudable. Of course, we haven't been able to locate every contact, it's not like these guys gave out their names and home addresses, but I think we've been able to put a lid on it. For the time being anyway."

"Where is she now, the OP?" asked Karl.

"In the Workhouse," answered Betsy. "Three months for aggravated soliciting." The Medium Security Institution out on Hall Street, also known as the Workhouse, was one of two city jails.

"Have you been out for a Re-I?" wondered Joe.

Betsy consulted her notes. "The last interview with her was, oh, the week before last. She named one more, a semi-regular customer, Buzz, drives for Sooner Freight out of Tulsa."

Karl looked to Joe. "We've forwarded it to the Tulsa HD."

Joe nodded. "Go out there again, see if her memory's improved. Do it this week."

Meanwhile," said Betsy, "we've spoken to the Flying J people as well as others at truck stops in the metro area, apprised them of the situation, and asked that they post signs on the premises warning about the danger of solicitation on the premises. You know, in case other ladies get the same idea. Karl and I are working on the wording."

"How about 'Please Don't Feed the Hookers,'" said Tut, coaxing a few sniggers.

Laird Cantwell, the lone state employee, offered, "'Today's Special: Blue Balls–Twenty Bucks!'"

Said Leo Schuler, "How about we make the pros walk around wearing a sign, like a sandwich board, big letters that say *caveat emptor*." This met with blank or puzzled looks, so Schuler quickly added, "Latin. 'Let the buyer beware.'"

"These truckers don't know Latin," laughed Betsy. "Maybe pig Latin."

Joe cleared his throat so all would hear. "How about we put as much effort into contact elicitation as we do making wisecracks. Good job, Betsy. Who's next?"

Tut raised his hand like a schoolboy who can't wait to be called on.

"Mr. Tutweiler," acknowledged Joe, "you have something to share?"

"Yeah," said Tut, "a woman came in the clinic last week. She had every condition in the book— GC progressed to PID, trich, crabs, yeast, chlamidiya. Probably cooties, too. Know what her name was?"

"Mrs. Tut," Arnold, deadpan.

"No ... Glorious Bunche," said Tut, grinning like a fool.

"A fitting name to be sure," said Karl. "So how did the interview go?"

"Oh, I didn't interview her," said Tut.

"Then why are you presenting this case?"

Tut, still holding that big, dumb grin: "I just thought the name was funny."

"Jesus H. Christ," muttered Joe, shaking his head in dismay. "Okay, who's got something other than a joke? Arnold, what's on your plate these days?"

Arnold got up and went to the chalkboard. He drew a goofy face with jug ears. He pointed to the ears and said, "You can't underestimate the value of being able to hear. I mean, how do you communicate with a contact if he can't hear what you're saying? That was the challenge with Fate McKinley. The OP, a twenty-four-year-old black woman, GC positive, named him as a frequent contact. She had the location of the laundry where he works, she had the make and model of car he drives. She knew his hours, where he goes for lunch.

"But she failed to tell me that he's stone deaf. Okay, so I show up at the laundry. I speak to the manager, explain the situation. Manager points to a tall, slender fellow pressing shirts, puffs of steam rising around him. I approach, tap him on the shoulder: 'Mr. McKinley, may I speak to you for a minute in private?' He puts a finger to one ear and makes a motion, like 'Come again?' I show my ID and repeat the line, a bit louder. He does the same thing. Then I get it, his world is quiet.

"What do I do now? I'm no good at pantomime and I don't know deaf-speak, so I go out to the car and get my notebook. It took a while, the interview. The manager gave us a small room in the back and we sat at a table, me writing notes to him explaining that he'd been exposed to gonorrhea and must be treated. To everything I wrote, he would just nod and smile. I wasn't sure he was even literate. Although, one thing I am now sure of: The deaf can't hear you any better when you raise your voice. So finally, the manager comes back, sees that we're having a problem and offers to help. Turns out that for the benefit of this employee he's learned sign language, basic stuff like 'You need to go to the health department with this man.' So we get back here, I run him through the clinic side and he turns up positive for GC."

"You did the interview how?" asked Joe.

"We called CID, arranged to have a deaf interpreter come by," answered Arnold. CID was the Central Institute for the Deaf, over near Barnes Hospital, one of the oldest such institutions in the country. "I know you're wondering about confidentiality, letting an outsider into the process, but Karl took care of it."

"I made up a form for her to sign," said Karl, "stating she would not disclose any sensitive information elicited from the patient, particularly names and whereabouts of contacts."

"Thinking on your feet," said Joe. "I like that."

"Well, he did name the OP, but no one else," said Arnold. "Actually, he wrote her name down, only the first name, in a barely legible chicken scratch. Seems that if you're totally deaf you never learned how to speak either, not unless you had training at a place like CID."

"Yeah, well, we've got a problem here and I think you all can see it. She's naming only him and he's naming only her. So where did it come from?

There's a third party out there, walking around infected, and I need you to find him. Or her. Arnold, you Re-I the OP and if that doesn't pan out, call that interpreter back and do the deaf guy again. All right, who's next?"

"I guess I am," said Malloy, rising from his chair. He walked to the chalk-board, flipped it over, and there on the obverse was a busy diagram, executed ahead of this meeting. His current case. "Last Friday, at the end of a long day," he began, "I fell into a syphilis case. Around four-twenty Wasserman calls over from the clinic and says, 'Come here, you've gotta see this.' I walk down the hall and he shows me an RPR that was strongly positive for syphilis. He tells me that the RPR was a stroke of luck. The guy came in with dysuria, and the clinician mistakenly ordered an RPR. So they check the guy more thoroughly, and he's just beginning to break out—penile lesions. Okay, so now happy hour is canceled, and I'm preparing to do a full-on interview that takes as long as it takes. We were here until six-thirty. Fortunately, the OP was pretty cooperative and didn't try to BS me."

"So you say," said Joe, always skeptical of the veracity of any OP. Deceitful bastards.

Malloy considered himself a good judge of character and there was every indication that this OP was truly motivated to tell the truth about the activities that led to this infection, being forthcoming as he had been with names and times and places, but he wasn't going to argue with Joe. That would just get him branded as naive and gullible.

Malloy continued. "His name is Randall Hoffman. Thirty-one, single, works at a brokerage downtown. Lives in South City, nice apartment—I've been there. So, how it went down: we adjourn to the conference room—it's after hours, the interview room's too claustrophobic for a lengthy one-on-one. We get comfortable, coffee poured, an ashtray for his cigarettes. I give him the motivational talk, stress confidentiality, show him the pictures in the Green Book. Got my notepad and ER forms laid out, my pen ready to write, and we go to it. Right off he names three contacts in the last three months, professional people like himself.

"One of them is a sort of boyfriend, weekends on occasion, but the other two are chance encounters he met at this house in Lafayette Square. Randall goes there to party, and during the course of this party people head off to certain rooms and get it on. It could be a couple or a group, he says. What's different, if not alarming, about this is that these gatherings are actually arranged for the express purpose of facilitating sexual encounters.

The homeowner and host of these gatherings is a guy named Bryson Vonderhaar III, who apparently runs a social club called Man 2 Man. Randall
says that Vonderhaar places ads in gay-oriented publications around the
country, saying essentially that if you are a discreet gentleman coming
through St. Louis, please feel free to take advantage of his services. Advance notice required. There's also a membership fee, as you would expect
with any private club."

"How much?" wondered Schuler.

"Randall balked at that," said Malloy. "He said it wasn't relevant to his
situation, and I agreed. It's got to be out of your price range, though. No,
seriously, according to Randall, these are well-to-do gays, educated, professional. They likely pay a good deal for the opportunity to mingle with their
own kind."

"Mingle, there's a euphemism," said Betsy. "It's basically a bordello, is
what you're saying."

"Oh, yeah, red lights and all, right in the middle of cultured Lafayette
Square," laughed Malloy. "Okay, probably some law is being broken, but I
think you'd have to show an exchange of money and be able to prove what
that money was intended for."

"Get back to Hoffman," said Joe, impatiently. "What's the quality of
information on the two chance encounters?"

"First names only, decent physical descriptions. One, a 'Carl from Phoe-
nix,' passing through, and the other a 'Jerry from Montreal' also passing
through."

Joe rolled his eyes at this. "What is this, a parlor game? 'Carl from Phoe-
nix,' my ass." He shook his head disgustedly, then asked Malloy what he'd
done so far.

Malloy was ready for this question, for he had done a lot so far and
was proud of himself for having gone the extra mile. "Right, okay, after we
concluded the interview, I had Randall ride with me to Lafayette Square
where he pointed out the house. And it is more than a house, it's a mansion by anyone's definition. It's a three-story Victorian, probably seven or
eight rooms per floor, must be hell to heat. After that, we came back here
for Randall's car. We agreed to meet the following afternoon at his place for
a follow up interview. The next day he was still in the cooperative mode. I
pressed him further and he gave up more names, but they're outside of the
critical period. I initiated them all the same. Then I drove to the boyfriend's

house and informed him of the situation. Jake Fromson, his name, is a paralegal in a downtown law firm. He was concerned and agreed to see his private physician asap. I'll follow up on his diagnosis. Next, late Saturday afternoon, I went to Vonderhaar's with the intention of interviewing him as an associate. I must have banged that big brass knocker for ten minutes and no response. Sunday was a day of rest, but I'll go back today."

Joe nodded approval. "Do we have a place of employment for this Vonderhaar?"

"Oh, I forgot. The OP says he goes by Trey. Get it? Bryson Vonderhaar the Third. Think poker. Three of a kind, treys. But to answer the question, the OP thinks he works at home, something with the stock market."

"Day trader," guessed Joe. "Those guys can do pretty well if they're privy to the nuances of the market, but they've got to be quick on the trigger. Split-second timing is the name of the game." Everyone looked at Joe, somewhat surprised that he knew anything about something as big and mysterious as the stock market.

Martha Warrick, another city hire, broke in. "Shaun, your OP, he's not passing through. He lives here. How did he break into this clique?"

"He says he heard about it at Robusto's, sitting around the bar. It came up in conversation, stories about this fabulous residence in the city where sex is a commodity. Randall was interested and contacted Vonderhaar directly. Sent him a letter of inquiry."

"Something stinks there," said Joe. "He didn't come a-knocking out of the blue. He's got a friend who's already in, someone to vouch for him. A fuck buddy. Find out who it is. Don't let up on this guy because you think he's spilled all there is to spill. You know better than that."

Malloy did know better and he assured Joe that he'd be on the OP like "a fly on shit," knowing that the phrase would prick the ears of his boss who was often heard spouting colorful bumpkinisms.

Not everyone had something worthwhile to present. After two more show-and-tells the meeting was adjourned, and the investigators filed back into the epi room to make phone calls and plan their day. As usual, Joe and Karl remained in the conference room to discuss what they had just heard and, presumably, to evaluate the resourcefulness and dedication their staff demonstrated just now.

Knowing they were being talked about made them slightly paranoid.

Karl was all right, riding herd over them daily, giving helpful advice here and there, and, really, not so different from them, but Joe was another story. They all kept their distance from Joe, a mercurial man prone to spittle-mouthed rants, who, historically, had shown no compunction about firing people for seemingly petty acts of insubordination. Lois Castro, for example. City worker, solid investigator, congenial, came here straight from Mizzou. One day Joe told her he wanted her completed ERs from a current syphilis case on his desk at the end of the day. Instead, she turned it in the following morning, thinking: Hey, a little late, no big deal. Wrong! Fired. Just like that. The thing was—and while they all suspected some of this, none of them knew the full extent of the man's deep-down prejudices—namely, that if you were a minority, a Yankee, a Jew, a Catholic, a liberal, a queer, or a woman who did not find Joe's leering glances utterly charming, then it was points against you. Also, he tended to cut more slack in the discipline department if the offender happened to be a fellow CDC employee.

Most recently, Steven Cox had tested Joe's limits. The former Steven Cox, whose vacant desk in the epi room was a constant reminder to the investigators that they had better keep their wits about them. Cox had lapsed into some variety of mental illness, gone buggy from total immersion in the STD experience, sordid as it was. A fed, Cox was the star investigator, enthused, indefatigable, once forcing his own brand of relentless epidemiology on a close-knit party of homosexuals, all with Teutonic-sounding surnames, and ridding them of a pesky outbreak of syphilis. After it was done, they actually sent him a beautiful floral arrangement, which he kept on his desk until it wilted.

Then he plunged into another major outbreak involving male prostitutes, one that took him deep into Rough Trade culture on both sides of the river and he saw things that curdled his blood. Eventually, his dreams were haunted by all manner of lurid scenes. Like a nefarious maggot, these disturbing images had eaten away at his psyche and one day he simply cracked. As breakdowns go, however, it was rather benign. He started clipping his toenails in the office, doodling enigmatic pictures on steno pads and taping them to the walls. He talked about starting a clinic where everybody, regardless of their malady, would be treated with the all-purpose ointment Unguentine. Got the clap? Unguentine. Syphilis? Unguentine in suppository form. Herpes? Unguentine and aspirin. Joe had warned him several times: "Pull yourself together, man. You're embarrassing yourself."

The last straw came when Cox was overheard telling a young black man that more taffy in his diet would likely prevent another infection of gonorrhea. Fraternal feelings aside, Joe had no choice but to let him go. A month later, the epi section got a postcard from Baton Rouge; Cox had become a clown in a traveling rodeo. Cox's empty desk was also a reminder that the turnover rate was high with no less than 13 investigators come and gone in the last three years. And it was a shame—a shame and a damned nuisance, because the epi section could not afford any drain on manpower. Eight overworked investigators were not nearly enough to even make a dent in the riot of STDs in the city.

Malloy, head down, thumbing through a stack of ERs, felt a tap on his shoulder. It was Karl. "Hey there one-sixteen, now would be a good time to pay that call on Vonderhaar." The investigators had names, of course, but they were also numbers. Malloy supposed this was for the sake of brevity when filling out the never-ending stream of forms. Malloy was 116. Arnold was 118. Betsy was 135 and so on. Karl used names and numbers interchangeably; he was quirky like that.

"I'm in the field this afternoon," said Malloy.

"Not a problem," said Karl. "You can switch with one-thirty-five."

Betsy, hearing the change of plans, said, "I've got a Re-I scheduled over in Dogtown in one hour. This guy is squirrely, I had to practically beg to get him to see me again."

"Fine," said Karl, scanning the room for another option. He fixed on Tut, reading a *Mad* magazine and chuckling softly. "Tutweiler, I believe you have field this morning. You will switch with Malloy. Okay?"

Tut shrugged what the hell. "Sounds good, boss. The people I'm after don't start moving 'til noon anyway."

Karl said to Malloy, "There you go, hotshot. It would be really nice for me, but especially to Joe, if you brought back some tangible results."

FIVE

TEN MINUTES LATER Malloy was heading out the door. In the lobby, just inside the front doors, Franklin and James, the building maintenance guys, were standing around, bullshitting as usual. Seeing Malloy, James lit up. Malloy went through the motions of an elaborate soul shake, what the brothers in his Army unit had called the Dap. "My man!" yelped James, grinning ear to ear. "What it be like? You gon' hunt down some wild poon?" He winked at Franklin.

Malloy understood that these guys saw him as a sort of safari hunter, looking to bag some trophies. The city streets were his jungle, and infected or at-risk humans were his big game. "Tell you the truth, it's a bitch, trying to get a handle on the love disease. It be like bailing out a sinking ship with a teaspoon."

"Yeah, yeah," chimed Franklin, grinning hugely, "tha's right, but you the man to do it. You the king, Malloy. The king!"

"Thanks, guys. Got to go, get my hunting gear." And looking over his shoulder, "Don't work too hard now." The last he heard, they were laughing their asses off.

He went to the parking lot to get his car. The lot was about the size of a football field that ended on the seventy-five-yard line, and situated between the health department and the symphony hall. It held fifty-six vehicles on a good day. In the middle was an aluminum-frame shack, like a prison guard tower without legs. Inside that shack was Timothy Clarkson, better known as Timba, the lord of this domain. With the morning rush, if you could call it that, over by nine and the afternoon activity not starting again until four, Timba had a lot of time on his hands. Other parking lot attendants might have played solitaire. Still others would have brought in one of those battery-operated portable Japanese TVs, watch the soaps all day. Timba enjoyed reading.

Malloy walked up, caught Timba engrossed in a paperback. "What're you reading?"

"*Forty Lashes Less One*," Timba told him.

"Ah, a pirate novel: 'Aye, me bucko, tie that scurvy dog to the mains'l and give him forty lashes—no, make that thirty-nine, one for each mate he's buggered.'"

Timba laughed, and tilted the cover up so Malloy could see it. "Naw, it's a Western, set in Yuma Prison. Two guys facing death, one black, the other

Apache half-breed. They get a pardon if they can bring in five dangerous outlaws. Right now, they're after number two."

"Good stuff, huh?"

"Elmore Leonard, man, he can't write a bad novel. I'm taking my time with this one, savoring it. I don't want it to end."

"I'll remember that name when I finally have time to read."

"Man, you ought to find time. Reading is very therapeutic."

"If that's true then you must be the most grounded dude in St. Louis."

"Hey, if that's a compliment, I'll take it. I guess you want your car?"

Timba went and moved a Camaro so Malloy could get to his Datsun. Malloy thanked him and pressed a dollar into his ham-sized mitt.

"Hey, listen," said Timba from the side of his mouth. "You're a newbie to this place ..."

"Three years," Malloy protested, "that's something."

"Hell," said Timba, "you gotta live here at least twenty years before you call yourself a native."

"You think I'm not St. Louis enough? Try me."

"All right. What is the square beyond compare?"

"Checkerboard Square—Ralston-Purina."

Timba shook his head in disgust. "No, man, it's a slice of Imo's Pizza. Where you been? Next: On what ship did Cooky and the Captain do their thing?"

"I heard of the Captain and Tennille ..."

"Fuck the Captain and Tennille!" spat Timba, whose raw nerve Malloy had apparently struck. "Those two asswipes couldn't even swab the deck of the S.S. Popeye. Every kid in St. Louis couldn't wait to get home from school to watch Cooky and the Captain on the S.S. Popeye."

"How'm I supposed to know that?"

"My point exactly."

"All right, all right," said Malloy, hands up in surrender. "I'll brush up on my local lore. You can try me again in ten years."

"There's no brushing up," corrected Timba, "it seeps in by osmosis, takes a good long time. Now where was I? I was about to say something impor-tant ... oh yeah, if you ever need a favor, something done, something that you yourself can't do alone, something, oh, I dunno, *illegal*, you call on me. I got the resources and the wherewithal. Just sayin', okay?"

"Can you get me a date with Chuck Berry?"

Timba slugged him on the bicep. "Smart ass, you better get in that rice burner of yours and hit the streets. I'd like to see you park that thing in front of the Teamster's Hall, those jokers would do a nice job of decorating."

"If it isn't American, the hell with it. There's an open-minded attitude that'll take us far in the world economy. See ya," called Malloy, driving off.

"Wouldn't wanna be ya," Timba called back.

Malloy had one stop before Vonderhaar, a GC contact on the near Southside. He drove down Vandeventer past the warehouses and vacant storefronts, turned left on Tower Grove and left again on Blaine. A few blocks down he saw the white squad car parked at the curb and a cop walking up to the house where the contact lived. He'd been here twice before, the stench from the interior overwhelming him as he knocked to no result. He'd also left several come-to-the-clinic cards that actually gave her an appointment, and those were ignored. This day he was determined to speak to her in person. Apparently, so was the cop.

Malloy walked up as the cop was still knocking. He stated his purpose and the cop, in turn, told Malloy that he wanted to speak to someone in this household, name of Pennington, regarding the whereabouts of a young man, same surname, who was a suspect in a robbery. Same name as my contact, Malloy offered, probably a brother, cousin, or uncle. The contact, LaShelle, was nineteen; he didn't think she was married.

Just then the door opened and a young woman stepped into the sunlight, squinting. The cop got down to business. Malloy sat on the stoop, giving them some space. He would get his turn before long. He was taking in the local squalor when a utility truck pulled up and parked behind the squad car. A guy emerged wearing a Laclede Gas uniform, tools and other hardware dangling from his belt. He walked up to the porch and actually interrupted the cop, asking was Elsie Pennington there?

The cop and LaShelle just looked at him, like, where did you come from? Finally, the girl said, "No, but I'm her daughter."

"Well, you haven't paid your gas bill in three months. We've left notices on the door, no reply, so I have orders to shut off the gas. Sorry."

"Wait a minute," she cried. "We just paid that bill a few days ago. The check's probably back at your office. Won't you hold off?"

"Sorry," repeated the gasman as he walked around to the back.

The cop wasn't done questioning her about her brother, as it turned out, but before he could pick up where he left off, she noticed Malloy sitting there. "Who the hell're you?" It was a question tinged with contempt.

"Shaun Malloy, ma'am, health department. I'm the one who's been leaving those cards at your door for the past week."

She stood there glaring at him, shooting poison darts his way, and he was glad the law was there. "Oh shit," flippantly, "that ain't nothin' but a mistake. I'll tell you about it when this man through with me."

"That's fine, I'll wait." Malloy sat there enjoying the Indian summer morning. He closed his eyes, pretended he was on a promontory overlooking a sweeping valley with a river below and the trees showing blazing fall colors to infinity. He loved fall in the Midwest and he promised himself he would get out into it. This weekend. He opened his eyes to the same old beat down neighborhood, every house in disrepair, same downtrodden young woman being asked to give up her brother, being told her heat is gone, being told she might be infected. Then it dawned on Malloy, here was the perfect example to give credence to the old saw that poverty, crime and disease are common bedfellows.

SIX

Bryson vonderhaar III felt that familiar twinge of arousal, back in the game, poised as he was to take his profit. Any moment now and he'd call his broker. Sell my position, sell it and cut me a check today! He got filled a little after open on the New York Mercantile. Just a single little oil contract, and if things went right he'd net about seven grand—not bad for a morning's work, if indeed it did happen. Six hours earlier, in the middle of the night, he had watched Standard buy the crude oil market on his home ticker. Standard had bought on the European floor which gave him a five hour advantage. He would ride the wave. A robust upward move would seriously fatten his wallet and the risk was limited. He checked the figures one more time and called Eugene, his lightning bolt of a broker. It was 9:25, shortly after open on NYM.

"Hey Eug, Trey Vonderhaar here. I'm watching crude. What's the noise in the first fifteen minutes?" Yelling into the phone over the roar in the background.

Eugene told him the price at that moment: $29.70. "Okay, I want ten contracts at market, buy stop thirty dollars thirty cents with a sell stop of twenty-nine forty to hold till canceled or touched." Eight minutes later, Eugene called back, telling him he was filled and the money would be deducted from his account plus fees. Typically, Eugene did not compliment or caution his clients' decisions, but today he expressed approval, saying only the signs looked good.

Trey hung up and took another stick of red licorice. He glanced at his charts on the wall, his homework that just might net him a nice gain. Another notch on the bedpost of lucre. His money was smart money. All smart money had stakes in the futures market. It was what made the world spin. Stocks were puny in comparison.

A home ticker had been installed in his third floor office by a fellow trader who was also an electronics wizard. The device gave him delayed quotes on commodities as they moved up or down. The delay was five minutes past real time, and for anyone not actually on the floor that was as good as it got. Right off, the contract started moving his way; tick, tick, tick, the bulls were off and running. He considered calling in an increase but that would go against his system and he never went against his system. That would be gambling and he wasn't some schmuck sitting at the blackjack table; he was the dealer. He was The House. Gamblers had no plan. Gamblers were losers.

The market dropped a few points and he could almost hear the bedlam in the oil-trading pit. He was definitely in suspense, but not seriously nervous about losing money. He had his sell stop order in place. He was protected. Not that he minded getting stopped out with a little loss anyway, happened all the time. Little losses. Playing the market was all about shouldering lots of little losses and then knowing when to grab the occasional huge win. That's what he sensed was happening now.

The market had stalled for a while, but now it began to move again, his contract value ticking upward by fits and starts … thirteen points … fifteen points … oops, back to thirteen, a momentary stumble … then higher and higher to a whopping eighteen-point gain. Again he did the numbers on his calculator. Should he sell now and take close to $5900 profit or hold off, hoping it would continue its trajectory and hit $6500? That would be sweet, but now he was getting the feeling that the commodity would soon lose steam. He had seen it before, the bulls coming out of the gate in a burst of speed only to peter out by the second turn. Maybe he was wrong, but the words of his financier father, Bryson Vonderhaar Jr., would make his mind up nevertheless. Those words were "Get out while the getting's good."

Trey called Eugene. He picked up on the second ring, shouting into the phone, "Yeah?" Trey heard the noise on the floor. It was loud and loud was good.

"Eug, sell my position now!"

"What say?" shouted Eugene over the din.

At that moment, he heard the sound of the doorbell. Whoever it was could just wait. "Eug, you there?" Again, the doorbell rang, this time with an urgency, repeated over and over. "God, that's annoying!" he sputtered as he walked over to the small plastic box on the wall, pressed a button and spoke into it.

"Yes, who is it?"

Outside, Malloy heard the voice but did not see where it was coming from. Then he saw the speaker on the wall beside the door frame. There was one little switch at the bottom and he began jiggling it.

"Don't play with the intercom," the voice said. "Now state your business or go."

"Um, Shaun Malloy, City Health Department. May I speak with you for a minute?" A pause. He wasn't sure if he was being heard.

"You have the wrong residence." The voice sounding nasally and snotty.

"No, it's Bryson Vonderhaar I need to see. He goes by Trey."

"How dreadful. What on earth could you want with him?"

"I can't discuss it with someone I can't see. I'll brief you in person when you come to the door."

"Not now, and probably never," said the voice.

"Listen, this is a serious matter. Your health may be at risk. We need to talk. Now."

"Don't give me that claptrap. My health is perfectly fine, and if there was something wrong I would certainly see my own doctor."

"I can't do the interview this way. Confidentiality, I need to ..."

"Your time is up. Now get off my porch, peon."

Malloy leaned in to the speaker, the better to be heard. "Screw you, man. Who do you think you are?" he said. But it had become a one-way conversation.

Bryson Vonderhaar III returned to his desk, thinking to tell Eugene he needed to get a hearing aid. The phone, still off the cradle, was dead. He looked at the ticker and hit the ceiling. His position had fallen 11 points from its high and was falling some more. Frantically, he redialed Eugene, listening to the distal end ring and ring. Acchhh! The insipid exchange with that idiot had cost him at least three thousand dollars. Damn the cursed luck, and damn the health department.

The following day, a Tuesday, Malloy was back for another shot at Vonderhaar, only this time with Karl in tow. Upon returning to the clinic, he had walked into Karl's office, stood there with one hand on the doorknob, and waited until Karl finished his phone conversation with someone about some misplaced gonorrhea cultures. Finally, Karl hung up and attended to Malloy.

"Well?"

"He refused to come to the door, and then he called me a peon. Through an intercom. Guy's a real douche."

"Asshole at the very least. Tomorrow we'll go over there together."

And so it was, just after ten, they got Karl's Cadillac Seville from the lot, tipped Timba a buck, put the top down, and headed for Lafayette Square. It was a beautiful morning; before calling on Vonderhaar, Karl wanted to drive around the Square. "Just look at these homes," he was saying to Malloy, playing around with the radio. "You don't see beauties like these just anywhere. Look there, that one with the man in the yard, Queen Anne design, and there, two doors down, Italianate."

Malloy looked, nodded comprehension. Sort of. "How do you know this stuff?" he asked.

"Oh, my father was an architect and we made our home in Charleston, a city even older than this one."

"Why do some of them have fences on the roofs?"

"Those are widow's walks," said Karl. "It's more of a New England thing, where supposedly the pining wife would stand looking out to sea, waiting for the return of her sailor husband."

"Widow's walk," repeated Malloy. "Makes perfect sense, a thousand miles from the nearest ocean."

"Architects borrow features from every society and culture," explained Karl. "Look at those carved stone pineapples on the porches, a symbol of hospitality that dates to Columbus's voyages to the New World. You see?"

"Yeah," said Malloy, "it's all one big interchangeable mishmash, but back to the widow's walks for a second. To have a widow you'd have to have a couple. Married, as in husband and wife. I don't see much of that around here."

"Plenty of same-sex couples," agreed Karl. "Lafayette Square as a neighborhood is even more gay than the Central West End. Because of that, it's spurned by the family values crowd—you're not going to see a lot of kids around here—and I think the residents like it that way."

They circumnavigated the park, and Karl stopped at the southeast entrance, in front of a brick building with old-time gas lamps at the entrance. Karl got out to read the plaque on the fence, a series of black, chest-high wrought-iron pickets that spanned the perimeter of the park. "It says this park was established by city ordinance in 1851 and that building was once a police station," he informed.

They drove on and Malloy pointed out Vonderhaar's residence at the southwest corner. "Absolutely gorgeous," lavished Karl. "A true Victorian mansion with a German Baroque exterior, it's got to be the largest house in the Square." Actually, Karl was mistaken. The house was French Second Empire, and that was what attracted financier Bryson Vonderhaar Jr. to it back in 1970 when he bought the colossus for a mere $78,000; with a few improvements, it was now worth triple the purchase price. Karl continued, "You think about back when this park was a destination for Victorian society, back when St. Louis was a premier city, and this house was the most important address on the park. Someone wanted to feel very important living there on the corner, because most of the other homes on the park are townhouses. It's at least a hundred years old, and well-kept it seems. Probably worth a fortune on the market."

"I'm so happy for him," said Malloy.

They parked in front on Missouri Avenue, about as wide as a thoroughfare can be and still be called a street or an avenue. At the curb there was a large stone block, the name Nulsen inscribed on it.

"Stepping stone," said Karl, "for passengers in the carriage. That first step could be a long one."

"An artifact to bang your shins on," said Malloy. "It's part of what makes this place so charming, right?"

"You got it." As they were walking up the long steps to the porch, Karl said, "You see that turret at the front corner above us?"

"Looks like something out of a fairy tale?"

"Yeah," said Karl, "just now I thought I saw a face at the window."

Just as they reached the top, the door opened and a young man stepped out. They stopped. "Hi there," he said with a smile. "May I help you?" Intelligent hazel eyes, close-cropped wavy brown hair, a thick, luxuriant mustache framing a wry half-smile, he looked like Freddie Mercury from the band Queen.

"Do you live here?" asked Karl.

"Not in this big old thing, I'd get lost trying to find the broom closet. I live in the carriage house out back."

"We came to see Mr. Vonderhaar," said Karl.

"Do you have an appointment?"

Malloy pulled out his photo ID, thrust it at him. "We're with the City Health Department here on official business."

The man nodded. "You just show up unannounced, I see. Well, I'll tell you what, if you just wait here I'll go see if Mr. Vonderhaar is available." He turned to go back in the house.

"And you are …?" asked Karl.

He pivoted gracefully "Oh, I'm sorry. That was impolite of me. I'm Freddie DuCoin"—stressing the kwon—"Mr. Vonderhaar's amanuensis."

"'A man you insist.' I'm not familiar with that term," Malloy, dubious.

"Oh, it's just another way of saying secretary. All right then. Now if you wait right here, I shan't be long."

They watched him go through an oaken door so formidable it probably could have withstood the force of a battering ram. It closed behind him with an authoritative thud. They waited on the wide porch where mums bloomed in ornate concrete planters, until Freddie came out, a chapfallen look on his face. "I'm sorry gentlemen, but Mr. Vonderhaar is indisposed. I explained your need to speak with him and he said he would take it under advisement."

Karl and Shaun just looked at one another, not believing what they were hearing. "What the hell does that mean?" asked Malloy.

Freddie shrugged. "I can only speculate, but I think 'taking it under advisement' means he'll think about it. He did ask that I tender this." And with a flourish he handed Malloy a business card. In embossed scripted letters it read: F. LAUGHTON DUNAWAY - ATTORNEY AT LAW. "Mr. Vonderhaar asks that any questions you have for him be directed to his attorney."

"Well, that's just so much bullshit," Malloy asserted. "You tell His Highness to get down here *now*."

Malloy started to get in Freddie's face, but Karl quickly grabbed his shoulder and turned him. He saw that Malloy was fuming and whispered, "Get a grip, will you?" Then Karl did the unthinkable, he offered a handshake; Freddie accepted. "Goodbye, Freddie, and thanks for trying."

But Malloy couldn't get all peaceable like Karl. "You tell Trey we'll be back. Tell him you can't flout the health codes."

Freddie smiled graciously. "I'll certainly convey that, Mr. Malloy. And just so you know, only his friends call him Trey."

Halfway down the steps, heading for the street, Malloy turned and saw Freddie standing there, arms crossed, still smiling.

"Why are you smiling?" demanded Malloy. No response. Again, "Why are you smiling?" He wasn't sure why it bothered him so, the guy smiling like that, like he was lording it over them. "Yeah, brother, keep it up," he called, "but remember these three words: to be continued."

SEVEN

DAYS PASSED. It was business as usual in the clinic: Guys being fatalistic about their diagnoses, accepting it as a foregone consequence of promiscuity; guys going nuts over being told they had a sexually transmitted disease, vowing to kill the bitch who gave it to them; gals seeming to take the news more to heart, breaking down in the interview rooms and using up half a box of tissue; clinicians scrutinizing genitalia like so many grapes in a bunch, looking for pathologies, all the while checking their watches, counting the minutes until smoke break; clerical staff, all female and the oldest being thirty-seven, discussing the plots of prime-time television shows, comparing husbands and boyfriends, and wondering what to order for lunch; investigators feeling swamped and frustrated at so many loose ends that their collective caseload looked like a box of tangled kite string.

Drug dealing in the restrooms; partying in the waiting room; serious heart-to-heart talks going on in the halls; a cacophony of baleful cries, raucous laughter, and choice imprecations heard throughout the second floor.

Joe Sargent had listened to the recounting of the Vonderhaar attempt and he was not surprised at the thought of someone in the upper echelon of society, which he presumed this guy was, living as he did in a vast house with a servant, not surprised at all that he would make himself unavailable, likely considering himself quite special, far above the hoi polloi subject to health codes so carefully written with public welfare in mind. In short, wealthy gays were the worst.

"Screw this guy," said Joe. "He's an associate, not a contact. He's not worth the trouble. We've got other fish to fry, so just let him be. For now."

Okay, that was that. Malloy took a bite of crow and closed him out. So be it.

Later that day, Malloy spotted the pro the old man had named ten days prior. It was close to three and he was heading back to the clinic from a foray in north city. He chose Olive because it was so perfectly seedy and because in the back of his head he thought maybe he'd see some working girls. He was studying their ways, he told himself—after all, he had majored in anthropology. He remembered when there were lots of girls working the Stroll, a four-block stretch of Olive from Euclid to Boyle, standing around flaunting it, short shorts and bikini tops in the warmer weather, flagging down passing motorists like so many taxis. That scenario was before November 15 of last year, the day that Officer Jim Masterson, sitting in an unmarked car hoping to make a bust, was shot and killed with his own service revolver. As fast you could spit, city vice had swept the Stroll clean, jailing a good dozen hookers. This, in turn, caused some to give their douche kits a rest—only temporarily—while others scattered to riskier locations. Only in the last couple months did some girls begin to return, nothing like the previous onslaught out in the open but you would see them lurking in gangways, half-concealed, selectively soliciting. They usually worked in pairs with a pimp close by, in a parked car watching or sitting at a window of a nearby apartment building, 40-ouncers and blunts on hand to help pass the time.

But here was this lone woman standing on the corner of Olive and Boyle in broad daylight, not even trying to pretend she wasn't a pro. In parts of the city they solicit the passerby by blowing kisses or licking their lips in a manner they undoubtedly deem seductive, but which only reminded Malloy of a scene from *The Wild Kingdom*, a hyaena licking its chops, about to tear into a buffalo leg.

This one was far more aggressive. She wasn't looking in his direction; he sort of sneaked up on her by accident, and when she saw the bare left arm hanging out the window and realized that a lone white guy had passed her up, she yelled, "Hey!" It was the most compelling hey! he had ever heard, part indignant and part command. She motioned frantically for him to stop.

Malloy pulled over. He still had her in his pouch, the compact, two-ring binder used to hold ERs. He checked the description provided by the old man with what he saw: Caucasian, twenty-two to twenty-six years of age, five foot six or so, pudgy, stringy blond hair. Yep, yep, yep, yep and yep. Brenda, the old man's "speckled pup," and none other. Already she was approaching, sure he was a customer because he had stopped. Malloy waited, let her speak first.

"S'up babe, lookin' for a date?"

A white girl talking black dialect, this piqued the anthropologist in Malloy. He decided to play it out just a while before he told her. "How much we talking about?"

She glanced up and down the street, judging the coast was clear. "Twenty for a straight fuck," she said, "twenty-five for a suck and a fuck."

Malloy hesitated and she took that as reluctance, so she quickly added, "Or just twenty for everything."

"Where do we go? I mean, we don't do it here, do we?" She indicated a bleak-looking four-family flat at the corner and said she had a room there. Pay when they got to the room and, no, he wouldn't have to wear a rubber. This made him feel sorry for her; she didn't even have the sense to protect herself from disease. And pregnancy was not a consideration. Repeat infections of gonorrhea, "the prostitute's friend," would see that she never gave birth.

Malloy couldn't stand it any longer. "I hate to break it you, but you see that big brown building over there? That's the health department."

Her eyes formed into slits. "You trippin' on me!"

"Ah, no, I'm not. On the second floor of that building is the VD Clinic and that's where I work. See?" He showed her his ID. Dubiously, she looked, took in the name and title: SHAUN MALLOY -VD CONTROL. She shook her head, no way.

Malloy got out of the car. "Don't do anything stupid like run off. The reason I'm here is that one of your johns came into the clinic with gonorrhea. The clap? Now, I'm not saying you gave it to him, but the very fact that he claimed to have been with you is a good enough reason for you to be examined. Think you could take an hour out from your work? I'll ride you there."

She stepped back, regarded Malloy with serious contempt, and just as he was about to say "Well, how 'bout it?" she screamed "Your ass!" Then she took off, knees pumping, bee-lining it to the four-family.

Malloy watched her disappear inside. What could he do? Leave and forget the whole thing? That wasn't him. He followed. The building was the pits, literally falling apart, brick lying on the sidewalk having fallen away from the mortar. The first floor must have been a beauty salon because there were still signs in the window, faded from the sun, one advertising Cut-N-Curl $10 on Wednesdays, another showing the Breck Girl in all her flaxen glory. Malloy knocked at the blank door: nothing. He tested the door, it was open. So what? Going in uninvited was not only unlawful entry it was a great way to get iced. He did, however, crack the door and shout, "Anybody home?" Which, after he thought about it, was pretty ridiculous. He went back to knocking and did so until his knuckles smarted, then took out his Barlow jackknife and knocked with the butt of that. Failing results, he started knocking and yelling. Loudly. He was nothing if not dogged.

It was only then that he heard movement inside, the shuffling of approaching footsteps. Malloy stepped back just as the door creaked open. A guy peered out. Diminutive, long black hair, baggy pants, wife-beater top, probably Hispanic but with some black features. Her pimp.

"What you want?" Annoyed.

"I'm looking for the girl who ran in here ten minutes ago. Name's Brenda, I think."

His look of annoyance changed to suspicion. "What you want with her?"

Normally he kept his business confidential, but here was a man who seemed as though he could be discreet with incriminating news about Brenda so, without getting too specific, Malloy stated the nature of his call. "Hmm," the pimp mused thoughtfully, "wait here." He receded into the bowels of the tenement, cursing as he went. Soon, Malloy heard more curses, cries, and the sound of general ass-kicking from within and how 'bout that? The pimp brought the girl out. She was a bit disheveled and pissed as hell, though he was glad to see there was no blood or visible marks of injury.

"Please, Ricky. I don't wanna go with him!"

Ricky shook her so her teeth almost rattled. "You go with him or else. Ain't no unclean bitch stayin' here with me."

"Will you come along?" she pouted.

Malloy saw his cue. "Yeah, Ricky, it wouldn't be a bad idea for you to get a checkup, too. It's free and confidential."

"Confidential like you tole me her business, huh? Shitfire, I know *I* don't have nothin' but if she does, then tell me and I'll go in."

"Fair enough."

Ricky stepped out into the daylight, watching as they walked over to Malloy's car. As they pulled away, Malloy gave a gratuitous thumbs up. An awkward minute passed. Finally, he turned to Brenda, scrunched up against the car door, sitting as far from him as possible. "I'm sorry this happened to you," he told her.

Malloy didn't just mean the here and now. In his mind he was expressing consolation for all that had happened to her—the crappy upbringing she probably had, the puppy she never got, the thousand cuts of parental neglect, the abusive boyfriends, the series of poor choices she'd made that led her to Ricky and peddling her ass on that street corner.

Her burning eyes caught his glance, tears beginning to well. "Kiss my ass," she said.

EIGHT

A LITTLE BEFORE FIVE, work behind him, Malloy rang Teri at her office.

"Yeah?" She sounded rushed.

"It's me. You up for a drink?"

"Sit in that chair and don't move!"

"I am sitting."

"Not you. I've got to get the cuffs back on this guy. Somehow he slipped out of them … I said don't move, goddamnit! Shaun, I'll *need* a drink after this. Let me call you back."

Teri Kincaid was a bail bondsman and his best friend. They had met a couple years before at a Mardi Gras party in Soulard, she draping a garland of plastic beads around his neck and playfully cautioning against throwing them to beckoning women eager to flash their boobs.

"Why beads?" he'd asked. "Why not confetti or paper airplanes?"

"Because, dear, beads are the established currency and they're so easy to throw."

"Don't you find it a double standard," he went on. "The guys throw beads to the women who in turn lift their shirts, but that doesn't work the other way around. Guys flashing for beads."

"Of course it doesn't work and it shouldn't. That would be unattractive, bordering on gross. We don't want to see a guy's junk flopping around. Breasts, on the other hand, are ideal for exposing. Smooth, shapely, jiggly."

"With a cherry on top."

As salacious as their initial conversation was, they had never become an item. Teri had a thing for bikers, the burlier the better. She owned a 1977 Harley Super Glide and on weekends went for day trips and poker runs with the boys. Every August she loaded up her saddlebags and took off for Sturgis, South Dakota to join thousands of other sprocketheads in the Black Hills.

This left open a unique opportunity for both of them. Without the drama and intensity attached to sexual relations—although Malloy secretly harbored rich, vivid fantasies—they found in each other a pal, a sounding board, a confidant.

"Go on! You caught crabs in the VD Clinic. That's hilarious!"

"It was especially funny when I was pulling them out with a nit comb and slathering myself with Kwell."

Teri took a gulp of her screwdriver, and leaned over to talk right in his ear. "Okay, so let me get this straight. This girl, Adrienne, who you met a couple times while out and about, she comes to see you at the clinic, not as a patient but a social call. It's closing time, but you have her wait until everyone is gone and then you bang her right there in your office?"

"Well, pretty much, except it wasn't premeditated. I was giving her a tour and we got to the interview room, which is secure and private, and then we looked at one another and read the thoughts: 'Hey, why not?'" Malloy tilted his pint of Guinness, licked foam from his upper lip. "And everyone hadn't gone. We were on the table, right in the middle of the act, you know, and here's this knock at the door: 'Hello? Cleaning lady. You be in there for long?'"

"Go on!"

"Yeah, and we stop and I say, 'Uh, just finishing up. Please come back later.' So we wrap it up and go out for a drink. But here's the thing: I like her just all right, but I'm thinking enough is enough. I mean, we've tried each other, maybe that's all we wanted to start with. Anyway, two days later, I'm at my desk, I start itching. I go the john, drop trou, and there they are, a platoon of tiny invaders.'"

"Believe it or not, I can relate," said Teri. "I got them, too, the crabs, from using someone else's sleeping bag."

"That's breaking news for science, because you don't get crabs from inanimate objects. You get them from close contact with other people who have them."

"Oh ... well, go on. You told her, right?"

"You're gonna like this. I wrote a note, sealed it in an envelope with her name, walked down to Saint Louis University, where she works. She was at lunch and I gave it to a coworker, who said she'd be sure to pass it along. I must've spent at least two minutes on that note. It said 'Roses are red, violets are blue. I've got the crabs, and so do you.'"

Teri laughed, shook her head. "You're too much. She must've turned three shades of red when she read that. Poor girl."

"Poor girl? She's living with a parasite and didn't know it? Wonder how many other guys she   gave it to."

"It makes you feel like each new sex partner, you better see that they've been checked out and have a clean bill of health before you climb between the sheets."

"Yeah, and that clean bill of health had better be very current, like the day of. There's so much VD out there, it's scary."

"You ought to know, but c'mon, isn't your take on it a bit skewed because of your job? I mean, you're in the trenches. You see it day after day. It's on your mind."

The bartender was within calling distance so they ordered another round, this time Malloy switching to a Bud longneck with a Jameson chaser. They were in Pete's Seventh Inning Stretch, a bar next to Teri's bail bonds office and overlooking the open expanse of Memorial Plaza. City Hall and the Civil Courts Building could also be seen from the big plate glass window in front. Normally they would have met at McDowell's or some place up in the West End, but Teri had to get back to work. This drink was it for now, because somewhere in this big city there was a bond jumper out there thumbing his nose at her.

"What were we talking about?" he wondered.

"Me saying that you're exaggerating the STD problem because you're in the thick of it."

"It's prevalent, no doubt about it. St. Louis is number one in the country for gonorrhea. I'm simply saying you can't be too careful. You don't have a steady relationship with the guy you're about to get naked with, you better be sure he straps on a condom."

"I carry a couple in my purse," she said. "I'm not trusting the guy to have one."

"There you go, an ounce of prevention. But you're right about this work having warped my mind. It's true. I've done VD talks so often that now when I see a woman walking down the street I no longer envision lovely curves, the shape of her legs and hips, the size of her breasts, the color of her nipples. Now I see a diagram of the female reproductive system. It's a bit disheartening, that's all."

She laughed. "That's got to be one of the strangest job liabilities ever."

"Well, look at you, pouncing on people like a cat catching mice. We both have jobs like no other. You living out the old cops-and-robbers scenario and me getting paid for poking into the sex lives of other people. Words, pictures, and three-dimensional models are my ammunition. In order to be effective I've got to know when to bluff, when to be sincere, when to flatter, when to intimidate, when to shut up and listen."

He swigged his Bud and acted like he was done with that topic. Teri nudged him. "I'm shutting up and listening. Please continue."

"Well, it's an art, epidemiology, though it's no less an applied science. Methodical, empirical and sometimes scatological. The work is endless, identifying those with venereal infections, educating them about their condition, interviewing them for names, location, description of their bed partners and the systematic tracing of these people to get them into the clinic for exam and treatment. Then it starts all over." He rubbed the back of his neck. "But you know what? It doesn't get boring at all if you play it like a game, giving yourself so many points for marginals, associates, suspects and contacts brought in, with a bonus score for each one who is actually infected. And there are plenty out there—infecteds, I mean. My score keeps climbing."

"Whatever it takes to get you through the day, that's my motto. I could tell you how I staked out this house in Wellston from dawn to well past lunch, waiting for this fool absconder to come out so I could nab him and collect my reward, but I don't want to go into it because I'm tired of talking shop."

"Don't tease me like that. Just a few details, like how you passed the time?"

"Radio, magazines, cigarettes. I wrote a letter to my sister in Pittsburgh."

"What about potty breaks? You had to go, right? A guy can pee in a cup if he has to, but a girl?"

When she only stared at her drink, he thought he knew the answer but wanted to hear it from her. "You made a trip to Walgreen's beforehand, didn't you? The adult needs section?"

She looked at him, cheeks blushing. "Depends aren't so bad once you get used to them," she said, laughing at the thought of what she'd done. "It was weird as hell, but necessary. I didn't have a backup. The minute I'd leave to use the gas station toilet, that's when he would've come out, got in his car and drove off."

"Kind of take you back to the days of Gerber foods and teething rings, did it? That first release into the diaper, regressing you back all those years? Did you have your blankie there with you?"

"Oh, shut up! Anyway, I've got to head out. Nice talking ... I think."

She drained her screwdriver down to the ice cubes, stood up and said, "Ciao."

"Purina," bantered Malloy, proud of himself for knowing the punchline.

NINE

MONDAY MORNING CHALK TALK, November 21st edition, had Leo Schuler center stage with Derald Tutweiler on deck. Everyone was present, all seated, coffee and doughnuts near at hand, ready to tackle any issue to arise in the fascinating world of epidemiology. There were several mini-conversations going on simultaneously until Schuler cleared his throat demonstratively.

"Okay, all right," began Schuler, wiry, bespectacled, encased in a beige cable-knit turtleneck sweater and wearing enough Hai Karate aftershave to gas a cockroach. For all his fastidiousness, Leo reminded Malloy of some prim librarian who knew the location of every book in her domain. "I am currently working the case of Larry Finch, reported to us with primary syphilis by his private physician. The initial interview was done here last Tuesday. Larry is fifty-four, a family man, father of three, grandfather of two, a GS 15 for US Army Aviation. Larry travels extensively for defense contracting, has input on the new Black Hawk helicopter, also testifies be-fore congressional committees. He's away maybe a hundred and fifty days a year, staying mostly at hotels and motor inns in Alexandria, Boston, and Stratford, Connecticut. Travels ninety percent of the time with a Colonel Higgins. Larry did not beat around the bush. He claims two infidelities in twenty-seven years of marriage, once four years ago and most recently on October twenty-eighth, both with anonymous females at the same motor inn in Alexandria.

"Sounds unlikely, I admit. One-time-only extramarital in the last four months and he's caught syphilis? We talked for nearly two hours, I told him his story belonged in the BS category. He swears he's telling the truth. I tell him that ninety-nine percent of all syphilis cases involve men naming men—exaggerating the numbers—so why doesn't he just come out of the closet and admit that he's gay? He laughed at the idea."

"What! Me gay? Wait 'til my hairdresser hears about this!" Pam Grady firing the first shot in the usual volley of sarcasm.

"Well, something isn't right," Schuler went on. "His story is fishy on two counts: first, the one-time exposure, with a white female no less, and second, his period of incubation was uncommonly short, only eight days before he went to his PMD and got the diagnosis, and yet minimum duration is ten days. I tell him this and he looks at me, an intelligent and genuinely nice guy, with big sad eyes, and says, 'I've told you the truth, what else can I say?'

"Larry claims he is positive only because he was infected by the pick-up at the motel. He had sex with his wife only four days before and not after, he says, so he doesn't want her tested or treated. I say she will have to be, either by her PMD or by us. He freaks out at this. Also, I tell him we'll have to talk to his colonel about his lifestyle—confidentiality maintained, of course—if he can't come up with a better story than that. Hearing this, he goes to pieces, starts blubbering and pleads with me not to do it, that I'll wreck his marriage and ruin his forty-five-thousand-dollar a year job. I tell him that I certainly feel for him but sorry, the wheels are already in motion.

"He called on Thursday saying that he had told his wife and she had taken it hard. She said she would stay with him only for the sake of the children and grandchildren, but it would never be the same between them. Now she's giving him the silent treatment. He said that he had read Ann Landers' column the very next day, and if he had only read it earlier he would have never told her. He said he would have 'fought me tooth and nail'. Landers advised someone never to tell a spouse of an infidelity because it was guaranteed to destroy the relationship. Of course, there was no way he could avoid that. If he hadn't told her, we would have."

"Ann Landers, the philanderer's friend," cracked Malloy.

"Yeah," said Schuler, "and meanwhile the wife has gone through the ordeal of prophylactic treatment. No signs present. But here's the quandary, and this is significant. This man was diagnosed as a primary case by a PMD on the basis of a suspicious-looking penile sore and a reactive RPR. Neither Darkfield nor FTA was done, and these are the number one and number two most definitive tests for syphilis. The physician could've ordered these, but he neglected to. It's too late for a Darkfield and the FTA was ordered on my suggestion only four days ago, and results take up to ten working days. In other words, we're operating under the assumption that poor old Larry has syphilis. Until the FTA comes back we're just not sure. He may have told his wife of his infidelity for naught."

"Have you interviewed his colonel yet?" asked Joe Sargent.

"Not yet."

"Well, hold off on that until the FTA comes back, and my guess is it'll be positive. His story is too convenient and all too familiar. But as for the wife, that's the way the ball bounces. Sorry, bud, we can't afford to wait ten days on your wife. Great job, Leo, thorough and diligent. Okay, presenter number two."

Derald Tutweiler shuffled up to the front of the class. His quasi-befuddled demeanor and slovenly appearance brought to mind a duck hunter who has just stumbled out of the woods after being lost for two days.

"Last week," he announced, "I was staking out a house in north city, waiting for a GC contact to show up. I'm sitting in my car, eating a bag of chips, when I heard the sound of glass breaking and a while later two squad cars screeched up. Three cops jumped out, pointing guns at me. Pretty rude, I thought. They ordered me to get out of the car and lie on the ground. I asked them if I had to, that I didn't want to get dirty. They said, yes, I had to. So I did and my pants got muddy. What happened was that someone had been breaking into my contact's house while I was watching it. The neighbors must've heard it, too, and, seeing a strange white guy parked out front, they decided to call the cops."

Tut ceased his oration. He stood there serenely, arms draped loosely at his sides. Fifteen seconds of silence ensued. Some of the others began to fidget.

"Yeah, then what?" asked Karl.

"That's it. They let me go when they learned who I was and what I was doing there."

"That's your presentation?" said Joe.

"Yeah, that's all I've got," said Tut.

"Hell of a story," muttered Joe. "Who's next?"

"That would be me," said Malloy, already at the chalkboard. As before, he flipped it over, bringing up a scribbled diagram containing a shorthand of codified categories—contacts, suspects, associates, marginals, their levels of priority, and the known relationships between them. This time it looked more like a plan for a prison break than a football play.

"My OP Dirk Hansen came into the clinic Friday morning complaining of swelling in the groin. Upon examination he showed signs of secondary lesions—classic plantar rash, just beautiful!—and passed his RPR with flying colors. He's probably had syphilis for three months or more and, unlike Leo's ambiguous OP, Dirk is thoroughly gay and totally cool with it. He's thirty-three, Caucasian, works as a waiter at Ponce De Leon's and lives in Soulard with his lover, Peter."

Malloy indicated an arrow leading from a circle enclosing OP to a circle enclosing C1. "Dirk says he is faithful to Peter since they've been living together—April of last year—and he can't imagine Peter cheating on him." Malloy knew better than to say he believed his OP, which he did, but instead felt obligated to show them what a hard-bitten cynical investigator he was. "Of course, I didn't take him at his word. I pressed him for more contacts until he ran out of smokes and was losing interest. Nada, only Peter. Although, I did get several associates, mostly other waiters from Ponce's and Robusto's. His friends."

Malloy reached for his coffee mug on a table nearby, took a slurp, and continued. "Okay, so Peter needs to be interviewed ASAP. Dirk has no problem with that, but he wants to be there. Peter Marquardt is a branch manager over at Boatmens Bank in Clayton, which makes him nine-to-five, but Dirk works Friday evenings, a big night in the restaurant business. Dirk says he'll make Peter available on Saturday afternoon. Done. One o' clock the next day I show up at their house, a rehabbed three-story on Menard, close to the brewery. Absolutely beautiful inside, well-appointed, as they say. Persian carpets everywhere, an amazing photographic collection including some pretty unforgettable black-and-whites by this guy Robert Mapplethorpe, and on one wall they have shelves of antique radios that you ..."

"Save this shit for your swishy pals at the decorator store," grumped Joe. "Get on with it."

"Yeah, right. Well, we sit in the parlor and they're having Bloody Marys. I explain the situation to Peter, who seems uncomfortable. Peter by the way is a dead ringer for the actor Robert Hays, the handsome guy in *Airplane*, remember? Anyway, I show him the pictures in the Green Book, ask has he seen these sores on himself or anyone else. He says he did have a 'boo-boo' on his penis a few months back, but he thought it was just the result of some athletic sex he'd had. It went away after a week or so and he thought no more about it. So, this is good, right? I'm onto something right off the bat. I've got my notebook ready and start asking for names. At first he says no one else, only Dirk. I counter with the logical assertion that there has to be a third party, that Dirk is definitely infected, and he, Peter, is likely infected. Therefore, it had to be introduced by someone else. *T. pallidum* doesn't just spontaneously appear like dustballs under the bed. So now Dirk is giving Peter looks and Peter is clinking the ice cubes in his drink, stalling for time, working up to truth or consequences, and guess what? You're gonna love what Peter spilled."

"His Bloody Mary?" clucked Tut.

"All over the Persian carpet," added Arnold.

"No, he had a three-way back in August, a little party held at the home of one Bryson Vonderhaar the Third. Men's night, party of twelve, members only, locals and out-of-towners. Cocktails at seven, dinner at eight-thirty, adjourn to any available bedroom sometime after ten. Peter hooked up with a Daniel from Hyannisport and a Steve from L.A."

"I'll be damned," said Joe. "This is the same guy who's too important to talk to us directly, wants us to go through his lawyer. I've never heard of such shit in my entire career. Karl, you call that lawyer today, set up a meeting with him and his client. I want you and Shaun there and I want it done this week. We're going to put a crimp in this guy's hose."

"Did he name Vonderhaar?" Karl wondered.

"That would be nice, but no, although he did say that one point Vonderhaar came in the room and offered them some poppers and chocolates.

Then he stuck around for a while, taking in the action, but not participating. Voyeur maybe."

"Full names, locating on these contacts to Peter?"

"No, and that's why this operation of Vonderhaar's is so outrageous. As I said before, when presenting Randall Hoffman, it's a club where affluent gays pay a membership fee to be hooked up with other birds of a feather. If they happen to be traveling through, say, on business, and give advance notice, then Vonderhaar will put on his social director hat and start arranging one of his dinners. Peter says he has a rule: first names only, although addresses and phone numbers may be exchanged if the parties so wish. And since Peter was in it only for the evening and already had a boyfriend, he didn't pursue it."

"How did your OP take it?" asked Betsy, typically concerned about the feelings of others.

"You know, not as hard as you might expect when you think of a normal person who's just found out his partner has cheated. 'Was that the night you said you were going to the play?' Dirk asked him. 'Why did you think it was all right to trick me? I wouldn't have done that to you.' Stuff like that. Dirk was, I would say, miffed. Miffed and hurt, as opposed to livid. When I left they were close to kiss- and-make-up."

Malloy turned, studied his handiwork on the chalkboard for a moment. "Any questions? Comments?"

"Yeah," said Joe, "that was a bonehead move, letting Dirk sit in on the interview. It automatically puts a muffler on the situation. With his boyfriend present, Peter could have just as easily clammed up and not breathed a word about this thing over at Vonderhaar's. I'm sure this was covered in epi school. With rare exceptions such as Arnold's deaf guy needing an interpreter, the interview is one-on-one, period."

Malloy knew that Joe was right and said so.

"Did you say if Peter was a member or a guest of this club?" wondered Martha. "If he's a member, he probably knows a lot more than he's letting on."

"He says he's an old friend of Vonderhaar's, they went to Country Day together."

"Well, lah-de-dah," opined Tut, himself a graduate of Roosevelt Public High School on the Southside.

"He says he's not a member, but that Vonderhaar invites him to the party on occasion in hopes that he'll become a paid member. Which he says will not happen because, quote, he's 'just not into all that debauchery on a regular basis.'"

"Any clinical results on Peter yet?" Karl asked.

Malloy consulted his watch. "Right about now Peter should be getting poked and prodded and injected with penicillin out at County Health, which is close to his bank in Clayton. He wanted to go to his PMD, a Brock Silber in the West End, but I talked him out of it. Didn't want to have to re-do the treatment." Several investigators nodded agreement, every one of them knowing firsthand what a hassle it was to have to tell these patients that they had to be treated all over again, that their private physician wasn't up on the most current guidelines and the shots they endured or the pills they took were just not adequate to cure their disease.

"How's this tie in with Hoffman?" Joe asked.

Malloy knew this question was coming, knew there was likely a connection but damned if he could find it. Joe would have him go over the puzzle again and again until he could connect the dots. "Yeah, that is quite a coincidence," he agreed. "Two yuppie types, both in the financial industry, catching a case in the same location but at different times with a different cast of characters. Vonderhaar as master of ceremonies being the only common denominator. To answer the question, Joe, in a phone reinterview I pressed Randall Hoffman, the first OP, about this and, still, he continues to name the same persons as before. Without giving away Peter's identity, I planted the suggestion of his introduction into Vonderhaar's love nest coming by way of another in his own profession—which would make sense, Hoffman sponsoring Peter or vice-versa. Hoffman stuck with his story that he came to the club on a cold call, so to speak, writing a letter of introduction and waving a check."

"Keep at it," urged Joe. "There's more to this, a collusion of some sort. Run it down, no stone unturned."

TEN

THE TWO OF THEM sat there at the dining table just off the kitchen, notepads and photographs spread between them, a large tray of pastries within reach. A fresh pot of coffee was made and Trey Vonderhaar poured himself another steaming shot. On one side of the coffee cup was the Latin phrase

Faber est Suae Quisque Fortunae; on the other side, the translation: "Every Man is the Artisan of His Own Fortune."

It was 9:30 on a Tuesday. The morning sun was streaming in from the large, curved, east-facing window in the front parlor, facing Lafayette Park. Freddie was dressed for the day, brown slacks and a light-blue pocket Oxford by Ralph, but Trey still wore his tartan plaid pajamas with his fleece-lined slippers. Trey's two-year-old Jack Russell terrier, a box of nerves named Roscoe, paced the room seeking any diversion that might evoke prolonged yipping and yapping. A nimbus of cigarette smoke hung over the table like a random thought. Freddie's exhalations; Trey didn't smoke.

To the casual observer they might have been taken for another set of same-sex couples sitting down to breakfast after a lustful night between the sheets. But no, these two were not lovers. Associates, yes. On the same page concerning wealth and the acquisition of it, yes. On the same page as regards good taste in attire, art, and food, yes. Yet they were not equals; far from it. One did the other's bidding, whatever he desired, no arguments brooked, no questions asked unless it was to clarify the assignment. So it was that the employer and his employee were in the midst of their weekly planning meeting.

"I'm thinking we pair David from Orlando with David from Houston," said Freddie. "They both expressed an interest in experimenting."

"'Novel sex,' as David from Orlando put it," said Trey, checking his notes. "Hmm, that could be anything from light bondage to rectal insertion with a telephone receiver."

"Not my telephone, I hope!" laughed Freddie.

"I say we put them in the Oscar Wilde room with a box of toys and let them work it out. 'David, meet David. Play nice, have fun!'"

"All right, good. That's taken care of. Now how about these others?" Freddie checked the notes both he and Trey had made while speaking to these various men by phone over the course of the last ten days. Once they knew St. Louis was along their route, Man 2 Man members would phone, asking if a soiree was available. While a certain number of members made the guest list based on a travel itinerary that was incidental, others upon personal request might be enticed to jump on a plane bound for St. Louis expressly for a fabulous evening at the home of Trey Vonderhaar. To complete seating at the dining table, nine to twelve persons being optimal, there were local members who might be called to fill in. Man 2 Man currently had 122 members from the continental US and Canada, each of whom paid $3,000 per year for at least six events, although some of the more interesting clientele were regulars. This handsome sum of collected dues allowed Trey to spare no expense in throwing his parties. Thus, he had all bases covered with the help of a capable support staff including a chef, a caterer, servers, bartenders, parking attendants, two chamber musical quartets on call, and a post-party cleaning crew.

"Paul from Tulsa and Steve from Windsor have both expressed interest in *menage a trois* so we need a third party for that. Someone local, don't you think?"

"We could phone Peter Marquardt, the banker who was here last month. See if he's available. He handles himself well and has those movie star looks. He's just the sort of fellow we need around here to make a good impression."

"Yes, good call," said Freddie. "If he's available, I'll put the three of them in the Sal Mineo suite with the king bed and the ceiling mirrors."

Trey nodded approval. "Here's one that gave me a chuckle. Zach Gershon has expressed interest in attending the next soiree. You remember him, the tall, older gentleman from Louisville, distinguished looking, owns several high-rises there. I received this letter the other day. Here, read the part I highlighted."

Freddie took the letter, smoothed out the creases and read the pertinent passage aloud. "And while my experience with Man 2 Man has been nothing short of exhilarating, I yearn for something out of my box, a bird of a different feather. In short, I would love to be introduced to some hot young twink of legal age with a gym body, torn jeans, a wife-beater top showing off his tattoos, backward baseball cap, and smelly white socks. Possibly a greaser, but, please, no bad or missing teeth. For that, I would pay a surcharge. Can you help me in this regard?"

"Can you believe it?" asked Trey.

"Oh, I believe it," said Freddie. "Opposites do attract, but who could this be? We don't have anybody like that."

"Not on our regular rolls, but there are hot young twinks to be had if you know where to look. I thought of all the young men in our orbit and I came up with one likely candidate: Drew Conger. You see him out and about at the parties, the openings, chums with several people we know, looks like he's game for just about anything. I want you to approach him, lay out the plan. I'm sure he'll agree to it, especially when you offer him

$250, seeing that Gershon's surcharge is going to be $1,250. Then it's just a matter of costuming him. I want you to make sure he looks the part well before the soiree and then the day of you can bring him here early and he can get ready in one of the rooms upstairs."

"He'll stand out among the other guests," offered Freddie.

"It will be something different, something nouveau. It'll show them that we're not just a stuffy dinner party."

"But Gershon wants a tattooed body. Conger probably won't go that far. Besides, new tattoos take time to heal, they have scabs."

"Oh come on, Freddie. You haven't heard of henna tattoos? They look like the real thing, but they're not permanent. You and he go to the novelty shop and pick out a few. Get something a grungy biker would likely have."

"Once again, you show an amazing aptitude for problem solving. It's a real pleasure working with you."

"Why, thank you, Freddie. Okay, moving right along, have you seen this little item?" Trey handed Freddie a piece of paper, the Man 2 Man questionnaire, rudimentary as it was. It had just been returned a few days ago, carefully filled out in precise penmanship. Under the heading Preferences was the notation "coprophilia."

Freddie made a face. "Oh dear! No, I hadn't seen that one. We haven't had one of those before, have we? Watersports, yes. But poop eaters, not that I can think of. What are we going to do?"

Trey showed Freddie the photo that Ted from Atlanta had submitted, a middle-aged white man, glazed-looking bright blue eyes, smirking at something. "Well, he is a new member and so we are not necessarily committed. We can either refund Ted from Atlanta his money or we prepare a room especially for him, line it with plastic and fumigate it afterwards. Frankly, it's a tough call. It seems like a lot of bother for one man's fetish."

"Unsanitary fetish, I may add. When the others learn what he's into, they may shun him. It could be awkward at the dining table. Whose poop does he eat anyway? His own or someone else's? Does he need an audience when he does this?"

"Your first question, I don't know. As far as the audience, I'm guessing yes. Otherwise he could do his thing solo, in the privacy of his own home. In fact, he may not even eat feces per se. I've heard that some of these guys get off just watching someone defecate. But, you know, even as we're giving this serious thought, part of me is thinking how ludicrous this actually is.

When it comes right down to it we really don't need a scat fetishist."

"His money may be green, but his fingers are brown," laughed Freddie. "Then it's the boot?"

"The old heave-ho," confirmed Trey, "although I do hate to lose the income. Do we have any new prospects on the horizon?"

They paused to replenish their plates. Trey reached for a glazed cruller. Freddie took a thimbleberry Danish. They took their bites, chewed for a minute, and finally Freddie said, "Walter Jamieson has been putting in a good word for Terrance Stowe-Douglas ... the sculptor? You see his work in some of the better homes, works in stone, abstract shapes, had a show at Phillip Cantor Gallery a few years back."

"I know him," said Trey, "met him at the St. Louis premiere of The *Boys in the Band* at The Rep. Nice fellow, but he can't afford us."

"Well, Walter's making noises like he really wants him in and that maybe we'd be willing to take some of Terrance's artwork to defray the full cost of membership."

"Not a chance," sniffed Trey. "I don't care for his art. Too—oh, I don't know—otherworldly, reminds me of a disjointed dream, puts me on edge to look at it."

"I see. But you're not necessarily nixing him as a new member, right? If the money is there, then it's a green light for Terrance?"

"That's correct."

At that moment, Freddie felt Roscoe on his leg. "Trey, Roscoe is humping my leg again."

"You'd better stop him before he ejaculates," said Trey, helpfully. "That stuff will stain your clothes."

Freddie wrested the animal from his leg while in mid-stroke, setting him off to the side. The headstrong Roscoe started to advance once more, but Freddie held out his hand like a traffic cop and the dog got the message. "Where were we? Oh, right, I'll speak to Walter. He may want to shell out for his young protégé. He adores Terrance, you know."

"Walter has an extra three thousand laying around?"

"Could be. We know he came into a huge endowment from the family trust. Since we've known him, he's never had to work. I think he's good for it."

"Freddie?"

"Yes, Trey."

"I've seen Walter's endowment, it's not that huge."

At Walter's expense they had a good laugh, Trey sounding out with a series of under-the-breath chuckles that seemed to issue from no deeper than the throat while Freddie's genuine hilarity had its roots in the diaphragm. Finally, Trey held up his hand, turned serious. "I'm glad we got our jollies out, because this next thing is not at all that comical. I got a call from Frank Dunaway, our battling barrister, who says that an official from the VD Clinic at the health department contacted him and is demanding to speak to us, meaning me. According to Frank, they claim that some of our members have come down with syphilis and they may have caught it here. They won't reveal who these diseased persons are, but they want the names and addresses of our members so they can test them."

Freddie shook his head in disbelief. "That's insane, we can't possibly give out our members' private information."

"That's what I told Frank," said Trey. "Those two that came to the door last month? You came to me and I gave you Frank's card to give to them, make them go away. Well, apparently, they're not going away. One of them or maybe a supervisor went to the law office and spoke to Frank, showed him some law that says something to the effect that citizens must cooperate with public health officials to stop the spread of communicable disease."

"Except we're not citizens," protested Freddie. "Citizens are people who hold down jobs, work on their own cars, mow their own lawns, worry about layoffs and foreclosure."

"I hear you, believe me. Nor are we some common business that is accountable for its employees. We are a private club whose members pay handsomely for certain privileges and expect a level of security in return." Trey leaned forward slightly, cradled his chin with a free hand and assumed the look of Rodin's famous statue. "On the one hand, I admit that I am concerned if there is syphilis being spread under this roof. Word of that gets out it could taint our image. Conversely, as you say, we can't just hand over the membership roster, say, 'Here you go. Round them all up, these bankers, restaurateurs, CPAs, developers, community leaders—nefarious persons, all of them. No, they won't mind being told they may have VD.'"

"What a dilemma," put in Freddie. "And there's no way out of this?"

"Frank says we have to at least agree to meet with them, and that it would get us off the hook if we would provide some information. Maybe then they'll go away. He wants to set up a meeting at his office this Friday."

"That's our next soiree. We need that time to get ready."

"Yes, we do and you're in charge. I'm going to this meeting by myself. We'll set it up for mid-morning and I'll be back in time for lunch."

"So what are you going to give them?"

"There's the large and looming question. To answer that I have to imagine what they're going to ask. Apparently, they cannot reveal names of infected persons who have entered their radar. So, I imagine they'll have to beat around the bush a bit, ask if I saw anyone having sex in my home, or do I have knowledge of certain people who may have symptoms of this syphilis—not that I even know what those symptoms may be. Things like that. They may even come out and ask who am I doing, but Frank says I don't have to answer that question since I'm not infected."

"Then how will you play it?"

"I'm going to have to throw a couple members under the bus. No way around it, I'm afraid."

"I see, and which names come to mind?"

"That's what we're about to decide, you and I. If only we knew who they suspect of having been here, we could hand over that member and be done with it. Think, Freddie. Who among us is most likely to get syphilis?"

"Jeremy Alt perhaps. He always looks a bit peaked, and he trembles."

"I think that's just his normal condition, but we'll put him on the list. Who else?"

"Nathan from Springfield. He's one of our most regular visitors, an odd duck, too. He told me once that he would screw anything that walked, which I took to mean he practices bestiality. Think of all the diseases you could pick up from screwing animals."

"There are certainly a lot of jokes involving sex with barnyard animals so it must actually happen. Can you imagine one of our members showing up, saying, 'Good evening, gents, uh, I hope you don't mind but I brought along my sheep.'" They chuckled at this as Trey wrote down Nathan from Springfield. There was quiet for a spell as they both ruminated. Freddie lit a Marlboro; Trey doodled on his notepad when suddenly a name appeared: Geoffrey.

"Who's the biggest lush?"

"It's a tie between Geoff from Baltimore and Jason from Chicago," answered Freddie.

"I'll go with Geoffrey. He arrives three sheets to the wind and leaves four sheets. I don't even know that he remembers a thing the next day. He could be seen as a liability to us. Didn't he knock over the serving platter, tortellini all over the floor? I sometimes imagine him having an accident out front here, drunkenly telling the police he was coming from this house."

"Except he always takes a taxi."

"Oh … right. Still, I nominate Geoffrey the Lush. He's our man. But he doesn't have sex by himself. Who shall his partner be?"

"Rainer from Seattle," offered Freddie, bemused.

"The late Rainer from Seattle?"

"Exactly. It puts a cul-de-sac on their avenue of inquiry. We didn't know he'd died last month in that avalanche in Innsbruck. Let them find out and when they do, well, case closed."

"Freddie, you're brilliant. Have another Danish."

"So Geoff and Rainer it is? You think only two names will get them off our backs?"

"Let's ask the oracle," said Trey, rising from the table and going to the fireplace mantle. He returned with a black sphere that fit neatly into his cupped hands. He upended it a few times and posed the question out loud: "Shall we, for the good of our operation, turn over to the overbearing health department the names of two sacrificial lambs—specifically, members Geoffrey the Lush and the conveniently deceased Rainer from Seattle?" Trey shook the Magic 8 Ball once more and in the little window appeared SIGNS POINT TO YES. "Good, that's settled. One more question, Great Oracle: In doing this, will we be free to operate without harassment from authorities to pursue our goal of providing great sex in tasteful settings, sumptuous dinner included, to only those who can afford it?"

Again, the Magic 8 Ball spit out an answer, but it wasn't one they cared to hear: DON'T COUNT ON IT.

ELEVEN

UNLIKE HIS COLLEAGUE Leo Schuler, Malloy was not one to wear cologne, deodorant or anything that might mask his natural smell. He had hippie tendencies in that regard, having somehow arrived at the conclusion that whatever happened to ooze from his pores was essentially a good thing. Nor was he interested in washing away this organic patina; he liked to let it sit a while, and therefore daily bathing was not his thing. Besides, those

German girls he dated while in the Army, they certainly didn't wash every day, didn't shave their legs or pits either, and he was okay with that, eventually came to find it sexy. There were those who actually told him that he needed a shower—"no offense, man"—and he took these suggestions good-naturedly, answering, "Yeah, I'll get to it one of these days."

But in fact he felt sorry for these people who were so concerned with hygiene, as if they had nothing better to do than obsess about bacteria forming on their bodies. Why couldn't they see there was hardly ever such a thing as an offensive odor, just a different one. And women. Women were the test of his philosophy on this matter. If, upon intimate contact, a woman suddenly withdrew her affections then Malloy chalked it up to her being another clean freak, telling himself that this prospect was probably not a good match for him anyway. But if she responded enthusiastically, her bouquet comingling with his aroma, then he knew he was on to something good. That's why he was titillated by those sexy words that Sheila had just whispered in his ear: "I like your scent."

Sheila Noonan, landlord, lived on the first floor of the three-story Victorian in Midtown. They were in Malloy's bed beneath the bay window on the second floor and had made fabulous love, first time ever, and now they were about to do it again. Before dawn they would have a third go and then Sheila would get up, put on her clothes, kiss him goodbye, walk downstairs and make coffee in her bachelorette kitchen. But now, while they were still locked in loving embrace, exploring each other with unabashed curiosity, Malloy was thinking that this was the best sex he had ever had. Which was saying a lot, he knew, but it had to be true because for months now he had had the most profound crush on Sheila and he had regularly fantasized over this very thing someday happening. Not that he ever hit on her—un unh, because common sense said you don't boink any female who holds a trump hand against you, be it your boss or your landlord. Even so, it had bothered him when guys came knocking, calling on her, taking her out or staying in for dinner and drinks. Sometimes he happened to be in the foyer and he would let them in, make their acquaintance. And snoop that he was, Malloy was quite aware when these guys would leave, if they left at all, and it killed him to think that they were getting what he so fervently wanted.

But this just happened by chance. What did they call it, serendipity? He wasn't necessarily one of those who believed that things happen for a reason, but it was happening because she apparently lusted for him just as he had been lusting for her. Hurray for serendipity!

It was Thanksgiving, a day he never cared for, what with everyone pretending that family was the greatest thing on earth. His family, consisting of a neurotic mother and a few aunts and uncles and cousins, were far away in Kokomo and he wouldn't dream of driving six hours just to hang out, gorge himself on turkey, and listen to Uncle Ken talk about appliance repair. Instead, he spent his holiday solo, in his new hometown, doing things that were fun. First he took a long walk through the West End and Forest Park, leaving from his apartment after breakfast and returning just before noon with salami and cheeses from Kopperman's Deli. Then he checked the *Globe* for what was playing and he decided to catch the one-fifteen showing of *The Road Warrior*.

It was set in a post-apocalyptic Australian wasteland where a band of survivors—decent people—were enclosed in a compound, holding all the petrol which was better than gold or anything else because there were no more gas stations. The holed-up survivors were surrounded and constantly taunted by really scary psychos on choppers and muscle cars, some of whom reminded Malloy, in appearance only, of the butch gays at Chaps, a leather bar where he did STD screening on Wednesday evenings. The psychos were constantly on the lookout for any opportunity to inflict pain on the decent people, pillage their settlement, and take their petrol for their ravenous machines. The Road Warrior, another burned-out cynic but decent somewhere deep inside, was the self-serving, inadvertent hero in this bleak story. Malloy thought that this new guy, Mel Gibson, played the character perfectly, and what fun to get to be in a movie like that. He also thought that if a guy were to have a crush on another guy, not suck him off or anything like that, but just hang out, get to see what makes him tick, then this guy would be it.

Afterwards, he went to a Welsh pub on Euclid Avenue, sat at the bar drinking stout and solving the world's problems with John the bartender who wore a long, craggy face and a droopy mustache like some lawman in the Old West. After polishing off an order of rarebit, he walked the six blocks over to West Pine Avenue, his apartment.

He was having a pretty good day by himself, not needing or wanting anybody. Then, as he was capping the evening with a bottle of Pinot Grigio, sitting at the kitchen table for two, pondering the universe, he heard someone out in the hallway. He went to look and saw Sheila coming down from the third floor. She had just put in a new bulb. They made small talk there in the hall. How was your Thanksgiving? Yeah? Did the day on your own, good for you. Mom and dad are divorced so I had two dinners to attend. So much food! And so on. There they were, two single people, who had never really socialized until now. Standing there in jeans and T-shirt, wavy brown hair framing an angel's face, she was prettier than ever and Malloy's heart was melting. He invited her in for a glass of wine. Without hesitation, she accepted.

They sat at the little table, glasses in hand. Malloy had gotten out the things from Kopperman's along with some crackers. He felt lucky that he was able to offer her something nice, the wine and deli nosh paving the way to something. A half hour passed and already he had learned about her background, her turn-ons—David Mamet plays—and turn-offs—littering—and her aspiration to be a fitness instructor. There was a break in the conversation, Sheila masticating, and even with her having a mouthful of Genoa salami Malloy was getting the hots so badly he worried that steam was coming out his ears. He couldn't believe she was here in his apartment and they were having, like, a date.

"What?" she said, slightly alarmed.

"What what?" he wondered.

"Why are you looking at me that way?"

"What way is that?"

"Like you want to do something."

"Maybe I do."

It got good after that. He moved in on her, they kissed as lovers kiss for the first time, eagerly, excitedly. He left her only for a moment to switch off the lights and then they flew onto his bed, actually no more than a mattress on the floor. He helped her disrobe and she went down on her knees, slowly removing his. First, the shirt button by button, and teasing him a little, unzipping his jeans, his cock ready to spring like a jack-in-the-box, then pushing it back in and toggling the zipper back up. There was no awkward groping, and not much foreplay. They went at it like a choreographed dance, him on top, her on top, doggie style, and a new way they had just invented. Slow grinding strokes, piston-like strokes, until they crumpled on the mattress, panting and spent, filled with pleasure.

Just after Sheila had complimented him on his scent, she said something else which had Malloy scratching his head. She was lying on her back, the streetlights shining in through the bay window, illuminating her petite and luscious torso. She reached over with her left hand and scratched the side of her right breast, the one closest to him, and said, "I've never done it with a tenant before. And though I like you, I don't want to make it a habit."

"Your call," said Malloy, thinking that would be a shame but at least he got this out of his system.

"We still have tonight," she said

"Yeah, we do and I'm loving it." He got up and returned with the wine. He drank straight from the bottle, then handed it to her.

By now they were sitting up. She reached in her jeans pocket and got a smoke. She asked for an ashtray. He complied. They finished off the bottle of Pinot. He went to the fridge and brought back two Bud longnecks, apologizing for having run out of wine. She said that was all right; beer was good, too. He told her a joke he had just heard about a boy and girl who worked in a Chinese take-out. They were in a parked car about to get hot and heavy when the boy asked for sixty-nine. The girl was really insulted, saying, "What, you want chicken chow mein now?" Sheila laughed and the laugh turned into a cough which sounded to Malloy like bronchitis. The cough continued until she hacked up a loogie and spit it into the ashtray.

"Sorry," she told Malloy, daintily dabbing at her mouth with a free hand.

"It happens," he said, slightly sad that the pedestal he'd placed her on had just developed a crack at its base.

"One more thing I should mention," she said, "and please don't get offended."

"Shoot."

"I hope you're not expecting a rent reduction because of our little escapade here tonight. That would be a mistake."

"You're kidding, right?"

"No, I mean it wouldn't be nuts to think that a tenant such as yourself might assume that because we chose to get intimate, we were suddenly on some special arrangement with the rent. I just don't want you to think that."

Malloy chuckled lightly. "Sheila, I promise not to bring up the rent. Except this once, right now, and that is to say that two-hundred a month for this place is a great deal. I am so glad I found this. I love my apartment."

"It is nice," she agreed. "And you're so much better than the previous tenant, Mr. Conklin, always cooking his cabbage. I had to air the place out for a week after he left."

"I ate a lot of sauerkraut in Germany. It's an acquired taste."

"Don't you go boiling cabbage in here!" she chided playfully.

"Don't worry, I'm a soup and sandwich guy. 'We chose to get intimate'— those were your words."

"Yeah, what about them?"

He traced a wet finger around her areola, saw the nipple perk. "Well, I'm choosing to get intimate again."

She reached over and touched him, semi-erect and growing. "Hello fella, ready for an encore?"

TWELVE

MALLOY RARELY gave much thought to his attire. Insofar as work went, it was usually a light-colored shirt with dark-colored pants or the other way around. Contrast was the thing; you didn't want to wear all white or all navy blue. That would look really dumb. The belt and the shoes, however, were always the same, brown leather.

But today was different. He was going to meet Trey Vonderhaar at his lawyer's office and he thought it wouldn't hurt to make a good impression even if the guy had been a jerk up until now. Sifting through his meager wardrobe he chose his least wrinkled khakis, the ones with the pleats, and a button-down, blue cotton pinstripe to go with it. Ties, he had only a few. One with shamrocks, his annual St. Paddy's Day pick; one in paisley; and a club tie, diagonal yellow stripes on a navy blue field with little red yacht flags. He chose this last, given to him by an ex-girlfriend whose father did actually belong to a yacht club. To complete this ensemble he chose his gray Harris Tweed sport coat, the one with the flaps on the side pockets *and* the breast pocket, a small but distinguishing feature.

He was in fine shape for this meeting, having been up all night making love to Sheila and now hungover to boot. But a regimen of strong black coffee, toast and jam, three aspirin, and a hot shower had mitigated the deleterious effects, and he felt he could at least function well enough to carry off the interview. The meeting had been called only two days ago. Karl had come to Malloy's desk on Wednesday, saying that Vonderhaar's lawyer had agreed to make his client available for questioning—in the interest of public health, of course—and that this meeting would take place on Friday morning, the day after Thanksgiving, and that since he, Karl, would still be on vacation in Charleston, he, Malloy, would be going alone. "I think they're motivated now," Karl had said. "They know we're not playing. It's a safe bet you'll be walking out of there with some names. Good luck, and don't let them snow you."

The law office of F. Laughton Dunaway was downtown in the Frisco Building on 9th Street, between Olive and Pine. Malloy walked into the spacious lobby, went to the desk where a jolly black woman in a guard uniform asked him his business and told him to sign in to the visitor book. Usually Malloy took the act of signing in as an opportunity for a practical joke, a way of messing with the system. He would laugh inwardly, imagining someone whose job it was to actually read these names: Who have we here? Peter Gozinya, what kind of name is that? Jimmy Crackcorn—a character from a song? How odd. Today, he wrote his name as Clem Kadiddlehopper, the clueless rustic made famous by Red Skelton. The guard directed him to the penthouse suite, "Hit PH in the elevator, it don't go no higher."

A receptionist greeted him, and said Dunaway would be with him shortly and would he care for some coffee? He sat there drinking the coffee and going over his notes on the case, knowing full well that he didn't have a hell of a lot of leverage with Vonderhaar since he wasn't a contact but merely a person whose residence was being used as a breeding ground for pestilence. Still, Vonderhaar was an enabler for the spread of contagion. If this was 200 years ago, he would be pilloried in the town square.

A dapper man in a three-piece tailored suit with dark tousled hair just long enough to be hip entered the reception area, strode up to Malloy and extended his hand. "Frank Dunaway. You must be Shaun Malloy." Malloy rose, matching the lawyer's grip. "It's a shame Mr. Benda couldn't have come," he said. "We seemed to have such good rapport on the phone."

"He took a much-needed vacation," said Malloy. "I'm hoping we can have good rapport as well. It's been my case all along."

Dunaway gave a bland, insincere smile and said, "Mr. Vonderhaar is already here. Please follow me to my office."

Walking in tow down the long hallway, Malloy tried to erase the image he had created of the person who spoke to him so arrogantly through the

intercom that day. He was willing to wipe the slate clean and start afresh.
As they entered, Trey Vonderhaar stood facing them. In the spirit of diplomacy, Dunaway introduced them properly.

"Oh, hello there," said Vonderhaar with strained cordiality, not liking
what he saw, thinking, *this is the miscreant who cost me three grand.*

Malloy gripped Vonderhaar's outstretched hand, thinking, *this is the
little twerp who disrespected me.*

Trey Vonderhaar was not an imposing figure. With his thin lips, wispy
brown hair conservatively cut, and stooped shoulders, he could have been
a clerk in a retail store with a feather duster sticking out of his back pocket.
To Malloy, he looked like he could stand to work out some. At odds with
this milquetoast appearance, however, was a mercenary, almost feral look in
his eye; the man was cunning, it was there. At six one, Malloy was a good
six inches taller, and he found himself speaking to the crown of Trey's head.
"Hello yourself," he said. "We meet in person, finally."

From a corner of the room a small dog trotted out wearing a snazzy
mini-sweater with fall colors; the material looked like cashmere. The animal went up to Malloy and started sniffing his leg. Vonderhaar intervened,
"Oh, Roscoe, leave the man alone. He doesn't need your attention."

"You brought a dog to this meeting?" Malloy, dubious.

"Why, yes, but not just any dog. Roscoe is a purebred Jack Russell terrier. Both his parents have taken honors at Westminster. When I leave the
house, I take him with me."

Dunaway moved around the large desk stacked with papers and accordion files and knick-knacks. He paused momentarily to straighten a framed
document that hung behind his desk, one of many such framed documents
filling his entire wall—diplomas and licenses to practice in both Missouri
and Illinois, issued by this or that august body, all attesting to his superb
prowess in the legal arena. In fact, he had graduated from the Washington
University School of Law, class of 1968, somewhere in the middle. Not
that class ranking mattered to Frank Dunaway. He came from old money
here and he was going to get a cushy penthouse office no matter what. That,
and he was in with other old eggs from the same basket, deep pockets such
as Trey Vonderhaar, people he could count on for business. Anytime they
needed a problem to disappear, such as pesky health officers pounding on
their doors, he was their man.

He plopped down in his leather high back chair, templed his hands as if in prayer, and said, "Take a seat, gentlemen, and we'll get down to business."

Dunaway started out by summarizing the situation as he understood it. He had a way of stating the situation that made both parties feel that they were not unreasonable in the stances taken. Vonderhaar, a respectable businessman whose office was in his home, typically did not respond to unannounced visitors. Even though Malloy had said he was calling on official business, that may have been a subterfuge. As far as his client knew, that person standing at his front door could have been a down-on-his-luck minority hoping to solicit funds for his next bender, or even a Jehovah's Witness, trying to lure the householder out so as to foist Jesus on him. Malloy could see that, right?

And Malloy, a hard-working public health officer, was only doing what was required, in this instance following a lead in a case of—what was it, syphilis? That's still around? Anyway, Mr. Vonderhaar, it appeared, was not a direct suspect in this outbreak, not someone who the health department believed had caught the disease or passed it on, but merely someone who may have knowledge of persons who were possibly involved, yes? Understandably, Malloy was eager to talk with Mr. Vonderhaar and, since he did not have a phone number, he had no other choice but to simply show up and hope that Mr. Vonderhaar could spare a few minutes out of his busy day. But that did not happen and things got a bit dicey and, well, here we are.

"The standoff is over, I believe. My client has every intention of cooperating with your investigation. Within reason, of course. Go ahead, Mr. Malloy, ask your questions."

Malloy turned his chair to face Vonderhaar. "May I call you Bryson? It'll save time. I'll cut to the chase, Bryson, if that's all right with you. Do you run a private club out of your home in which the common interest is men meeting other men for the purpose of sex?"

Vonderhaar gave a scornful snort. "I don't know where you're getting your information, but you couldn't be more mistaken. I am the founder of a benevolent organization in which members look to better their worlds and that of society as a whole by thought and deed. We meet as the mood strikes, no particular schedule, coming together in the spirit of fraternity, enjoying the pleasures of fine dining, good music, and stimulating conversation."

"And if a few of these members, from time to time, run off to the nearest bedroom for a little cornhole action, that's to be accepted, even encouraged. Am I right?"

Dunaway jumped in. "Mr. Malloy, there's no need to use that sort of vulgar language, it's unprofessional."

Malloy acknowledged the rebuke, but kept his eyes on Vonderhaar. "It's a moot point, I guess, because we all know this is what happens."

"You don't know a thing about what goes on inside my home," Vonderhaar, fuming.

"Let's keep this cordial, shall we?" Dunaway, playing referee.

At this point the dog came over and started to lift his leg in Malloy's direction. "Roscoe," broke in Trey, "don't you dare!" The dog promptly retreated.

Malloy looked at Vonderhaar with wonder. "Bring an animal to a serious meeting? Perfect. Okay, chase time again. It boils down to this: since we've had not one but two individuals who tested positive for syphilis and these individuals both say, in strict confidence, they were involved in sexual activity with other men *in your home*, then what I need are the names of every member so that they may be tested at the very least and, depending on results, treated properly. It's the only way we're going to get a handle on this situation."

"I'll speak for my client on this, Mr. Malloy. What you ask is simply out of the question. You've heard of police officers being hauled into court for stopping motorists without probable cause, merely because they *looked* as though they were up to something? That's what your proposal amounts to, a sort of hunting expedition. But instead of taking careful aim at one particular target, you're taking pot shots blindly and hoping you'll hit something."

"It's called the big net approach, and it is done ... maybe not with the members of an entire club, but within social circles when one or more persons are infected."

"Mr. Malloy, your dedication to your profession is admirable and, rest assured, you are not going to walk out of here empty-handed. I told you that my client was willing to cooperate and he will. Trey?"

Vonderhaar passed over a sheet of ruled paper, folded in half. Malloy opened it and saw names, addresses, and phone numbers, neatly printed. "Two names? Just two, that's it?"

Vonderhaar nodded assent. "That's it, two of our members who just couldn't keep it in their pants, I suppose. They found an empty room and decided to act upon their desires. I happen to know because I caught them *in flagrante delicto* … in the act."

"I know what it means," said Malloy, getting rankled. "But where there's smoke, there's fire. These aren't the only members who're, as you so delicately put it, acting upon their desires. I'll need more names, even if you only *think* they may have been screwing at your place. This is your group we're talking about, your pals, this benevolent organization that you preside over. In providing their names, you show that you have their welfare at heart."

Vonderhaar shrugged helplessness. "I can only tell you what I know and these two are all that I know. This sort of indiscretion is not something that occurs at one of our dinners. In fact, it is frowned upon. We tell our members, many of them from elsewhere, that if you want to go beyond the conviviality of the evening, get to know each other more intimately, why, there are plenty of fine hotels in the area. There's no health code violation in that."

"For some reason I don't … what the hell! Your dog is on my leg!"

"He still has puppy behaviors," Vonderhaar explained, snapping his fingers twice. "Roscoe, come here." The dog continued to hump Malloy's right leg. Malloy reached down and went to grab the collar, intending to separate him. The dog snarled and kept at it, making short, raspy grunting sounds.

"He's getting off on me," said Malloy, rising. He tried several quick motions of his leg, and still the dog hung on, standing on his back paws, working towards a climax. This was getting embarrassing. Vonderhaar too, rose from his chair, going for Roscoe, but it was too late: Malloy, a former soccer player, sent Roscoe sailing across the room, banging mightily into a credenza. Vonderhaar rushed to the dog's aid, picking him up like a hurt child. The dog appeared stunned as his master stroked the back of his head, whispering, "there, there," all the while glaring at Malloy.

"Get that animal neutered," Malloy told him, checking his pant leg for anything amiss.

"Not until he's sired his first litter!"

"You are so full of shit," said Malloy, instantly regretting it.

Dunaway circled his desk and got between them. "Well, gentlemen, that concludes our session. Mr. Malloy, I thank you for coming and I trust you'll find your way back out. I'm going to have a word with my client now."

But Malloy didn't move. He stood there picking at some loose thread on the sleeve of his sportcoat. Then he made a show of clicking his pen a few times and carefully clipping it to his shirt pocket. It appeared as if he hadn't heard Dunaway.

"Mr. Malloy?"

"Oh, one more thing," he said, coming out of his trance. "I ask that Bryson here get tested for syphilis. It's standard for anyone who has been in the same environment where the disease has been found. He can either come into our clinic and we'll have him in and out within an hour. Or he can go to his own physician, but we'll need to see the test results."

"I have no problem with that," said Vonderhaar. "I take care of myself with the help of my excellent doctor, Brock Silber. I'll see him this week and I'm sure he'll forward the test results."

"That would be peachy," said Malloy. "I'll give you a week to have it on my desk."

The elevator door opened to the spacious lobby and Malloy stepped out. He wondered if he needed to sign out on the visitor book. The jolly guard was at her station, engrossed in a magazine. She probably didn't care who came or went or what time they did, she was just passing time in the big city. He headed for the glass revolving doors and just before he walked into them he heard her booming voice, "Goodbye, Mister Kadiddlehopper!"

THIRTEEN

ANOTHER DOWNBEAT DAY in the epi room, shortly before nine, all investigators were present. Several were on the phone attempting to get contacts to come to the clinic on their own without having to drive to their homes and personally badger them to do so. Betsy and Martha were comparing notes on their separate cases, suspecting correctly that they were connected; there was a copulator common to both. Martha would assume both cases. Malloy was getting ready to go in the field, a Wunnenberg's Street Guide laid out to map his stops, trying to be logistical in his foray. Arnold was on the phone with some poor schlub who apparently was in denial over his sexuality, Arnold saying, "Look, James, I spoke with your doctor and he says you have a lax sphincter. Now why don't you just come clean and …."

This was the calm before the storm.

At precisely 9:09 Joe Sargent blew into the room like a hurricane. Malloy was just walking out when Joe stopped him with a forcefully planted palm on his chest: "Siddown!" This caught everyone's attention and those still on the phone were heard saying, "Uh, I'll call you back later." Joe had just stormed out of Karl's office after he and Karl had gone over the monthly stats that Karl tabulated and diligently recorded. Each month, on or about the fifth, which this day was, the final numbers for the previous month were ready. The investigators were well aware of the effect that the stats could have on Joe, and now—surprise!—they were seeing the fearsome mask of the creature they most dreaded: the royally pissed Joe.

The thing sticking in Joe's craw was the terrible news that the epi staff had interviewed only thirty-six percent of all positive GC seen in the clinic for the month of November, as opposed to the sixty-one percent interviewed during the previous month. Joe tended to take this indolence personally.

"Every one of you is to blame! Every one of you could've done more, found time for one more interview. Lazy, complacent shits, all of you!" He was just warming up, they knew. He began pacing the room, a Kodiak bear disturbed from his hibernation. "You sit here chatting to your friends on the phone, clipping your nails, while these positives are walking out the door. Is that good policy? Is that our answer to the epidemic of gonorrhea in this city?" No one said a word. "Well, is it?"

To Martha's horror the angry bear was looking at her for some reason, demanding an answer. "No, sir," she said with as much surety as she could muster.

"You're goddamn right it isn't!" he thundered, and for emphasis Joe kicked a small coffee table, which upended and clattered on the tiled floor, one of its legs barely hanging on. Then he left, and they heard him kicking the wall out in the hall. Then he was back in the epi room, face beet red, scowling, cursing, saying how he'd push them twice as hard.

"From now on it's teams A and B," he said with a snarl. "Each team must spend four hours a day in the clinic and each investigator will do a minimum of four GC interviews per day. Got that? GC is now equal priority with syphilis except GC contacts do not have to be seen within three days. Betsy, Arnold, Shaun and Derald are the new members of Team A. The rest of you make up Team B." He cast his eye around the room looking for signs of dissent. "If that doesn't work, if we don't pull up our stats in a big way, then I'll have you working nine-hour days with five GC interviews minimum. And if it comes to that, don't go crying to your union about being overworked, because you don't have a union. Instead, you've got me!"

They sat in their chairs regarding Joe warily, hoping like hell he was done. He wasn't. "You ever hear of the proactive approach? That's where you don't sit on your ass and wait for the problem to come to you. You go to the problem. What this means in your case is that you don't wait for the clinicians to call over and say, 'We've got one for you. Can you come get him?' No, if you've got time you walk down the hall and go in that clinic and you ask around if anyone's got a positive for you to interview. That's how we're going to get things done, got that?" Now he seemed to be looking at Tut.

Tut knew all too well that he did not have a way with words; he felt he should keep his mouth shut. Joe, however, would not be ignored, not by the biggest slacker of the lot, the one on the verge of getting fired. "Got that?" he repeated with even more menace.

Tut gave a half-ass smile which Joe took as a smirk. He said, "You won't find me remorse in my duties, nope."

Joe's eyes grew wide with incredulity. "Remiss, you idiot! It's remiss in my duties, not remorse. Get it straight! But, hey, if it's remorse you want, how 'bout this?" Beside his desk, Tut had an REO Speedwagon poster tacked to the wall. Joe walked over and ripped it down. That felt so good that he went over to where Betsy sat and from her area pulled down a picture that her six-year-old daughter had made showing a house with smiling people in the windows and trees with green leaves in the yard. Betsy was aghast and put her head down, feeling shamed at the malice welling up inside. Joe was on a tear now, looking around for his next conquest and finding it on the wall next to Malloy, a picture of a man and a woman pushing a little girl on a swing in a park. The couple was smiling, the little girl was having a ball, all was right with the world. The caption read: VD IS FOR EVERYONE. YOU CAN'T BE TOO SAFE. GET CHECKED OUT TODAY. Joe went to tear that down, too, but hesitated, seeing how the message related to the mission he was preaching. Then he changed his mind, pawing at it, balling it up to the size of a grapefruit, and pitching it into a wastebasket halfway across the room. A three-pointer.

"That's that," he said, wiping his hands as if they were dirty. "Now get back to work."

With Joe gone, it felt as if he'd taken all the ions with him. The epi room was still and unnaturally quiet. All they could do was to stare at one another, a few lifting eyebrows significantly. Malloy was the first to speak. "Damn, that was inspiring."

"A prince of a guy," added Arnold, "a model of patience and compassion in employee relations."

"He's going to have a heart attack," said Betsy.

The new members of Team A got together and conferred, deciding that since their day was already planned out, and some of them had appointments with patients, they would start the new schedule tomorrow. Malloy grabbed his things and headed out once again. In the stairwell he ran into Terry Fallon, the local pop star who'd had several Top 40 hits back in the day. Fallon liked the clinic, found the staff capable and professional. Best of all, the service was free. Malloy had interviewed him a few times, always for GC contacts.

"Uh-oh! At it again, old man?"

"Hey, man," greeted Fallon, middle-aged, wearing a hangdog look. "I think I caught a case. Started dripping this morning."

"Bummer," said Malloy. "You'd think by now that you'd have some sort of radar for that thing, a little voice to say, 'Watch out for this one, she's got the clap.' Or you could wear a rubber and not worry."

"Can't do rubbers, man. It's like taking a shower with a raincoat on. It's all about the sensation. I'd rather keep the feeling and take my chances, dig?"

Malloy chucked him on the shoulder. "Your chances haven't been that good lately, but go on up. They'll take care of you."

"You know it, man. You guys get all my business." He laughed at his own dark joke and continued up the steps.

He went to the parking lot, got his keys from Timba who was engrossed in a Ross McDonald novel, *The Blue Hammer*. It was a fine day for early December, sunny and mild with the promise of a productive time in the field. He had contacts to call on in north city and the Southside, some getting stale in his pouch—the reason being a combination of no one ever home; no response to the cards he'd been leaving; family members assuring him, falsely, that the contact in question would show his or her face in the clinic forthwith; family members saying they were not responsible for the actions of the contact and please, from now on don't be coming 'round knocking so early. And so on.

But first he had to take care of a little matter of blatant non-compliance. Chris Dickerson had been contacted and told that he'd been exposed to GC and that examination and possible treatment was required. That was two weeks ago and still no action taken. The OP, a thirty-five-year-old grade school teacher with her hair pulled back in a bun, had wept bitterly in the interview room, naming only him. After three days of waiting for Dickerson to either show at the clinic or provide proof of treatment elsewhere, Malloy went to his job, Lumberman's Pickup down near Lemay, where Dickerson drove a forklift. He first went to Dickerson directly, attempting to flag him down, but the man just waved Malloy off and kept on rolling down the aisles of the massive warehouse. This left Malloy no other choice but to go to the supervisor. Not all supervisors were amenable to public health officers asking for help in enforcing health codes on uncooperative employees, but Mike Shotwell was. Shotwell checked Malloy's credentials, listened to his telling of the problem, Malloy saying only that Dickerson had been exposed to a communicable disease and that, after being told of this, he still was not lifting a finger toward that clean bill of health. Shotwell, who likely knew it was some type of venereal disease they were talking about, said he just didn't understand that sort of bullheadedness, a guy like Dickerson was only hurting himself. Malloy said that it happens a lot, guys sometimes get it in their head that it can't happen to them or that if they do have something it will go away on its own.

Shotwell took a walkie-talkie, pressed a few buttons, and got Dickerson on the horn. "Chris, would you stop what you're doing and come to my office for a minute? Never mind what for, just get in here." He clicked off. Shotwell pointed to an adjacent office on the other side of a glass window and said to Malloy, "I'll let you two talk in private, but I'll be right there if you need me."

Dickerson walked in, saw Malloy and spat on the floor in contempt. "I told you leave me alone, and now you come to my job. What the fuck is wrong with you?"

It was not Malloy's nature to be intimidated by hulking, overbearing chowderheads. He looked Dickerson in the eye and said, "If you had gone to get checked out like I asked, then I wouldn't be here."

"Yeah? And I told you, tell me who gave my name and I'll get it taken care of."

"You know I can't do that. The names are totally confidential, the same as your name will never be given out."

"Bullshit, it can be only one person, the girl I've been seeing for damn near two years. But I want to hear it from you. How many guys did she name?"

"Can't tell you that either. What I can tell you, though, is that you need to come with me to the clinic right now. This is serious, no more putting off."

At this, Dickerson started cursing and blustering until Shotwell came in. "Listen, Chris, I know a little about what's going on and I think it's in everyone's best interest that you cooperate with this man. I'll give you the time off with pay if you'll see the doctor and make sure you're all right. I mean, I had a cousin who had some kind of lump in his groin area and he let it go and it turned into a hernia."

"I don't give a shit about your cousin's hernia. I don't have what this guy thinks I have, and I ain't seeing no doctor."

"Chris, you're a good worker and I like you as a person, but you need to go and get checked out and don't come back until you do."

That was a week ago, and as far as Malloy knew the ultimatum was still in effect, yet Dickerson had done nothing to comply. Besides walking around with gonorrhea and possibly infecting others, he was flouting the law. Now here he was back at the man's job, about to apply leverage—again—on Dickerson via Shotwell. Malloy was pretty sure things were going to get ugly.

He parked out front beneath the big plywood sign and went straight to Shotwell's office. He rapped on the door frame. The supervisor looked up from some paperwork he was doing: "There he is, the pubic health officer. Looking for some pubes to check are you?" He gave a hearty laugh. "What's up?"

"Same as before," said Malloy, stepping into the office. "Last I heard Dickerson was maybe going to see his own doctor and get back to me with the results. I'm still waiting."

Shotwell leaned back in his chair, huffed, and said, "Well, you can keep on waiting because he never came back after that day. I guess he decided his pride was more important than his job. I told you he was bullheaded."

"Damn!"

"Damn is right. You set the wheels in motion when you walked in here and Chris wound up falling off the truck. He was a good worker, too."

"Now I've got to find him. You have his application, his home address?"

"Give out personal information from an employee's file? I can't do that. You've got your confidentiality and I've got mine. You guys must have all sorts of resources, you can find him on your own."

Malloy drove out of the lot and got on a stretch of South Broadway where there's not much in the way of housing for several miles clear down to Carondelet. The river on his right, the occasional gas station or brick yard on his left. He drove along, arm out the window, listening to "Bette Davis Eyes" by Kim Carnes, and when that was done the playlist went straight to Rick James' "Super Freak." He was feeling good despite the letdown back there. He knew not to take it personal, that Dickerson wasn't intentionally deflating his better-than-average percentile of cases closed out, all contacts located and treated. He still might find that ornery bastard, still might be able to close out the ER on this case favorably. One thing that bothered him, though. The OP named only Dickerson and yet Dickerson acted as though she had cheated on him. If Dickerson did turn up infected and in the resulting interview named only her, then things would get dicey. He would not let up until the truth came out.

Don't take it personal, he told himself again. But that's not always possible, an inner voice shot back. Case in point: Trey Vonderhaar. Right from the get-go, the guy had been playing him for a chump. Demeaning him through the intercom, refusing to come to the door, sending a lackey instead. And when finally they met in person, that superior air, projecting the vibe that he was too important for health department business, and, when pressured to deliver, dangling a couple of bullshit names in front of him like he was that easily duped.

Those names turned out to be worthless, epidemiologic dead-ends— one guy, who owned a chain of liquor stores in Baltimore, tested negative for syphilis but got treated anyway, and the other guy, what? A human popsicle. After weeks of waiting to hear from his counterparts in the Seattle Health Department where the ER request had been forwarded, he finally got word that one Rainer Wolbeck had perished in an Alpine avalanche during a skiing trip, his presumed syphilitic condition perishing with him. A dead contact, how convenient. He was sure that Vonderhaar would have known. But the loose thread in this case was not to be tied off any time soon, for he, Karl, and Joe had met in Joe's office specifically to address this problematic case. After floating a couple of ideas, including bribing Freddie DuCoin to copy Vonderhaar's little black book—it was there somewhere—Joe decided that they had gotten all they could from Vonderhaar. Let it go for now, he'd said, reluctantly.

He made three more stops, with varying degrees of success, then returned to the clinic. That afternoon he exceeded his mandatory four interviews, doing six; four guys and two gals who collectively named fourteen contacts, an average of two point three. No surprise there; they were young and sexually active. When four o'clock came, he cut out early because this was Wednesday and he had screening tonight at the Stadium Hotel.

He pulled up to his apartment just as Sheila was walking up the steps to go inside. She had her back to him, carrying a couple bags of groceries. She set them down while unlocking the front door, and Malloy, now out of his car and walking toward the house, called out her name. She turned, and seeing it was him, gave the merest nod of recognition. Then she picked up her groceries and went inside. Not even a "Hey, how ya doin'?" She must be having a bad day, he thought.

FOURTEEN

THE STADIUM HOTEL on 20th Street, next to the once-bustling Union Station, could rival any establishment in any city in America for sleaze.

The building itself dated to 1892. St. Louis was at the top of its game, a player in the arena of muscular capitalism, and Union Station was the hub of that arena. Over the entrance, colorful tiles set in limestone spelled out YMCA, but it had long ceased catering to the needs of young Christian men. The basement housed a leather bar called Chaps, while a former ballroom just off the lobby housed a dimly lit bar, Martin's, which opened at six.

Above this menagerie were three floors of cheap rooms, once the domain of bachelor railroad workers and now the abode of aging men living month-to-month on social security checks. By day, the lobby of this hotel was the haunt of these codgers, who occupied ratty, piss-stained couches, chain smoked, popped Sen-Sens, and watched soaps with only each other and their tubercular coughs to keep them company.

But at night it was a different story. The place transformed into a raucous, throbbing venue for gays who were hot into disco, in the case of Martin's, or torch songs, in the case of Chaps.

As usual, Malloy and Mike Wasserman set up their makeshift testing site on folding tables in a laundromat off in a corner of the basement. Sometime before eight, they had schlepped in two large cardboard boxes of stuff. GC testing was done by inserting a calgi swab into a urethra and then transferring any little beasties picked up by the swab to a shallow culture plate with a burnt umber-colored medium that *gonococci* found yummy. The culture plates were taken to the lab on the ground floor of the health department, placed in an incubator, and three days later—voila! GC or not GC.

For syphilis testing there were needles, syringes, alcohol prep pads, elastic bands for tying off veins, gauze pads and surgical tape for covering the puncture, glass tubes with rubber stoppers for blood, metal racks for the tubes, and a centrifuge for running RPRs. The centrifuge was the heaviest and most cumbersome piece of equipment they carried, but it could give results in less than 30 minutes. Results were either positive or negative for the presence of the disease. If positive, it would not differentiate whether it was a new infection or an old infection that had been treated; like other diseases from measles to yellow fever, once you caught syphilis, you had the antibody for life. To try to determine whether a positive blood was a current infection, Malloy would do a cursory examination of the individual's mouth, palms, torso, anus and genital area, looking for signs.

"Please lift your arm," he told a shirtless man. The man lifted and Malloy took a close look at the area just beneath the axilla. "Hmm," he said, palpating the area with a latex-gloved finger. "Could be a lesion, but more likely a pimple. Okay, now drop your pants."

"All right!" With his bristling black beard and strapping physique, he could have passed for a northwoods lumberjack. It wasn't easy disrobing in this janitor's closet / exam room. The guy dropped trou and Malloy recoiled. The head of his penis, the coronal sulcus, was purple and swollen and skewered with an open-ended metal ring, a miniature bent barbell. Malloy had heard of Prince Albert piercings before, but had never seen one.

"Hardware … didn't expect that."

The hirsute one hoisted his member for a better look. "It's new," he said. "Do you like it?"

Malloy took it in hand. Grasping lightly, he turned it over; it looked worse on the underside. "Ow!" he winced. "That's got to hurt."

"Just at first, a day or two, but that's good because pain is what it's all about."

"Pain is overrated," Malloy, no trace of sarcasm. "But why do that to yourself?"

"For the greater glory of my fabulous cock, why else?"

Malloy digested this for a moment. "I'm glad you hold it in such high regard. Now, let's take a quick look here." A half minute later, he snapped off the gloves. "Okay, you're good to go. No apparent signs, but I'm not a doctor or a nurse. I've got your information and we'll see you in the clinic tomorrow for a more definitive diagnosis, see what the RPR is really telling us."

The guy gave no answer but instead was studying Malloy intently. Finally, it came out. "Has anyone ever told you that you look like Nick Nolte—*Rich Man, Poor Man?*"

"I thought it was Redford," said Malloy.

"Redford's just a pretty boy. Nolte's got some stones, and so do you."

In the two and a half hours they were expected to be there, Malloy wore two hats. He acted as clinician, drawing blood, taking swabs, giving those samples to Mike Wassermann, standing nearby. Malloy also acted as public health officer, offering education or counseling on STD concerns to those who asked. If a patron turned up obviously positive, sporting a fresh syphilitic chancre, say, there was no time to do an interview. They were not there for that. The investigator would get the name and number and address, and stress the need for immediate treatment.

Mike Wassermann, a great lab tech but as socially facile as a badger, had but one job and that was to run the tests. Wasserman was a very odd duck. His five-foot-eight frame carried about 240 pounds, much of it packed in a belly that strained against the polyester fabric of button-down K-Mart shirts. Every now and then one of those buttons would go flying off. He wore a white lab coat, even here in this extremely casual setting, and horn-rimmed glasses with thick black frames. Adding to the mad scientist look was a shock of wavy, black hair, an asymmetric affair which he himself barbered without much care. Supposedly he had bipolar disorder and took lithium carbonate for his condition, which might explain the white, sometimes frothy residue that often formed at the corners of his mouth.

Wassermann had been with City Health for ages and in addition to the bipolar baggage, he had OCD, which made him extremely thorough in his work. If he got to know you, he would proudly tell you that he was the great-grandson of August Paul von Wassermann, the German bacteriologist who developed the Wassermann Test or Wassermann Reaction, an antibody test for syphilis based on complement fixation.

Malloy was Wassermann's favorite investigator because he didn't treat him dismissively or say unkind things behind his back like some of the others. Wassermann actually looked forward to these screenings at the gay bar. Malloy would pick him up at home and drop him back off, and they would joke in the car and bond a little more each week.

They both favored the Stadium Hotel much more than the Club Baths, the other pest-hole they went to regularly. At the gay bar at least they could drink. Now that he had a free minute he was going down the hall to Chaps to get another round, a Bud for himself and a Shirley Temple for Mike.

As an anthropology major, Malloy found Chaps a gold mine of human study. The basement bar was the clubhouse of the Gateway MC, a hell-bent-for-leather bunch of middle-aged guys who shared a taste for macho posing, motorcycles, and ball-busting sex. Their uniform implied the rebel-outlaw lifestyle—tight, faded jeans to accent the bulge at the crotch, wide leather belt with plenty of metal studs, a batch of keys jangling from a belt loop on the right or left side, depending on sexual preference. Above the belt, a distressed leather jacket with club colors and insignia, and billed leather cap. The intended effect, deliberate or not, was to pattern themselves after Brando and company in the 1951 biker classic, *The Wild One*. No one had suggested this comparison, but it was obvious to Malloy, that movie being one of his favorites, although Lee Marvin, not Marlon, was his man in that flick.

These butch bikers weren't nearly as gruff as they looked, Malloy knew. At the core they were nothing more than teddy bears. It was a tender scene to see them standing around the Wurlitzer, plunking down quarters, weeping openly to Crystal Gayle's "Don't It Make Your Brown Eyes Blue?"

At one end of the floor they had a tricked-out chopper, a 1961 Harley Fat Boy, gleaming chrome with buffed leather saddlebags. Mounted on a raised platform, it was cordoned off, inaccessible to greasy-fingered mortals. It was the bejeweled idol, the golden calf, of this subterranean sect. At any given moment a small service was in progress with several acolytes gathered round, beer in hand, paying homage to the dream machine on its altar.

Malloy also made the announcements. He had just made one here in Chaps, his own clarion voice making do for a microphone, and now he was heading upstairs to Martin's Bar to make one last announcement for the testing. The bartender reluctantly cut the music, stopping The Village People mid-track, and prompting a chorus of "Aw, c'mon!"

The bartender gave an effeminate wave and spoke into the mic. "Health department, fellas, this guy just can't stay away."

Malloy took up the mic. He looked to the crowd on the floor, bathed in multi-colored beams from the twirling disco ball on the ceiling. "May I have your attention? This is the last call for free and confidential tests for syphilis and gonorrhea. We're set up in the laundromat downstairs. Some results will be made available tonight. C'mon down, we need the company."

The bartender grabbed the mic, turned to Malloy and said, "This is your third announcement tonight. You know what I think, guys?"

In unison, a resounding "What?"

The bartender smiled wickedly. "I think we got ourselves a microphone queen!"

Malloy dropped Mike off at his apartment then turned north and made every green light on Kingshighway from Gravois all the way to West Pine, where he turned to get to his own place. He was bone-tired as he climbed the steps to the ornate wooden door that opened to the large, lighted foyer of his apartment building. It was nearly 11:30, everyone asleep. He walked right in his apartment, door unlocked as usual, because everyone here was cool. He switched on the light and saw an envelope on the floor where no envelope had been before. He put down the box of blood samples, picked up the envelope and opened it with a sense of dread. As he read the hand-written note a sinking feeling came over him.

> Dear Mr. Malloy,
> I have just learned that my cousin Roger is moving here from Providence, and he will need a nice place to live. I have offered him your apartment. Please make arrangements to vacate by the end of the month.
> Sincerely,
> Sheila Noonan, Landlord.

Malloy crumpled the note into a ball and punted it across the room.

FIFTEEN

THE NEXT DAY after work Malloy went to the Italian restaurant on the corner. Fortino's was just one of the many reasons he loved his location. It had been there since the '50s, occupying the basement floor of a large apartment building, the Melrose. The ambiance was something else—signs in different languages, paintings, Italian movie posters, antiques including old crank-handled telephones, knickknacks and bric-a-brac covering every square inch of wall and ceiling, which was so low that you had to bend at the waist walking through if you were over five ten. The lighting dim and the smells wonderful. He knew everyone there and they knew him, knew that he chased VD for a living and knew that he liked his linguini with chicken livers in the white sauce, not the red. Malloy, for his part, thought it utterly amazing that they even offered linguini with chicken livers in two different sauces. Today, though, he was sitting at his usual booth near the door, drinking Chianti and mulling his options.

The end of the month was only twenty days away. How was he supposed to find a place by then, and what kind of place would that be, so hastily chosen? And what were the chances this apartment would have anywhere near the charm of his current digs or the convenience of a supermarket just one block over, even if that supermarket was dirty and didn't carry certain items he craved and he was often accosted by aggressive panhandlers in the parking lot? Nor would it likely be in a neighborhood like this one, where he could stroll around in the evening, winding up either at Fortino's or the cafe on the other corner where they had live music on the patio, weather permitting. No, he wasn't going to chance into something as good as this, which meant that his happiness, and therefore his mental health, would be compromised. Hell, it was already compromised just sitting here thinking about his situation.

He could berate himself for not listening to that tiny voice in the back of his head telling him it was bad policy to screw your landlady. Or, he could berate that voice for not speaking loudly and emphatically enough—stupid voice! But that vixen Sheila was as much to blame as he. If she hadn't kicked her husband out last year, if she hadn't always looked good enough to eat, if she hadn't chosen to change that light bulb when she did—

and now that he thought about it, the timing was deliberate. She *knew* he would hear her and come out to say hi. If all that hadn't transpired the way it did …

It was futile to assign blame, he knew that. What had happened was an inexorable attraction of a man to a woman, a magnetic force, which had been going on for eons and which had a mind of its own. You couldn't stop it; you might as well try to stop the tide. It was well documented: guys would risk everything they cared about—livelihood, personal welfare, even family ties—just to get their rocks off with someone new. The engorged phallus was the very definition of self-absorbed, monomaniacal, striving toward gratification, no matter the cost. It did not think ahead or weigh consequences. It had no morals, no conscience, although it did have recriminations. And how!

As Malloy sipped his Chianti, a thought entered his brain and it was not the first time either. The thought was part rueful, part wistful, and it was this: that he was every bit as promiscuous as the men and women who showed up to the clinic day after day, asking to be cured of their affliction but not the behavior that caused it. They didn't want to curb their sexual appetites. They just wanted the burning or the ache or the swelling or the lesion to go away so they could look around for another try and hope like hell they wouldn't catch something the next time. Malloy was no different. He'd had the clap in college and, though it scared him, it did not scare him into wanting a steady relationship with anyone. At least, yet. At twenty-nine, he was still acting like a horndog, still doing the one-night stands, a lifestyle choice that sometimes turned around and bit him in the ass.

Claudia Stellini, for example. When was it, a couple Halloweens ago? Walking down Euclid, witnessing the spectacle of latter-day bacchanalia—women in stiletto heels, fishnet stockings and loosely laced bustiers; guys in nothing but sneakers and sequined jockstraps leading other guys on leashes; dogs dressed as people, people dressed as dogs; everyone moonstruck, ratcheting up the absurd. Suddenly, a tall, striking redhead blocked his path. He liked redheads. She looked him up and down and nodded approval. "You're just what I've been looking for," she said.

Malloy was used to doing the soliciting, but he didn't mind the flip-flop every now and then. There was something in her eyes that told him she was half a bubble off plumb, but he went with it because she looked good and it was kind of a turn-on being around someone who was so sure of what they wanted. Plus, he couldn't wait to see what she looked like in the buff. That opportunity came sooner than later when she suggested they go to her apartment nearby. There they cracked a bottle of vino and got down to business. He wasn't at all disappointed in her body, not with rosebud nipples capping off a stunning pair of thirty-eight Ds and "down there" a furry landing strip of auburn that said, "Climb aboard, sailor." She said she liked a lot of foreplay, but got bent out of shape when he played with her extra nipple.

"Leave it alone, would you."

"It's pretty interesting," he said. "I never saw one before."

"It's called a supernumerary nipple and they're not that uncommon. My roommate in college had one, too."

It was an inch below her true nipple, on the side of her left breast. "Can I tongue it?"

"No!"

She moaned and groaned and drooled during sex, and when it was over they fell asleep. In the morning, he awoke and felt icky. Not from any misgivings about the sex, but because her bed was full of grit or sand or something, as if an animal slept there. She was a respiratory therapist at Barnes-Jewish, and he would have thought a respiratory therapist would keep her bed clean. He couldn't wait to get out of there, so he kept looking at his watch and saying how he was late for an appointment. A goodbye smooch and he was out the door, never to see her again. That's why they called it casual sex.

Two weeks later, a guy came into the clinic, dripping. Malloy interviewed him, a stonemason with arms like an orangutan. He didn't play games, naming two women during the critical period, one who worked checkout at the Southside Schnucks and another, less findable, who was "a nurse or something at some hospital." They had met in a bar and he had taken her to his place. He called her Carla. As Malloy pressed him for details, he became more and more certain that it was Claudia.

"Did she have any distinguishing features?" The guy had already described her pretty well, but Malloy was fishing a little deeper. Maybe it had been dark and he didn't see it.

The guy laughed. "Well, now that you mention it, she did have a third nipple. It was the weirdest thing. God, she was sensitive about it, too."

Bingo.

After the stonemason left, Malloy filled in the woman's correct name and address on the ER, took it to Arnold and asked that he run it, citing "conflict of interest." Then he walked over to the clinic side and asked Del Goodwin, the physician assistant, for a shot, 2.4 million units of aqueous penicillin in each cheek. Friend that he was, Goodwin complied and never inquired as to the reason for this act of masochism. He didn't need to.

The waiter came over with a bottle and offered to fill his glass. Malloy thanked him and felt another pang at the thought that when he left Fortino's would no longer be his place. He caught himself. Wait—not when he left, but *if* he left. He might reason with her, although Sheila seemed like one of those women who, when they decide something, decides for good. Still, he had to try. If it was the sight of him that was bothering her, he would promise to stay out of sight. She wouldn't even know he was there. He would mail her the rent, not ever knocking at her door. He could also offer to pay more rent. He could afford another hundred a month, anything.

Filled with resolve, he drained his glass and went outside. It was still light. He could see his place from Fortino's front door. He walked across Sarah Street and as he got there a UPS truck pulled up. Delivery for Sheila Noonan. Malloy accepted it. Here was an excuse to talk to her. He was doing her a favor, signing for her package. That cold shoulder of hers would warm right up.

He knocked at her door on the first floor. No response, but she was in there because there was loud music going on with a male voice giving directions of some sort. He tried the knob and the door was unlocked. He opened the door a few inches and called her name, then opened the door all the way and went in. He passed through a parlor and went to the source of the noise, a large studio, her sanctum sanctorum. Now he saw her, in tights, squatting and thrusting to a workout tape, her back to him, facing a wall of books and records. The music, kind of a rumba beat, was booming and a male voice was saying, "That's it! Now bend, deeper, crunch those abs …" He was twenty feet behind her, booming, "Sheila! Hey!" She still didn't hear. He walked up and tapped her on the shoulder.

She spun round like a dervish, eyes filled with rage. He had startled her, understandable. "It's just me," he shouted. He was thinking that she looked pretty sexy all sweaty like that, a stray damp lock of hair curling over her lavender headband. Adorable, really.

With a prizefighter's jab she punched him square on the sternum, then she slapped him hard. "You prick! What the fuck are you doing here? Get out! Now! Now! Now!" Each "now" growing in volume. She was shoving him toward the pocket doors that led back out. The voice on the tape saying, "That's it, squeeze those buns—tight, tighter!" Just before exiting he turned and tried to give her the package. She took it and threw it in his face, nailing him square in the eye. With one final shove he was out, Sheila sliding the pocket doors together with a bang. "Asshole!" she yelled after him.

Then he was back in the foyer. Walking up to his apartment, the one eye really tearing up, his ego crushed like a grape, his plan shot to hell, he told himself that he'd better get packing.

SIXTEEN

THE CALL on line twenty-five asked for him by name. He pressed the tab and the blinking light went off. "Hello, Shaun—may I call you Shaun? This is Sherri Voss, remember me? I was in your clinic a couple weeks ago with an infection and we talked."

"I remember you well. You named one person, a Chris Dickerson, a real piece of work, that guy."

"You said it was confidential," a tone of betrayal in her voice. "Anything I told you was between us."

"That's right, it was. Just between us. So what's going on?"

"He's been here, to my house and to my work, threatening me, saying I went out on him and now he's lost his job because of it. You must have told him, how else could he know?"

"Yeah, I told him. I *had* to tell him, but your name never came up. I only told him that he'd been exposed to someone who'd been diagnosed positive for GC, I mean, gonorrhea. I guess he surmised that had to be you, sorry."

"This is bad," she said. "He is not a nice person. Now I'm worried about my safety."

"What you need to do is go to the adult abuse office—I forget, you live in the county or city?"

"City."

"Go to the city courts, the adult abuse office, apply for an order of protection. The court will issue one and if he can be served, he'll have to appear before a judge. The judge will give Chris a chance to explain himself, and because whatever comes out of his mouth the judge probably won't believe, the judge will put the protection order into effect and he'll be forced to keep away from you."

"And if he doesn't?"

"He can go to jail. Listen, you've *got* to do this."

"All right, I will, but in the meantime I'm worried."

"You see him, call me. I still need him to get to a doctor, get him treated prophylactically."

"He doesn't use those."

"You're thinking prophylactic, a condom. Prophylactically means preventively, as in I need Chris Dickerson to get treated—preventively or curatively, either way."

"He's on the loose. Good luck finding him."

"I know, I've been to the address you gave, the place on Keokuk. I looked through the windows and it looks empty. I've left messages, that's about all I can do."

"He moved out after he lost his job. He won't say where he's staying. He just drives around in that big truck of his, like some desperado. And it's weird because he's sort of religious, he's got one of those Christian symbols on the back of his truck."

"A Jesus fish?"

"Yeah, and he once told me that he could see himself as an avenging angel if anyone ever messed with him."

"Just steer clear of him as best you can and get that protection order. Otherwise, how you doing?"

"Oh, coming along, you know. I'm due for a follow-up this week, maybe I'll see you when I'm there."

"Yeah, that'd be great. Know why?"

"Why?"

"Because you named only Chris and when I spoke to Chris the news really hurt him, as if someone he trusted had been unfaithful. I could see it in his eyes—I'm psychic like that. A minute ago you mentioned that he accused you of going out on him. Maybe there's truth to that, huh? I haven't interviewed Chris because we only interview positives and I can't find him anyway, but if I did interview him I'll bet he'd name only you as a sex partner. Funny, because there's got to be at least one more person in this equation. So, you want to give me his name now, over the phone, or do you want to wait 'til you come in for your follow-up?"

Silence at the other end, then a click.

"Nice play," said Arnold who had eavesdropped.

"How's that?" asked Malloy.

"The way you turned tables on her. Beautifully executed. Like I always say: you're the maestro until someone else comes along."

Karl walked in, looking around to see who was available. "Well, if it isn't Team A—alert, motivated, ready to vanquish all venereal disease." He was rubbing his hands together like he was excited about something. "We just got a call," he declared, "the Club Baths of all places. They've got a guy there who's apparently very sick. He's been there a while, like thirty-six hours or something, and he doesn't want to leave."

"Call an ambulance," said Malloy.

"That's what I first suggested, but Mike, the manager there, says he doesn't need the drama of medics carrying a patron out on a stretcher. But here's why we're going there right now: Mike says this guy, in addition to looking like a truck ran over him, has penile lesions—but Mike didn't say 'penile lesions.' He said 'sores on his peter.' Mike inspected him, I suppose. And what do we do with sores on someone's peter?"

"Call an epidemiologist?" guessed Tut.

"We dark field," said Arnold conclusively.

"That's right," said Karl. "We're going to dust off the dark field microscope that's been sitting there in the closet for who knows how long and we're taking it to the gay bath house. Sound like fun? Now, who hasn't done one?"

In epi school, they all had done hands-on training in dark field microscopy, a two-hour session meant to demonstrate the fundamentals of viewing a live specimen of *Treponema pallidum*, the causative agent of syphilis. But in real life the opportunity rarely came up, mostly because the syphilitic chancre disappears after a relatively short window. By the time its owner grew concerned enough to do something about it, it was gone or going away. Also, the sore was painless; if it appeared on the inside of the labia or around the anus, its owner might never know it was there.

Betsy said she hadn't done one. Karl said this was her lucky day. Betsy said fine, but added that she wasn't confident doing the procedure by herself and could someone accompany her?

"I wasn't going to have you go alone," assured Karl. "We don't want a female investigator in a room alone with a naked man anyway, no matter how competent she might be. We're not too busy right now, so Shaun will go with you. He's done a few of these and knows the drill."

On the way out they ran into Mohammed Shafi, the medical director of the clinic. He had a coffee in one hand and a bag of candies and chocolate bars from Woolworth's in the other. Seeing the sturdy wooden box that Malloy carried by its handle, he asked what they were doing and, when he heard, he said in his trillling Middle Eastern accent, "Oh, wow! I've always wanted to see a dark field examination. Can I come along?"

Well, sure, why not? The Palestinian doctor would bring his own car so he could leave at will. Malloy and Betsy waited for Timba to get Malloy's Datsun out from behind an Impala and a Newport, yachts compared to Malloy's dinghy. Malloy tipped Timba and they were off, with Shafi trailing.

Malloy was no stranger to the Club Baths. He and other male investigators before him had been screening there for years. By arrangement with management, they showed up every month on a particular evening and were given a small cubicle with one bare light bulb, a space normally reserved for wanton sex. In this sad excuse for a clinical setting, they would either draw blood for syphilis testing or swab throats, urethras and rectums for GC testing. It smelled awful, and it felt germy like you didn't want to touch anything. Malloy thought of it as a way station in Dante's Inferno.

They walked in and Mike Deerfield, the amiable day manager, met them in the lobby. "I didn't know you were bringing a group," he said to Malloy, eyeing Betsy and Dr. Shafi.

"It's not often that we get to do one of these," Malloy told him, lifting the box with the microscope, "so we see it as a teaching exercise. And thanks for calling. So, where's the patient?"

"He's a patient already? You guys are quick. He's down that hall in a room, the same room he's been in since yesterday afternoon." Mike lowered his voice and said, "Tell you the truth, I'm very upset with the manager on duty yesterday for even letting this guy in. Christ, what a mess. I've seen corpses that look better. I've been in to talk to him several times and when he's not out of it entirely, like conked out, I've been able to gather that he's been jilted by his lover and he decided to come here to sort of throw it all away, get even with this lover, I guess, by doing anyone who came along. Thing is, he looks so bad, I don't think he made it with anyone at all. No one will go near him, and I don't blame them. The guy's a walking fungus. I mean, who wants to catch some horrible disease?"

"Did you get a name?" asked Betsy.

"He signed in as Dorian Gray."

"Dorian Gray is a character in a novel," said Malloy, who knew something about signing in under false pretenses.

"Figures. He's not one of our members, he's a walk-in. Anyway, follow me and I'll take you to him." Mike chuckled lightly, "The patient in room fourteen."

They walked down a hall that could have been a floor in some shabby office building, blank beige walls with doors spaced about twenty feet apart. It was before eleven but a few early birds had already arrived, and they passed a couple apparently going to their room, holding hands, nude except for bath towels draped around their paunches. Some of these doors were part way open and they saw flashes of skin and movement within. One man, seeing them pass, stuck his head out the door, called, "Who let the cat in?"

"Just humor them," said Mike to Betsy. "We don't get many women in here, like zero." He stopped at a door that was barely cracked, and opened it. The light was off and the room was dim. "Dorian? Hey man, I brought you some company, some people from the health department. Dorian, you awake?"

A lumpish figure huddled in the corner on the only piece of furniture in the room, a waist-high platform resting against the wall, brown vinyl cushions, kind of a cross between a cot and a massage table. He wore a white sheet draped around his torso like a toga. They entered the room, switched on the light.

The man cried out as if stabbed. Mike switched off the light.

"That better? Look here, these people are going to check you out. This guy's a doctor—didn't you say?"

Mohammed Shafi moved in a bit and said, "That's right, Mr. Gray, I am a doctor and I'd like to take a look, if you don't mind. But first, how are you feeling?"

Now the door was wide open and the light from the hall illumined the room. The man was either shitfaced or really sick. He was about Malloy's age, Nordic in appearance, fine blond hair, deep-set blue eyes, shot red, with a distrustful look to them. He blinked twice and wrapped his arms around his chest. "I'm cold," he said.

"We do have blankets," said Mike, "I'll go get a couple."

The doctor unzipped his L.L. Bean lambswool sherpa sweater. "Meanwhile, you can use my vest."

The man took it gratefully. "What day is it?" he wondered, struggling with the mere act of donning the garment

"Wednesday, a little before noon," answered Shafi, who had taken charge. Malloy opened his blood kit and handed the doc a pair of latex surgical gloves. "You've been here a while, have you?"

"Long enough to wish I was dead," said Dorian Gray, coughing weakly.

"Oh, it can't be that bad, can it? Let's have a look and see what's going on with you." Even as he spoke, Shafi was already examining him, palpating here, probing there, wishing he had his magnifier. At least he had his stethoscope. "Breathe deeply," he told Dorian Gray.

"I'd say pneumonia or pleurisy right off the bat. That's fairly obvious, but you see here? Swollen lymph glands in the neck, a major infection going on." Shafi invited them to feel the nodes for themselves, the patient looking on with mild interest. "And look here, on the face and nose, these reddish macules. I've seen this before." Now that the doctor mentioned it, Malloy and Betsy noticed the man's face was spotted with what looked like boils or infected pimples. Lower, from mid-trunk on up to the base of his neck and around the collarbone were a series of purple-black blotches.

"Weird," said Betsy, "the configuration of these bruises look like the Hawaiian islands on a map."

"I've gotta go with the Azores," said Malloy.

Malloy opened the wooden case he'd brought and took out the dark field microscope, a solid, black piece of instrumentation about sixteen inches tall. It had a metal band affixed to its base imprinted with the name of the manufacturer: Zeiss. He set it on the cot-table next to Dorian Gray, not even close to an ideal place because the surface wasn't stable, but it was what they had. Carefully, he laid out various things alongside of it—swabs, syringes, gauze pads, glass slides, and more. Shafi was just getting to the man's crotch. The patient had offered no resistance to being examined head to toe, everywhere except the nether regions, and now with his toga folded around him like a diaper, he seemed dubious.

"We're going to take a look at your private parts," said Mohammed Shafi.

The patient cast a disheartened gaze at the floor. "Oh, that's not a good idea. You don't want to see. It's not pretty, not anymore."

"We do want to see, because by knowing what it is then we can help you."

"And her?"

"She's part of our team. Think of her like a nurse."

"Could just as well be a doctor," asserted Betsy.

"Allow me to unfold this sheet," said Shafi. "There, that's the way. Let me get a look. Okay, what have we here? A couple lesions just below the glans, the one about a centimeter in diameter, looks fresh, too. Okay, let's see, any more lurking about? I'm just going to lift your testicles. Shaun, you're blocking the light. All clean there. Now I need you to turn over and spread your cheeks."

But Dorian Gray was too weak to do anything as gymnastic as turning over and spreading them. They had to help turn him, and Dr. Shafi did the spreading. He took a pen light from his shirt pocket, gripped it between his teeth, and got nose-to-nose with Dorian's fundament. "Uh huh, uh huh," he murmured, the tiny beam of light darting here and there. The others leaned in for a better look. Shafi removed his gloves then took pen light from his mouth. "No lesions that I can see, but you do need to wipe your bottom, Mr. Gray. Okay, you two, you're up. I think we're ready for the dark field."

Gray put up no more fuss. Whatever they had to do, he would lay there, genitals exposed, and let them do it. Mike had not returned with the blankets and, though Gray still wore the doctor's sweater vest, he was starting to shiver.

Shafi put a comforting hand on his shoulder. "Those sores on your penis? That's a sign of syphilis. You've heard of syphilis, yes? A communicable disease spread through sexual contact with someone else who already has it."

"Yeah, a big bitch named Arthur Tottingham Jr."

"We'll get to specific names a bit later," said Malloy.

The doctor continued. "Anyway, we suspected that you had this disease and so we brought a special microscope to be able to actually see the germs that are causing this disease. These trained epidemiologists are going to take a sample from that sore. Don't worry, it won't hurt a bit."

Betsy slipped on another set of latex gloves and went to work, Malloy talking her through it, Shafi standing off to the side, watching every move. "Grasp the shaft of his penis with one hand, hold it steady, and take the sample with the other hand. You see how it's oozing? The organisms are right on the surface so you just dab it a few times, roll the swab gently across the area. That's it, you're doing great."

Dorian Gray hadn't had multiple persons attending to his penis since that drunken Fourth of July bash at Carlyle Lake, before he ever had the misfortune to meet Art Tottingham. Despite his enfeebled condition, he started to feel a tingle in his loins. "How about that," said Malloy, "he's starting to get some wood here—Dorian, you may be a hetero, after all—and a little wood is good, it presents the lesion even better. Go for it, Betsy. There you go, that's probably a good sample. Now apply it to the slide and we'll take a look."

While they were prepping the sample, Dorian Gray seemed to grow concerned over what they might see. "Is it like a parasite?" he asked.

"You could say that," said Shafi, delighted to explain. "It's a spirochaete bacterium that needs a human host. Its scientific name is *Treponema pallidum* and the 'pallidum' comes from pallid or pale. This germ is so pale, so faint to the eye that it wasn't even observed until 1897. Not to get too technical here, but this microscope gives a type of illumination needed to enhance the contrast in unstained samples, especially one such as *T. pallidum*, which absorbs little to no light and in fact does not stand out at all with standard illumination techniques." The doctor saw that he had lost the young man. He tried again. "We call it dark field microscopy—think of the dark field as a black background. This very-hard-to-see germ shows up nicely against this black background. You'll see for yourself in a minute."

Betsy clipped the slide with the smeared sample to the stage of the microscope. She made some final adjustments, turned the focus knobs back and forth a few times, and then let out an astonished whistle. "They're here, I see them moving."

After Betsy had her fill, Malloy took a look. He saw what he had seen maybe four times before, tiny corkscrews twitching and jerking, actually in the throes of death, having been removed from their human host. That is, if these primitive organisms could even be thought of as having something like a life and death. And so far as their movement, they were always twitching; undulating would be far too graceful a description.

The doctor stepped in to peer down into the lens. After oohing and ahhing, he announced, "This is the most beautiful sight I think I've ever seen."

"Really?" said Betsy.

"In the medical world, yes. It's impressive how these organisms find a way to pass themselves on, person to person, century after century.

They thrive on our lust and frailty, wouldn't you agree? Anyway, this man has syphilis all right, and pneumonia, but the signs indicate some other condition as well. These blotches on his chest and macules on his face ..." He turned to the patient. "Sorry, I didn't mean to refer to you in third person. You're as much a part of this as we are. Those signs, I think, are not indicative of syphilis. I said I had seen this before, and believe it or not it was in Sicily.

"Several years ago I spent a summer there, medical officer on an archaeological dig, and I saw the same signs on some of the old men living in and around this village where we stayed. What you present, Mr. Gray, looks quite similar to what I saw that summer, a form of cancer known as Kaposi's sarcoma. But what's odd is that Kaposi's tends to be chronic, affecting elderly men from the Mediterranean region. Of which you are neither."

"Great," muttered Dorian Gray, "I've hit the trifecta. Want to try for a fourth disease?"

Shafi, trying put on a positive spin, "What I'm saying is that we'll get you to a hospital where specialists will take up your case. That's the best plan."

Dorian Gray guffawed. "I'm not sure if I still have health insurance, and my sugar daddy just dumped me so there goes that handout. I'm not kidding myself. I'm alone. Alone and dying, okay? It sucks, it really does—how would *you* like it?—but I'll deal with it because I have to. Now can I have a look at those things in the microscope?"

He slid off the cushions and stood at the waiting instrument. He bent over, gazed through the lens, and saw the same thing they had seen. He gagged thrice in succession, his pallor somehow deepening. "I think I'm gonna heave," he said.

SEVENTEEN

ARTHUR TOTTINGHAM JR., known by his friends as Art, had met Trey Vonderhaar at a seminar titled *Living With Wealth and Loving It.* The gathering of approximately twenty-two suits and a few skirts was called to order at nine sharp on a weekday morning in the Starlight Room at the top of the Chase Hotel.

Trey had signed up for the seminar not because he needed better advice on how to enjoy his money, but because he thought it would be a good opportunity to meet other well-heeled gentlemen and possibly recruit a few into his organization. *Living With Wealth* was sponsored by the city's premier brokerage firm, of which Art was a senior advisor. Art was also billed as a featured speaker on the program, the presenter of "Spend It Like You Mean It," a topic that caught Trey's attention.

Before the event got underway, the attendees gathered around the coffee dispensers, schmoozing and glad-handing. Art had walked up to Trey and said, "I knew your father well. There was a man with a purpose, to make fortunes for his clients and ride their coattails to his own fortune. Bryson Vonderhaar Jr. could smell a lucrative investment opportunity through a brick wall. He also enjoyed life immensely—how about you?"

That got the ball rolling, and the two became fast friends. The shrewd young entrepreneur and the seasoned financier more than thirty years his senior, sharing a proclivity for the acquisition of wealth without having to work too hard for it, lavish living, and menus extraordinaire. So it happened that when the seminar ended at noon, they went to the four-star restaurant off the hotel lobby and got a table near the window. Art ordered a bottle of Pouilly-Fuisse and oysters Rockefeller for starters; Trey would not have expected anything less.

They weren't ten minutes into the conversation before Art made it known that he was queer by bringing up the Gateway Men's Chorus, a performing ensemble that had been gathering admirers for several years now. Trey said yes, he had been to a few performances and they were nothing short of spectacular, Art replying, Well, then, you must have seen me, the balding fellow in the last row, trying to sound mellifluous but in reality probably croaking like a frog—ha, ha! Once Art opened the door, the conversation quickly turned to matters of modern homosexuality, its joys and its tribulations, including the clandestine nature of the lifestyle.

Art, more than Trey, had no qualms about opening up and divulging some very personal information. "Sometimes I feel like I've got to have it—right then, you know?" There was no one near their table, but Art took no chances, leaning in to Trey, speaking in whispers. "It might be a stockholder's meeting, and I'm sitting there, looking the picture of the polished professional, pretending to pay attention. But really, I'm looking around the conference table, gay-dar honed in, prospecting for a likely candidate. You know? Getting off, just imagining. My desires, at times, overwhelm everything else. I may be a card-carrying AARP member," he confided, "but my libido is that of a twenty-five-year-old."

Trey wasn't sure if Art was coming on to him. The man had already indicated that he would fuck, or possibly be fucked, by practically any swinging dick out there. No matter; he wasn't interested in this withered old toad, not for sex anyway. He took a sip of his Pouilly and decided to seize the moment. "It's coincidental that you bring this up, because I happen to have a circle of friends with interests similar to yours, a private men's club, quite exclusive, and we meet in my home, oh, once or twice a month for drinks, dinner and an evening of social pleasure."

"I like the pleasure part," said Art, with a lecherous wink. "Count me in next time you party."

"We call them soirees and, sure, I'll put you on the guest list. You'll be contacted by mail or phone, depending on how much lead time we have. Very often the mix includes out-of-town guests and it happens that there's not much advance notice, what with people on the go so much these days. I try to keep it to under fourteen guests, so if you can't make one particular soiree, no problem, I'll invite someone else. But not to worry, there'll always be another."

"It sounds like work," said Art, "playing host week after week. I hope your members appreciate it."

"Oh, they do. We get rave reviews, and we try to keep it fresh. Varying selections of music, for instance. One evening it might be Ravel, another evening it could be Copeland. And always a different entree with an accompanying wine. No one has ever complained of a boring time."

"You keep saying we. Who is we?"

"Myself and my assistant Freddie DuCoin. We started Man 2 Man four years ago after looking around the city and finding no outlet for discriminating gentlemen to indulge their, shall we say, carnal interests. Throw in the collective charm, wit, and intelligence of the hand-picked members, the elegant setting of my Lafayette Square home, *and* the anticipation of a new encounter, and you have quite the experience."

"It sounds so ... cultivated," said Art, "I can hardly wait. But you're leaving something out."

Trey smiled. "I won't play coy. There is a fee, otherwise I couldn't provide the level of splendor that the members have become accustomed to." Trey stopped there, wondering how deep Art's pockets went. Up until now membership fees had stood at $3,000, but today Trey was willing to make an exception for his father's old friend.

Art rubbed his thumb and two fingers together, the age-old sign of monetary transaction. "Well? Are you going to tell me the price tag or shall I offer a donation of my choosing?"

"It's four thousand for one year," he answered coolly. "And for that you get your own monogrammed bathrobe…kidding! About the bathrobe only."

Art's face lit up. "Oh, *now* I see why you do it. Very clever, young Vonderhaar, you give new meaning to the word exorbitant. I do believe your father would be proud."

Trey put on his hurt face. "It's not the money, Art. I'll tell you right now I am independently wealthy, and have been since I came into my inheritance at twenty-one. So, money, while always welcome, is of small consequence in the overall scheme of things. I do it because I like doing it. Truth is, I don't go out much so I like drawing fascinating people into my circle, into my home. They come, we have a nice time, then they go. I like it that way. But look, it was just an idea. You struck me as someone who might be receptive. Think about it, no hurry at all. Get back to me if you decide this is something you'd entertain."

"I have thought about it," he said, pulling a checkbook from the inside breast pocket of his Milan-tailored, eighteen-hundred-dollar Armani suit, "and I thought that this membership fee that I called exorbitant is actually a good way to keep the membership exclusive, as you say. So, I'm in, the newest member of Man to Man. Do I make the check out to you?"

"Make it out to the club, and that's Man 2 Man with the number two in the middle."

Trey sipped his Pouilly and scooped another oyster from its bed, watching as Art wrote the check. Just like that, huh? He congratulated himself on an easy extra thousand—he would never think of it as a con or a swindle—and promised he would try to attend more of these financial seminars.

EIGHTEEN

Two DAYS before the investigators found the wretched Dorian Gray in the confines of a seedy bath house, hoping to hurt the feelings of Arthur Tottingham Jr. by servicing any stranger who might chance by, the shit hit the fan on Midvale Drive in the affluent suburb of Frontenac. For one thing, Arthur Tottingham Jr. did not have feelings, at least not toward Douglas March, a.k.a. Dorian Gray, any longer.

When first they met at The Loading Zone on a raucous Friday evening there was electricity between them, the young department store salesman quite taken by the suave older man with his craggy looks and commanding personality. For his part, Arthur Tottingham Jr. saw the firm, fit, and seemingly unjaded Douglas March as a possible replacement for his previous live-in lover, who had gone out for smokes one day and had never come back. Having drank themselves silly at the bar, Tottingham took Douglas home with him that evening for a test drive. Douglas passed with flying colors, following Tottingham's suggestions without question, wanting only to please in the bedroom. The man was insatiable, Douglas would give him that, insatiable and diverse in his preferences. He liked head, giving and getting, and he liked buggery—not so much the giving, but the getting, which, according to Art, was "sublime, a pleasure so keen it is barely tolerable."

The next morning at breakfast, young Douglas March was interviewed by his host. Who did he currently live with? Ah, another clerk from the same department store, I see. Was he, Douglas, a good roommate? Responsible? Did they split the household chores? Did he consider himself a neat person or a slob? Was he an early riser? Was his car reliable? Was he on good terms with his family? Did he visit them on holidays? Was he prone to taking long showers? Did he make sure to put the cap back on the milk? Would he always remember to shut the lights off and lock the door before leaving the house? Could he be trusted alone in this house?

Finally, Arthur Tottingham Jr. took Douglas in his arms and gave him a playful slap upside the head. "It does get lonely here and you have a nice way about you, not to mention an impressive boner. You're a little rough around the edges, but we can work on that. How would you like to come live with this old man?"

Douglas could hardly believe his luck. Forever, it seemed, he'd been looking for a plum situation like this, being kept by an experienced older

man with lots of money. He jumped at the offer, gushing all over Tottingham, telling him how he could make eggs Benedict and whip up the best
fondue imaginable. "We'll have so much fun together, you'll see. We'll be a
couple that everyone talks about, we'll be envied! Oh Art—may I call you
Art?—you've made me the happiest man in St. Louis!" Suddenly, Douglas'
mood turned from elated to serious. He looked into the cool, calculating
eyes of his newfound lover and said, "Just one question from me, and it's an
important one. Will you be true? Will you? I don't think I could stand it if
you ever cheated on me."

Arthur Tottingham Jr. laughed heartily at this. Again, he took Douglas
in his arms, giving him an affectionate bear hug and tousling his hair. "I
don't fault you for asking," he said, "but the question is completely unnecessary. By me asking you to share my life here, that implies my willingness to
be faithful. You can see that, can't you? But to address your concerns, the
answer is no, I wouldn't dream of cheating on you."

If Douglas could have seen behind Art's back, he would have seen that
he had his fingers crossed.

Weeks passed, and like Douglas had hoped, they were happy. The week-
days seemed to fly by, both of them toiling at their respective jobs, morning
to evening. The weekends were greatly anticipated, especially by Douglas,
who had never done the sort of activities that Art enjoyed—polo matches
at St. Louis Country Club, plays at The Rep, lazing at Art's condo in the
resort village of Innsbruck. Douglas worked hard to polish the rough edges
that Art pointed out. He made quick studies of Art's cultured friends, and,
in his own chameleon-like way, worked at emulating those attributes he
believed would lend him some much-needed *savoir faire*. Alone, he would
practice some particular manner of speech that he had observed, making sure to incorporate important-sounding words such as fiduciary and
variable annuity and arbitrage, terms that he had overheard while with Art
and his cronies. In short, he attempted to talk like them—these overstuffed
bigwigs—walk like them, act like them, and think like them, but it was
hard to take the salt from the earth.

One day while Art was out, Douglas was going through the top drawers
in Art's dresser, looking for a picture that Art had once showed him, the
two of them together at the Missouri Athletic Club's Gentlemen's Repast.
Douglas wanted to get that photo enlarged and framed, and surprise Art

by putting it in the den with all the other pictures illustrating Art's amazing journey through life. Moving things around, he uncovered a small envelope addressed to Mssr. Arthur Tottingham, Jr. It was already opened and
the note inside was partially sticking out, so Douglas didn't feel too much
like a snoop when he plucked it out and read the invitation.

YOU ARE CORDIALLY INVITED
TO AN EVENING OF SOCIAL PLEASURE
AT THE HOME OF BRYSON VONDERHAAR III.
CASUAL DRESS WITHIN GOOD TASTE.
VALET PARKING AVAILABLE. REGRETS ONLY.

Douglas studied the note. The stationery was fancy with an embossed
monogram centered atop the sheet. The letters were done in some stylized
font that probably was the work of a print shop. Another of Art's friends
flaunting his impeccably good taste, thought Douglas. But it was the date
of this event that caught his eye and sent a stab of pique through his heart:
Saturday, January 5, 1982. That was three months ago, after they had been
living together for a month. Douglas remembered the evening. Art told
him that afternoon that he was going out for drinks and dinner with an old
friend, a former classmate from Andover who was in town for one night
only. It would be just the two of them, the better for reminiscing. "You
understand, don't you?"

He understood all right, the man was double-dipping. Art didn't get
home that night until close to three. Douglas was sure about that, because
he waited up for him. When asked whether he had a good time, Art went
into a lengthy explanation of the evening, what a wonderful conversationalist this friend was, how he had carried sad news about the demise of
certain cherished classmates, and even what they had had for dinner. But
restaurants close before midnight, what had he been doing since then? Oh,
we just drove around and hit a few late night bars. We were having such a
good time, we didn't want it to end. "You understand, don't you?"

Douglas put the note back in the envelope and returned it to the exact
location where he'd found it. He noted the return address with its city zip
code. He decided not to confront Art with this, hoping that he was wrong
in his assumption, and besides, he was in no position to give an ultimatum:
you stop this running around or I'm leaving! That was the last thing he

wanted, to wear out his welcome here, to go back to his old blasé existence. Instead, he would watch Art a little more carefully and not be so gullible.

What Douglas couldn't foresee was the effect that this poorly concealed note would have on their relationship. Even though he thought he did a good job of pretending everything was fine, deep within things were not fine. A vile feeling slowly came over him, a rancor that he fervently wished would dissipate and yet, try as he might, he could not dispel it. He found himself sniping at Art, finding fault with his choices of restaurants, turning away from him in bed at night.

It took time for this rift to develop, but it became more and more apparent; eventually the household had the ambiance of a rendering plant. Art became aloof around Douglas and this, in turn, caused more resentment, which fueled the estrangement.

The boil burst at the breakfast table on a Sunday morning. Art called Douglas' Hollandaise sauce lumpy and burned-tasting and pushed his eggs Benedict aside. Douglas blurted, "If you don't like it, make your own damned sauce!" Art said no fucking way, he was tired of eggs Benedict every weekend. He'd had it with eggs Benedict.

"And while we're at it, as far as variety in the kitchen, you're a one-trick pony, aren't you? A bit stunted in the imagination department. You ever hear of a cowboy breakfast? Steak and eggs. There's a meal that'll put some stiff in your prick—not that you'd much care, Mister I've Got a Headache."

Tears welled up in Douglas' eyes. "You get so much joy from hurting me," he said. "It's sad the person you've become."

Art was unmoved by the young man's pain. In fact, in addition to the eggs Benedict, he thought maybe he was done with the lackluster eggs' creator as well. "You really should watch your step," he warned sternly, "and now it may be too late. You know that I brought you into this house not just as a warm body to share my bed, but as a ward. It's been five months now, and I feel you're not living up to my expectations. So, my dear boy, the quick and short: perhaps it's time for us to part."

Douglas was horrified. "You can't mean that, not after we signed up for that Caribbean cruise!"

Art shrugged. "I'll take some other enchanting young man."

"Oh, someone like Bryson Vonderhaar the Third? Hah! You thought I didn't know. You've been seeing someone else all along, you cheater!"

Art arched an eyebrow at this. "I see you've been into my drawers, and

I'm not surprised. White trash is sneaky by nature, always skulking around looking for opportunities, something to pawn perhaps?"

"No, it wasn't like that!"

"Please shut your stupid mouth and get the hell out of my house. And take that hideous skin rash with you."

"Look who's talking. You've got one, too."

"True, but it's not as bad as yours and mine is going away while yours only gets worse."

Douglas balled his fists in the air, and he shook them at Art. "Oh, I could just scream!"

"Do that on your way out the door," said Art.

NINETEEN

MALLOY LOOKED out the window of his apartment and saw coming up the street a pair of Vietnamese kids carrying a six-foot pole on their shoulders. Hanging from the pole were several plastic grocery bags, bulging with items from the Schnucks down the block, with the stylized red logo of the store emblazoned on the bags for everyone to see. He knew the kids were Vietnamese because, well, they looked Vietnamese, and because neighbors had told him that boat people were moving into the neighborhood.

Boat people, he gathered, were refugees who had fled the chaos in the aftermath of the Vietnam War. He had seen pictures of boats so jam-packed with human beings, crammed so tightly that a sneeze would have knocked someone into the drink. They were hoping to go somewhere, anywhere but Vietnam, but the boats were so top-heavy that it was a wonder they didn't swamp and sink. In fact, a lot of them did. But the ones who made it to America were pretty lucky. And smart, too. They knew to string a pole—it looked like a curtain rod—through the handles of grocery bags and place that grocery-laden pole on their shoulders, chugging along, as if coming back from the hunt with the carcass of a bush pig.

That this neighborhood had Vietnamese did not surprise him. It had Mexicans and Bosnians and Afghans, too. There were restaurants and markets with foreign names all along South Grand and, at times, exotic smells in the air. Malloy wondered if his former neighborhood had boat people. He really missed the old place, especially Fortino's with its red-and-white checkered tablecloths. But now he was in the land of backyard barbecues, guys in muscle shirts sitting on their porches drinking beer at two in the afternoon, and roving packs of teenagers who didn't think twice about hurling insults. He was a Southsider now. It was all right.

As for the living quarters, this place had a Murphy bed, a definite improvement over a mattress on the floor.

The health department was still convenient, just a straight shot down Grand past Tower Grove Park and Saint Louis University, a ten-minute drive if you didn't stop for coffee. Today Malloy made his own coffee. He wasn't going straight to work, but to Alexian Brothers Hospital to re-interview Douglas March.

They had taken him there from the bath house when he said that Alexian Brothers on South Broadway was the designated health care provider for employees of Famous-Barr. That was when he was still pretending to be Dorian Gray. That little ruse ended quickly at the admitting desk when he was asked to show identification. Once the paperwork was settled and they sat in the waiting room twiddling their thumbs, Doctor Shafi tracked down the ER physician on duty and briefed him. March had syphilis and needed treatment, that much was certain. Shafi then told the ER doc that March likely had something in addition to syphilis, describing the signs he'd observed but leaving out his own speculative diagnosis, and that he needed a thorough work-up.

Now it was two days later, and March was still hospitalized, still undergoing tests, still puzzling the doctors who came to look him over. As Malloy waited on the elevator to take him to Ward 5B, he did not feel particularly optimistic about eliciting new contacts. During the original interview conducted at his bedside once he'd been admitted, March had come across quite sincerely that this Tottingham character had been his only sex partner these last six months. Then what had he been doing holed up in the Club Baths for nearly two days, playing pinochle? Yeah, he could see how it looked, he was the biggest slut in St. Louis and, yeah, he did go to the baths to drown his sorrows in semen but that's not how it played out. Prospects came and prospects went without so much as a lousy handjob. Once they saw him unclothed, they beat a hasty retreat from the room.

That interminable interlude was his crucible; he'd confronted his demons, then decided he didn't like what he saw. He turned tail and ran, but the demons caught up with him and devoured him. His self-image had gone from spurned lover to vagrant, and the blemishes on his body as well as the sores on his genitals had definitely blossomed during that stay. The purely carnal atmosphere of the baths, the negative auras of so many men, each intent on starring in his own porn flick, had somehow entered his system and spurred the germs on to do their wicked work with an even greater vengeance.

That was his theory anyway, and he was sure he'd be dead if Malloy and company hadn't come when they did. Then, he said he was so tired that he couldn't continue, and he fell asleep.

When Malloy walked in, Douglas March was sitting up in bed, picking at his breakfast. On the mounted TV screen at the far end of the wall, Phil Donahue was listening to Gore Vidal recite a litany of offenses by the hated Norman Mailer, Vidal especially galled by Mailer's claim that he could "write him under the table." They said hello but didn't shake hands; March still looked pretty sick. They talked about his case and March asked if Malloy had caught up with Tottingham yet. Malloy said he'd gone to the brokerage where he worked the same day that March had named him. He was told that Tottingham was out, not to return until the following day. Back at the brokerage the next day, he was told that Mr. Tottingham had called in sick. Now he supposed he would have to go to his home, talk to him there. What was that address again?

Dutifully, March recited the address, feeling a pang of remorse at having been ousted. It could have been so wonderful, their life together as a couple, but for Art and his sneaking around.

"Did I give you that other address," he wondered, "the one in the city?"

"Which one is that?"

"Where he runs off to when he gets a wild hair, some rich guy's place. I found a letter inviting him to a party there. He went by himself, kept it secret from me. I took a drive there to see what it was. It's a mansion, nothing less. There's a carriage house in back that's bigger than a regular house in Dogtown or somewhere. A blue Beamer parked in the drive. You might find him there. I don't have the exact address with me, but it's on a corner of Lafayette Park, you can't miss it."

"Believe it or not, I know the house," said Malloy. "I've been there a few times."

"On business, huh? That makes sense, VD coming out of there. It's probably how I got it. Wait—so if I've got syphilis then Art's got it, too?"

"Yeah, that's how it works, unless there's someone other than him."

"No, I swear! Then you've really got to find him and tell him. God help me, I still care about him."

Though he'd just woken up, Douglas March was ready for a nap. Malloy said goodbye and they'd be in touch later. He walked down the hall to the nurse's station, asked for the physician on duty. Seated at the console, a young brunette in a white lab coat looked up from some charts and said, "I'm Doctor Hettenbach, how may I help you?"

Malloy showed his credentials and said he was inquiring about the patient in Room 526. The doctor looked at his pedigree on the laminate, saw the appellation CDC, and took Malloy as a colleague. "I'm going to the break room for a cup of coffee," she said, "would you care to join me?"

"It's actually horrible stuff," she said, setting his cup on a table. "Slightly better than industrial sludge. Now, about Mr. March, what would you like to know?"

"We brought him here two days ago with a chancre the size of bottlecap on his penis. I'd like verification of treatment for syphilis, for starters. And I'd like to get an idea of his overall condition."

"That's right, we did treat him for syphilis according to current CDC guidelines, and the lesion has already cleared up. The skin and membranes in that area are returning to normal. So that's taken care of, but there are other concerns and that's why he's still here."

Malloy took a sip of coffee and made a face. "Ugh, you're right. This *is* bad." He pushed the cup away. "So, these other concerns. It's obvious he has something other than syphilis."

"Yes, and we're working on it. His Tine test was positive for TB, that much we have. He's also been diagnosed with pneumonia, which may explain his profound fatigue. His immune system must have been at low ebb, because you just normally would not see these things in a thirty-year-old man. Then there are the skin problems. Are they related to tuberculosis or pneumonia? During rounds this morning our senior physician thought that it might be some form of cancer, possibly a rare form called Kaposi's sarcoma. Bottom line: the man is a wreck, and we're keeping him here for a while for observation."

"Then I'll know where to find him. Of course the TB will be reported to the health department and the TB people will want to talk to him, too."

"Let's hope we don't find anything else wrong with him, the poor man."

"Compassion, a good trait in a doctor. By the way, I know a little about

TB. Routine Tine test for all health workers. I turned up positive last year, and I'm still taking pills for it."

"Sure, combination therapy—isoniazid, rifampin and the rest. There's a good efficacy rate as long as you remember to take your pills every day."

"Every day for a year and not drink—yeah, like that's gonna happen."

She bestowed a smile. "So … you just heard me say that TB is not real common in young people. You look to be the same age as our patient in 526. How do you think you picked it up?"

"I *know* how I picked it up. Sitting in the close quarters of an interview room on the second floor of the health department, being coughed at and sneezed on by street people, soup kitchen workers, itinerant musicians, ten-bucks-a-pop hookers, and anyone else who might come along, all sitting three feet across the table from me. You think someone would have told them it's polite to cover your mouth when you do that."

"Occupational hazards, Mr. Malloy. We've all got them."

"Yeah? What's yours?"

She gazed at her coffee cup, gave it a frown. "Bad coffee. Life is just too damn short."

"I'll drink to that," he said, "with something other than this gunk." He looked at her hopefully; she knew what was next. "You want to do something sometime?" He was thinking along the lines of playing doctor.

She seemed amused, but not taken aback. "Only if you can get more specific than that."

TWENTY

"WHATEVER YOU'RE SELLING, I already have it." Instantly, Malloy knew that this guy who'd answered the doorbell was going to be a hard case. Brusque, irritable and looking like hell, how could he talk such a person into letting him in and agreeing to sit down for a frank discussion of his sex life? Start with the basics. "I'm not a salesman, I'm a public health officer and I've come here to inform you that someone has contracted a serious communicable disease, syphilis, and this person has named you as a contact. You'll need to be examined and treated as soon as possible, like today. May I come in so we can talk further?"

The man stood there in his doorway, wearing a terry-cloth bathrobe on a beautiful April afternoon, scowling at this news from a total stranger.

"Who the hell do you think you're talking to?"

"Arthur Tottingham Jr.," answered Malloy.

"There you're wrong. Arthur's gone to St. Bart's. I'm house-sitting until next week."

"Please cut the crap. I know you're Tottingham, I have a picture of you," he lied. "We can talk out here, but it'd be better if we go inside, more private."

And so it went, Malloy, quite persuasive when he needed to be, breaking down the barriers that Tottingham was putting up, little by little, until the man had admitted his identity and wondered aloud what circumstances had brought a health officer to his door. "Couldn't we have done this over the phone?" he sighed. "No, I guess not. Well, I'll let you in, but under protest. You leave when I say so."

"Agreed," said Malloy.

They sat in the kitchen, perched on wooden stools at a long copper countertop. Tottingham didn't offer Malloy so much as a glass of water. No matter, he launched into the standard spiel of how the disease is spread, what it can do to the human body, how it can be easily treated with penicillin, and the importance of naming one's sex partners. Normally, he wouldn't interview anyone who wasn't already shown to be clinically positive—a new case—but with Douglas March's vehement assertion that Tottingham was his only contact, Malloy felt he should try for names. Tottingham would turn up positive, he knew it, and he had him in his grasp now.

But first things first. He showed him the pictures in the Green Book— moniker for SYPHILIS: *a synopsis*, the U.S. Public Health Service's handy little volume of clinical porn—turning pages, pointing to syphilitic lesions in all stages on various orifices and genitalia, both male and female. "Have you seen any sores like these on yourself or others?" he asked repeatedly.

And more than once Tottingham told him to go to hell. "I'll tell you if you'll tell me who gave my name," he repeated for the third time. It really annoyed him that he couldn't have this information. That was the way it worked in his world: you give information to get information.

The very fact that he was fishing so ardently told Malloy that he'd had multiple partners in the last six months, and he was dying to know which one was infected. Another thing, the terry-cloth robe had fallen open, exposing some bluish-black, scabbed-over lesions below the neckline; they were awful to look at.

"Are you on blood thinners?" Malloy wondered.

"I wouldn't tell you if I was," Tottingham answered.

"Do you mind if I take a look at whatever that is on your chest?" asked Malloy in his most professional manner.

As Malloy leaned forward, trying to get a better look, Tottingham clenched the folds of his robe tightly around his neck. "I sure as hell do mind! It's a skin rash and it's under treatment by my doctor, thank you." Tottingham stood up, pointed to the door. "You may go now," he said sternly.

"Fine, right after you tell me the name of your doctor. You'll tell him you were contacted by a health officer as a person exposed in an active case of syphilis. I'll need to know your test results and verify your treatment. That's the law."

For a moment, Malloy thought Tottingham was going to give him the bum's rush toward the door; he was big enough to do it. Instead, he said, "My physician is Brock Silber, down on Maryland Plaza. Very capable fellow, I'm sure he'll answer any more questions you may have. Just don't bother me any more."

Malloy now had the perfect chance to drop a name; he had to see the reaction. "Doctor Silber, sure, I know of him. Isn't he a pal of Trey Vonderhaar?"

Tottingham stiffened at this. "I'm sure I wouldn't know who his friends are."

"But you know Vonderhaar, don't you? Been to his house a few times, caught a little action in the Boom-Boom Room, or whatever they call it?"

Tottingham turned a nice shade of crimson. "Go!" he commanded. "And get that shitcan out of my driveway!"

He chuckled. "You insult my ride? That's pretty low."

"Oh," menacing now, "I can get lower, much lower."

TWENTY-ONE

As the summer of 1982 approached, certain reports were circulating that had both St. Louis health officials and the local gay community abuzz.

On the vernacular side, that of the people, there was talk about a new disease that attacked mostly gay men. It was dubbed the Gay Killer or the Gay Plague and it was definitely lethal, the person literally wasting away, sometimes in the span of a few months or even weeks. It started with a flu, might lead into a long spell of fatigue, victims tired to the bone and not caring about much of anything. No one really knew how it worked, except that in some it morphed into pneumonia while in others it developed into a cancer with nasty-looking sores on the body, usually below the neckline.

Supposedly, Haitians had brought this scourge into the country. Others were just as convinced that the disease had originated in Africa, where men and monkeys had had sexual congress—really?—or else the contagion "jumped" without benefit of monkey sex from animal to man. Presently it was concentrated in the metropolises of New York and L.A. where intensive care units were filling with victims of this strange disease; a few celebrities had already succumbed to it. Nobody knew the contagion factor, but it was clear that it was only a matter of time before it found its insidious way to the Midwest. Though most understood that this talk might be classified as idle, speculative, or even gossip, everyone concerned very much understood that at least some of it was true. No one was freaking out, not yet. Just knew that this thing was coming their way, and they'd better watch out.

In the clinical world, these reports did not remotely resemble gossip. Mention of the new disease was found in the pages of the *Morbidity and Mortality Weekly Report,* a periodical in the form of a four-sheet pamphlet published by The Centers for Disease Control and disseminated to virtually every health department in the nation. The well-documented articles addressed every aspect of public health and communicable disease. Much of the time it sat on the investigators' desks, among the steno pads and stacks of forms, but sometimes a headline would catch the eye and they would discuss it. This morning it was Joe Sargent who brought a particular article to their attention.

"Morning, people," he called, as his massive frame passed through the door of the epi room. A few wary investigators called back. Casually, Joe sat on the edge of Pam's desk, the better to peer down her open shirt as he spoke. "Did you happen to see this story in the *MMWR?* The one about the connection between this rare type of pneumonia and gay men. It's a synopsis of what they've found in the last year or so. I'll assume you haven't read it, as busy as you are, so I'll read some of it to you. Not that I enjoy reading morbidity reports to a bunch of grown men and women who should be reading this on their own, but this is something we need to be aware of.

"Okay, some of you may have heard about this new disease of the immune system making its way into the gay community. And if we know about it then the gays sure as hell know about it, so we need to keep on top it if only to clear up rumor and maybe quell panic.

"The timeline dates to June of last year when a cluster of *Pneumocystis carinii* pneumonia, known as PCP, turned up in five homosexual men in L.A. Tip of the iceberg, right? Quoting here: 'In this report, the Parasitic Diseases Division of CDC's Center for Infectious Diseases had become concerned about other reports of unusual cases of PCP. The division housed the Parasitic Disease Drug Service, which administered the distribution of pentamidine for PCP treatment. Because PCP was rare and pentamidine was not yet licensed in the U.S., it was available only from CDC. A review for requests of this drug had shown that PCP in the U.S. was almost exclusively limited to patients with cancer or other conditions known to be associated with severe immunosuppression. Requests for this drug from physicians in California to treat PCP in patients with no known cause of immunodeficiency had sparked the attention of the Division staff.' End quote. You with me so far? This pneumonia normally only seen in cancer patients with severely compromised immune systems starts turning up in gay men who don't have cancer."

"A new STD for us to worry about," said Leo Schuler, despondently.

"Maybe," said Joe. "As you know, pneumonia is an opportunistic infection. Well, this article goes on to say that shortly after the first report, that is, the five guys in L.A. with PCP, additional cases of other life-threatening opportunistic infections—OIs—as well as a malignant cancer known as Kaposi's sarcoma were reported among gay men in California *and* New York City. So now it's on both coasts.

"This is July of last year. CDC is not an agency to sit on its ass and watch as a potential epidemic starts to ignite. It's going to try to douse the flames. So immediately it forms a Task Force on Kaposi's and OIs to begin surveillance and do epidemiologic investigation. It says that thirty CDC Epidemic Intelligence Service officers participated in this task force in the Summer of 1981. Some of you may recall Jim Fisk, who worked out of this clinic for a week back then. He was one of those EIS guys, but since his work was only in the preliminary stage I never got to learn what he found here. But it does say what the task force took away from the exercise as a whole. Again, quoting, 'The key underlying factor for the disease appeared to be severe depression of the cellular immune system. The OIs initially reported were life-threatening and often fatal. Although Kaposi's sarcoma was a known but infrequent cancer in the United States, the classical form of the disease was rarely life-threatening and typically occurred among elderly men.'"

Malloy looked to Betsy and said the name Douglas March. Betsy nodded affirmatively, adding "The late Douglas March."

"I thought of him, too," said Joe. "Okay, wrapping it up. There's a lot more, but this paragraph sums it up: 'By the end of 1981, one hundred fifty-nine cases of Kaposi's and *Pneumocystis* pneumonia had been reported in the U.S., with the earliest cases retrospectively identified in 1978. Seventy-five percent of those cases were reported from New York City or California, and all but one case were men." Joe paused to let that sink in. He read the next lines with even more emphasis. "Within six months it was clear that a new highly concentrated epidemic of life-threatening illness was occurring in the United States. The co-occurrence of Kaposi's sarcoma and OIs suggested that the epidemic was one of immunosuppresson and that Kaposi's and OIs were a consequence of the immunosuppression.

"There you have it," said Joe, stealing a peek at Pam's melons. "They're not coming right out and saying that this is something being spread through sexual contact, but what other logical assumption is there?"

"Look at Hep B," said Arnold. "We didn't know that was sexually spread until recently. Needles were the cause, then all of a sudden we're seeing it in the gay community alongside syphilis."

"Yellow as a school bus," put in Tut.

"It all goes to transfer of bodily fluids," said Arnold. "Maybe not every bodily fluid, but blood and semen for sure."

"Don't short-change vaginal fluid," said Betsy, mindful of gender parity.

Schuler tapped his pencil on his desk for attention. "Like I said, another STD for us to deal with. No problem, right? Our case loads can handle another disease. Hah!"

"Don't put the cart before the horse," cautioned Joe. "Even if it's proven this is a communicable disease, it could be a long time before we're mandated to do epidemiology on it—if, in fact, epidemiology can be done on it at all. Anyway, it's now on our radar."

The death of Douglas March was still fresh in Malloy's head, for it was only a month ago that he'd stood at the young man's bedside and watched him go. When he'd called the hospital to check on him, he'd been told that March's medical information was confidential. The nurse's station wouldn't even confirm if he was still there as a patient. Malloy checked himself; he knew better than to try to get information over the phone. You had to go to the hospital or the factory or the school, whatever the establishment, act authoritative, flash your ID, and *then* you got the information you want.

He asked for Dr. Hettenbach; they put her on. "Mr. Malloy, how are you?"

"Just all right, but you sound chipper, good for you. Hey, I won't keep you. I just called to check on Douglas March."

"Right, you're following up on his condition as it relates to public health. An important job. Well, Mr. March is not doing well. As you know, we treated him for the syphilis and that cleared up just fine, but those other things that you saw and that we talked about? Something very pernicious there. We gave him the full regimen for the pneumonia, and that didn't help. We tried a couple alternate antibiotics and that had no effect either. The skin cancer you can't do much about, it's going to do what it's going to do. In short, Mr. March continued to fail and we reached a point where the best option was palliative care. We had him transferred to our hospice where he's living out his final days, I'm afraid."

"That was fast," said Malloy. "He was admitted only two weeks ago."

"Yeah, sometimes it happens that a disease comes on so strong—layman's terms—that it just saps a person's vital energy and leaves them without a will to live. You're welcome to visit him at the hospice, and he'd probably enjoy that. He doesn't have much family. Do you have something to write with?"

St. Dismas Hospice, named for one of the many patrons of the dying, was located in a residential neighborhood, not far from Alexian Brothers. A middle-aged woman with a plain gray dress and a large, shiny crucifix around her neck answered the door. Her name was Sister Fran, and she was as nice as could be. She led Malloy up a winding staircase and down a hall to a door partly ajar. "Knock, knock, Mr. March. Company." Sister Fran eased the door open. The room smelled of Vick's VapoRub and tangerines. March was lying in bed staring at the ceiling. There was a fruit basket on the tray beside his bed, within reach.

The tag attached read: BEST WISHES FOR A SPEEDY RECOVERY —
YOUR CO-WORKERS AT FAMOUS-BARR.

After some small talk, Sister Fran left. Malloy pulled up a chair. He
didn't talk just yet because he didn't know what to say. At least he'd had
the sense to refrain from saying what he'd normally have said: "How're you
doing?"

March led off by asking why Malloy had come. Another interview?

"Nah," said Malloy. "We're done with that. I just came because, you know,
I wanted to."

March asked if Malloy could put some pillows behind him, against the
backboard, to prop him up. Malloy complied, grasping his armpits, pulling
to help scooch him up. He saw that March was only just a skeleton in his
young body.

"You came to say goodbye," he rasped with a voice like paper. "Thank
you for that. That's a kind act from someone I barely know. Art hasn't even
been here. So selfish and cruel, he'll break my heart to the very end."

Again, Malloy didn't know what to say. He merely nodded.

"But you got him, right? You told him about the disease, what I have and
how he gave it to me. What did he say?"

"I caught up with him at his place. He wasn't exactly receptive to my
visit, but he did agree to see his doctor." Malloy gave a look of exasperation.
"Now that's a whole 'nother story, this Dr. Silber, trying to get information
out of his office, information that he's required to report. I'll never understand this foot-dragging, what's the big deal? Just tell me the diagnosis and
show me proof of treatment. What, you want me banging on your exam
room door, disturbing your work?" He caught himself short. "Sorry, I got
carried away."

But March wasn't really listening to Malloy's rant about Silber. His blue
eyes, sunken in their sockets, needed something to cling to. "Did he say
anything about me?"

"Who, Tottingham? Yeah, he said that he was sorry if he hurt you in any
way, and that he wished you wouldn't hate him for the things he's done."

"He said that?"

"Yeah."

He saw tears coming down Douglas March's cheeks. "I don't hate him. I
just feel so stupid. I was faithful—foolish me. Look what it got me."

TWENTY-TWO

MALLOY FELT it was high time he paid Silber a visit and got some answers. It had been several weeks since Tottingham had supposedly gone to see the doctor and, Malloy still hadn't heard the results. He couldn't formally interview Tottingham until he had a positive diagnosis. For that matter, he wasn't satisfied with Silber's communique on Vonderhaar's condition either, a faxed form on the doctor's letterhead that said only NEGATIVE. If they were going to use their private physicians, at least they could pick a doctor who was responsible enough to report properly.

And now Karl was breathing down his neck for test results on Tottingham, too. Phone calls didn't work either. A bored-sounding woman who called herself the answering service would only take his number and relay it to the doctor. The doctor must have been extraordinarily busy, because he never returned any calls.

Silber's office was on the first floor of a former palatial residence, now converted to commercial space, located in the heart of Maryland Plaza. It was flanked by other mansions turned to offices and across from a grandiose working fountain smack in the middle of Maryland Avenue that sometimes developed a foaming case of soap suds when pranksters got in the mood. Silber shared his office with another physician, Dr. Larry Gould.

Malloy entered the waiting room and went to the sliding glass window. A sign told him to sign in and have a seat. He tapped on the window. A hand slid open the panels. "Yes?"

"I'm here for Dr. Silber."

"Do you have an appointment? There's no one scheduled for this time."

"I'm with the health department. This won't take long."

"I'll tell him you're here, but it's going to be a while. He's in the middle of a procedure."

Malloy signed in as Boo Radley and took a seat. The waiting room was empty. He picked through the magazines and settled on Andy Warhol's *Interview*, which featured candid, insightful banter with rising stars in the world of fashion and entertainment.

He read a piece on Mel Gibson, the guy who played the burned-out Road Warrior in that flick he'd seen over Thanksgiving. He learned that Mel had grown up in Peekskill, New York, and his family had moved to Sydney, Australia, when Mel was a teen. He thought that was kind of unusual, a family emigrating from America instead of beating a path to

America. Also that Mel came from a family that was devoutly Catholic, something that Malloy could relate to, his mom with her holy cards and his dad, a lifelong member of the Knights of Columbus, with a beer gut to prove it. He flipped through more magazines and looked at his watch. Thirty-five minutes gone by. Waiting room, yeah, right. How about waiting-for-nothing-room?

He rose to tap on the glass window again. Just then a door that presumably led to the interior medical suites opened and a dark-complected man with John Lennon spectacles walked out. He acknowledged Malloy with a friendly nod and a hello as he headed for the door.

"Dr. Silber?" Malloy inquired.

The man halted. "No, I'm Dr. Gould."

"I've been waiting for Dr. Silber. Could you please tell him that Shaun Malloy from the STD Clinic is here?"

"He must not have known you were here," said Gould, "because he left about fifteen minutes ago. Sorry."

"What! I didn't see anyone leave."

"He went out the back door—that's where we park, in the back. I'm just going for a stroll in the neighborhood. Fresh air and sunshine, the best panacea, and free."

A half hour earlier, the receptionist had padded down the hall to Brock Silber's office. Seeing he was on the phone, she took a nearby pad and wrote on the first blank page: "Health Dept guy here to see you." She handed it to him; he glanced at it, and made the Okay sign with a circled thumb and forefinger. She left and he kept talking. "Then we're set: nine thirty, table for six. And Bernard, not too close to the back, somewhat near the bar so we can people watch, you know? And don't forget the floral touch. Yes, I know you always crown each table with a tasteful bouquet, but at ours tonight I'd like something really eye-catching. All right then? Toodles until this evening."

The procedure that Dr. Brock Silber happened to be in the middle of was booking a table at Robusto's. He had invited five dear friends to share in his birthday celebration. Nothing complicated, merely the act of wining and dining and being seen at the trendiest bar-restaurant in St. Louis. It wasn't every day a man turned thirty-seven, and he wanted to do it in style. They would raise their glasses and toast both a successful physician and an urbane denizen of the Central West End. The man of the hour, virile and debonair, sought after by handsome men and beautiful women alike. He would positively bask in the attention. Oh, it was going to be an evening to remember.

He picked up the note that Charlotte had left. Health department, what a bother. It had to be this fellow Malloy who'd been leaving messages about Art Tottingham. What were his test results? Had he been treated yet? Would he please specify the regimen used? As if he had nothing else to do but answer piddling questions coming from pushy public servants. The truth was he didn't quite know how to treat Art's condition. Ditto for the similar conditions of certain other men that Trey had referred to him. It was hard, trying to make sense of the sores and unsightly skin rashes. He was no dermatologist.

If Stephen Lipkin were here, he would know what to do. He would perform the exam, make a well-founded diagnosis, and prescribe the proper treatment. For his part, Silber would scribble his name at the bottom of the prescription pad, offer the patient some words of encouragement, and hand him a big fat bill—a bill he would pay gladly, without flinching, for the patients Trey sent him were always well-off.

Stephen Lipkin was not a physician, but he may as well have been. He had gone through the physician assistant program at Duke University, considered to be the best PA program in the nation. He came to Silber through a mutual friend, a professor at the Washington University School of Medicine. Lipkin started on the Tuesday after Labor Day in 1980, when Silber was in his seventh year of private practice. In the thorough and proficient Lipkin, Silber saw a wonderful resource. Lipkin could cover for him while he took time out for three-hour lunches and afternoons on the links with friends who also had serious time on their hands.

Brock Silber was a social animal at heart. Everyone knew it. He was charming, well-spoken, adept at the art of repartee and never at a loss for an amusing *bon mot*. He was in demand at so many social functions that he had to be quite selective; only invitations from the most prominent or at least most interesting people would merit his RSVP. One week it was a Derby Day party with waiters carrying trays of mint juleps and young boys in jockey outfits working the crowd, taking bets. Another week it was Men's Night Out at The Racquet Club, an evening of fine cigars, gaming, the best single malt scotch, and gents in top hats and tails walking arm-in-arm with dazzling women wearing nothing but earrings and high heels.

Yes, he was quite the socialite, but he was not a very good doctor.

And then, just a few months ago, after nearly two years, Lipkin quit. There was no falling out, no personality conflict. Lipkin said he wasn't happy and wanted to move on. Silber offered to raise his salary from $19,200 a year to $19,700 a year. But it wasn't the money, he said; it was the mission.

Silber's mission was about curing the ills of a bunch of degenerate, wealthy old farts. Lipkin had found a different mission, a calling. He was going to work for a doctor who ran a clinic in a dirt-poor community in the Ozarks. He was switching the class of patients he would minister to, from the upper crust to the burned and stubborn lower crust which tended to stick to the pan. Just as well, thought Silber. Lipkin had gotten noble, a trait Silber found despicable.

Now he was on his own again and, frankly, what little competence he'd had—having graduated third from the bottom of his class at Wash U. School of Medicine, but voted Most Winning Personality—he'd lost through inactivity and a waning interest in his chosen profession. Essentially, he was out of practice.

But he did like the money it brought, and he was going to have to figure out what to do about patients like Art Tottingham, who had loads of money but puzzling medical problems. If he didn't cure a fellow like Tottingham now, that fellow might not return when he has some other malady down the road. Or, he might not return because he couldn't, because he had died. From being misdiagnosed!

Adding to this anxiety over not knowing what to do, the health department had gotten involved and was demanding answers that he did not have. Tottingham had come to him saying he'd been told that he'd been exposed to syphilis. Apparently, this Malloy who was now staked out in his waiting room, had told him that. Though Silber didn't know syphilis from herpes, that sounded like a diagnosis from someone in the know. A presumptive diagnosis, but good enough for now.

On a shelf in his office were two books that he consulted, when he consulted at all. One was the *Physician's Desk Reference*, 1972 edition, a compendium of drugs for medical use which was written for consumers as well as physicians. The other was *Larousse Medical Illustre*, 1937 edition, by Drs. Galtiere Boissiere and Anatole Burnier. An appreciator of art in all forms, Silber loved the look of its cover, a brown leather spine on green boards with gilt lettering. This medical dictionary had belonged to his grandfather, Uriel I. Silber, M.D., who had barely escaped with his family from Lyon, France, in 1939. As his grandfather used to say, "We were going out the back door as the Nazis were coming in the front."

Silber recalled that day with Tottingham, the man on the exam table, a loose sheet draped around his flabby torso, grousing that he shouldn't even be there, he had better things to do. Just give him the medicine and send him on his way. Silber gave him a quick once-over, punctuating the silence with "uh huh" and "aha" and "that doesn't look good." He then told the patient to wait there, he'd be right back. In his office, he thumbed through the *Larousse* until he found syphilis. The pictures nearly had him gagging. How could someone go on living with deformed genitals like those poor bastards in the book?

Tottingham didn't have anything like that, although he did have some weird bruises on his chest. Maybe his syphilis was a mild case or maybe the signs had come and gone. The book was written in French, but Silber could comprehend just enough thanks to his family clinging to their heritage after coming to the States. He saw that the treatment listed for syphilis involved ingestions of bismuth, arsenic and mercury. Of course, the heavy metals. No germ could stand up to that.

He felt better now, having at least stumbled on a plan of action. But shouldn't this treatment be buffered by something else? Penicillin was often given for various infections. Maybe he should prescribe penicillin in addition to the other stuff. What was that saying? A pound of cure is better than an ounce of prevention. He looked up penicillin in the *PDR*. Oh no. There were so many kinds, and worse, some were to be taken in pill form and some were administered by injection. He decided on ampicillin. It came in pill form and was taken three times a day for ten days. His patient was already pretty grumpy; think how he would bitch upon being told that he would have to get a shot.

Art Tottingham studied the prescriptions that Silber had given him. He was getting dressed and Silber noted how much better he looked with his clothes on. "Where do I go for the mercury and bismuth and arsenic? A pharmacy or a college chemistry lab?"

"Just follow the instructions on the label, and take the medicines without fail," said Silber.

"Arsenic? Come on, are you sure? That's a poison. Haven't you seen

Arsenic and Old Lace? Cary Grant. His sweet old aunts are killing people with arsenic."

"Mr. Tottingham, I assure you that this is the correct treatment for your condition. You see that diploma on the wall over there? It says Doctor of Medicine. Doesn't that instill confidence? Sure it does. Don't worry, you'll be fine. Oh, and you can make the check out to Brock Silber, M.D."

And now this health department person was waiting for him, expecting him to account for his actions, second-guessing his decisions. This Malloy hadn't been to a prestigious medical school; what did he know? He would have none of it. He was taking an early lunch today, and maybe a well-deserved massage after that. Without telling anyone, he exited through the back door of the medical offices, climbed in his cherry red Audi Quattro, and drove off.

TWENTY-THREE

ST. LOUIS' CENTRAL WEST END extends well beyond both sides of the north/south-running Euclid Avenue in the vicinity of the Chase Hotel and Barnes Hospital, but when people talk about the Central West End or simply the West End, they are usually talking about that seven-block stretch between Forest Park Parkway on the south and Washington Avenue on the north.

It was an urban pageant, a stimulating mix of commercial enterprise and residential life. Along the way there were restaurants and cafes of every imaginable taste; styling salons, high-end art galleries where on a Friday evening opening one might meet Julian Schnabel or Cindy Sherman, magazine stands, floral shops, boutiques selling the latest fashions from the runways of Milan and New York, antique shops, confectioners, delis, and bars.

Yes, probably two dozen bars on that stretch and branching off into a few side streets, from old school watering holes like The 34 Club where serious drinkers showed up after lunch and claimed their barstools to upscale places like Robusto's where the crème de la crème of society gathered to sip cocktails, flaunt designer labels, and regale one another with tales of personal conquest. Euclid itself, lined with European-style homes, featured the likes of buskers, dog walkers, panhandlers, cops on bicycles, young mothers pushing baby strollers, skateboarders, tourists, and locals going about their business.

It was an entertainment district, of course, and the strip shut down after last call at one —"Get out! Go home!"—and awoke with a yawn at six when the coffee shops and breakfast cafes opened their doors. Visitors seeing the West End for the first time said it reminded them of parts of certain East Coast cities, Baltimore in particular; others were just as sure it had a French Quarter feel. But of course it was neither an East Coast or Southern locale; it was uniquely Midwestern.

Hemingway once famously called The Ramblas, a series of streets in Barcelona that lead to the sea, "the finest walk in the world." Malloy thought the same thing about Euclid Avenue. Especially now that it was early June and the fragrance of honeysuckle vine tantalized and the clop-clop of horse-drawn carriages filled the evening air. He was bar-hopping by himself, having a pretty good time with a thirst for spirits and the means to enjoy them. He'd hit three bars in the last two hours and now he was heading to Robusto's for a nightcap or two. Robusto's was both a bar and a restaurant which specialized in French cuisine. You entered through glass doors and there was a maitre d' station. If you wanted a table you worked it out with the maitre d', then you went to the bar to wait for your call. If you didn't have a reservation it would be a while, several drinks worth. If you only wanted to drink, you simply walked past the maitre d' and looked for a spot at the bar.

The restaurant was large with several dining rooms connected to the bar, which was also large. Standing in the bar, you could see any and all parties coming from their tables or going to them. Once Malloy had seen a limo pull up out front. A chauffeur jumped out, opened doors, and five glam boys spilled out. As they paraded through the bar, meeting a waiter who ushered them into the back and out of sight, Malloy asked a nearby patron what's the deal with that? Duran Duran, she said, they just played the American Theater.

Another time he was in the mens room, pretty toasted, when a guy with hair all spiked up like Rod Stewart circa 1973 walked in and took the urinal next to him. Then he heard the guy speak, that English accent. Damn, it *was* Rod Stewart. But Rod neglected to wash his hands after handling his dick, and Malloy thought he'd have some fun with that.

After a quick wash of his own mitts, he followed the soccer player turned singer into the dining area and saw him take a seat at a large table along with a sizable party already working on some appetizers. There was an empty chair near the foot of the table; Malloy nonchalantly occupied it. He waited for someone to say something, like, "Who the fuck are you?" When that didn't happen, he settled in and relaxed.

He took a sip of someone's water. He eavesdropped as best he could. At length, it began to dawn that this was Rod's band, that they must have played The Arena or Mississippi Nights and now they were winding down. Wasn't that Billy Peek over there beside Rod? How cool was this? A waiter came by and he ordered a Glenfiddich, the very thing to get him just right. Waiting for his drink, he leaned over to the guy beside him, tapped him on the shoulder, and said in a whisper, "Did you know that Rod Stewart doesn't wash his hands after peeing? That's bad form, yeah? Now look at him, eating calamari with his fingers."

The man, likely a roadie or a sound tech, stopped in mid-chew as he regarded Malloy with utter disdain. "Who the fuck are you?" he scowled.

This evening he was standing there, watching Flash the bartender shake and pour another exquisite concoction into a fresh martini glass. He himself had ordered a Guinness with a chaser of Tullamore Dew.

All around people were jabbering loudly, having to shout to be heard over The Police. There was a giant mirror on the south wall, the biggest damn thing anyone had ever seen, and it took in nearly the entire sweep of the bar. He saw knots of people out on the dance floor, and he took note of a small party of unescorted women, although he was not really on the prowl tonight. On the other side of the room, he saw Ken Westermann at the waiter's station, white shirt and black bowtie, waiting for his drink order. Once upon a time, he had gotten to know Ken a little too well after the balding career waiter had turned up positive for secondary syphilis. Turned out, Ken was a chicken hawk, made a regular practice of picking up guys half his age.

Out of the corner of his inebriated eye he caught a familiar face down at the end of the bar. Bryson Vonderhaar had just come from the restroom and he was talking to some others, yukking it up. Malloy was not one to kid himself: he didn't like Vonderhaar and therefore he did not like to see the man having a good time. In fact it pained him to watch, for not only was Vonderhaar an insulting little prick, he was personally responsible for gay men in this city breaking out with syphilis and this other new, un-known thing. What slime. Look at him. Starched jeans and pressed-cotton oxford shirt, that patch of seaweed plastered to his miserable skull. And now, to Malloy's eager attention, Bryson Vonderhaar was heading his way.

Vonderhaar made his way slowly, squeezing between people on the floor and those standing at the bar. Just as he was about to pass, Malloy stepped out and blocked his path. "Hey there, where you going?" Vonderhaar looked at Malloy, blinking. "Come on, Trey, you remember me. The peon who came to your door last fall. We also met in your lawyer's office. Your dog tried to fuck my leg, remember?"

Vonderhaar's face went dark. His eyebrows bunched, his mouth formed a tight oval. "You!"

"None other," replied Malloy, cheerfully. "Tell you what, let me buy you a drink and we'll talk about this Man Club of yours and what it's doing to your circle of friends."

"We'll talk about nothing," he asserted in a patrician tone. "You have no business with me here, and I'll thank you to get out of my way."

He went to sidestep past Malloy, who grabbed him by the sleeve. "You idiot, let go! You'll tear my shirt."

Malloy leaned into him, spoke to his ear. "Don't run off, Trey. We're going to talk, now or later, and you're going to see the light. You're going to shut down your high-class whorehouse until we can sort out who's infected and who's not. You're going to give me your little black book of members and we're going to contact every one of them and insist they get examined by a doctor. How's that sit with you?"

During this discourse, Malloy held Vonderhaar by the wrist. It looked as though they were holding hands, something not unseemly in this bar. Now, Vonderhaar jerked his arm and broke free of Malloy's grip. "You're a damnned fool if you think that could ever happen," he said through gritted teeth. "Oh, you people are just so ..." Vonderhaar turned and walked off in a huff. Malloy watched him recede, thinking, *What have I done?* Which was followed by, *Hey, in for a penny, in for a pound.* He drained his Dew and followed.

Vonderhaar walked past the waiters' station and into the restaurant. He took a seat at a table with five others, four men and a woman. He was in the middle of saying, "My god, you won't believe what just happened," when he looked up and saw Malloy standing over him. Vonderhaar stood and addressed his tormentor. "You cannot do this," he said firmly, emphatically, as if speaking to a disobedient child. "This is a restaurant and I am with friends."

"Oh, are these the same friends that pay you for the privilege of contracting sexually transmitted disease, and making my life hell in trying to clean up your mess? They look like they could afford the membership fee to your club—what is it, a couple grand? How about I throw in a door prize? A free STD with every act of unprotected sex."

One of the diners, a tanned, vigorous-looking man with a pin on his lapel that said BIRTHDAY BOY, started clapping and said, "Bravo! And what lunatic asylum did you escape from?"

Another fellow with a caterpillar of a mustache intoned, "I think we've had enough of this boorish talk. I'll thank you to leave our table, and if you don't I'll call the police."

"Don't get your nose outta joint," retorted Malloy, going for one last dig. "I'll leave all right, but words of wisdom," placing a hand on Trey's shoulder, "you'd better watch this one. He's bad news."

"And you're drunk," chided Vonderhaar. "A pathetic, ill-bred lout who can't handle his liquor, and then it comes to this, accosting people you don't even know at their very table."

Malloy took in that pronouncement, shrugged maybe so. "You've got a way with words," he told Vonderhaar, "I'll give you that."

TWENTY FOUR

"I THINK I REALLY STEPPED IN IT this time," said Malloy.

"It'll blow over," said Teri, nudging him. "It was just a misunderstanding ... well, a lapse of judgment, anyway. That sort of thing goes on in bars every day. Bad vibes, angry words. People don't take legal action for something like that."

"These people will," persisted Malloy. "They've got everything they need to strike back: time to stew over what happened, money for lawyers, and unrelenting vindictiveness."

"Yeah, maybe you're right," agreed Teri, "but since it's now out of your hands, let's just have another round and try to forget about it."

They were in McDowell's on 12th Street. It was a little after five on a Friday, two days after that mess at Robusto's. Malloy had gone to Teri's bail bond office and they'd taken her car. They walked in and took seats at the bar, facing the stage where Irish musicians played every evening. Lucky, the bartender from County Donegal, looked at them studiously and said in old sod brogue, "Well, well, if it isn't Mister Venereal Disease and Missus Bail Bonds, a couple a fookin' Micks lookin' to slake their thirst in the finest bar in the city. What'll ya have?"

They had their customary libation, she a screwdriver and he a Guinness. They were now on their third round and had pretty much caught up on certain items of interest in their crazy lives. At the moment they were silent, enjoying the warm wash of the booze over their bodies, neither in any particular rush to resume the conversation. At length, Malloy said, "Have another round and try to forget."

"What's that?" she asked.

"A while back you said 'Let's have another round and try to forget.' People do use alcohol as a way of blotting out memory, especially if it's something they shouldn't be doing or that they're ashamed of." He lifted his proper pint of Guinness and spoke to it, "You're a fine one, aren't you? First, you release inhibitions, then you give the green light to do stupid shit, then, when the deed is done, you conveniently allow us to tuck it away in some secret back vault of our minds under lock and key."

"Okay, so why are you on this track? Did you do something awful? You didn't kill anyone, did you? Molest some high school girl, the plaid jumper and white stockings too much to resist? You don't have to drink yourself silly to be absolved of guilt, you know. There're friends to confess to. So, go on, I'm all ears."

He laughed. "You don't look much like Father Garrity from fourth grade back at St. Cletus. And besides, any confession I would make, you'd have to order out for lunch, that's how long it'd take. Actually, I was thinking of an interview I did and how that drinking-to-forget thing really backfired on me. This guy was a contact to syphilis. He and the OP, the original patient, lived together and he was the only one the OP named.

"In fact, the OP died—not from syphilis, but from something else—and he swore on his deathbed that he was true to this older guy, Art, so you know Art got it from somewhere. Yeah? So, it took way too long to get a diagnosis on Art, and that's another story, but when the diagnosis finally was made and it showed positive, then I got to interview Art. Of course Art didn't want to be interviewed about his sex life, because he feels he's pretty goddamn important, and it took some doing to get him in a one-on-one. So now it gets interesting because I know that he goes to this place in the city, like a private club for wealthy gays where they feast like kings and then have a circle jerk afterwards. But I can't tell him that I know he's part of this orgy scenario because the OP told me and he can't know from me who the OP is, although he does know. You follow?"

"Crystal clear," she, sarcastically.

"So, we're doing the interview in a secluded corner of a bar near his work—he can't deal with the riffraff at the STD clinic—and naturally he names the OP thinking that'll get him off the hook. We talk some more, he feels like he's done. I say what about group sex in a private setting, has that happened in the last year? I don't name names like that dickhead I confronted in Robusto's the other night, I don't suggest a particular location such as a mansion in Lafayette Square. I just put it out there and wait for a reaction. At this point he knows that I know about this men's club and after a certain amount of badgering he breaks down and admits that, yeah, he's gone there on several occasions and had great sex with multiple partners from all over the country.

"So, now I'm thinking, All right, we're getting somewhere. But the great sex is all he knows because every time I ask for details like names, descriptions, locating on these people, he says, 'I was too drunk to remember.' He must've used that twenty times: 'Sorry, I was too drunk to remember.' I walked out of that bar with zip, and what really bugged me was that this guy Art was bullshitting me. He had to remember something, but I couldn't motivate him."

Teri wagged her head in resignation. "What're you going to do? You tried, be content with that."

"Makes me wish we could use torture on these guys who conceal their contacts. Put their feet to the fire."

"There's always the whipping post," she added. "Let the townspeople take turns until they fess up."

Suddenly, he got this amused look that comes when a certain memory dredges up visions of wild and reckless youth.

"What's up?" she wondered.

"I was just remembering how I once held back. I had the clap in college and I went to the public clinic in Bloomington. I got treated, but when it came time to talk to the investigator, I ran out."

"Wow! And then you became that guy only to have people run out on you. Or, at least hold back."

"Yeah, it's ironic, huh?"

"That's what they say. What goes around, comes around. Tell me about it. Was she pretty?"

"She was very pretty, but you know what? I can't talk about this right now. I shouldn't have brought it up. Can we table it for another day?"

"Sure, no prob, Bob."

"One more, what do you say?"

"Only if Lucky's pouring," she said to the grinning barkeep standing there. "Lucky, same again."

"He does pour a stiff one," said Malloy. "Maybe I should switch to Jameson's."

"Speaking of stiff ones," said Lucky, wiping off the bar in front of them. "Why does the pope wear his underwear in the shower?"

"He's modest?"

"No, he doesn't want to look down on the unemployed." Lucky laughed genuinely even though he'd probably told that joke a dozen times in the last few days. Their laughter echoing his, he turned to fetch the drinks.

Teri slurped the dregs of her screwdriver, said, "Yeah, well, you watch out with those 'stiff ones' yourself. No more banging the landlady."

"No chance of that this time. The landlords live downstairs. Joe and Ethel, nicest people in the world, pushing eighty. I see Ethel in the backyard, tending her garden. She'll wave, say hi. There's a hole in the front of her mouth where her teeth used to be."

TWENTY-FIVE

DRIVING TO THE NEXT BAR, Malloy was playing roulette with the radio stations, and, coincidence of coincidences, Todd Rundgren popped up singing "Hello It's Me." The song that was his and Pam's back in college, the song that they both said couldn't have fit their situation any better if it tried, especially the "spend the night if you think I should" part. He had opened the lid to that box of emotions back there at McDowell's, and then suddenly closed it. Teri didn't seem too curious. It was good that she didn't press him because … why? Because, it still hurts, he had to admit, his first real heartbreak. Six years ago and it still bothered him.

"It's positive for gonorrhea," stated the nurse, far too calmly. She should be hysterical over the news. Inwardly, he was freaking out. He'd taken human reproductive physiology in college. He knew what the clap did to your equipment, scoring the urethra, the epididymis and all those intricate pathways through which the sperm travel. What if the infection had gone on too long and those insidious invaders had done irreversible damage? What if he were to end up like Uncle Dave? To hear Malloy's dad tell it, when Dave was a sailor he'd caught the bullhead clap in a Singapore brothel. Back then they didn't have penicillin; that miracle of science wasn't used until 1943. Despite his willingness to undergo cures of the day—protracted periods in the steam cabinet, a solution of calomel and oxyquinalone benzoate injected into the urethra—Dave's clap smoldered for months until his otherwise vigorous body made an uneasy peace with the nasty germ. Uncle Dave and Aunt Ruthie never did have kids, which gave him concern, for he liked the thought of a bunch of rugrats running around his imaginary house, getting yelled at by his imaginary wife.

In the here and now, there was penicillin and the nurse was just about to give those little buggers the one-two knockout punch.

He dropped his drawers again and she stuck him in each cheek with a needle and syringe, each one containing 2.4 million units of aqueous penicillin G. That was a big dose and it hurt, but it was a welcome hurt. It was the cavalry coming to the rescue. The big guns being brought to the front.

"Well, my job is done," she said, inserting the business end of the syringes into a needle cutter. "Now, you'll need to see Mr. Langdorf, our epidemiologist. He'll ask you some questions about the source of this infection."

Malloy recalled being puzzled, hearing the word for the first time, a noun whose definition he would one day personify.

As to the nurse, she was a dish, flaming red hair and freckles, not even five years his senior. He didn't see a ring. She also had a great sense of humor. "What are your symptoms?" she'd asked as she entered the examining room. And he stated the god-awful truth: "My thing feels like it's burning." To which she replied, "That just means somebody's talking about it." He found a sense of humor to be quite sexy. Would she even consider?

"The source?" he parroted.

"You have a debilitating communicable disease. This is a public clinic. Public health laws say you have to be interviewed to try to determine where you picked this up. And let me tell you, it didn't come from a toilet seat."

"Yeah, no problem. It's the right thing to do, yeah?"

"It's how we stop the spread of it, only it always manages to stay two steps ahead of us."

She escorted him to a room down the hall. It was barely big enough to fit a table and two metal chairs. It looked like one of those interrogation rooms in the crime shows on TV where the cops grill the suspect as he's crawling out of his skin because he needs a fix. On one wall someone had scrawled in pencil, "love hurts." But it wasn't where he wanted to be, so he decided to scram. He knew that to do so was probably a violation of some kind and that they might come after him, the public health police. He'd put down his address on the intake form. Maybe he'd come back, turn himself in, but only after talking to his so-called girlfriend about this business. He didn't see any compelling reason to get anyone else involved just yet.

He cracked the door, stuck his head out and peered in both directions. He sensed the waiting room and the stairs to freedom were to the right. He strode down the hall at a fast clip, just rounding the corner when a voice yelled after him, "Hold up! You need to wait!"

The clinic was in Bloomington. He lived outside of town, in a farmhouse on a road where the buses don't run, with four other guys, also students at IU. The drive there gave him time to mull the situation. He'd been with one girl for the last two months. The hot piss and tingling hadn't started until two weeks ago. That pretty much incriminated Pam as the source. It didn't necessarily mean she was cheating—not that they'd ever made a pact to be exclusive anyway.

He wasn't totally clueless on the subject back then. He knew that often women can have gonorrhea and not be aware of it. She might have caught it from a guy she slept with months before she met me, he thought. For all he knew, she could be the Typhoid Mary for the spread of clap on campus. And damn it to hell, she was the prettiest girl he'd ever slept with and you don't imagine getting the clap from someone who looks like a *Cosmo* cover girl. Maybe girls who ride on the backs of motorcycles, but not girls as pretty and sanitary-looking as Pam.

Malloy laughed inwardly at such naivete. Now he was quite aware how such beliefs are a towering fallacy and that gonorrhea is an equal opportunist. But back then, well, he just couldn't fathom that someone like Pam might be booby-trapped.

Next he had to figure out how to approach her with the news. He was indignant as hell, but if she really didn't know she was infected he did not want to come off reproachful or try to embarrass her publicly. He had to be reasonable about the matter. Then he had to decide whether they were through or would he forgive her and resume sleeping with her. After she got treated. She was really fun in bed. That decision would depend on how she reacted once he told her. What a mess.

Whatever he would tell Pam could wait. He wanted to be alone for a while. He retired to his upstairs room in the farmhouse and played records, read magazines, cracked a few textbooks and tried not to think about the prospect of never having kids because of this thing. On top of that dour thought, he was feeling *dirty*. That wasn't called for, he knew. Deep down he knew he was still the same unjaded product of Midwestern upbring-ing—well, not really, but at least as a kid he'd been fed a diet of wholesome television shows such as *Make Room For Daddy* and *Father Knows Best* and *Ozzie and Harriet*. So he had that going for him, clean living by osmosis. Still, he couldn't help feeling tainted. After all, he had the same disease as cheap hookers, freewheeling gangsters, and depraved politicians.

On the second day of being mired in self-pity, there came a knock at the door. It was Harold, the chubby, hair-down-to-his-ass, bong-puffing transfer student from Perdue.

"Hey, you hibernating or what? There's no solitary confinement in this house. C'mon, up and out, there's a kegger over at The Barrens. Oh, and Pam called for you, couple times. Says give her a shout back."

"I've decided I'm done with women. They're bad juju."

"Right," said Harold. "And I'm done with Panama Red and all other tasty contraband I can get my hands on."

He gave Pam a shout back, and they agreed to meet at The Barrens in about an hour. Bummed as he was, he couldn't pass up a kegger. Bonfire, beer, and bullshit in the Great Outdoors. Nothing like a kegger to lift your spirits.

The Barrens was a huge tract of pine trees planted in nice straight rows. If they were planted with thoughts of a future harvest, whoever had done the planting must've died or forgotten about it because those pines were now massive. The aisles between the pine rows were big enough to drive a car through and, by the time they arrived, there was already a fire and a dozen cars parked in the clearing in the middle of it all.

He was on his second beer when Pam and her girlfriends came along. With her wavy blond hair, green eyes, and confident stride, there was no mistaking her. She looked so good it was criminal, and she had on that outfit he liked so much—a brown hemp skirt that came down just over the tops of her cowboy boots, denim jacket and a cashmere scarf the colors of fall. She walked right up and gave him a bear hug and a kiss. She smelled good, too.

Over the next three hours they stood around the fire talking, joking, sloshing beers all over the place and getting fairly looped. There was a banjo, a guitar and a harmonica. Some guys had a car on its last legs, a junker, and they were driving it down the rows, sideswiping trees and laughing like hell. When the car quit running, they all coaxed it to the perimeter of the pine forest and pushed its battered carcass down into a ravine, hooting and cheering as it came to a final stop in a creek bed. In south-central Indiana in the mid-seventies, this was excellent entertainment.

Friday night, the rigors of college were on hold and the thought of a career in the workaday world, of marriage and a family, well, that was as distant as a constellation. The here and now was so delicious he was loath to spoil it. What if he didn't say a word about the clap, just pursued this promising relationship with Pam as if nothing had ever happened? But he couldn't do that, he knew, and the reason was more selfish than altruistic. She wasn't cured yet; how many copulations would it take before she reinfected him? In fact there was every indication that she wanted a sleepover this very night. So, the time for truth-telling was nigh. Problem was, as Malloy recalled, he wasn't the most suave guy around. Then or now.

"Hey, you feeling all right lately? Down there, I mean."

She looked at him quizzically. "'Down there?' You mean here?" She clicked the heels of her cowboy boots.

He chuckled. Good. Maybe she would take this thing lightly. "Ah, no. I mean, to use clinical language, in the snatch region. That is, the vagina and all that's connected to it."

Then she got serious. "Yes, I am feeling all right down there, and every other place. And why do you ask?"

"I went to the city earlier this week, paid a visit to the VD Clinic there. I have ... *had* gonorrhea and you're the only one I've been with."

"Like hell!"

"It's true, why would I lie?"

"To hurt me." And she started weeping, causing heads to turn.

He put his arm on her shoulder for comfort, but she pulled away. "Lots of times girls don't know they even have it," he said, trying to soften the news. "I'm telling you so you'll go to the doctor and get treated. I'm already treated."

She was listening. "You could see the school nurse on Monday. They keep it confidential."

"That fucking Odin," she blurted.

"Odin? Why him?" Odin was the biggest hippie on campus. He was majoring in sitar and free love. At the beginning of the semester, when several students collectively freaked out in the Quad one sunny afternoon, having collapsed during some strange dervish dance and all rushed to the hospital, it was Odin who was fingered for supplying them with peyote laced with strychnine or some shit.

She turned in to him, discomfited, and he lifted her chin. "I was with him a few times before we started hanging out. He told me he'd had something, but he'd gotten rid of it."

"Yeah, he probably thinks he can get rid of it by passing it along. I think I'll have a pow-wow with Odin."

"He's really a nice guy, Shaun. I worry how you'll handle it. Please, let me talk to him."

"Not if I find him first."

A few days later Malloy got his chance.

The improbable figure of Odin—long frizzy hair parted in the middle, red bandanna on his forehead, beads and arrow points and feathers around his neck—was hard to miss. Malloy saw him fifty yards off, going into the student center and ran after. When he got there, Odin had already gotten a a cup of ginseng tea and was starting to roll out his blanket near the open hearth. He walked up. Odin regarded him with curiosity.

"What's up?" Malloy standing over him.

"You, man." Odin held out his hand for a soul shake, the gesture ignored.

"Look, I don't really know you so I'll just cut to the chase. Pam, you know Pam? She told me you guys had a thing for a while, had gotten it on a few times."

Craning his neck, looking up at six feet of Shaun Malloy, Odin said, "Look man, I can't talk to you when you're up there. Come down to my level and we'll rap about Pam."

He got down on the floor, but couldn't get cross-legged as Odin had. "Oh yeah, that was a good movie," Odin went on. "And we definitely got it on, more than a few times. I introduced her to the ways of Tantric yoga. She was an enthusiastic student."

"Yeah, great. I just came down with the clap which I got from Pam which she picked up from you."

Odin was pensive for several beats. "That's not my clap. My clap was purged."

"Oh? You mind explaining that?"

"I had the symptoms, the discharge and all that. I went to the doctor for it, only this doctor was a shaman, a Native American, over near Whitehall. He set me up in a sweat lodge, gave me some herb and 'shrooms and agua. I was in that place for two days, man, meditating, traveling out of body, experiencing nirvana. And by the end of it, I was cleansed in spirit *and* body."

This didn't surprise him, Malloy recalled. What did surprise is that he thought somehow he could talk to this idiot. "You are the worst kind of fool," he remembered saying. "You can't meditate away the clap. You need penicillin."

"That is not the Yaqui way."

Now he understood. Odin had been reading Carlos Castaneda, who wrote of spiritual quests under the tutelage of a mystical Yaqui Indian named Don Juan whose sacraments were peyote and other hallucinatory drugs. The books were huge on campus, especially among the quasi-enlightened.

"I'm telling you flat out. The sweat lodge didn't cure the disease. You may think it's gone, but it's still lurking in your ... your loins. You've got to get to the clinic and get conventional treatment. Otherwise, you'll spread the clap all over campus and no one will be safe."

"My loins, man, are my own to do what I want with."

With that, he popped Odin on the beezer.

"What the hell'd ya do that for!" The words thick yet sharp, his nose and mouth staining red.

"Well, I had to do *something*," Malloy said, rubbing his knuckles.

This time there were only two dozen gloomy-looking young men and women in the waiting room. Maybe he could get out in two hours. Halfway through the newspaper, his number was called. He walked up to the window. "I think I'm wanted," he told the receptionist. "Last week, I ran out on Mr. Langdorf."

"You're the one," she affirmed. "They *are* looking for you. I believe the matter was turned over to the police. We take absconders very seriously here."

"Is that what I am? Sounds dangerous. Well, I'm here now, ready to face the music. Bring on the interrogator."

"Have a seat and Mr. Langdorf will be with you."

"Fine. Could I see the nurse, too? The one with the red hair and freckles. I need her to check me out again and I have something to ask her."

"I can't promise you'll see that particular nurse. They're all equally qualified."

"No, it's got to be that nurse. It's a personal matter, personal *and* confidential."

TWENTY-SIX

DELICIA JACKSON LOOKED LIKE A PRO, busting out all over her tube top and short shorts. She was what the brothers call "healthy." Said she came in for a routine checkup and turned up with GC. When Malloy interviewed her, she claimed she'd had sex with 200 to 300 men a month at ten bucks a head. All anonymous, of course. Sarah and Washington was her spot.

They both knew she was lying. She used that smug go-fuck-yourself smile that seventeen-year-olds put on when confronted by bothersome adults, her peacock-blue makeup cracking a little. Malloy wasn't having any of it. "How about that guy you were talking to out in the hall before we came in here? When's the last time you got it on with him?"

"Today." Again, that smile.

"What's his name?"

"Kenny."

"Is he your pimp? He'll have to be checked out, you know."

"Why'nt you go ax him yourself."

So that's what he did. He told Delicia to wait in the room. Kenny was still there, out in the hall with his entourage. He was not a big fellow but his lid made up for it, one of those black fuzzy Stetsons wrapped in plastic so the rain wouldn't ruin the fake fur. Kenny refused to cooperate, wouldn't even speak to Malloy in private. Finally, to get him off his back, Kenny offered to come in the next morning for a checkup. "But you be wastin yo' time," he added, "'cause I ain't got no bugs on me." Delicately, he picked an imaginary louse from his sleeve. A comedian.

Kenny's pimps-in-training laughed at the way Kenny was playing this fool social worker or whatever he was. Kenny was not the biggest mo-fo to ever come out of the hood but he was one of the baddest, having once hung a criminal dog from a lamp post because it wolfed down Kenny's Slim Jim when he wasn't looking. They stood by the elevator and would've left long ago, but Delicia was still being held captive in the room down the hall. The more Kenny dug his heels in, the more insistent Malloy became, his authoritarian mode switching on. Having it out right there, their voices rising, people from the waiting room filing into the hall, forming a crowd.

In his office, Joe Sargent heard it, too. He closed his girlie magazine, and with a grunt, rose from his chair and went to investigate. Joe rumbled up, put out his arms in a "calm down" gesture, and asked what the commotion was about. Malloy answered succinctly, "This guy's a contact to a hot case of GC—OP's here now—and he won't cooperate in the least."

Joe nodded. He understood. All too goddamn well. Joe had already sized up Fuzzy Hat, a pint-sized punk armed with attitude. Still, diplomacy must prevail. Putting a paternal hand on the man's shoulder, Joe asked in his not-so-gruff voice would Kenny please step into his office and they'd settle this whole matter. Now Kenny saw his great opportunity; he was nothing if not a consummate showman. He reached up and flicked Joe's hand away as if it were a waterbug. Then he stepped back and looked the six-foot-four, 280-pound Joe Sargent up and down. He tilted his chin up, a study in defiance, and said, "Get yo' motherfuckin paws offa me, boy!"

Onlookers murmured. Kenny's entourage applauded the brilliant riposte. Malloy winced, thinking how this wasn't going to end well. Joe Sargent, chief of epidemiology and a proud son of the South, could not fucking believe that a punk nigger had just called him "boy" in his own clinic. Motherfuckin, all right, maybe. But boy—he'd even emphasized it!—that really boiled his broccoli. In fact, that three-letter word had an amazing effect on Joe, who began to flush and tremble, the pressure cooker within ratcheting up his blood pressure to the danger zone. He could barely restrain himself, closing in on Fuzzy Hat, pleading with him to "just touch me."

"Excuse me. Excuse me, can I get through here?" A man in civilian clothes but with a brown nylon Sheriff's Department jacket and a clipboard in hand was pushing past the ringside of onlookers into the fray itself. He went up to Joe asked, "You in charge here?"

It wasn't easy for Joe to suddenly switch horses, but he came up with "Yeah, why?"

"You got a Shaun Malloy working here? I need to see him."

"He's standing next to you," said Joe. "What's up?"

The deputy acknowledged Malloy with a "Hey," and asked if he could step away for a moment. Joe said he was coming, too, and the deputy said not a problem. Malloy saw Kenny heading for the stairs, passing Tut coming from the opposite direction. Malloy called and Tut walked over.

"What's up, man? Someone in trouble?"

"Nah," said Malloy, "but turn around, see that big black hat going down the steps? I need you to follow him to his car and get me the plates. Can you do that?"

"Shit, I don't have a screwdriver."

"Jesus, Tut, I mean write it down, the plates. Now go."

The deputy and Shaun followed Joe into his office. Joe shut the door. There was no preamble, the deputy simply saying that he had court papers for Shaun Malloy and he handed them over. He didn't say "You've been served" or anything dramatic, although he did point out a court date.

"You mind telling me what's this all about?" said Joe, looking over Malloy's shoulder at the document with its 22nd Judicial Circuit stamp.

"It's a summons, an order of protection," said the deputy, a hefty white guy, late thirties. "It's what they call an 'ex parte', meaning that this other party, Vonderhaar, is alleging that you've been bothering him or stalking him. I emphasize alleging because it could be bullshit, sometimes people take out these orders, make up stuff, just to screw with someone they've got a beef with. Anyway, you get your chance to go before the judge and tell your side of the story. The judge may grant the protection order or he may decide there's not enough merit. Either way, until the court date, you have to stay away from the petitioner and that means no contact in any way. It's all in there, just read it carefully, you'll understand." The deputy stepped away. "Okay, I'm done here. Have a nice day." But then, at the door, he added with a tired smile, "This job is probably somewhat like yours, it never fricking ends. At least it's not boring."

Joe's irritation was palpable, sending some sort of prickly static bouncing off the office walls. It was impossible to know where the run-in with Kenny left off and the embarrassment of having an employee served in his office began, but the two events together were causing the volcano in Joe's body to act up. It was so obvious that Malloy said, "Joe, I know you want to tear me a new one but maybe that should wait. Why don't I just go to my desk and you call me when you've calmed down and you're ready to discipline me proper."

Joe fixed him with an intense gaze. Why did it have to be Malloy? A fucking cowboy out in the field, but overall his best investigator. "I don't need any of your fucking lip," he barked. "What I need is a five-thousand word essay on some aspect of public health on my desk in two days, that's Thursday eight AM sharp. Collegiate format, footnotes, bibliography, anything else. And there'd better be five thousand words because I'm going to have Danielle count every one. Got that? Now get out." Malloy was one step from disappearing when Joe called out, "And take a goddamn shower once in a while, will ya? You smell like a goose fart."

Alone again, Joe went to his desk, opened the bottom left drawer, took out a fifth of Jim Beam and a smudged glass that read DIRTY NELL'S ROADHOUSE. He poured himself a nice shot and felt it light his belly. He followed with another, and what do you know? The volcano started to quiet down.

Malloy went back to his desk and saw the sheet of paper torn from a spiral notebook laying there atop of everything else. MO WC 5-454 banged up Eldorado / black / mag wheels / Magic 108 sticker. Glad to help, Tut.

TWENTY-SEVEN

MALLOY WORKED long into the night to produce Joe's 5,000-word assignment, culling his essay from sources as diverse as the British Journal of Venereal Diseases and the King James Bible. Of course, he threw a good deal of his own thoughts into the mix. It was titled ON THE ORIGIN OF VENEREAL SYPHILIS.

"Many realize that their infection is due to a recent sexual exposure," he wrote, "but how many realize that both they and their pathogens are subject to the same hereditary processes, that all living things have parents and exist only because their entire line of progenitors was able to reproduce successfully?

"This raises intriguing possibilities. For instance, it is possible that one's distant ancestor may have harbored the ancestral treponeme which now infects a distant twentieth century relative, or that one's disease is brought on by pathogens descended from a sinuous line which at some point may have passed through the bodies of Cleopatra or Attila or even a Neanderthal named Og. A small consolation to victims, but nonetheless fascinating."

He was just getting warmed up. He hit the return key on the ancient Hermes 2000, passed down from his grandfather, and forged ahead.

"And yet there are those whose curiosity runs deep, asking tough questions such as 'who was the first?' If the Bible is to be believed, then Eve must have passed on all venereal disease to Adam or vice versa. They were the first people, so it had to originate with them. But literal interpreters of Holy Scripture have it that venereal diseases are divine punishments for man's failure in the Garden of Eden. This moralistic view can only add to the existing stigma attached to victims of venereal disease, a stigma that is not only backward and harmful, but is contrary to the realization of quality public health for one and all."

From there, he went into the introduction of New World syphilis to Europe, with that stalwart Italian mariner as unwitting conduit.

"The Columbian or New World theory surmises, by historical record, the appearance and sudden spread of a new form of syphilis in late fifteenth-century Europe. On his second voyage, Columbus left Seville in August 1492. He and his crew sailed to Haiti, then known as Hispaniola, where, among other adventures, they had sex with native women. They returned to Palos Bay in 1494, infected, as Columbian theory goes, with Haitian syphilis. Then, with six sailors and six Carib natives, they traveled by land to Barcelona. This company, plus the sailors who remained at Palos, are believed to be the nidus for the syphilization of Europe.

"It remained for kings and armies to provide the disease with a strong foothold. In late 1494, King Charles VIII of France, seeking a Byzantine empire, invaded Italy and besieged Naples, where syphilis was said to be already present. The Neapolitan armies were composed in part of mercenary soldiers, some of whom hailed from the port cities of Spain. The historian Roswell Tarr states that Naples was defended by the Spaniards, whose army was accompanied by a host of harlots. He further cites the account of the noted sixteenth-century anatomist, Fallopius, that the cunning Spaniards deliberately sent their debauched women to meet the French army. Eventually, both armies were so weakened with disease that the siege simply fell apart. Naples fell and the armies dispersed, spreading syphilis as they went. Thus began the first great syphilis pandemic of Europe.

"That endemic Caribbean syphilis first reached Spain via Columbus' crew is fairly certain. A Spanish physician, Ruy de Isla, revealed in a 1539 treatise that forty-five years earlier he first recognized signs and symptoms among that crew docked in Palos Bay. At that time, syphilis was apparently a very acute disease, frequently fatal in the secondary stage. That this acute and severe form of syphilis became attenuated or weakened within the span of one human generation to the more chronic form of today indicates that it was a *new form* of syphilis. Else, why would Old World syphilis, already in the population, suddenly become epidemic and develop manifestations never before seen?

"The demographic drift of syphilis at the turn of the sixteenth century is well documented. In addition to de Isla's findings, an edict issued by the Diet of Worms in 1495 refers to the new disease as 'the evil pox.' By 1497, it had appeared in Scotland; Vasco da Gama, in 1498, had reported it in India. By 1505, it had appeared as distant as Canton, China. According to Columbian theory, syphilis was spread throughout the Western world within twelve years of its introduction to Spain."

Malloy went on to point out every coin has a flip side, and that the pre-Columbian theory, also known as evolutionary theory, may vindicate poor Columbus. In this alternate postulation "... syphilis was present in Europe prior to the voyages of Columbus, but was either unrecognized, confused with other diseases, most likely leprosy, or was present in a much milder form. This theory holds that syphilis is not a disease in itself, rather a form of trepanematosis. Other forms are known in various parts of the globe as yaws, pinta, and bejel. All forms are caused by *Treponema pallidum*, although symptoms vary with regard to environment and even culture."

He took a moment to go over what he'd written, and what he read pleased him, that A in English comp really paying off now. It was getting on midnight. Up to now, the beer fueled him and so he went for another. He returned to the table, notes and articles spread everywhere, salient passages highlighted. It took but a moment to pick up the thread.

"Some scholars look to the Bible, citing what they believe are the first references to syphilis in the Old World. Isaiah 3:16-17 describes a possible outbreak among certain lascivious persons. 'Moreover the Lord saith, because the daughters of Zion are haughty and walk with stretched forth necks and wanton eyes, walking and mincing as they go, and making a tinkling with their feet. Therefore the Lord will smite with a scab the crown of the head and … discover their secret parts.' That sounds ominous," he editorialized. "In those days, you had to be careful whom you minced and tinkled around."

Too flippant? he wondered. Nah, leave it. He continued. "In addition, prehistoric human bones as well as mummified Egyptian bodies have been found bearing scars of such a disease. The argument, however, becomes moot at some point. Microscopes and serologic testing, the ablest tools for definitive diagnoses, would not be available for many centuries. All we have to go on are descriptions of signs and symptoms preserved in record from the period. That, and conjecture."

He added one last paragraph about "Old Joe"—or haircut or lues or Irish mutton or French gout or whichever of its numerous appellations you chose to call it—being just as sneaky and opportunistic today as it was in the time of Columbus. Then he went to bed thinking how Joe would like it.

TWENTY-EIGHT

"It's obscene, the way you guys demean the term Hoosier. I'm a hundred percent Hoosier and proud of it. How'd you like it if I called St. Louisans river rats or boneheads or, oh, I don't know—*culturally backwards?* In other words, would you please stop using Hoosier as a pejorative, at least in my presence?"

"Shaun, believe me, I didn't mean nothing by it," said Tut, palms out in appeasement, "didn't realize you were sensitive about it. But the guy really was one. Only a stupid hoosier would call the VD clinic and ask if you can get the clap by masturbating into a dirty sock."

"And you humored him by asking if it was a right or left sock," said Betsy.

"But why does he have to be a Hoosier?" persisted Malloy. "Why can't he be just a dumbass?"

"We don't know how that got started," said Tut. "I'm from here, I've heard it all my life. It's probably been around since way before my grandpa was born."

"He's right," said Arnold. "We know that a St. Louis hoosier is different from an Indiana Hoosier, but the one here? It's kind of like calling someone a hillbilly, only they live in the city not the country. You see a guy on a sunny day, wearing his baseball cap backwards and squinting because the sun's in his eyes? That's a hoosier."

Laird Cantwell, another native, got in the act. "You see a pair of legs sticking out from under an old beat up truck? That's a hoosier changing his oil. And he doesn't think to catch it in a pan. That oil is running down the curb, headed for the drain and eventually the water supply."

"And there's always a can of Busch nearby," said Arnold. "Unanimously, it's their beverage of choice, probably substituted for mother's milk when they were babes."

Said Betsy, "My husband the lawyer likes to say that if you're a hoosier and you don't mind a bench warrant or a civil judgment, you rule the roost in South St. Louis."

Put in Tut, "You know what a hoosier's last words are? 'Hey, watch this!'"

"Okay, okay," said Malloy, exasperated. "I can see I'm not going to change a timeworn idiom, as idiotic as that idiom may be. Just keep in mind that a *real* Hoosier is a proud son or daughter of Indiana. Kurt Vonnegut, Larry Bird and Florence Henderson, to name a few."

"Carol Brady can't be a hoosier!" said Tut, aghast. "She's hot, man."

"She *is* hot," said Malloy, "if you're turned on by middle-aged women who've had more kids than a litter of puppies. I'm going out, anybody want anything?"

"A week's vacation," said Arnold.

Malloy knew that things were getting weird when Darius, the homeless guy who worked at the newsstand down the street from the health department, warned him, "Be careful, man. They's some scary shit goin' round." Malloy said there was lots of scary shit going around, which particular scary shit was he speaking of?

Darius looked the part of a bum, dressed in too many shabby layers for the weather. His appearance was further enhanced by a bushy 'fro, mashed down in places, and speckled with bits of lint; nostrils so cavernous they could have concealed chestnuts; and his skin, so dark it shined. He could have been forty or sixty, who knew? But Darius was not a bum; he was a businessman. The newsstand was his livelihood. Mornings, he sold the

Globe-Democrat along with *The Evening Whirl,* "An uninterrupted crime-fighting publication since 1938," and a few other local fishwraps. Malloy had walked down to get the latest issue of the *Whirl* because often there was mention of some contact he had chased or was currently chasing.

Darius knew Malloy worked at the clinic, and felt that he could talk to him about this scary shit that had him worried. He looked along the street, spied no eavesdroppers, said lowly, "Some kinda sickness, grabs on to you and don't let up. In the beginning, it be like a flu and even if that go 'way, you got other problems. You gets tired, real tired, you start losing weight, they be swellin's here n' there and spots, man, spots all over. Red spots, white spots, purple ones—it be different with different people. I seen spots, scabs on faces and arms, legs, some the size of Kennedy halfs. That's when you know it gettin' real bad."

Malloy asked him where he had seen these things. Darius gave a mock hurt look. "What, you don't believe me? On the street, man. Vacant lots, alleys, loading docks, empty buildings, anywhere my peoples be congregatin' for some good times, you dig?"

A woman walked up and plunked down six bits for a four-bit *Globe.* Darius beamed. "Thanks a lot, lady. Yeah, anyway," he continued, "this thing ain't gon' 'way. One week you see a guy look like he on his last legs, all coughin' and tremblin' an' shit, next week he ain't around. You say, 'Where ol' Wilbur?' They shake they head sad-like an' say, 'Wilbur gone an' he ain't comin' back.' It somethin' else, man."

Malloy gave it thought. "How many has this happened to, people in your own circle?"

"Lessee, there was Wilbur an' Dano. And we ain't seen Pickaninny for a while, he probably gone."

"Pickaninny?"

"Tha's what we call him, big dumb, bug-happy son a bitch. Eyes wide open, hair long and rasty-lookin', all tied off in little ribbons, always singin' or dancin' like that damn fool in that ol' book, Unca Tom's Cabbage."

Malloy smiled at the misnomer, pressed on. "Okay, so tell me, were Pickaninny or any of these others sexually active? Maybe turn tricks?"

Darius' eyes narrowed to slits. "Shit, now you's wantin' me to narc on my brothers? What you gon' do with this information?"

"For now I'm just going to file it away in my head, but it might come in handy later. You're worried about it, worried it might happen to you.

Maybe down the line I can do something."

But Darius seemed dubious, wanted to know how in hell Malloy thought he might be able to make a difference in this bad-ass disease going around. There were millions and millions of nasty little germs and only one of him.

"Don't worry about it," said Malloy, "just answer the question."

"Yeah, yeah," said Darius, "you gon' get information from me and you gon' keep it on the sly, hear? Aw right, den. Of them I mentioned, jus' Pickaninny was up to what you talkin'. Trickin' like that. We'd be over at the Gateway Diner—'cross from Tower Grove Park?—an' he'd say, 'You know, I think I need me some cheeseburgers and fries.' Then he'd walk out, cross over Grand into the park, disappear about a half-hour an' come back lickin' his lips an' say, 'Gimme a big plate of cheeseburgers and fries.' So I'll let you guess what he was doin' over there in that park."

"Yeah, I've heard that before," said Malloy. "Any given day there's someone cruising the east end of that park looking for a blowjob, ten-dollar bill burning a hole in their pocket. What's Pickaninny's real name?"

"Lawrence somethin'. No need to know real names, not in my world. Shit, man, you don't even know *my* last name."

A man walked up and wanted a copy of yesterday's *Post*. "Don't sell the *Post* here," Darius told him. "They's a box on the corner."

The guy walked off and Malloy said, "But this is a *Post* newsstand. It says *Post-Dispatch* on the front."

Darius looked at Malloy like he was stupid. "*Post* comes out in the afternoon."

"Yeah, so what?"

Darius spat on the ground. "Hawkin' that thing cuts into my drinkin' time."

"Good point. Anyway, I may want to look into Pickaninny and for that I need his name. What about relatives?"

"You might wanna try Produce Row," said Darius, "he was a swamper down there, part-time, when he could get off his ass for some honest work. Try Franklin Produce or Mantia Fruit. You let me know what you find." Darius let that settle a moment, then he looked at Malloy and said, "Now, Mistah Disease Detective, you gon' buy that newspaper or try to steal it?"

TWENTY-NINE

On the phone Kenny cursed him out and swore he'd never come in, that he could take care of it himself. Yeah, right, and dogs can drive cars. Just because Kenny was able to skip out, having taken advantage of Malloy getting served, did not mean that Malloy was done with him. The clinic was affiliated with the Regional Justice Information System, REJIS, and all it took was a phone call followed by a few formalities such as stating his name, his employer, his security access code, providing the characters on Kenny's plates. And just like that he had Kenny's pedigree—full name, birthdate, driving record, home address with phone number. Thank you, Big Brother.

Yesterday he'd paid Kenny a visit at his mother's house where he spoken to Kenny by phone and his mom was pretty nice, saying Kenny didn't much stay there but if Malloy saw him would he please tell him there was some mail waiting here. Next he went to Delicia Jackson's house in The Ville. It was before ten and she came to the door in a sheer negligee, nipples and bush apparent though the filmy gauze. He asked about Kenny and she tried to shut the door, but Malloy had his foot in it.

"I know he's in there, why don't you cut the crap and let me talk to him?" No sooner had he said that when Kenny appeared at the door, smoking a doob in his skivvies. Malloy went into his best motivational spiel, but Kenny was unmoved. He shoved Malloy back, and with an almighty thud slammed the door.

Malloy stood there, pondering his next move. Then he saw Kenny at the window and went over and tried to convince him some more. This inspired Kenny to draw a pistol and wave it menacingly on the other side of the glass, swearing that he'd shoot Malloy in the face if he ever came around again. Malloy backed off. He walked to his car, drove around the block until he saw a white city squad car. He honked at it, the cop stopped. Malloy explained the situation and when the cop heard brandishing a weapon he got on the radio, saying, I've got a ten thirty-two here, request additional support. Malloy led the cop back to Delicia's place. The cop told him sit tight; Malloy found a vantage point and waited for things to unfold.

Soon cops were all about and they had their weapons trained on the door. Open up, police! Open up Kenny did and Malloy never saw a body shake so. Kenny claimed there was never a pistol, that this guy, Malloy, had it in for him, he'd made it all up. The cops didn't believe one word he said, but without evidence of a weapon it was just one person's word against another's. They would, however, ensure that Kenny got to the clinic just as Malloy intended. They stood by as Kenny, bitching up a storm, got in Malloy's car and then they followed Malloy two miles to the clinic and watched as the public health officer and his indignant patient entered the building. Waiting for the elevator, Kenny said he needed to go back because he'd forgotten his hat. Malloy said no way. Kenny said Fuck you, I don't go out in public without my hat. Malloy replied that if Kenny tried to walk off again he would personally give him such an ass-beating that he would run crying to his mama. Now get in this elevator.

That was yesterday, when the cops were his friend and the system was on his side. Today was a different story. Today, he was going to court to tell a judge that he really wasn't a public nuisance, that his freedom to pester people such as Trey Vonderhaar should not be curbed in any way. He did not have a good feeling about it. He already imagined the judge granting the protection order, which would keep him from having any contact with Vonderhaar for the next six months. Okay, so how bad was that? If Vonderhaar's name surfaced again in a syphilis investigation or as part of this new thing that seemed to be spreading alongside syphilis, he could still work him, he'd just have to do it through Betsy or one of the other investigators.

Division 14, Adult Abuse and Domestic Plight, was everything he expected. The defeatist looks of the characters milling about in the hall waiting for the docket to thin out. The stone-faced bailiff monitoring the courtroom, just waiting for an outburst to happen, handcuffs ready. The lawyers in their hundred-dollar Joseph A. Bank suits, sitting at their table between the bench and the gallery of fidgeting defendants, everyone wanting to get the hell out of there. It was taking a long time, that was for sure.

A person served with a protection order doesn't really need a lawyer. The order is alleging misconduct, bothering another person. It's not as if he were being charged with a criminal act. But if the judge grants the order and the defendant then violates that order, well, then it rises to a criminal offense and that defendant can be arrested and jailed. As far as Malloy could tell, most of the waiting defendants did not have lawyers. They were probably going to accept their fate resignedly and any defensive argument would be feeble at best—"But Your Honor, we're in love. She just doesn't know it, yet!"

No, for most of them the presence of a $150-an-hour lawyer in their corner would only pour salt on their psychic wounds. With or without a lawyer, they wouldn't win because the judge granted ninety-eight percent of these orders. Asses would be covered. The judge couldn't chance it that some hothead he let slide last week wouldn't break his girlfriend's jaw this week. And then the spotlight would be on him, the cries of an outraged public: *you could have stopped this!*

Malloy saw Dunaway at the lawyers' table and he assumed correctly that he was here for Vonderhaar, who was *in absentia*. His turn was coming up and he wished he'd hit the john when he'd had the chance. He tried to put aside the urge to pee by listening to what was going on at the bench.

One by one, as their names were called, the defendants walked up to the judge. The Honorable John Henry Pugh would read the allegations and spice it with certain passages that the petitioner had written detailing the defendant's horrible acts. Now there was an obese white guy, around 40, standing before the judge, who was glaring at him through spectacles on the end of his nose, asking whether these things were true. Malloy strained to hear the dialogue, but then the defendant blurted quite audibly, "It is definitely untrue. I am *not* a pervert. The only perverted thing I've ever done was to jack off my dog, and that was consensual."

Then Malloy's name was called and both he and Dunaway approached the bench. They nodded in recognition. For the twenty-third time that day, the judge read the charges to yet another defendant. "It says here that you chased the petitioner through the dining area at Robusto's and then you berated him in front of his friends. Is this correct, sir?"

Ever the contrarian, Malloy replied, "I wouldn't say *chased*, Your Honor, it was more like followed. And *berated*, such a prejudicial term. I would change that to addressed."

The black-robed judge raised his wiry eyebrows, digging little furrows into his forehead. "Good Lord, we have a semanticist here. Well, for all your fine-tuned definitions, I'd say these allegations are correct. Robusto's is a very nice restaurant, as you are likely aware. Many prominent citizens pay good money to dine there, my wife and I included. The Beef Wellington is superb, and their Dessert Mont Blanc—positively decadent. The settings are impeccable, and the service is without equal. And to this oasis of fine dining you bring your crude behavior?"

Malloy saw he was going down fast, said, "I had to take it somewhere, Your Honor."

Judge Pugh did not find this amusing in the least. "It's people like you who taint the notion of civility. You, sir, are an ill-bred lout and this is why you stand here before me. You are well advised to take stock of your behavior before it lands you in even more serious trouble."

There was that word again. Lout. Vonderhaar had called him that, now this puffed-up personage was pulling it out. Must be the preferred derogatory noun of blue-blooded St. Louisans.

The judge looked to Dunaway and said, "This protection order is granted for a period of six months. Mr. Malloy, you understand that you are to have no contact of any kind with the petitioner, and that means stay away from him."

"What if I'm out somewhere and he walks into my space?"

"Then you leave, simple as that."

"Doesn't seem fair," said Malloy.

"Who said anything about life being fair?"

Dunaway thanked the judge and asked that the order be in effect for a full year.

"Let's take it six months at a time, see how Mr. Malloy here comports himself. Meanwhile, your client should rest more easily. Be grateful for that." Judge Pugh looked to his bailiff. "Next case."

Out in the hall he ran into Sherri Voss, the love interest of a certain nettlesome contact. She had a nice shiner on her left eye. "Ouch," said Malloy. "Which door did you walk into?"

"Very funny," she said. "I can't find enough makeup to camouflage it, and an eye patch might get me mistaken for a pirate."

"You could blacken the other eye and pose as a raccoon." He took a closer look at the shiner. "I suppose this is the handiwork of a certain Chris Dickerson?"

"You got it, and this was *after* he was served the protection order that you told me to take out. Today is our court date, but of course he's not here. The judge granted the order, and when he saw what Chris did he also put out a warrant for his arrest."

Even with her face marred, Sherri was attractive. He wouldn't mind getting her between the sheets sometime if the fates allowed. He put his arm around her, gave a friendly squeeze. "No need to tell you how important it is to put out your feelers when you decide to take up with someone new.

The signs were probably there, you just overlooked them in that rosy glow of a budding relationship."

"You're right. Eight months together, and I never saw a violent side to him. He wouldn't even swat a bee in my kitchen, he had to capture it and take it outside. I just don't get it. Now, he's become a woman beater and some sort of outlaw and for what?"

"He could have easily taken care of the problem and moved on," agreed Malloy. "Some guys have a lot of pride, which is their downfall ... listen to me, I sound like a preacher."

"You know what he said, just before he punched my clock?"

"I'm almost afraid to know."

"He came to my house. Like a fool I let him in. He had the protection order in his hand. There were daggers in his eyes and he said, 'You think this piece of paper is going to keep me from you?'"

THIRTY

BRYSON VONDERHAAR III loved late payments. His debtors had a three-day grace period after payments were due at the beginning of each month. After that, each day delinquent meant $25 tacked on to the principal. These debtors were not legion, but they were precious in terms of providing a healthy stream of income.

Long ago, his financier father had taught him the value of making loans to otherwise flush persons temporarily down on their luck, people who would rather spend a day in a snake pit than walk into a bank for help. Presently, he had but seven promissory notes to collect on. They ranged from a piddling $3,000 lent to an out-of-work actress-model who was likely to land a role in an upcoming Spielberg movie, to a not-to-be-sneezed-at $19,000 with a local car dealer who needed to keep afloat until the new 1983 models came in.

And though Vonderhaar II had been a ruthless businessman, his son had done him one better in the loan shark department. Whereas Pater— God bless his flinty soul—had been satisfied with five percent interest, filius saw 12 percent as a proper figure. Hey, take it or leave it. He'd read *The Merchant of Venice* and was quite impressed with the usurer Shylock. There was an enterprising fellow!

Trey had only a few rules concerning this aspect of his growing empire:

he avoided doing business with known gamblers or drug addicts. And once the contract was signed and the money changed hands, he would never again deal directly with that debtor; that's what Freddie DuCoin was for.

"What's the word on Ingersoll?" Trey wondered.

Freddie had to wash down a bite of bagel with lox and cream cheese before he could answer. "The payment arrived by mail yesterday with an extra hundred twenty-five bucks and a note saying it wouldn't happen again."

"Of course it'll happen again," mused Trey. "Procrastination is such an endearing human trait. How about Wunderlich? He still riding the bad luck train?"

Ryan Wunderlich was the president and lone employee of Chimney Pot Enterprises, an architectural salvaging company that specialized in the collection of ornament from buildings slated for demolition—his Soulard warehouse was filled with cornices, finials, marble balustrades, Corinthian columns, elaborate reliefs, even bigger-than-life statuary. He was the darling of the preservation movement for saving artifacts that otherwise would join the rubble heap. Trey Vonderhaar didn't give a hoot in hell how much of a hero Ryan Wunderlich was to certain moonstruck urbanites. If Wunderlich couldn't sell his product then he couldn't pay his premiums, and he was just another deadbeat. "Our boy wants to know if he can skip this month's payment and double-down next month, says he has a major client from Chicago taking delivery late this month."

"We've already given him a couple reprieves," snapped Trey. "He should have put something aside to keep on schedule. No, I'm not going to enable his lack of self-discipline. Call Dunaway and tell him to start the proceedings, that'll get his attention."

Upon Trey's behest, F. Laughton Dunaway would draft a breach of contract lawsuit demanding immediate payment in full of the promissory note plus punitive fees. If the case went to court with Trey getting a judgment, and if Wunderlich still failed to make good, then Dunaway would apply for a writ of execution. Writ in hand, the sheriffs would come to confiscate Wunderlich's treasures and Trey would take possession. He was already imagining the auction he would have. A Sunday afternoon, semiformal dress, the cream of society milling about the warehouse. He would serve cocktails and canapés, bring in a real auctioneer who would stand on a plank spouting rapid-fire gibberish the way they do. It would be quite the lark!

"Okay, will do," said Freddie, adding that he would make a deposit at the bank later today.

Trey, chewing on his thumbnail, seemed distracted. "While you're there," he instructed, "get balances on the accounts."

"It's a pretty pile, I can tell you that without a note from the teller. It keeps growing, too. When are you going to make a serious withdrawal and do something nice for yourself?"

Trey regarded Freddie with genuine fondness. This wholly capable man had been at his side for five years now. Freddie knew every aspect of his operations, knew his mind on many matters both business and personal. As his man Friday he was nothing less than indispensable. They both knew it, and therefore it would not be out of place for Freddie to believe that he was in line to some day receive a good portion of his "pile."

Fat chance of that. Never mind that he, Trey, had no immediate family and certainly no heirs; Freddie was not getting a penny of that pile. No qualms about that. Freddie's salary was ample and the perks of this job were covetous; his own charming carriage house for one, and connections to certain well-placed homosexuals for another. Between the day trading, the money lending, and Man 2 Man—not forgetting the unsparing inheritance that paved the way for all to come—Trey Vonderhaar had amassed a fortune. He had plans for his money all right, and it didn't include charitable donations to loyal underlings.

"That's kind of you to think about my welfare," ventured Trey, "but for now I think I'll just watch it grow. It's got to be up around six hundred by now, the combined accounts."

"Four hundred seven thousand and some change last time we checked, plus another hundred eighty over at A.G. Edwards locked up in investments. You might want to think about moving more funds over to the brokerage, the return is so much better than the bank's."

"Oh, you're my financial advisor now?"

"Sorry," shot Freddie, "I just …"

Trey waved him aside mid-apology. "No offense taken, Freddie, and you're right, of course. But that six figures in the bank is there for a reason. I like to have the feeling of being able to go liquid any time I want, say, tomorrow."

"You're going somewhere?"

"No, but it could happen. I could decide to go orchid hunting in Paraguay or study calligraphy in Japan, take a fat pay-out, stay for six months, recharge my batteries. You think you could take the helm while I'm gone?"

"You know it," said Freddie, gamely, "it would be an honor and I'm perfect for the job."

Trey reached for the clay teapot and refilled his cup with a spot of Earl Grey. "Speaking of jobs," he said, I've got one for you, an unusual one."

"Yeah?"

"Oh yeah. Our soiree tomorrow evening is all set with ten confirmed guests, but Ron from Nashville has suddenly canceled and normally one cancellation would not be a problem except that Tory from Manhattan had his heart set on hooking up with Ron."

"You can't substitute?" asked Freddie.

"From all reports Ron is the only one in the group who enjoys anal sex, and Tory is strictly back door. There's no one else I can offer Tory and you know what a good client he's been, all those referrals he's given us. So … "

Freddie caught his direction and his anus involuntarily puckered. "You're asking me to get buggered by Tory from Manhattan!"

Trey nodded in his resolute way. Even as they spoke, the matter was a *fait accompli*.

Still. "Begging your pardon, but I reject the notion that Ron is the only one who likes it from the rear. These are men with experience, surely one of them is more than happy to take on that role. Have you even asked?"

Trey stared back impassively, not even offering a courteous reply. Freddie despised this Trey, the cold, heartless version of his otherwise cordial employer.

Finally, Trey spoke. "Freddie?"

"Damn it, Trey, that's not in my job description!"

Trey gave him a smile that a viper would appreciate. "Your job description, Freddie, is whatever I say it is. You can take one for the team."

"Easy for you to say. The thought of it is enough to make me want to switch teams."

"The assignment accepted under protest, perfectly understandable. I'll introduce you two at the start of the evening. And Freddie?"

"Yes, Trey."

"I'll need you to act super gay."

"Truman Capote gay?"

Trey shook his head. "Too bland. You ever hear him talk? You feel like you want to smack him. Tory likes them flamboyant. Think Elton John primping in his dressing room, trying on feather boas."

THIRTY-ONE

THE GATHERING at The Asylum, a bar on Euclid Avenue, couldn't really be called a party. It was a send-off for the artist Ren Peters, who was on his last legs from this new disease. Malloy had met Ren a few years ago at a gallery opening also on Euclid.

Ren was the picture of a hot new artist then, standing before one of his outrageous sculptures, regaling newfound groupies with an inside look at the artistic process.

"Art today is not about aesthetics," he proclaimed, "it's about ideas."

His modus operandi: "Basically, I make it up as I go."

The incredible amount of work devoted to each piece: "It's ninety percent thought and ten percent doing."

His high regard for the gallery owners and art reviewers who touted his work: "Just a bunch of cheese-eaters."

And finally, the effect that his formidable sexuality had on his work: "Gay is to art as bees are to honey."

Malloy was a fan, too. He couldn't afford one of Ren's pieces, but he did buy him a beer at the after-party down the street. Ren was a great conversationalist if you wanted to talk about his art.

Now the idea was that he was dying and over a swell pouring he wanted to be feted by his friends and followers one last time. Malloy had never heard of a wake where the soon-to-be decedent was able to hold a cocktail in one hand and shake hands with the other as he said goodbye, but times were changing and nothing these days was too overstated. Malloy stood before the mirror, worked his thin black tie into a Windsor knot, finished his Dewar's rocks, and headed out the door.

Across town, Drew Conger dressed for sex. He wore tight chinos, Tony Lama boots, a pressed white long-sleeve shirt open at the collar to show a hint of chest hair, and a dove-colored vest that had once been part of an Italian suit. A sterling silver band set with a turquoise stone held his ponytail in place. Sure, it was a wake for Ren, poor guy, but there would be lots of pretty packages there. He might get lucky. Drew often got lucky.

The Asylum was three stories of anything goes across from Robusto's.

The downstairs was a lesbian bar, Girls Go Down. The main floor was an afternoon hangout for older queens, sipping their Grand Marniers and flicking ashes from elegant cigarette holders. The upper floors housed a chest-thumping nightclub which opened at seven, had a cover for DJ Ray-gay, a dreadlocked white guy with a fondness for The Wailers, Grace Jones, Ryuichi Sakamoto, and Blondie. Off to the sides were restrooms ideal for doing drugs or quick sex or both.

The wake was in the bar on the main floor. Most of the old queens had already gone, having drunk themselves into stupors. Malloy walked in, got a smile from the he/she taking the $10 "Suggested Donation." He passed through several knots of people on his way to the bar, nodding. He was in a good mood, and these people seemed all right.

He got his beer and scanned the room. Ren wasn't there yet, but he did spot someone he knew. He walked over and greeted Killian, his friendly server from the Down Street Cafe, a hipster hangout in Soulard. Killian was with a group of friends talking about the pressing topic of the stricken Ren and this thing that was going around.

"They're calling it AIDS now," said a thin woman with streaked hair and a ring through her nose. "They just had a meeting in Washington of gay community leaders, doctors, researchers, and some high muckety-mucks from the CDC, and it was decided to replace GRID with AIDS."

This was news to Malloy. He was really out of the loop, an epidemiologist with the very organization she had mentioned and he had never heard of GRID or AIDS. She seemed to know what she was talking about.

"Where did you hear about this?" he queried.

"It was in the *Post* today," she said.

That explained it. Malloy was a *Globe* reader.

"So what do those letters stand for?" Killian asked.

"GRID is gay-related immune deficiency," the first woman said, not missing a beat, "and AIDS, I forget, except that it also has immune deficiency in it. They changed it to AIDS when they realized that the disease wasn't just for gays."

"Okay, great," said a stubby male version of a fire plug, "so it got a new name but what are they doing to cure it?"

No one had an answer. Several of them studied their drinks waiting for someone to pick it up again.

At last, a Jim Morrison look-alike chimed in, "I think we all know it's most likely a new STD, and if that's true then it's even more reason to use condoms."

"A full body condom," put in one wag.

Said a tall brunette with perfect teeth, "If you listen to Jerry Falwell and his followers, it's God's will, a punishment on gays for their wicked ways."

"What a jerk," added Fire Plug. "I'd like to wring his fat, ugly neck."

"So misguided," added the brunette, alarmed that the others might think she was in Falwell's camp. "It's just another example of how narrow-minded the religious right can be."

Malloy was looking at the woman with the ring through her nose, thinking about hitting on her later. He had never been with a woman with a nose ring.

"It probably is sexually spread, this AIDS disease," said Killian, "but needles are a cause, too. You're doing needle drugs or dating someone doing needle drugs, you're pretty high on the list." They all agreed.

"But that's not how Ren got it," said Ms. Nose Ring, a fount of information. "He's in with that group here on Euclid, and some of them have it, too." She lowered her eyes. "So sad, so incredibly sad." Most of them knew what she was talking about, a close-knit bunch of guys working along the strip as waiters, florists, hair stylists and shop owners, all of whom shared a taste for hard-ons and jizz. Gossip had it that no less than five waiters from Robusto's were already afflicted.

"You know what they're doing," asked Fire Plug, "the ones who learn they're infected? They max out their credit cards on luxury items and travel, get it while they still can. You know Andrew and Brandon, waiters over at Ciao Bella? They took an extended vacation, a world tour on American Express, all the major cities, the best restaurants, exclusive clubs, the works. By the time the bill catches up with them, well, good luck collecting."

"Some of them, it hits hard right away, they couldn't do anything like travel." Jim Morrison leaned in, lowered his voice, "You remember Danny from the bookstore, black guy, about thirty, big toothy smile? One day he got sick, real sick, had to move in with his mother while he wasted away and finally died. Watching him go like that, it almost killed his mother, too."

"Whoa," said Killian, incredulous, "that's what happened to Danny? I wondered where he went."

"You know, the last time I saw Danny he was with Ren," said a man in a white shirt and a vest, his long brown hair in a ponytail, "they were closing down the bar at Milano 390. Those two and a couple others, getting silly, had the bartender mixing every drink he knew. That was maybe four months ago."

"You see what happens," said Killian, looking past the others, "you start talking about someone, then they show up. Hey Ren, glad to see your face in the place."

Ren Peters came tottering up on three legs, two of his own and a tapered cane. He simply stood there with no particular expression. His wavy black hair had lost its luster and no amount of Redken could restore it; pale and cavern-eyed, he had the haunted look of a condemned man. "Wouldn't be anywhere else," he answered, looking around, taking in the place wistfully. "There's been a lot of good times here, a lot of crazy times half-remembered the next day. New York's got nothing on us, right?"

There were rejoinders of "You got that right," and a short discourse on the St. Louis club scene being the equal of New York or Chicago if only for the abundance of free parking. Small talk went on for a minute. No one was willing to break the ice about Ren's condition or the reason they were here. Until someone said, "Nice cane."

Ren held it up for a better look. "I think of it as a walking stick," he said. "Cane often has that curved top to it. This was made for me by Rob Lasch, the woodworker? It's red oak with a unique feature that some would call macabre." Theatrically, he shifted it from one hand to the other, indicated the grip, a stylized skull of bronze. "A death's-head," he declared, "like you see in those old cemeteries. It was my idea, Death being such a close companion these days. I thought I might as well embrace the situation instead of try to shoo it away. Makes sense, don't you think?"

This admission, of course, opened the spigot. In a gush of sentiment they told him how brave he was to deal with it head on, what a tragedy it was that he and others were being taken in the prime of their lives. A few were weeping openly.

Ren acknowledged their compassion and said, "It's stalking us, you know." He looked from face to face. "But then, there's so much hedonism in this society, what do you expect?" This gave them pause. No one knew quite what to say until Ren added, "And I, for one, was an enthusiastic participant. God, what a time we had!" He turned to Killian, "Be a sweetheart and get me a drink. Vodka martini, dirty. Tell Ginger it's for me." As Killian made for the bar, Ren took her place in the loose circle of well-wishers.

"Glad you could make it," he said to Malloy beside him.

"Never turn down a chance at good company."

"You know it's a party when the health department shows up," he said openly. "Did you bring some penicillin? I'm sure there's a few here tonight who could use a dose."

Failing to detect a jocular tone, Malloy was worried that Ren, for some reason, had it in for him. He was right.

Ren pivoted to better face Malloy. Leaning on his walking stick with both hands, he said, "You're a character in this play, did you know that?"

"I definitely feel like one right now," answered Malloy, trying not to sound too much on the spot. Suddenly, eyes were upon him. He was glad that Killian wasn't here to see this.

"I don't think you realize," Ren reproved. "Let me tell you what your role is. First person I lost was my boyfriend, Sacha. Sacha was a ballet dancer who was featured on the Harvey Edwards posters with destroyed ballet shoes, dirty worn-thin tights and gritty scenes of sweat and hard work. At first I didn't believe it was him on the posters until he showed me the original duct-taped dance shoes in his closet.

"I was smitten, but it wasn't to be. He joined the Royal Danish Ballet, went to Copenhagen, caught pneumonia. Or so they called it. He came back to St. Louis and died within a month. I was at his apartment every day, taking care of him.

"You have no idea what that's like, watching someone you love deteriorate. Then one day you hear a knock at the door. I look out the window and it was you. We chose not to answer, because we sensed it was something unpleasant. *And*, because this is America and we can fucking well expect some privacy in our own homes. But you kept knocking and coming around and leaving notes about having to report to that stupid clinic of yours. My lover is dying this horrible death and you're on his case about some fucking VD you say he has!"

Ren might have continued this tirade, but his emotions had stirred up his bronchitis. He grabbed the drink of a woman on the other side of him and hacked a bolus of phlegm into it. He handed it back to her.

Malloy recalled paying several visits to the home of Sacha whatever-his-name-was, banging on that blank door until one day a neighbor came out and said that Sacha had gone to Denmark to dance. Malloy remembered wanting to tell the neighbor, Fine, let the Danes deal with his syphilitic ass.

Ren Peters recovered momentarily and Malloy braced himself for round two, but the artist seemed to have gotten it out of his system. He gave an imperious wave of the hand, a signal to the others to put away the stink-eye. He put an arm around Malloy's shoulders, good-buddy style. He gave him a friendly squeeze and said, "Karma will catch up to you and your storm trooper tactics, that will be on you. Meanwhile, I'm dying and it won't do to harbor bad feelings or grudges. I forgive you. You were just doing your job ..." He was on now, as on as on can be. " ... as fucked up as that job may be. So, we part company, no longer friends but at least not enemies." Ren scanned the small audience, gave a wink. "Drinks on Shaun, here, what do you say?"

There was applause and several demands for cocktails with premium spirits, "none of those rotgut well drinks." Damn, that meant he couldn't leave.

The ponytailed guy in the white shirt and vest walked up, and Malloy accepted his offer to help carry the drinks. At the bar, they got acquainted. His name was Drew and he was an account exec at a classic rock station, which meant he sold ads. He had a cockapoo named Oscar which he loved to spoil, and a mom over in U City who loved to spoil him. Drew knew Ren from the art scene around town. He went to the openings regularly and in fact he had a photo show coming up at the Eden Coffeehouse. He might even sell a couple, which would be great because he could always make more. And yeah, he'd try a Guinness, same as Malloy.

Malloy paid the bill and they took the drinks over on a tray. Ren had moved on to another group. Those remaining took their drinks, some saying thanks. Drew suggested they get a table, Malloy said why not.

They sat there listening to loud, world beat music played over JBL loudspeakers installed about every forty feet on the ceiling and walls. Malloy did not feel a need to talk. Drew Conger did, though.

"Do you really track down VD suspects?" he tried.

"Yeah, I do, but we call them contacts."

"That must be exciting, huh? A little dangerous, too."

"Exciting, no, not in the least. Dangerous, maybe. You get on the wrong side of those drag queens, they'll try to scratch your eyes out."

"That's right, you must come in contact with every sort of sexual flavor out there. The s-and-m crowd, queens, butches, femmes, trannnys. Is there one area you specialize in?"

"You're assuming I'm working mostly gay cases," said Malloy, reluctant to talk shop, "but actually it's the other way around. In 1979, there were approximately three million cases of gonorrhea in North America compared to only one hundred thousand cases of infectious syphilis. Gonorrhea is largely a straight disease while syphilis these days is more in the gay community, about seventy percent. So what does that tell you?"

"That you're knee-deep in VD?"

"Up to my elbows."

"I guess you're pretty careful about who you screw."

Malloy gave a sort of rueful laugh. "Not as careful as I should be."

This was good news to Drew Conger, who had already envisioned giving Malloy an invigorating rubdown with warm baby oil. "I hear you," he confided, "there's so many hungry men who want this particular thing or that particular way and you want to please but you're a little cautious, I mean, you don't know who they've done last or what they're carrying that's not obvious on the surface. Just because you're young and healthy-looking doesn't mean you can't be infected."

"Ren Peters, case in point," said Malloy.

"I really long for the old days when you could just screw anyone you wanted and not have to worry about catching something that might turn you into a walking cadaver."

They drank to that, and Malloy said, "I wonder if this is how the burghers felt during the Black Plague of the thirteen hundreds in Europe. They estimate thirty percent of the population was wiped out, but nobody really knows except that people were dying faster than they could bury them. Not saying this AIDS thing will be anything along the lines of that, but I'm seeing now that it *is* an epidemic and we're riding the first wave of it. The time will come when everyone will know someone or know of someone who has it."

"I knew someone," said Drew tentatively. "My friend Bruce—Bruce, gay stereotype, right? He had the lisp and the limp wrist, too, but he was hot and he had a stand-up comedian's sense of humor. Bruce was a graphic designer, had a studio down on Washington in an old button factory. We'd get together about once a month for drinks and see what would happen next, you know?

"Thing was, he used to complain about his weight even though he looked trim and fit. Then one day I stopped by the studio and he really was thin,

thin and worn-out looking. He said he was recovering from a bad flu, and that he'd be all right before long. Next week I called him at work and a guy said Bruce'd had a relapse and was in the hospital with pneumonia. When I went looking for him at the hospital, his family was in the room, standing around his bed. They looked at me as if I was the killer or part of the bad crowd that had led him down the wrong path. That was the last I saw of him."

Drew blathered on for a few more minutes, but mercifully Chrissie Hynde and The Pretenders drowned him out with "Back on the Chain Gang." Malloy was thinking that it was very sincere of Drew to tell that story, but at the same time anyone he told it to would know that he was exposed to AIDS and possibly infected as well. Was he naive or unusually forthcoming?

"How long ago was this?"

"It was cold, there was snow. I guess six months ago."

Why aren't you infected? thought Malloy. *Maybe you are.* "It must be hard," he offered. "Sorry for your loss."

"Oh, Bruce wasn't my boyfriend, but we did enjoy each other every so often. How about you, you got a main squeeze?"

Malloy looked at Drew for several seconds before answering. "I don't want to go into my personal life with you right now," he said. "Let's just drink our drinks and listen to music."

"Okay, no problem. Sorry." At least a minute went by before Drew said, "I'll bet you get it anytime you want, a good-looking guy like you."

Malloy chuckled wryly. "You're persistent, huh? No, I don't have a 'main squeeze' or a significant other. I get bored with a steady girlfriend. Before you know it you've got to meet their friends, their family, go to a certain restaurant she likes, see a certain movie that she wants to see. Maybe it's that I'm too selfish or maybe it's that I like variety, probably some of both. I like to sample them, you know? The first time is really exciting, after that it goes downhill. A few more turns over the next week or two, and I'm ready to move on. You wanted to know, so there it is."

"All right! You're talking my language," said Drew.

"Yeah, but the people we go for have different plumbing."

"You can't tell me you're totally straight."

"I come from a long line of heteros."

"But this is a gay bar. You come to a gay bar not expecting to get hit on?"

"I came to a gay bar thinking to say goodbye to a friend—so I thought—before he goes into that long sleep."

They people-watched for a while, speakers blasting The Psychedelic Furs' "Sister Europe." They drained their pints. Drew ordered another round, changed his to Bacardi and Coke. Malloy said thanks but no thanks, he was leaving. Drew placed an arm on Malloy's sleeve, said, "You know who you look like?"

Here we go again. "Nick Nolte?"

"No, Robert Redford. The Sundance Kid. Totally. You watch that movie?"

"Yeah, it's great."

"I could be your Butch Cassidy."

Malloy rolled his eyes. "I don't think so. Those guys were buddies, having a good time being outlaws, not queers."

"Nope, there was definitely an undertone between them. Didn't you see them holding hands when they jumped off that cliff into the river?"

Malloy remembered that scene, remembered thinking it was cool that they did that.

"They both thought they were going to die, why not hold hands?"

"It goes to what I'm saying. They're strong masculine guys who have a thing for each other which they won't openly admit, their culture won't allow it. But it's there. That holding hands part was a sweet expression of their love."

Malloy really didn't want to think of Butch and Sundance in love. Just the idea of it was bumming him out. "Have it your way," he said. "I'm going to hit the head and then I'm out of here. Good talking with you." Drew watched him walk off, then got up.

Malloy was mid-piss when Drew took the stall next to him and un-zipped his fly.

"You too, huh?"

"Tell you the truth," said Drew, eyes locked on Malloy's manhood, "It's not so much that I have to piss as much as I want to check out the goods. And what do I see? A nice piece of meat and, oh, you're cut—circumcised—that's good. I'll bet that thing looks great when it's hard!"

Malloy held his unit with his right hand. He thought to shield it with his free left hand, cover the object of Drew's lust, but that would be silly. Yet, how to handle this weird situation?

"I like to piss in private, so step away." Drew, totally intent on ogling the prize, seemed not to hear him.

"Back off, I said!" Malloy in command voice.

But Drew was oblivious to his peril. "Oh, c'mon! I've seen yours, now check mine out." Malloy told himself don't look, but he did anyway. Drew had his out, erect, grasping it at the base, pointing it at him. "Would you like to touch it? Go ahead."

"You just don't listen, do you? That, and you're a whiner and I don't like whiners." He pivoted to the left and with the remaining urine left in his bladder, sprayed Drew, getting him good from the crotch to the bottom of his chinos. Then he shook it off and zipped up.

Drew stood there looking down at the dark stain on his pants, mouth agape in astonishment. "Now how the hell am I going to go back out there?" he chided. "Everyone will see this. That was uncalled for."

Malloy, almost out the door, looked back and said, "I call 'em as I see 'em. You're a big boy, deal with it."

But Drew Conger had the last word. Malloy was already ten steps into the bar itself, when he heard the high-pitched, hate-filled scream from within the restroom: "Bitch!"

THIRTY-TWO

THERE WERE TWO REASONS Trey Vonderhaar remained healthy and unin-fected while various members of his club sometimes didn't.

First, he was monogamous with a man who lived far away, in another country, and was rarely around. Second—and this was a corollary of the first—although he was often present in certain rooms in his home during scenes of vigorous if not kinky sex, he never ever jumped in despite fervent entreaties to do so; he liked to watch.

And so it was that at the climax of an evening's merrymaking, with some having retired to their assigned rooms for an engagement, Trey found him-self at the door of the Walt Whitman Room with a silver tray balanced on one hand. The tray had party favors: thin white lines of cocaine, crushable vials of amyl nitrate, an assortment of the finest chocolates from Bissinger's, and small bottles of mouthwash "for personal use." No drinks; each room had its own wet bar.

Trey rapped lightly on the door and then entered without invitation.

Both men were quite naked; Freddie was sitting on the bed with a pillow placed modestly over his lap, and Tory from Manhattan stood before the bed, a few feet away, gazing down at his flaccid member through a tangle of gray pubic hair.

"It's just not working," he lamented. "I don't understand. It worked this morning in New York."

"Probably a case of drunk dick," Trey, acerbic, setting the tray on a coffee table. "The before-dinner drinks, the after-dinner drinks, the stress of travel. Don't worry, it's only a temporary condition."

Balefully, "Yeah, but I need it now."

"Fellatio doesn't help?"

"We did that and this young man here was fantastic, very attentive, and there was a half-hearted boner for a minute but then ... back to the old limp noodle."

Freddie gave a good-natured shrug and said, "We gave it the old college try, but the lead just won't stay in the pencil."

"Well spoken," said Trey, "you succeeded in using two cliches in one short sentence. Anyway, I believe I have a solution."

"We've already decided to call it a night," interjected Freddie. "Isn't that right, Tory?"

"Well, let's hear what he has in mind." Then, suspiciously, he added, "It doesn't involve inserting something in there, does it?"

"You mean like a swizzle stick?" laughed Trey. "No, it involves an amazing array of sex toys, dildos to be exact. Wait just a moment. Oh, and help yourself to anything on the tray."

Trey returned with a box labeled DOCTOR JOHN'S NOVELTY BOUTIQUE and set it on the bed. "I don't know about this," said Freddie, a residue of white powder on his upper lip.

"Oh, shush," said Trey. He opened the box and several fake phalluses poked their strange heads out, each one different in shape, size and color. "They don't all have names," said Trey, "but I believe this one is called Anusaurus Rex, hard yet pliable rubber, eight inches long and nearly two inches thick with an enlarged head."

He handed it to Tory from Manhattan, still quite naked, who put it through some quick back-and-forth thrusting motions as Freddie rolled his eyes. "It's got some heft all right, but purple is not my color."

"A discerning fellow," said Trey, ready with another pick. "Hung like a horse. Have you ever wanted to live up to that adage? Well, here's your chance. This thing is molded to resemble an actual horse penis in both size and shape. At thirteen inches it's way too big for the average rectum, but to each his own."

Freddie looked mortified.

"Or how about this beauty?" Trey was getting into the role of huckster, having fun with the presentation. "I present the Incubus. Overall length, nine inches with seven inches insertable. You see the thick veins on his long shaft? That's going to drive him nuts, guaranteed."

Tory from Manhattan looked down at himself in a clinical way. "I just wish I could do it with my own equipment. It's a sad reality," he added, "all the money in the world can't raise a cock if it doesn't want to rise."

Freddie said to Trey, "Please tell me these are new and never before used."

"Some are new and some have seen some mileage." Like a pendulum, he waved a crimson model with an exaggerated head. "This one here was passed down to me from my Aunt Tess. She called it Frenchy. It's a bisexual dildo," he chuckled.

"They've all been sterilized?" asked Freddie.

"Washed in soap and water. I don't know that you can sterilize rubber."

Tory from Manhattan looked at Freddie askance. "What's with all these questions? You want to do it or not?"

"Oh, he wants to do it all right," assured Trey. "He's just a bit of a ger-mophobe, that's all." Trey reached down into the box and brought out a monster cock. He handed it to Tory, who held it up as if he were giving a toast. "Okay, you didn't care for purple, but maybe black is more your style. Meet Mandingo. It has a flared head that's flexible and, according to the directions, you really feel it going in and out. Well, no kidding. Eight and a half inches overall length and two to four inches thick. It goes without say-ing, use caution and plenty of lubrication."

"I like it," said Tory. "Does it come with a harness or something that I can strap it on?"

"That's more of a lesbian thing," replied Trey.

"Oh, yeah, right," Tory said, sheepishly. "I knew that."

"Well, you two have a good time."

"Thanks a lot," said Tory.

"My pleasure, I'm glad I could be of help." He picked up the tray and offered them further items. Tory took a handful of chocolate cremes.

Freddie declined, but shot him a look. "Trey?"

"Yes, Freddie."

"Fuck you very much."

THIRTY-THREE

IN THE FINAL decades of the twentieth century, Western civilization was deciding whether to go down the tubes all at once, or perhaps linger with the intent of lingering some more. Shaun Malloy, a mere grain of sand on the beach of this highly dysfunctional civilization, was deciding whether to check Jimmy Bowers as a six or a four on his report.

Barring the fact that there was no number for "deceased," the next closest option was a six, "unable to locate," but it meant no points for him on the epidemiology scoreboard. That left the four, "located, refused treatment," but that wasn't right either. He'd think on it some more.

The near Southside was one of the most vice-ridden sections of the city, a street university for pimps, pros, perps, and players, and also the turf of the Insane Unknowns. If Malloy thought hard, he might be able to remember a time when not one of the gang was being summoned for a VD check, promiscuity being their badge of honor. One of the pledges new members make and abide by is to bone as many females as possible without revealing their identities. So when a young GC patient told Malloy or any of the other investigators that the boy wouldn't give his name, they automatically suspected one of the Unknowns. With a good description they could usually figure out which one it was, and this time it was Jimmy Bowers.

Malloy parked his Datsun alongside the basketball courts at 39th and DeTonty. There were seven guys on the court, practicing layups and jump shots, the taller ones stuffing the ball in the hoop without a net, showing a lot of style and grace, too, despite the shitty condition of the court. Malloy recognized Melvin "Porkin' Babe" James, whom he knew to be an associate of Jimmy's. He called him over and Melvin came without a fuss. The Insane Unknowns trusted Malloy and accepted that he was not just any honkie.

"Jimmy? What you want with Jimmy, man? He got VD or somethin'?" Melvin snorted nervously. Malloy sensed that something was wrong.

"Melvin, you know I can't go into specifics. Just say it's a health matter."

"Health matter, shee-it! Ain't nothin' you can do for Jimmy's health. He dead, man."

"Dead! How?"

"You read the papers, man?" asked Melvin. "'Cause the story be in there last week. Law and Order section, man. Jimmy, he live upstairs in this four-family flat, and this ol' dude downstairs be grillin' pork steaks out on his deck on a Sunday morning. Jimmy get this idea he gonna steal the man's food. He get his fishin' pole and when the guy goes to take a piss or whatever Jimmy lets down his line and snags one of them pork steaks right off the grill, reels it in like a floppin' fish," Melvin laughing at the thought.

"The ol' dude comes back and sees one of his steaks missin'—no one around, hmm? But he figures it out. He goes back in the house gets his double-barrel sixteen-gauge and waits just inside his door. 'Course Jimmy tries again, he can't be happy with just one. Jimmy leans over the upstairs balcony, doin' his thing, ol' man waits for the right moment, comes out and lets him have it with both barrels. Jimmy done before he hits the ground."

"Wow, that's cold!" said Malloy.

"You goddamn right that's cold, now Jimmy cold, too. He wanted a nice grilled pork steak and life handed him a shit sandwich."

"Hey, that's pretty good."

"I know, I be waxin' eloquent once in a while."

"I'm sorry, Melvin."

"Yeah, you, the rest of the guys, and about twenty bitches he was doin'."

"He sure liked the ladies," Malloy said, "and he paid for it. He was what you call a regular at the clinic."

"We gonna miss him, that's for sure." The guys on the court were calling his name, so Melvin trotted back to his squeaky sneaker world. Malloy drove off with a head full of thoughts, one of which had to do with the finality of death.

Jimmy Bowers was now in the category shared by three out of four of his grandparents, certain neighbors, a boyhood friend named Jinx, various pets from his childhood, and several fellow soldiers who lost out to misadventure. That's just the way it goes, he told himself, some are in it for the long haul and some cash out early. Thing is, every one of them leaves you something to remember, so you could say they really aren't gone. Like Jimmy talking up his own peculiar pharmacology, street diagnoses and cures that should be included in every physician's bag of tricks.

Fondly, Malloy recalled Jimmy explaining the "earwax test" for gonorrhea. "Yeah, man, all you do is dig a little earwax out, put it on the tip of
your long finger and without her gettin' wise to what you doin', you slip that
finger up her snatch and if she's hot it'll burn her and she'll jump or yell."
They shared laughter there in the interview room, but what they didn't
share was an absolute belief in this method.

Jimmy went on to talk about the "sniff test", probably the most valid in
his curative arsenal. "It's a sure-fire thing, man. You gets your nose right
down there and, if the smell don't knock you out, you knows it's okay to
plunge in."

"The nasal appraisal. It stands the test of time, huh? Got any more?"

"You know the one they call bad blood, where you get sores on your
johnson?"

"You're talking about syphilis."

"That's it! That be one bad ass disease, man. I had that once, but I cured
it at the Mobil station."

"Yeah?"

"Yeah, just as soon as that sore show up I went to the pumps and doused
it with gasoline. That sore be gone the next day."

"What, regular gas does the trick?"

"No way," smiling so wide his gold gleamed, "it's got to be high octane,
nothin' else."

Timba was waiting as Malloy pulled in the parking lot. The attendant
stood near as Malloy gathered his things. When he got out of his car, Timba took his keys and handed him a pulp soft cover, *Amazing Stories*. On the
cover was a frightened yet voluptuous woman in scant clothing, chained to
a wall, and an obviously mad scientist about to pull some levers that would
probably turn her into a mindless robot assistant.

"There's a grisly story in here called 'You Can't Kill Mike Malloy,'" he
told Malloy. "It's about a bunch of drunks in New York in the 1920s who're
trying to murder another drunk for insurance money. It's from true life," he
added, "there really was a Mike Malloy, ex-firefighter, who survived numerous attempts on his life by five of his so-called friends. If you look at the
inside first page you'll see it's from 1962. I got it at Amitin's, thinking you'd
like it, maybe this guy was your uncle or something."

"Killing an Irishman can be tough," Malloy agreed, "we're either too stubborn to give it up or too drunk to care. I'll read it, thanks."

As they were talking, Betsy drove up and parked her car alongside. She got out in a huff. Her mascara was running and she wasn't her cheerful self. When asked about it, she said she'd been jumped in the projects, in a hallway of the Darst-Webbe. She'd been after a GC contact on one of the upper floors. She didn't have her purse, so they took her ring, snatched it right off her finger. No, she didn't call the cops, that would mean she'd have to go back there. And no, she wasn't all right, she was pissed as hell and she wanted a drink.

Malloy looked at his watch. "What do you know? Beer-thirty. There's a table waiting for us at Humphrey's. Let's recruit a few more and head over there."

If Humphrey's was 100 feet to the north it would be on the campus of Saint Louis University. There were two levels, an L-shaped bar on the ground floor, and tables and more tables on the upper floor with dart-boards and foosball in one corner. Both up and down stairs, there were pictures on the walls of various local sports figures in action, and the restrooms were chock full of graffiti, some of it even clever. The entire place had a patina of grease and sloshed beer.

It was a five-minute walk from the health department if you cut through the campus, and a few of them did walk, despite the cool drizzle that'd started to fall. Seated at a table on the first floor, the bartender within shouting distance, were most of the investigators plus the lab tech, Mike Wassermann. There were two pitchers of Budweiser before them and nachos were on the way. It was not intended to be a staff meeting but that's the way the tide turned, beginning with discussion of what had happened to Betsy. It was longstanding policy that female investigators with business in the projects would arrange for a male counterpart to go along. You didn't have to clear it with Karl; you just looked to see who was available.

"I decided I wasn't going to buy into that double standard," explained Betsy. "Shaun or Leo isn't expected to come to me and say, 'Hey, can you take time out of your day to come with me to the projects? I might need back up.'"

"And you did need that," said Arnold earnestly. "It's no big deal for one of us to come along. Me, I love the smell of urine in a dark hallway."

"What I needed," rejoined Betsy, "was a fresh canister of pepper mace and you can bet I'll be getting one very soon."

"That's not going to faze those people," said Tut. "They probably eat pepper mace for breakfast, sprinkle it on their Cocoa Puffs. You might wanna think about a handgun, they've got these Lady Derringers, fit right in your handbag."

"What do you mean 'those people'?" reproved Martha. "You're talking about *my* people, people of color who can't afford a house of their own and have to live in government-subsidized slums? *Those* people?"

"Touchy," said Schuler.

"Touchy my ass," Martha shot back. "You tend to get touchy after being black for forty years and hearing ignorant comments way too often. That really rubs my fur the wrong way."

"Assholes come in every color, Martha," said Arnold.

She scanned the table, softened a little. "Look, I don't want to mess up the party here. I know Tut didn't mean anything by it, just an unfortunate choice of words."

"Whew," said Tut, "thanks for letting me off the hook, Martha. I mean it. But I've gotta say, it's gonna be hard if I have to think about everything I want to say before I say it."

"Amen, brother," said Malloy, raising his glass. "A toast to saying what you mean and meaning what you say."

They were in the middle of telling stories about Joe when the server brought their nachos.

"I thought we said jalapenos on the side," protested Mike Wasserman. "There's jalapenos all over it, stuck into the cheese."

"I don't remember saying jalapenos on the side," said Arnold, "but I thought we ordered wings along with the nachos."

Malloy and a few others were already going for the loaded chips on top. "Jalapenos give me heartburn," said Wassermann.

"Any problem can be solved," declared their server whose nametag read TRENT. This got their attention, and they wondered what Solomon-like solution he had in mind. "You can delicately pick out the offending item," he told Wassermann, "or I can get you another order, sans jalapenos. As for the wings, no problem, but it's going to be about fifteen minutes. Deep-fried or grilled, and house sauce or honey mustard?"

Serious debate ensued, and they decided on two separate orders of wings. Wassermann grumped that he would pick out the peppers, which prompted Trent to throw out a timeworn line about picking a peck of pickled peppers.

"I don't get it," said Tut, "who's Peter Piper?"

"Never mind," said Betsy, "just eat."

"Would you like some moist towelettes?" asked Trent.

They said they would wing it—ha, ha—and Trent walked off.

"Light," said Schuler.

"What?" said Arnold.

"Light in the loafers, our waiter."

"Well, yeah, probably, but what tipped you off—the earring or the affected manner of speech?"

"It was the way he said moist towelettes. Not only that, but no self-respecting straight guy would even dare to say 'moist towelettes' in public."

"You just said it," put in Betsy.

"You know what I mean," said Schuler.

"Aren't we judgmental?" said Martha. "So what if he's gay. He could be a flaming queen in a prom dress as long as he gets our order right."

"It's hard to tell these days just from looking," put in Laird Cantwell. "A straight guy might wear the jewelry because he wants to seem hip. Gays initiate a fashion trend, and the rest of us schlubs pick up on it."

Said Pam Grady, "Gays, the obvious ones, are always having fun. They seem to have a refreshing attitude on things."

"You think there's more gays now than ever before?" wondered Wassermann, inspecting his nacho chip for any hidden bits of pickled pepper.

"Definitely," remarked Tut, "they're everywhere. It's like they all got together and decided to come out of the closet."

"I had this Wash U professor," said Arnold, "a contact to a primary, who said that there's some formula to account for it. Essentially, the more gays who come out, the more gays who *will* come out. Action builds on example, which builds on previous action, something like that. He compared it to the magnitude scale for earthquakes."

"That means we'll all be gay within ten years," said Malloy.

"Unless this new disease wipes them all out," said Schuler.

"True that," said Arnold. "This is not a great time to be an active gay man."

"You know, we really need to talk about this as a group," said Betsy. "This AIDS thing is here, in our city, infecting people, maybe running rampant, and we know so little about it."

"It's got to be an STD," said Wassermann, "but is it exclusive to the gay community?"

"Gay men," corrected Martha, "lesbians are the least likely group to turn up with a venereal infection."

"Lesbians have other problems." said Schuler, "like remembering to put fresh batteries in the vibrator."

"Careful," warned Martha.

"What do you call a lesbian with fat fingers?" threw in Tut. Without waiting, "Well hung."

"Let's be serious for a minute," said Malloy, uncharacteristically. "I agree with Betsy. This thing has shown itself, we know it's out there, we know it's in some of the same people that we're seeing for gay syphilis. We're epidemiologists. You think maybe we could be doing epidemiology on this AIDS?"

"It's a noble idea," said Arnold, "but not very practical without known parameters like how exactly it's spread, how contagious it is, and what's the critical period. Otherwise we'd just be spinning our wheels."

Malloy countered, "Two years from now we'll probably know all that. You know CDC is working on it night and day. Meanwhile, normally healthy guys our age are getting sick, becoming emaciated, and dying too soon. I think we should try to do something."

"We could warn the at-risk groups," offered Betsy, "that would be doable. Make up posters and fliers, scatter them in the right areas."

"And what would these posters say?" Schuler, dubious. "You can't tell healthy promiscuous men in their twenties and thirties about monogamy or even abstinence, if that's what you're thinking."

"We could say something like there's this new disease in the gay community, it can be fatal, and to avoid it the best plan is to limit your sex partners and wear a condom."

"No bareback," put in Pam Grady, giving a mock finger-wag.

"Again, a very noble idea," said Arnold, "and something like a public health announcement definitely couldn't hurt the situation. Some of those guys need a reality check from the sexual smorgasbord they're living in. But back to science for a minute. We're not even sure if sexual contact is the only way it's spread. What if saliva is also a contagion factor?"

"Or tears," offered Mike Wassermann.

"How about snot?" from Tut.

"And then there's the possibility of non-human vectors," said Laird Cantwell, sipping his Dr. Pepper. "Mosquitoes come to mind."

"Right on," said Arnold. "Then how're you going to do traditional epidemiology if the thread is running in six different directions? Did he get it from screwing this guy over here, or from being sneezed on by that guy over there, or from being bit by that mosquito that just came from an AIDS blood meal? You see? Source and spread analysis is out the window."

Malloy could see the roadblocks in his half-baked plan rising up before him. "We use the epidemiologic model for tertiary syphilis, go back a year for contacts, round up suspects as well, see if they're infected, and if they are, and if they're not already on their deathbeds, then we, um, quarantine them."

"Oh that'll go over with a bang," said Schuler, sharply. "Why don't we also make them wear armbands with pink triangles like gays in the Nazi concentration camps? But it's really a moot point, isn't it, because even if you did find contacts to an OP with AIDS, what purpose would it serve, since there's no fucking cure and not likely to be one anytime soon."

"He's got a point," said Wassermann. "We're in the infancy of this thing, the proverbial tip of the iceberg. Trying to control it now would be like throwing darts at shadows."

"You know what I think," said Tut. "I think we need two more pitchers and where the heck are those wings?"

"You know what I think?" said Betsy. "I think that even if we did agree to do something proactive about this AIDS thing, try to do epidemiology on any infected patients who show up in our clinic, we'd have to do it on the sly because it would never get past Joe."

THIRTY-FOUR

"THAT IS NOT GOING TO HAPPEN," growled Joe Sargent. Malloy was reminded of Winston Churchill telling the Brits at Harrow School during the Second World War, "Never, never, never, never give in!" Joe's bulldog jowls were even shaking like Winston's.

But the comparison stopped there. Where Churchill was hoping to lift the spirits of bombed-out Londoners, Joe was bent on quashing any notion that might steer his investigators away from working established and approved venereal infections with every iota of energy they had. "Gonorrhea and syphilis in this town are already at epidemic levels and you want to chase down some phantom disease?"

"You were the one who brought it to our attention," asserted Betsy, "reading that article from the *MMWR*, remember?"

They were in the epi room, coming up on ten, Team B out in the field. Joe shifted his big butt, sitting on the edge of Betsy's desk; her knockers, straining against her blouse, were even bigger than Pam Grady's melons. "That's right, I wanted you to be aware of it, not fill out ERs on it." Feasting upon cleavage, imagining Betsy as the gatefold in the next issue of *Hooters*, he said with empathy, "I see your hearts are in the right place, but get the idea out of your head. It's not feasible, you should know that. When CDC says it's a communicable disease spread by sexual contact *then* we'll include it in our repertoire."

"We had to at least run it by you," said Malloy. "We talked about it over drinks yesterday and some of us thought it would be worthwhile to keep a lookout for people with signs of AIDS. That is, while we're already doing epi roundup of contacts in the gay community."

"And when you find these people, what are you going to do with them? Send them to a hospice? There's no cure for shit's sake."

"Yeah, there is that problem," agreed Malloy.

"Problem?" said Joe. "I'd say it's more like a big rubber stamp on the forehead of anyone that gets it, and that stamp reads 'Death Sentence.' And let me remind you, you are not the ideal person to be making inroads to the gay community, not when you're currently under a restraining order to keep away from a certain well-known member of that community. You think word doesn't get around? 'That health department guy, Malloy, he's bad news, harasses gays in restaurants.' That's what they're saying, so cool your jets, all right?"

"Sure, Joe, and thanks for the motivational talk."

"Smart ass."

As it happened, that was not the only heated exchange that Joe and Malloy were to have that day. Around 4:40, as Malloy was going from the clinic to the epi room, he saw a lanky, long-haired guy in the hall with a pencil behind his ear and a slim notebook in his hand. He seemed to be looking for someone. He took in Malloy's approaching figure like a zoologist encountering a curious new species. "You look like you work here," he said.

"I've been accused of that, yeah."

"Are you an investigator? I'm looking for someone who can talk about this disease they're calling AIDS that's going around."

"And you are?"

"Sorry, Urban Lehrer with the *Globe-Democrat*."

"Hey, Shaun Malloy. I've seen your byline. You did that story on the rat infestation up in North City."

"That's my beat, rats and VD," he chuckled. "After five years you graduate to graft and corruption. I've still got three more years to go."

"Your timing is good," Malloy said. "A bunch of us were just talking about AIDS yesterday over beers at Humphrey's. And what we concluded was it's serious, it's spreading, and there's not a hell of a lot we can do about it."

"That's the bare bones of it," Lehrer said. "I'm looking for insights, anecdotes, the human interest angle. I'd like it from someone who's in the trenches, not some desk jockey."

"Yeah, well there's a big ornery desk jockey named Joe Sargent who's somewhere in the vicinity, unless he's gone home early, and he really doesn't like any of us talking to the press. He likes to do the talking."

"Control freak, huh?"

"Director of epidemiology, GS-15 with CDC."

"I could talk with him to get an overview, but maybe we could talk for a half hour or so. How about at that place you mentioned, Humphrey's—that's nearby, yeah?" Urban Lehrer flipped open his reporter's notebook and was jotting something when Joe and Karl came around the corner. Malloy's earlier comment about Joe was a gross understatement; the sight of an underling talking to someone who was obviously a reporter made Joe hopping mad. In a second he was standing over them, demanding to know what was going on.

Lehrer introduced himself and explained his purpose. Joe, fuming, said he should have checked with him first. Malloy said that's just what Lehrer was about to do, that he was directing him to Joe's office when Joe walked up.

"Bullshit," said Joe. "You had your notebook open and you were taking notes."

"I was writing down your name and title in anticipation of the interview."

"I don't buy that," scowled Joe. "Let me see that notebook. Show me."

The reporter's notebook, long and slim, is designed to fit into a pocket, and that's where Urban Lehrer quickly put it: in the back pocket of his slacks. He stepped back from Joe and said, "You know I can't do that, reporter's privilege. You'll have to take my word for it. Can't we just forget about it and start over? You got a few minutes to talk now?"

"How about this. You go back to your paper, have your editor call me tomorrow, and if I'm still important enough for you to interview, we'll set it up then. Meantime, don't ever come barging into my clinic, doing unauthorized interviews with my investigators. Got that?"

"Loud and clear," said Lehrer.

Joe then turned his glower to Malloy. "And you, in my office. Now!"

Malloy pivoted in the direction of Joe's office and as he did he caught the reporter's attention, who silently mouthed "Humphrey's."

Lehrer's cue also caught Karl's attention and he half-whispered to Malloy in passing, "So you're a lip reader now?"

Lehrer had already claimed a table and was working on a pitcher when Malloy walked in. "Thanks for coming," he said, rising politely. "I hope you didn't get in Dutch for talking to me back there."

"Joe's bark is worse than his bite," said Malloy, filling an empty glass, "although he will fire you if he sees you as disloyal, disobedient, or a chronic fuck up. For my act of insubordination, I am to write a three-thousand-word essay on some topic that's 'pertinent to the noble profession,' as he put it."

"One of those? Disciplines by handing out writing assignments. My mom would do that. 'Urban, I want you to write "I will not sass my loving mother" fifty times in your best penmanship. Good training for a future journalist, getting used to writer's cramp. What will you write about?"

"I've got a magazine article and some medical journal printouts about famous people in history who have had venereal disease and how it affected their outlook, their work, and maybe even our lives as a result. I'll probably re-read those and cobble something together."

Lehrer studied the bubbles in his glass for a moment and said, "This new disease will also take a lot of people, some of them famous, and it will affect every level of society from corporate boardrooms to soup kitchens. It's going to change the way we relate to one another, and in some circles it already has. As news of AIDS spreads, gay men are being seen as modern-day lepers. People afraid to shake hands, share an ice cream cone, mothers don't want them picking up their babies. It's really stirring things up and I'm going to write about it as best I can."

Malloy's expression told Lehrer that he totally got it. "From a selfish point of view, it's a damn shame. Just when we were making good progress in the arena of sexual liberation, here comes this boogeyman to ruin it for everyone. Like, use my situation for an example. I like women and I'm sexually active. Not into the monogamy thing, okay? But if one of those women who happens to take me home has a guy in her stable that's bisexual, well, guess what: I'm in the same pool with Reggie over there who's down at the Club Baths three days a week. It was bad enough having to worry about herpes, now this thing. It sucks, it really does."

"You could say that it's the price of free love," said Lehrer, "the pendulum swinging back after a decade of all-out promiscuity."

"But I'm not ready for it to swing back just yet," grinned Malloy. "Not ready to give up the old tomcat ways."

"Good for you," said Lehrer, "keep the flame burning. So, what can you tell me about AIDS from your end? You must know some who've come down with it."

"You gonna quote me? I don't know that Joe can stand another fit."

Lehrer said he would take notes, but that anything which might appear in print would not be attributed to him as a public health officer. The name Shaun Malloy would not appear in any future story unless he gave his express permission. With that understanding, Malloy started to tell him about the one-sided romance between Douglas March and Arthur Tottingham, the Lafayette Square residence where the disease likely originated, and, most recently, the case of Ren Peters. Lehrer said that he'd heard about Ren Peters, and he was aware of additional infections among several others in Ren's social circle.

"Word on the curb has it that certain waiters from Robusto's are on extended sick leave," he told Malloy, "and there's Derek who runs Fleur de Lis Antiques, poor guy, on the way out. Danny from the bookstore is already gone. Between what I've seen and what I've heard, they've all come down with AIDS, and what do you know? All from the same pea pod, all working along Euclid, the same as Ren, and all playing fuck-buddy with one another."

Said Malloy, "One of our clinicians says AIDS gives its victims the three Ds that nobody wants: dementia, diarrhea, and disgrace." He looked out the window at a meter reader writing a ticket. "It'd be tough," he added, "seeing those first signs on your own body, suddenly realizing that your time is limited."

"You've got to die from something," said Lehrer, "but ideally when you're seventy, not thirty." He paused to light a cigarette. "Of course, this small group is just a microcosm of what's actually out there. There may be thousands of cases in the metro area and some of them are going progress slowly, people living with this virus as a chronic illness with no specific symptoms instead of dying right away."

"Like carriers?"

"Not quite. They're not feeling exactly chipper, just not having the full-blown signs and symptoms."

This made Malloy think of Drew Conger, who seemed to have fooled fate. "It's nice to talk with someone who's obviously studied this," he told the reporter. "Okay, so where are we going with this? What else besides who's got it? I suppose you're wondering what, if anything, the health department is doing about it. You might want to talk with Dr. Calder, Prudence Calder, the health commissioner, since all the big decisions flow from her office. As for the epi side of the STD clinic, we're already working time and a half on the two major STDs in this city, so, practically speaking, all we can do is keep an eye on this thing."

"I guess it's not possible to do epidemiology on AIDS, just like you couldn't do epidemiology on the flu because of how quickly it spreads."

Malloy nodded. "And if the causative agent is a virus, as they're starting to believe, then it's not going to respond to antibiotic treatment anyway. It's going to take a vaccine to knock it out and that could be years away." He paused to refill his schooner. "Think about this: people are dying of it in the early stages, but it may not stay that way. When New World syphilis was introduced to Europe by Columbus and company, it, too, was virulent at the onset, with a high death toll. It took about thirty years for it to attenuate, get acclimated, you could say. But after that it was chronic, something you didn't want but generally less than fatal."

"That's really interesting," said Lehrer, scribbling away. The reporter drew on his Winston and blew the exhaust toward the ceiling. "I think you're going to see a sharp increase in research and development of a vaccine for AIDS. The reason? Well, up until recently the attitude was these diseases are only in gays and needle addicts, misfits and scumdogs who didn't deserve any special attention. But new cases are popping up that don't involve those two groups. Now it's in the blood supply and hemophiliacs and others who need transfusions are inadvertently getting the disease. Newborns have gotten it through umbilical cord blood from infected mothers. You get the picture. With these so-called innocent victims now showing up, our government has taken due notice and decided to put some resources into the problem." He smiled knowingly. "Like any thorny problem which requires a great deal of money to fix, it all comes down to politics."

Malloy nodded in affirmation. "And it may be something as basic as Senator Smith's wife's niece, in the hospital from a car wreck, and she gets the disease from a batch of tainted blood. Now he's raising a stink on the floor of the Senate, demanding action to stem this plague in our society."

"Yeah, that's one scenario," said Lehrer. "But meanwhile, we've got to take measures to limit the spread. And that's where you and I come in."

"Oh," said Malloy, "so you're not merely an objective journalist. You're a crusading journalist."

"I follow my conscience, simple as that. So I am going to gather up thread, as it were, and weave it into cloth on my trusty IBM Selectric II. It's going to be a hell of a story, one that may even change policy at City Hall. Right now I've got three or four good sources and I'm hoping I can count you in. This is such an important story that my editors are giving me extra time, no specific deadline—a luxury, believe me. We can talk every so often. Or, whenever something pricks your ear, you can phone me at work or home any time of the day. What do you say?"

"Why do I feel like I'm being recruited into the CIA? I don't know that I want to work as a spy."

"Not a spy, an intern in the communications field. An under-the-radar intern, no one knows it but you and me. It'll be all right, you'll see."

"Let me think on it," said Malloy.

"You mentioned that men's club in Lafayette Square, that sounds somewhat suspect. What about that?"

It was a topic Malloy wanted to broach anyway, see what this reporter thought about an exclusive fraternity that spreads disease with impunity. So he gave Lehrer an earful about Trey Vonderhaar and Man 2 Man, his shield Frank Dunaway, and the bitter icing on the cake: the protection order currently in place.

"Wow," said Lehrer, "that sounds like a whorehouse in gentlemen's attire.

And it still goes on despite several cases of infectious disease linked to that address?"

"It's thriving, as far as I know," answered Malloy. "And you're right, it is essentially a brothel. But since it operates as a private club and whatever the members get for their money takes place behind closed doors, there's no proof of lawbreaking."

"You're convinced it's a danger to public health? Who else feels the same way?"

"The entire epi staff, my supervisor Karl Benda, and even Joe. But as I explained, it's really hard to pin anything on Vonderhaar. He's providing the setting, yeah, he's orchestrating the activity, he's whistling all the way to the bank, but he's never been named as a contact. I don't know why, maybe he's super careful. All we can do is attempt to interview him as a suspect or an associate to an original patient. Unfortunately, the public health statutes don't have any teeth when it comes to any category less than a bona fide contact."

Lehrer blew a pretty smoke ring and poked it mid-air with his forefinger. "Then if you want to shut down his operation, make the world a little safer, you're going to have to go with the whorehouse angle. If you could get someone, a disgruntled member who's pissed at Vonderhaar for whatever reason, to say that money was exchanged for the sole purpose of sex, then you'd have something. The vice squad would be at his door, ready to throw a turd in his punchbowl."

THIRTY-FIVE

TREY VONDERHAAR liked getting mail. The fliers and coupons and announcements of store openings, all the unsolicited stuff, went straight to the circular file, but occasionally there was something to really brighten his day. The hand-addressed envelope with the canceled stamp in the upper right corner was just such a thing.

The fairly large stamp in question depicted a brightly plumed parrot with a quizzical expression, "Brasil" emblazoned below it, and validated with a crisp postmark, proof of the correct postage to ensure its delivery from Rio de Janeiro to St. Louis. To Trey Vonderhaar, it was the adult equivalent of finding a special present under the tree on Christmas morning. He wanted to run after the letter carrier and plant a kiss on her big lips, but decided instead to slip her a tip at some later date.

The letter was from Eduardo Nunes de Siqueira, his former classmate, and if the Jesuits had known what they were doing nearly every night in the confines of their well-appointed dorm room, the pair would have never graduated from PUC Rio, the Pontifical Catholic University of Rio de Janeiro.

But graduate they did. Eduardo went home with a degree in art history, hoping it would fulfill his parents' dictum to "make something of yourself." Trey, the more studious of the two and with the added challenge of total immersion in Brazilian Portuguese, took his degree in finance and international business.

By then his mum had passed. His father, living in nearby Sao Paulo and managing a score of top-tier commercial properties, attended Trey's graduation, patting him on the back and telling him how proud he was to have a son who could walk in his formidable wingtips. Now, get back to St. Louis, he advised his only child, to see what spoils you might reap.

Trey and Eduardo parted ways, but first: a road trip.

Eduardo was the classic Brazilian playboy. His father, the extravagantly wealthy Luis Nunes de Siqueira, owned five percent of the arable land in the province. He put it to use growing cane for sugar and, to a lesser extent, coffee, which, when roasted, made up the family's blend sold only in the better stores. Thus, the de Siqueira household held back nothing from Eduardo and his older sister, Katrina. There was every amenity, every gourmet food item they might want, every imaginable whim granted. There were servants, chefs, and chauffeurs at their beck. Life was grand for the children of a Brazilian land baron.

By the time he reached eighteen, Eduardo had ascended to the zenith of the club scene in Rio, putting his family's vast financial resources to good use. He owned several hot sports cars, including a Maserati 3000, a vintage Chris Craft Catalina power boat, and a stake in a trendy new restaurant called Churra Scaria. His only care in the world was whether he might make co-captain on the polo team.

On that goodbye getaway, as they motored along the coast en route to Buzios, radio blaring "Radar Love," Eduardo turned to Trey at the wheel, and casually said, "You know, my friend, no matter what the Jesuits say, there's no such thing as sin below the equator. We don't suffer from the shame-based religious upbringing that plagues so many of your middle-class American families." He had been speaking Portuguese, but now he switched to a thickly accented English. "We do not have what you Americans call 'guilt trip.' We do as we please and damn the consequences."

Trey nodded enthusiastically, keeping his eye on the winding road, for the speedometer on the Maserati was pushing 160 clicks. *That's right*, he thought, *it was a stroke of luck to latch on to you, dear Eduardo. Not only do you have the dreamboat looks and the swagger to complement it, not only are you fantastic in bed with a body chiseled to perfection, but you have the wealth to make the party last as long as we want it to last.*

"You are more free-wheeling than I am," said Trey, "that's a given. You have your female fan club back on campus, a whole string of coeds waiting for the chance to take you to bed, and no doubt you have ... slept with some of them."

"Of course I have. Why shouldn't I indulge?"

"And then you have me. Don't you see that as a conflict?"

Eduardo shrugged. "I never thought it to be one way or the other. Why limit oneself? Would you be happy having the same dessert after every meal?"

"If that dessert was as delicious as you, yes."

Eduardo laughed delightedly. "Flattery, *meu querido*, will get you everywhere."

On the on that last evening of their jaunt, they found themselves at one of the outdoor tables at the Azul Marinho restaurant, overlooking the ocean, wavelets glinting with the last rays of the setting sun. Below them, on the beach, children were shouting, kicking sand at one another, while a small band of musicians had gathered around a fire and were pounding out a samba beat. The table held the remains of several plates of prawn pastels. They were on their fifth round of *caipirinha*, Brazil's national cocktail made with sugar, lime, and *cachaça*, a native spirit distilled from sugar cane. Trey remarked that this wonderful elixir they were drinking with such abandon may have had its humble origins in the de Siqueira cane fields.

"Oh, it is almost certain. Our cane makes the best *cachaça*, and we have the awards to prove it," slurred Eduardo, swirling the remainder of his drink. He paused to study the face of his friend, a face that was presently out of focus. "There are the haves and the have-nots, yes? It is very nice to belong to that first category, eh?"

"I can't even imagine being in the other category," said Trey. "Holding down a regular job, having to wait for things, saving up to make purchases, having to settle for below-par goods and services. Yuk!"

"So, today we are the princes of our domains. Someday we will be kings. Are you ready for that?"

"Sure," said Trey, "I'm looking forward to it. I intend to surpass my father in the financial arena. I'm already making plans, entrepreneur all the way, work for no one but yourself, eh?"

"You are just the one to do it," said Eduardo, snapping his fingers at a passing waiter. "*Garçom!* Two more," he called.

"It's a good thing we're on foot," said Trey. "I'd hate to see your beautiful car wrapped around a tree."

"That would be tragic," agreed Eduardo, "but not as tragic as this being the last night that you and I are wrapped around each other."

"It doesn't have to be."

"You're absolutely right! We are the haves and the haves can do what they damn well please. What's a plane ticket to St. Louis?"

"Hah! About as much as you lose at the horse track on any given day."

"That decides it," Eduardo confirmed. "We will keep the flame burning. I come to you or you come to me, whenever our hearts so desire. Once a year, once every five years—who knows? But at least this is not our final embrace. A toast!"

"To us!"

"To us."

And now, as Trey carefully unfolded the letter and began to read, he felt a flush of excitement wash over him. Eduardo missed him. Life in Rio had lost its allure, he needed fresh experience to rejuvenate his psyche. Yes! It was going to happen.

Eduardo was coming to visit.

THIRTY-SIX

"TELL ME AGAIN what we do when he comes out."

"*We* don't do anything," said Teri Kincaid. "You're along for the ride, to keep me company, remember? What I do when he comes out, *if* he ever comes out, is to jump out of this car and nab him before he realizes what's happening. Then, I put the cuffs on him, hopefully without much trouble, and I take him down to the Fugitive Window at City Jail and hand his ass over."

"Just a day's work, huh?"

Teri glanced at her friend in the passenger seat, legs propped up on the dash, a half-grin pasted on his mug. "Have another Altoid, Kojak."

They were parked outside a dingy-looking house on Wisconsin Avenue where it butts into Gravois, a downscale neighborhood that, from the looks of things, specialized in bars, radiator repair shops, and salons offering African braiding. Teri was on the trail of one Jerome Hauck, a no-show at his arraignment for burglary first. Teri had bonded him out for three grand and now she was on the hook for it. They were stationed outside of Jerome's girlfriend's place. His old beater was parked six doors down in a sorry attempt to throw off the cops or any bail bondsmen who might come around. Yet, here they were on a Sunday morning, poised for action. But there was no action; it was all about the wait.

Malloy picked up the Department of Corrections flier again. It had a mug shot of Hauck that made him look slightly brighter than a lemur. "These wanted posters haven't advanced much since the days of Wyatt Earp, have they? But I guess you don't need much, just the basics. Our guy described as white male, age thirty-four, six foot one, stocky build, brown hair and brown eyes. Pretty generic, probably describes half the white guys in South St. Louis. But here it gets specific: 'tattoo of a devil or demon on his left shoulder.' You think we'll get to see that?"

"If he comes out shirtless. And he could, it's warm enough."

"Says he has an alias: 'Fudge.' What the hell kind of nickname is that for a burglar? 'Fudge is the name, burglaring is my game.' It just doesn't seem right."

"Neither does being out three grand. Thank you, Fudge." She yawned and took another drink of water, just a sip. She wasn't wearing Depends this time, and she didn't want to have to leave for a potty break. "So what else've you been doing besides running down VD suspects?"

"I wrote an essay called 'La Vie Boheme: Syphilis and Public Figures Before Penicillin.' I put some research into it, who had it and how it affected them and those around them, maybe even us today."

"Was that for one of the local papers?"

"Nah, it was a punishment that Joe gave me for talking to a reporter without permission."

"That's funny, he disciplines by handing out writing assignments. My mom used to make me do that. 'I will not take things that don't belong to me. Write that one hundred times, Teri, maybe next time you'll think before you act.'"

"You were a thief?"

"A klepto, mostly candy bars, some comic books, a hamster once. But that's all in my rear view now. So, what'd you find that I can bring up at my next cocktail party?"

"All right, you asked, here goes. First off, encyclopedias and history books really skirt the issue. A look-up of twenty writers, painters, and composers in my *New Columbia Encyclopedia*, people thought to have had or known to have had the disease, syphilis is mentioned only once, in the bio of Paul Gauguin. But there were plenty of euphemisms—'misconduct' and 'excesses' for debauchery, 'severe illness' for late syphilis. This is understandable, because without modern-day diagnostics, the question of a certain disease like syphilis becomes speculative, although speculated on by learned physicians of the day. Also, biographers back then, unlike now, weren't on board with the 'warts and all' approach. They hoped to spare their subjects humiliation and so they left out the unflattering details. Good example: the German musician Robert Schumann was batshit crazy from syphilis. Literally. He imagined bats flying around his head, was heard yelling and trying to swat them away."

"Bats in the belfry for real, poor guy."

"Yeah, and at age forty-four, the height of his career, he went mad and threw himself into the Rhine in Dusseldorf after paying the bridge toll with his silk scarf. He fell beside a fishing boat and was rescued, only to die paralyzed at a local asylum."

"Aw!"

"He botched the job, but the *New Columbia Encyclopedia* was kind in saying that 'Schumann's life was clouded by a threat of insanity.'"

"This is good stuff," said Teri, "I'll be a hit at the cocktail party. What else you got?"

Malloy shifted his position for the fiftieth time that morning. "I think there's a bad spring or something under this seat. Okay, so understand that syphilis had been around for a long, long time and the vast majority of its victims were commoners, a lot of soldiers and prostitutes, who suffered no less than the public figures of the day who also had it—I'm talking kings, generals, tyrants, famous artists, clergy including popes. But it's the writings and lamentations of this elite, educated group that survives. Few diseases are better chronicled than syphilis."

"And there was no cure, right? So if you got it, tough luck."

"There was no VD clinic they could go to. Penicillin wasn't invented until 1943. They had cures, more like tortures. You'd have to be pretty desperate to take them. As far as literary references, there're some pretty good ones. Ever hear of Rabelais? A writer *and* a doctor. He wrote this book, *Gargantua*, a best-seller in 1532, and in the opening lines there's a speech that begins 'Most illustrious drinkers, and you, most precious syphilitics.' And then, a half century later, Shakespeare mentions it in his plays. 'A pox on it!' You've heard that. The pox is syphilis."

"It couldn't be chicken pox?"

"Not chicken pox or smallpox. Syphilis was called the Great Pox, because it can cripple or kill you. How about Casanova? The great lover that some guys want to emulate definitely had his share of venereal disease. He put it to paper, too. In his *Memoirs* there's a dialogue between a doctor and a military officer, a captain who had been a patient, and the doctor is thanking the captain for spreading his syphilis around and giving the doctor so many new patients." Malloy chuckled. "Souvenirs, that's what he called it. 'You had relations with Don Jerome's housekeeper and you left her a certain souvenir which she communicated to a certain friend.' The chain goes on from there."

"It sounds like they had a good sense of humor way back then. I guess if you're faced with no cure, you deal with it by poking fun at it." There was the sound of a door opening. They looked to the row of houses and saw a finely attired, black woman emerge from the house next to Hauck's. She got to the sidewalk and kept going. "In her Sunday best," said Teri, "on her way to church."

"You take one corner of every block in this city, if there's not a bar then it's a church."

"That's the truth," agreed Teri. "They're either getting God or getting tanked."

"You want to hear more or are you bored with it?"

"No, go ahead. I've got time."

"One of my favorites is Oscar Wilde. Very amusing guy, and what a life. Claimed he caught syphilis while he was a student at Oxford, from a hooker named Old Jess. What does he do? He dedicates a poem to her. But he didn't do women as a rule, he was notoriously gay, right? And he wound up in prison for his affair with Lord Alfred Douglas. But backing up here, even though it was no secret he liked men, he found a woman to marry him and they had two healthy sons who eventually disowned him. It was *after* the birth of the second son that the late stages of the disease began to show, but interestingly there was never any indication that his mind was affected. He kept on writing great plays and novels.

"Syphilis can affect the mind, as we know from Henry the Eighth, who belonged in the looney bin but instead happened to rule a country. Anyway, the mental deterioration can take years, or it may never happen at all. The only paradigm we have to go by is the infamous Tuskegee Study. Are you ready for this? This was a formal clinical study, a collaboration between my own U.S. Public Health Service and the Tuskegee Institute, where healthy black men were deliberately infected with syphilis just to see what would happen. The subjects were mostly poor sharecroppers who thought they were getting free health care from the government. Nice, huh? This study went on for forty *years*, if you can believe that, and the results were that about one-third of these guinea pigs developed neurosyphilis, a condition that disposes one to madness. So, there you have it. Our government in action. Medical science has been advanced at the cost of unnecessary human suffering."

"Amazing. You know what you just did? In one long breath, you went from Oscar Wilde, a gay English poet, to the misfortunes of poor, black sharecroppers. You're so full of it—random information, that is. So what happened to Oscar?"

"He served his time for gross indecency, the Victorian term for man-to-man sex, but he had fallen while in prison and developed a brain abscess which eventually did him in. After his release, he got this seedy apartment in Paris, where he entertained as best he could. As the story goes, he couldn't stand the wallpaper in his bedroom and, on his deathbed, his last words were, 'Wallpaper, one of us has to go.' At least he died a free man."

"That's a good line," said Teri. "I hope I can be so clever on my deathbed. Instead I'll probably be asking someone to run out and get me the latest issue of *Guns and Ammo*." Malloy chuckled at this, and decided to be quiet for a change.

After a while, Teri spoke up. "You said it a minute ago, 'man-to-man sex.' Isn't that what's-his-name's private sex club? The guy you're court-ordered to stay away from?"

"Yeah, Trey Vonderhaar and his Man 2 Man clique, a daisy chain of fun and frolic. 'Hey, everybody, last one in the orgy room is a rotten egg.' That place is a breeding ground for venereal disease including this new thing, AIDS. It's an affront to public health, and it should be shut down. In other societies or other times in history, it would've been shut down by now."

Teri arched her eyebrows with a smirk. "And the members put in prison for gross indecency?"

"Hah. No, we emphatically inform the members to stay the hell away."

"And you can't do that why?"

"Because we don't know who the members are."

"He's got to have an address book, a Rolodex or something, with a master list of all members. All we have to do is get our hands on that and start calling."

"We?"

"I can't see you doing a proper B and E by yourself."

THIRTY-SEVEN

"REALLY, you did Fredbird! What was that like? Was he in costume?"

The woman, with smoky eyes and copper-colored hair so luxuriant it begged to be stroked, registered surprise at Malloy's reaction. "I thought this was supposed to be ..."

"Sorry," he said, "Just pretend I didn't say that. Okay, I'll need a full description. You did see his face, right?"

"Of course, I saw his face," she said, somewhat peeved.

"I'd say you're one of the few. All that anyone else ever sees is this silly chicken in the ballpark, performing antics."

"Well, that's what he was doing with me, performing antics, in a hotel suite paid for by the Cardinals." Her name was Stacy Koons and she was an instructor at the Police Academy. She was brought in as a contact to GC, having been named by an infected cop assigned to the Third District. Once in the clinic, she turned up a positive smear which bought her an interview with the epidemiologist. So far she had named the cop who named her and had added the Cardinals' mascot as a bonus. The critical period for elicitation of GC contacts went back three months. She'd already named two casual encounters in the last month, so why stop there?

He only got Fredbird's real first name, Travis, plus a description—"tall, rangy, with a nose kind of like a beak"—and then he started fishing for more.

"Okay, who else?"

"That's it, there are no more."

He put his pencil down, gave her a serious look. "Stacy, I've been doing this long enough to know when I'm being snowed. The way I see it, you're young, pretty, and single, why wouldn't you be sexually active?"

"Because I'm not a slut."

"That's an antiquated notion," he told her, "that anything other than monogamy is somehow immoral. Freud dispelled that. He called it libido, which means sex drive or sexual appetite. And that was Doctor Freud's message, that it's okay to have a healthy libido."

"Do you have a healthy libido?"

"Absolutely, some days it's so healthy I feel I could ravish six women all at once."

She laughed and said, "Well, there is one more and, really, that's it."

In the epi room filling out his report, Malloy was thinking about one of the more intriguing aspects of epidemiology: namely, his role as confessor. That's what he was at times, someone who heard confessions of a sexual nature. And just like the transgressions whispered in a confessional, the names of sexual contacts given to him in the interview room / confessional were in the strictest confidence.

That he loosely performed the same function as a priest was a source of wonder to him. At St. Cletus Grade School, he attended Mass every morning with the other boys and girls. When it was time, he served several years as an altar boy, learning the magical Latin phrases that aided the priest in changing blood into wine, bread into flesh. And he went to confession every Saturday afternoon, telling his young sins to a shadowy figure on the other side of the grate. That was then, and since, well, many a former acolyte had abandoned his catechism.

Ditto for him. These days, he didn't necessarily believe in an afterlife or the existence of a deity that cares about our puny lives, but he still believed there was such a thing as sin, which meant being aware of one's misdeeds and trying to atone for them. Nothing wrong with that, he told himself, because unless you're amoral, you have to deal with your shameful behavior one way or another. You can get drunk, you can kick a chair, you can pay a shrink a small fortune. Or, if your religion provides, you can go to confession, the poor man's psychotherapy. Daily, in the interview rooms, he elicited and heard the confessions of men and women who blindly followed their lust wherever it took them; maybe he should start wearing a white collar.

Arnold interrupted his reverie by asking, "You want to hear something funny?"

"Lay it on me," said Malloy.

"Janelle just called with some bad news: she's going bald. I interviewed her last week, a walk-in, positive GC smear. She named three guys, including her husband. I contacted the husband right away and he got treated. Now she's losing her hair."

"*Alopecia areata*," offered Malloy, "bald patches on the scalp from undue anxiety. I had it when I thought I was going to Nam."

"Good guess, but that's not it. Her husband played a trick on her. He thought he'd get even by mixing her depilatory crème in with her shampoo, told her so." A big grin broke out on Arnold's mug. "Now he's calling her Yul Brynner, cruel bastard."

"Hell of a prank," said Malloy, laughing. "Human ingenuity knows no bounds."

"I told her the name of a good wig shop."

"God, it feels great to have a good laugh," he told Arnold, "but now I've got to shove off. Need to see a cook at a restaurant up on Broadway. Wish me luck."

"Luck," said Arnold. Malloy went to the coat rack in the corner. He got his jacket and strapped his backpack over his shoulder.

Timba was busy with some guy alleging that his car had gotten dinged in the parking process, so he simply tossed Malloy his keys and said, "Be safe." As he walked off, Timba was quoting from a notice posted on his shack that said ABECO Parking was not responsible for any vehicular damage incurred on the lot.

It was late morning, the clouds were breaking up and Old Sol was poking through. Heading north on Grand, he saw a group out front of

Midtown Music, dancing on the sidewalk to Jr. Walker & The All Stars blaring from the outside speakers. People sitting on chairs in vacant lots, drinking from 40-ouncers, solving the world's problems. People on porches, waiting for Fate to stumble by. And the way it looked to them: here he was, a stranger, alone in his car, slowing down or stopping. In his old Datsun, he didn't look like a cop. A social worker, a building inspector. Maybe. Nevertheless, they often mistook him for someone looking to buy drugs or sex. *I'm looking for addresses, you fools, or I'm consulting the street guide—that's why I'm slowing down or stopping.* It was hard enough trying to find a house when half the addresses are missing, but when you're being earnestly hailed at the same time: "Hey brother," they'd call out, "com'ere a minute! I wants to show you something."

Not long ago St. Louis cops located the scattered remains of a missing murder victim; they were tipped off after seeing a cur in the vicinity gnawing on a human femur. *No, brother, I don't want to see what you have. Not today.*

He pulled up to Diamond Cafe, an old-time eatery with a steam table and a lunch counter that had catered to working stiffs along this section of Broadway just north of downtown since the 1930s. In fact, the original 1936 menu, a wooden sign, was mounted on the wall. A "plate dinner" was thirty-five cents. He walked up to the man at the cash register, who looked like one of the Mario Brothers in that new video game. Politely, he asked for the contact by name, making it seem like he was a friend of the guy. You didn't need to get all official right off the bat.

The man took a customer's money first, rang it up, thanked him for coming, and then turned to Malloy. "You a friend of Harold's?"

"In a roundabout way, yeah," he replied.

"If you are a friend then you should know that Harold works the early shift. Comes on at three when we open, leaves at ten when Joe comes in."

"Oh, that's right," said Malloy with a snap of his fingers. "No problem, I'll catch him tomorrow."

"Tomorrow?" said the little man. "I don't think you're a friend at all, otherwise you'd know he's off Tuesdays, spends the whole day at the track during the season."

He sat in his car, window rolled down, thinking about which direction to go; he had contacts to pursue every which way. He found a pack of Big

Red in his jacket pocket and chewed that for a while, still pondering. Out from a murky cloud of thoughts popped the improbable figure of Darius, about to swat him with a rolled up copy of the *Globe*, saying, "Don't forget about Pickaninny." He looked around for a street sign and saw that North Market was the cross street. Two blocks to the east lay Produce Row, all thirty-five acres of it. He parked outside of one of two main buildings and walked in. It was a wholesale market, that much he knew. A sign at the entrance to a long row of stalls told him more: "Welcome to Produce Row, where produce arrives by 14,000 tractor trailers and rail cars 24 hours a day, 7 days a week, from 49 states and 76 different countries." And to unload all this tonnage you need manpower, ready and able, hungry for work, even more hungry for coin. Find the swampers, he thought, and you find Pickaninny.

The place wasn't all that busy just now, but he got the feeling it had been several hours earlier, around dawn. A regional wholesale market like this one had its own rhythm apart from everything else. He walked the aisle and on both sides were stalls with heaps of fruits and vegetables, all for sale but only in bulk. Broccoli by the crate, potatoes by the hundred-pound bag, pomegranates by the barrel. Here and there, guys who looked to be buyers from markets and restaurants were inspecting items, haggling with vendors. He walked through before making any inquiries, wanting to take it all in, yeah, but also trying to remember the names Darius had told him. Finally, he saw a sign for Mantia and realized that was one, but a check of the premises said nobody here. Coming back along the row he saw a couple guys who looked receptive to conversation. The sign over their heads read FRANKLIN PRODUCE — OWNER, FRANCIS CUSUMANO.

One guy was standing at a crate, chest high, using it as a desk. He had papers spread out before him, a pen in one hand and a foot-long stogie poking out his mouth. At Malloy's approach, he looked up, pushed his glasses back with a forefinger, and said, "What's up, Bub?"

Malloy told him who he was looking for, but not why. The guy seemed okay with not knowing why he was looking for a particular swamper, probably got approached about it routinely, detectives and parole officers seeking these guys out. "Go back out the way you came in," he said, pointing with his cigar toward the daylight, "you look to your left, toward the river, and down at the end of the street you see a big tree. That's their clubhouse, that's where you find the swampers." Malloy thanked him and began to walk off. The man called after him, "So you gonna walk right in and make yourself at home? They're a suspicious bunch, not exactly bubbling with hospitality. You tell 'em Brother sent you."

He saw the tree way down there, could've walked it easily but decided to drive so he'd have his stuff with him. There were maybe sixteen guys under the tree, near the tree, about half of them white, the rest black or Hispanic. There was a low campfire with a ring of tree stumps around it, a few chairs, and a folding table rummaged from somewhere. Off in the weeds stood the ruins of a house, systematically stripped over time for its combustible parts. Guys were sitting, standing, hands in their pockets, pacing, talking, joking around, poking the fire, playing catch, and thumbing through a copy of *Pussyrama*. But all eyes were on him as he walked up.

No one said hello, a few nodded. He could've been a guy looking to join them, start out on the bottom rung, take the shit work and pray that it got better. But he had a car so that couldn't be right; swamper don't have no car.

He moved in a little, got near the fire, stretched his arms out, palms down. This is a hobo camp, he thought. He had never seen a real hobo camp, but he was sure they had to look and feel like this. And what do hobos do? Try to take advantage of you, maybe gang up on you. He began to regret this ill-chosen mission, why did he need to find Pickaninny anyway? He was about to invoke the name Brother, when a baboon in a boonie hat sidled up. Out of the side of his mouth, "Bum a smoke?"

"Ah, no," he said. "Gum, you like gum?" He held out his Big Red.

"I hear that's bad for your teeth," he said as if he were an actor on a stage, grinning wide, showing the nubs of rotted teeth. "Toothless is the way to go," merrily, punching him playfully on the arm, "saves on toothpaste, I'll tell ya that." Everyone in earshot started laughing like hell.

That helped. He didn't beat around the bush in telling them he was looking for one of their own, said it was a health department matter. They all knew what that meant. They were all rough and tumble, used to just getting by; nearly every one of them had had the clap, the crabs, the croup, pink eye, or scabies at one time or another.

"What, you gonna swoop in and save his ass?" they asked.

"If Pickaninny has somethin'," said a short, stocky one, "it'll either go away or it'll kill him. It's his fate, why you wanna mess with the man's fate?"

"May be too late anyhow," offered someone off in the ranks. "We ain't seen his sorry ass for what ... two weeks?"

"Thought he might be vacationing at his retreat on Martha's Vineyard," said one joker. They all had a good laugh.

"He got one in Hawaii, too," said another. "You can try there."

"Okay," said Malloy, laughing along, "I can see it's no use. Wasn't that important anyway. If I can't get to him, I'll just wait for him to come to me."

The toothless one made an exaggerated study of Malloy's face, bobbing his head like a chicken. "Funny," he announced, "you don't look crazy, but you sure actin' like it. Ain't no one gonna come to you."

Malloy shrugged good-naturedly. He tossed them his pack of Big Red and walked off. He was almost to his car when he heard footsteps behind him. It was the short stocky one, hustling along. "Hey, wait up," he called. Malloy turned, waited. "I know where Pick lives," he said. "Fact, I was over there on Sunday, trying to find him, see what was the matter. Knocked and knocked, but no answer. Maybe you'll have better luck. If so, tell him Rowdy says anytime he's ready, I'm ready."

The house was on a side street off North Broadway in the Baden neighborhood. Rowdy didn't know the address, but gave a description: end of the street, second house on the left, dingy white wood frame, broke-down Pontiac in the drive. Two doors on the porch, the one on the left is his, goes upstairs. Malloy parked in front. Walking up, a young black kid sitting on the porch of the house next door watched him. It was before noon, kid should've been in school. He knocked and rang the bell, no bell to be heard. He knocked some more, called out "Hello!" The kid kept watching him, and when he looked to the kid the kid didn't look away.

Finally, the kid said, "It's open." Malloy said, "Yeah?" To which the kid replied, "Yeah, but you don't wanna go up there."

"Why not?" asked Malloy.

The kid made a funny face, said, "Do what you gotta do," and went inside his house.

Malloy tried the knob, it turned, and the door cracked open. There was mail for Lawrence Singleton on the floor just inside the door. He called his proper name as he went up the steps, feeling silly using the nickname when he didn't know the man. He got up there and called the name extra loud a few times, not wanting to be mistaken for an intruder, although he was. He walked down the short hallway, came to the kitchen, a plate of something on the table—SpaghettiOs? Whatever it was, it had hardened and formed mold. He walked over to the door that led to the back porch, unlatched the lock, opened it. "Stuffy in here, Lawrence," he bellowed, "I'm letting in some fresh air."

He went back up the hall, came to a door partly open. Had to be the bedroom. "Lawrence, you in there?" Silence. "There's people worried about you, man." Silence. "I'm coming in, okay?"

The shades were pulled and it was dim, only the natural light from the hallway filtering in. He stood in the doorway, letting his eyes get adjusted. Eventually, he made out a bed and a dresser. There was a lamp on the dresser. He found the little chain, pulled, and the room lit up. There, on the bed, a cocoon of blankets and sheets.

In one deft stroke he dismantled the cocoon to find the remains of one Lawrence Singleton a.k.a. Pickaninny, erstwhile swamper and gay hustler whose corpse was not exactly fresh.

He wasn't freaked out by dead people; he'd certainly seen enough of them in the back of his crackerbox ambulance as a medic in Germany. This one was on his side, frozen in semi-fetal position, one claw-like hand grasping a bottle of MD 20-20—Mad Dog—the other hand at his face, looking like he was scratching his scalp. His eyes were shut, thanks for that, but his mouth was open in a rictus of anguish. Just as Darius had mentioned, his hair was long, black and rasty, now standing out against the pale backdrop of dingy sheets. He was wearing only pajama bottoms and socks, his emaciated torso bare.

Without touching the body or moving it, Malloy made a survey and noted some of the same signs as he had seen on Douglas March, keeping in mind that the skin tones of the two men were as different as night and day. Then he thought he saw something in the man's mouth, a small movement. He took his pen and very gently probed the buccal cavity. A small, white moth fluttered out. "Holy shit!" he cried, and began laughing deliriously at the weirdness of it all.

THIRTY-EIGHT

AT FIRST, Malloy thought that Darius had flown the coop, but as he drew near he found him in the coop—or the cubby, whatever you called it. Malloy stood behind the newsstand and looked at Darius on his butt, arms around his knees, curled up inside. It was 8:05 on a Wednesday morning, the night's unseasonable chill still in the air, pushed by a noticeable breeze. He never knew if Darius actually slept in this metal box or if he laid his head somewhere else and just got here early. Copies of the *Globe* were stacked atop the stand, and Malloy knew that they arrived damned early.

"Hey man, you counting sheep or what?"

"Jus' passin' time, that's all. You wanna paper?"

"Sure, c'mon out, greet the day."

"Day don't need no greetin', not from me." Like some rusted machine, he slowly inched out. Malloy extended his hand and helped Darius up, who groaned as he stretched his arms and neck. "Got a kink," he explained.

"Could be the pillows they give you in this motel," said Malloy. "Hey, I brought you some coffee."

Darius grinned, showing what teeth he had. "Well, ain't you the thoughtful one. Thanks, brother."

After a moment, Malloy said, "That guy you told me about, Pickaninny? I found him."

"Yeah? What'd that sorry bastard have to say? He mention me?"

"Didn't say anything, he was dead. I did some asking around at Produce Row, like you said, and I was led to an apartment over in Baden. Let myself in, found him in his bed, full rigor mortis, probably been laying there like that for a week or more judging by the smell. I called the cops, they called the medical examiner, unmarked hearse came and got him and took him to the morgue."

"Huh, ain't that somethin'? Least he died in his bed. They say what got him?"

Malloy took a sip of the java he'd brought for himself. "You remember telling me there's some scary shit going around, and I said I was aware of it? I said I'd seen it in some of the same people who were turning up with syphilis. Well, Pickaninny had that disease, the ME confirmed it."

"Aw, shit," said Darius.

"Yeah, sorry. Listen, the body's still at the morgue, there's no one to claim it. If no one claims it, he goes into the potter's field out by the airport. He got any family?"

"I sure as hell don't know of any. We weren't that close."

"You want to claim the body? I'll help you get him a decent burial."

Darius spat on the sidewalk. "The man owed me seven dollar, why I wanna help him get buried?"

"I don't know, thought maybe you cared about him."

"Not that much. You still want that paper?"

"Yeah, *Globe* and a *Whirl.*" He held up the *Whirl.* "Great headline: 'Sean Slept While Burglars Crept.'"

"Ol' Ben Thomas, the publisher, he got a knack for rhymin.'"

"Okay, you won't help bury the guy ..."

"I'll go to the funeral if there is one."

"Great, but do me one favor now. I want you to think about anyone Pickaninny had contact with, and you know what kind of contact I mean, and I want you to make a list, write it out or just keep it in your head. I'll be back in a day or so, and we'll talk then. Deal?"

Darius snorted. "Deal means both sides get something out of it. What I get from this deal?"

"You get the satisfaction of knowing you helped curb the advance of acquired immune deficiency syndrome, a.k.a. AIDS, a.k.a. the scary shit that be going 'round." Malloy started to walk off, but turned, said, "Lawrence Singleton."

"Who?" from Darius.

"Pickaninny, the late Lawrence Singleton."

THIRTY-NINE

THE EX-JOCK from the Cardinals' personnel department explained that the team had just gone on the road and there wouldn't be another home game for eleven days. No, Fredbird didn't go along for away games, and no, he would not give out Fredbird's full name or home address. Malloy would just have to come back when the team returned, but he shouldn't bother the mascot before or during the game. He could approach Fredbird with this "business"—Malloy had shown his federal ID and said he was there on official business—only after the game, when he was out of character and finished with his job of firing up the crowd.

"What, does he change in the locker room with the rest of the players?" Malloy was in no way familiar with the workings of a professional baseball team.

"No, he has his own dressing room." The ex-jock was well-tanned, perfectly coiffed, with a haughty tone that was starting to really bother Malloy.

"Okay, I'll wait till he's done, but then I'll need someone to take me to him."

"As I said, you'll have to find him after he leaves the stadium. We can't have you bothering him while he's on our property."

An ogre inside Malloy's head screamed *arrghh!* "What're you, stupid? I can't approach him after he leaves, because I don't know what he looks like when he's not wearing his fucking chicken suit."

"I think we're done here," he said, and started to walk off.

"You have to make him available to me," Malloy called after him. "It's a law in Missouri."

The ex-jock turned and smiled thinly. "Fredbird is an independent contractor. He is not an employee of the Cardinals organization so I don't think that statute applies in this case."

"Who's your supervisor? I need to speak with him. Or her." But the trained monkey of the Cardinals' organization had already walked off.

It was only 9:45, and Malloy still had another couple hours before reporting back to the clinic. The investigators did not have to spend the full four hours in the field chasing down contacts, but they could and often did, even if they didn't have the workload to warrant it. If they wanted to run a few personal errands, grab a late breakfast, well, nobody would be the wiser. They were not accountable in that way, and, besides, they all worked the occasional evenings and weekends.

He found himself driving south along 14th Street, then west on Park, and, before long, he was in Lafayette Square. For the hell of it, he drove around the park. It was a typical nice day in St. Louis, and the sidewalk bordering the park was filled with runners. He noted they were all moving clockwise, and he wondered if that was some unspoken rule. If he was out there with them, prancing along like a ninny, he was pretty sure he'd be going in the opposite direction.

At the southwest corner of the Victorian park stood the house. Driving past slowly, he took special note of a car parked in front, a yellow VW Beetle convertible with the top down. He decided to circumnavigate the park once more and come to rest at a respectable distance from Trey's front door but close enough that he could keep an eye out. Just for a little while.

Meanwhile, another syphilis case had surfaced with ties to Man 2 Man. Jason Berger, a steward with TWA, tested positive for primary syphilis and was treated and interviewed the same day. Berger was cooperative, naming five contacts within the critical period, two of whom turned up infected.

Three of the five men named lived in Berger's layover cities; ERs on those were forwarded and STD investigators in those health departments had worked the cases. One of the two who turned up infected was a local, Jim DePuydt, a chemical engineer at Monsanto.

While Jason Berger had never heard of Trey Vonderhaar or Man 2 Man, Jim DePuydt had. He freely admitted to having attended a soiree this last spring, going as the guest of Emilio Borst, a longstanding member of Man 2 Man and second-chair violin in the St. Louis Symphony Orchestra. It was starting to look like a clusterfuck, and several investigators were working it as a team.

Malloy had been handed Borst, and, when contacted, the leonine violinist stated that he had been diagnosed and treated for his disease by Dr. Brock Silber, but still he was concerned because he was experiencing a "certain ennui," which, he felt, compromised his performance. To make matters worse, he had a hell of a case of diarrhea that never quite went away. And to make matters even worse, these purple spots on his upper chest and legs were getting worse. The musician was beside himself with worry.

This just pissed Malloy off, for he guessed correctly that any treatment Borst had gotten from that quack Silber was dubious at best. These people, trusting in doctors and medicine, deserved proper diagnosis and treatment.

Malloy had no better luck with Borst than he'd had with other *bons vivants* who had paid their dues to Vonderhaar. It wasn't so much that they were uncooperative, just that the information provided was so sketchy it was practically useless. Ah, but there was one sunbeam shining through the clouds: Borst did mention that at one point, while he and "Earl from Annapolis" were hard at it, their host came in the room, offering refreshments and sex toys. Borst recalled that Vonderhaar, lingering in the room as he and Earl from Annapolis resumed sex, took a "keen interest" in the horizontal passion play on the four-post bed. "He became aroused," said Borst, "and began fondling himself—through his clothing, mind you. We said that wasn't necessary: 'C'mon join us, three is a nice number.' But he declined politely, then took his tray and left. My guess is that he's a voyeur. And nothing wrong with that," Borst was quick to add, "every great performance needs an audience."

That was enough for Malloy. Among Borst's shadowy cast of carnal characters, he formally initiated Bryson "Trey" Vonderhaar III as a suspect. Of course, with an order of protection still in place, he couldn't run it.

Betsy could, though, and, par for the course, she had an appointment with Vonderhaar and his lawyer later this week. Good luck with that, he'd told her.

Now, as he sat in his Datsun watching the joggers and rollerbladers, thinking how cool it would be to invent a machine that could harness that energy, he was suddenly seized with a massive cramp above and behind his right knee. He tried to shake it out in the car, but it persisted, the muscle tied in a knot of pain. He jumped out and tried to walk it off, limping almost comically at first. He then groaned his way toward a mighty elm on the grassy parkway between the sidewalk and the street, cantilevered against it, and started doing a runner's stretch.

In Vonderhaar's front parlor, some forty yards away, they were wrapping up business. At Trey's behest, Jack Westhoff, one the more sought-after interior designers in the city, had dropped by. Trey was tired of the look and feel of the parlor and certain other rooms on the first floor, and he wanted Jack's advice on what to do. "You're right," said Jack, "the color in the parlor here doesn't complement the furnishings, and you don't want to upset the furnishings, splendid as they are. I suggest you go with a shade of tawny for the walls and a nice teal for the trim, make you think you're in a sunset meadow … oh, my! Look at that fellow over there, trying to push that big tree over. Will he do it?"

Trey looked out his picture window and saw what Jack was talking about. "Yeah, we get a lot of fitness nuts around here. The park is a freak show at times." Trey turned toward the breakfast nook. "Oh Freddie, come here for a moment, please."

Freddie DuCoin put down his coffee and newspaper and rose from the table. He went to the window. Trey pointed, said, "Do you see what I see?"

"A man pushing on a tree, but in street clothes. Obviously not a jogger. Weird."

"Look closer," said Trey.

Squinting, Freddie studied the figure in question. "Oh, *now* I see."

"Jack, would you excuse us for just a moment?" While Jack Westlake inspected an imposing grandfather clock over in the corner, Trey took Freddie aside. "Are you up for some fun?" he asked.

"As long as it doesn't involve screwing somebody," answered Freddie, tapping his wristwatch. "Too early for that."

"Freddie, you really amuse me at times. And yes, it does involve screwing

somebody, but not in that way. You see our friend from the health department out there, the one who's been ordered by the court to stay away? Why
do you think he's here?"

"It's no coincidence. He's probably spying on us."

"On the nose! Opportunity knocks, and you're my accomplice. So,
here's the plan. You put Roscoe on a leash, take him for a nice walk in the
park—he'll love that. You walk past Malloy there, he sees you, says hello.
You're happy to see him, you make small talk. He asks about me. You invite
him to come along on the walk. Because he'll do anything to get to me, he
agrees. Now, once you've gained his confidence, made him think you're
unhappy here, here's what you do …"

Jack was at the front door, finished with his survey. Trey saw him out,
saying they'd be in touch. Trey then moved to the picture window. He
watched Freddie and Roscoe approach Shaun Malloy, who was now back
in his car. He saw them stop and talk. So far, so good. He held up his
Magic 8 Ball, shook it vigorously, and asked, "Will he play along?" Through
a small portal at its base, the mute oracle coughed up an answer: YOU MAY
RELY ON IT.

FORTY

MALLOY WAS automatically suspicious of Freddie's invitation to a party
that evening in the tony West End.

He wasn't fit company for a fast crowd like that—"People worth meeting," as Freddie put it. He was cool, he knew, but in a Lee Marvin sort of
way. He didn't put up with pretentiousness, and he imagined he'd find a lot
of that at this party. A bunch of posers and wanna-be hipsters. Why would
Freddie even want him there?

But then, Freddie casually mentioned that certain parties from the Man
2 Man sphere would be in attendance, and he knew he was in. With that
disclosure, his mindset suddenly switched from that of the guy who might
show up at this phony-baloney party, have a few drinks, make small talk,
and bow out early to that of the guy who was there on a secret mission.
He'd seek out these shadowy figures, and, over cocktails, discreetly pump
them for information on Trey Vonderhaar and his nefarious racket.

He could have walked to the party from his old apartment. It was on
Lenox Place, an elongated horseshoe of a private street off Euclid Avenue.

As he drove through the open gates, a uniformed watchman in a parked car, BONDED SECURITY written on the side, motioned for him to stop. Malloy pulled up alongside, facing, gave him the single-digit address.

"And who lives there?" asked the guard, giving Malloy's car the once-over through aviator sunglasses.

"Henry Ambruster," he answered, short on patience. Malloy disliked most authority figures, never mind that he himself was one.

"Just checking," said the guard. "Nice ride," he ventured out of the blue. "Not quite old enough to be considered an antique, I suppose. Bet those wheels've eaten a lot of road, huh?"

"What's your point, man?"

"Just that you might want to park it somewhat out of sight, like under a big tree or something. At least not out in the open."

"Go to hell," said Malloy, and drove off.

The brass knocker on the oak door made a "ka-chunk" sound that probably reverberated throughout the massive Tudor. After one such knock, the door opened and an athletic, fair-complected fellow appeared. Mid-thirties, wearing jeans, a yellow V-neck sweater, and a Cheshire cat smile on his face. "You must be Shaun," he said, extending a hand, palm down, as if he expected it to be kissed. "Fantastic! Glad you could come. Freddie's told us all about you."

"And you are?"

"Oh, a thousand pardons. I'm Eric, Henry's partner." He took Malloy by the arm and led him from the vestibule where they stood, along a short hallway, into a large living room, and ... yikes! There were maybe a dozen men standing around, all eyes on him, making an entrance arm-in-arm with a virtual stranger. There was a disconcerting silence, prompting a prickly feeling of dread, and a trusted inner voice said, "Get gone!"

"Attention everyone," called Eric. "May I introduce our featured guest of the evening, Mr. Shaun Malloy." It was too late to bolt, for now he was shaking hands with Henry Ambruster, along with Stewart and Ray and Phil and Michael and Kip and Rafael and Rocky and Dennis and Jay and Drew. As in Conger.

"Nice to see you again," he said, unconvincingly.

"Where's the bar?" asked Malloy.

"I'll get it for you," answered Eric, brightly. "After all, I'm the host.

What'll it be? You look like a scotch on the rocks."

"Why not. Dewars if you have it. Rocks and a splash of water. By the way, where's Freddie?"

"He called to say he's running late. He had to get batteries for his video recorder."

"He's making a movie?"

"Yeah, you might say that. Freddie has many interests, some of them quite naughty," he laughed. "Be right back with your drink."

That first scotch went down so easy it was soon followed by another, then another. He found himself talking with Kip about some innovative investment opportunity called mutual funds, which was "bound to be a game-changer in the financial world." That was slightly less boring than hearing Michael ramble on about the films of Joanne Dru. This was not Malloy's idea of a party; it was more like a polite reception for a banker who'd just been promoted to branch manager. He wished that Freddie would hurry up and get here so that he could point out the Man 2 Man members in this mix.

Henry came by with a tray of hors d'oeuvres, nicely presented. Malloy popped a stuffed mushroom, pronounced it excellent, and asked for the bathroom. Down the hall, he was told. He locked the door behind him, not wanting to deal with Drew Conger barging in on him.

He looked flushed. Half a dozen scotches will do that, he thought; then, this isn't working. You don't have a playbill for the characters to know who's who, and broaching the topic would be just too flipping awkward: 'Hey, you been to one of Trey's little affairs lately? Soirees, yeah, that's it—leave your clothes and inhibitions at the door. Well, if I were you, I'd steer clear of that place for a while, like for the rest of your life, because there's some bad juju in that house. Take it from me, I'm a public health officer.' No, it was stupid to come here, definitely above and beyond the call of duty. Time to go.

He went back out and Eric handed him a fresh highball. Last one, said Malloy. Oh no, you can't leave! Well, yeah, he affirmed, it's been fun and all.

"Oh, stick around a little longer," Eric persisted, "the fun's just getting started. And look who just walked in."

Freddie walked up and extended his hand. "You look well lubricated," he said.

"You've got some catching up to do," rejoined Malloy. "Where's your movie camera?"

"I parked it out in the hall. That's for later on."

Freddie turned to Eric and said, "Is everything in order?"

"Any minute now," he declared.

"What're you talking about?" wondered Malloy.

"It's a surprise," said Freddie. "You'll see."

"I don't care for people speaking in code," said Malloy, listing to one side, "it's actually rude and you don't want to be rude to your guests … you know, it's really hot in here …why is the floor moving? And …"

Eric grabbed the drink from Malloy just as he crumpled to the floor.

"Nice save," said Freddie, observing Malloy's dumbfounded expression as he lay on the parquet floor. "Boy, those things work fast."

"It wasn't this drink," said Eric. "I put it in the drink before this."

Malloy was in dreamland. It was neither a pleasant nor unpleasant dream, but reminiscent of his mother telling him something that she thought was important.

Now that you're twelve years old, she was saying, *it's only a matter of time before you'll experience a nocturnal emission.*

His mom was like that, always using clinical terms, especially if it involved anything to do with sex. Even when he was a young boy and other kids were calling their dicks a pee-pee or a pee shooter, Shaun, under threat of reprisal, had to say penis. The sex act itself was never called anything but coitus. Not that talk of sex itself came up much anyway.

But here she was throwing out a new, ominous-sounding term. He was going to have a nocturnal emission. He asked for clarification.

Some people refer to it as a wet dream, she explained matter-of-factly, *because it usually happens when you're sleeping. Your body is making sperm and this sperm likes to swim around in semen, but sometimes this semen builds up and needs a release. So, it overflows the pot, you might say, it comes out of your penis and onto your pajamas. It's thick and sticky but harmless, a natural thing for young men to have. I'm telling you this so when it does happen you won't worry.*

When he came to, the first thing he felt was a draft around his crotch. He could see shapes in the room, moving, murmuring. He sensed he was sitting in a chair and there were people around him. Again, he wondered why there was a draft around his crotch. Then he understood that some-

204 CREATURES ON DISPLAY

one was fellating him, licking his cock like a lollipop. He stirred, tried to rise, but his legs were rubber. He struggled to understand what was happening. He did not wish to be fellated. Not here, not now.

His senses were coming together now, and he heard someone shout, "Do the Deep Throat thing." He felt his cock being consumed and it hurt. For the first time he looked down and saw the top of a head bobbing up and down between his legs. The head had long brown hair, and this confused him further; by now, he remembered where he was and he recalled seeing no women at this party. He took the long brown hair, gathered a fistful, and pulled. He saw the face of Drew Conger.

"Hey, watch it!" Conger had this crazy look in his eye, like a cat that's been given the remains of a salmon. He wiped his chin, and with renewed purpose went back down on his unwilling subject.

With a guttural grunt, Malloy kicked with his feet, feebly, but it worked. Drew Conger tipped like a bowling pin and fell away. Holding the arm rests, Malloy now rose from the chair, and caught sight of Freddie with his movie camera, grinning, pointing it at his erect pole. As he pulled up his pants and belted, he saw a gallery of leering faces, snickering and hooting, and he felt sick at his own humiliation. "Fuck you! Fuck alla you!" he mouthed, but to his ears it sounded like he was inside a box.

On unsteady legs, like a punch-drunk boxer, he went for the door, pushing a few bystanders aside. Freddie called after him, "That's a wrap, Shaun. Don't think it'll need too much editing. Gay porn is not that picky. Oh, by the way, Trey sends his regards. He had other business this evening, said you'd understand."

The watchman was standing near his fake patrol car, having a smoke, when Malloy rolled up. The guy signaled stop. Malloy stopped, not out of obedience but with hope the guy would start some shit. Sure enough.

"Done for the night?" he asked, walking up to the open driver's side window.

For the first time, Malloy saw the holster at his side. "What does it look like?"

"You look like shit, you know that? What'd they do, put you through the ringer?"

"They put me in a bad mood, not that it's any of your fucking business, asshole."

The guard placed a hand on his holster. "One more curse word out of your filthy mouth, I'll have the cops here so fast you'll wish you never saw me."

"Oh, really? Since when is it a crime to call a shit-for-brains rent-a-cop an asshole?" He took his foot off the brake and kicked up a batch of pea gravel as he peeled out.

FORTY-ONE

"I don't think your friend need worry," said Karl, "there's very little chance of picking up an STD from receiving oral sex. One time only? Gonorrhea, maybe, big maybe ..." Malloy could almost see into Karl's brain "... two percent chance. Five, tops. I hope it was at least good for him."

Malloy shook his head vehemently. "No, it wasn't good for him. They put a roofie in his drink and took advantage of him when he was passed out."

"How did he have an erection then, to get the blowjob, if he was passed out?"

"He doesn't know and that doesn't matter. It happened, and now he's worried about possible infection."

Karl gave a knowing nod. "I guess you can't stop a healthy cock from getting aroused, even if its owner is in lala land. Well, your friend can always come here and be checked out. If he's worried about being noticed, we can bring him straight back to the clinic and do the sign-in there."

"That's nice to know," said Malloy. He put a knuckle between his teeth, and looked away thoughtfully. "We can check for the routine stuff, sure. But what about AIDS?"

Karl tapped the eraser end of his Dixon Ticonderoga No. 2 pencil on a stack of reports, sounding out a military tattoo. It was the start of another work day, and they were in his office. "Nothing to offer there," said Karl. "They've got to know precisely what it is before they can develop a test for it. And knowing that is down the road."

"So, if he did pick up a case the only way to know is, what? Wait and see what develops?"

"You got it. Life's a bitch that way."

Malloy went back to the epi room. Arnold was on the phone asking some hapless person at the other end how long he'd had sores on his penis.

Betsy was talking to Martha about a stripper named Fanny Rose who might be a link between the GC cases they were currently working. Martha was going to lure her into the clinic by leaving a trail of one dollar bills for her to follow. There was a note on his desk from clerical:

> Shaun,
> This guy came by and said if you don't stop coming by
> his house and talking to his mom about his "condition"
> then he's coming back to fix your wagon (his words).
> He wants you to call him, but not before noon. What
> nerve these guys have (my words).
> Danielle

Malloy crumpled the note, aimed for the wastebasket and missed. He was sick of it all, really tired, I-need-a-year-long-sabbatical tired.

Of being outright lied to, of the coaxing and cajoling, of sixteen-year-old girls with pelvic inflammatory disease who will never have kids of their own because some thoughtless chump wanted to get his dick wet and move on.

Tired of the runaround from contacts, tired of telling doctors the current VD treatment guidelines, and just as tired of being disappointed in the medical profession as a whole. Tired of Joe breathing down his neck, of wisecracks from his fellow investigators, of verbal abuse in the field. Tired of the endless stream of patients marching into the clinic every morning, and tired of living and breathing VD day-in day-out, trying to instill a little quality control to their busy sex lives only to have half of them show up a few months later reinfected.

Tired of wondering where the last vestiges of his innocence went.

FORTY-TWO

A VOICE PIPED UP on the speaker of his desk phone. "Shaun, you've got a call on line twenty-eight."

He picked up the receiver, punched the blinking red light, "Malloy here."

"Hey there, it's Urban Lehrer. How's it going?"

"It's going. And you?"

"Still working on this piece about AIDS here, gathering thread as I said, and it's taking shape. Can you talk for a minute?"

It was 3:30, and work was winding down. Malloy looked around the room, saw the others busy putting out their own little fires, said, "Yeah, sure."

"This thing, what's being called the gay plague, is spreading, which is what you'd expect in a plague, and when it spreads fast enough and sickens enough people it becomes an epidemic. So ... I think we're on the brink of an epidemic, people succumbing not only on the East and West coasts, but here in flyover country, too. We're always a few months behind the curve, you know that. Everything trendy, from fashion to designer drugs, eventually comes to the Midwest, but on a delayed schedule."

Malloy could hear newsroom sounds from the other end, typewriters clacking, voices rising and falling. "AIDS is trendy? I don't think so, it's here to stay."

"Okay, bad choice of words," said Lehrer. "But the point is, it's now in the population, among us, and it's something we have to address. Because ignoring it and not taking precautions is no different than lining up for the gas chamber. When we talked at the bar, I said it wasn't getting a lot of attention from mainstream media because of who its victims were, but now that the blood supply is tainted, and hemophiliacs and other so-called in-nocent victims are getting it, complacency about this disease is turning into serious concern."

"I read that the mayor of New York had the bath houses shut down."

"That's right, they're taking measures in New York and San Francisco, shutting down gay bath houses, making more of an effort to control pros-titution, setting up hotlines, forming liaisons between the gay community and social agencies, getting the word out. At least trying to be proactive, which is something St. Louis needs to do as well. As I said, we're behind the curve. We don't lead the way. We tend to follow the lead of others."

That word again, thought Malloy. Both Joe and this reporter preaching proactive.

"St. Mary's set up a hospice specifically for AIDS patients, did you know that?"

"I do know that," said Lehrer, "and it's a good move. I also know that hospices in other cities are having trouble finding and keeping caregivers. When they found out their patients have AIDS, they worried about their own safety and in some cases refuse to provide care."

"The Sisters of St. Mary would never do that. They have a long history of ministering to the terminally ill, no matter how contagious they may be. It's their reason for living." Malloy heard himself sounding testy but he couldn't help it, for he greatly admired these nuns and their indefatigable good works.

"Hey, I believe you," said Lehrer, placating. "But we're really off point. Actually, I called to see if you have anything new to report. In all your traipsing around, coming in contact with some of the most at-risk people in this city, have you seen any more cases of AIDS? I know you're not able to talk freely right now, so you can just say yes or no and we'll take it from there."

Malloy immediately thought of Emilio Borst and his connection to Man 2 Man. To tell this inquiring reporter that the second chair violin of the St. Louis Symphony was likely infected with AIDS would be sensational, a major scoop, but it would reveal that the musician was a contact in an ongoing case and thus break confidentiality. Besides, to provide "news" such as this felt too much like gossip.

"Nah, nothing since we last spoke," said Malloy. "Just a lot of the same ol' same ol'."

The voice of Del Goodwin, one of the physician assistants on the clinic side, came through the intercom affixed to the wall above Malloy. "We've got two positives for GC here waiting for an interview with an investigator. Anytime you're ready."

"I've got to go," Malloy told Lehrer.

"What about that house in Lafayette Square," Lehrer persisted, "a real threat to public health, from what you said. Have you made any headway in curtailing that operation?"

"I'm working on it," said Malloy. "It's complicated and I can't do it alone. I'll keep you posted."

"Thanks, and here's a post for you. Mr. Vonderhaar must be having another of his soirees tonight, because I drove by there about an hour ago and there was a catering van out front. Maybe the health department could get there early, set up a VD testing station on the sidewalk there, intercept the guests as they walk in—how proactive is that?"

FORTY-THREE

MALLOY SAT on a folding chair on a small embankment in Lafayette Park overlooking wide Missouri Avenue to the west, and beyond that, Vonderhaar's place. He was not alone. His companion was down below, almost out of sight, sitting in her parked car. It was 7:20 and the sun was going down for the count, throwing long shadows from the cedar trees around him. It was neither chilly nor windy; except for the occasional mosquito, he was perfectly comfortable. A man and a dog approached. The dog saw him first and strained at the leash to get to him, but the man jerked on the leash and made a point to skirt around the strange man sitting by himself in the park at dusk.

He trained binoculars on the opulent Victorian home. With each passing minute, the interior became more defined. From the living room fronting the street, chandeliers lit the scene and several figures were seen moving to and fro, carrying various objects, making preparations. It seemed that company was coming.

A couple hours earlier, he had intercepted Betsy on the way to her car after work. Remember, he asked, when we all talked over drinks about trying to do something about the spread of AIDS? There was debate over what exactly might make a difference. Doing epidemiology wasn't practical, preaching abstinence was ludicrous, handing out rubbers, yeah, that would help but you can't be there to make sure they'll put it on when the time is right. You brought up the idea of communicating a warning, something to get them to stop and think about what they're getting into. Well, Trey Vonderhaar is throwing another party tonight, and if you still want to make a difference now is a good time.

He further explained his plan which involved her approaching the Man 2 Man members as they arrived and handing them a flier that would spell out the perils that awaited them in the House of Vonderhaar. He would be in the vicinity, at the perimeter of the 500-foot imaginary circle that kept Little Red Riding Hood safe from the Big Bad Wolf, but within earshot if any problem arose.

"That sounds like a great way to get fired," she said.

"There is that chance, yeah," said Malloy, "and with a job at stake I don't have any argument to talk you into it. You'll either do it or you won't. But if you don't, you're a big ..."

"Pussy?" she said, smiling. "Can't have that—I'll do it."

"You will?"

"Why not. I'm not long for this place anyway. Any day now I'm putting in my two weeks' notice. Going back to college."

"That's great! Never stop learning. Let me guess, you're going for a master's or doctorate in public health. You want to run the show, not have the show run you."

"Not even close," she said. "I'm done with public health and its built-in frustrations that don't wash off in the shower. Ornithology, Shaun, the study of birds. I'm going for a master's in zoology with a specialty in ornithology. I want to be a field scientist, discover new species. I'm already a birder, out every weekend with the Audubon Society, got my binoculars and field guides and sandwiches. Believe it or not, I've got a Life List of three hundred forty-three species and I've only been at it for three years."

"Good for you!" said Malloy. "Have you seen many goonie birds on your field trips?"

She smiled. "Are they like the elusive snipe? You hear about some gullible person being taken on a snipe hunt, searching for a bird that doesn't exist."

"Oh they exist, and you'll see several of them this evening, up close. But you know what I think? I think we should give Vonderhaar a chance to call the thing off himself. We're going to call him and state our intentions."

They left the parking lot and went back up to the STD clinic. A few clinicians were still working, double-checking test tubes and culture plates, doing quality control while puffing away on cigarettes—smoking in the clinic being a no-no. The epi room was deserted. Malloy had Vonderhaar's number, and he'd used it only once just to see if it worked. That time Freddie had answered, and Malloy said, "Oh sorry, wrong number." And Freddie had cracked, "Oh, were you trying to reach the sperm bank? The numbers are very close."

With the system set for conference call, he punched the seven digits. Trey himself answered.

"Yes?" He sounded harried, like he'd been in the middle of something.

"Trey, this is Shaun Malloy. Don't hang up until I tell you something important, something you'll want to think about."

"What is it, Malloy?" A bite to his tone.

"In a few hours you'll start receiving guests for another swell evening of drinking, dining, and socializing. That's as far as it will get. You will desist in allowing those guests to hook up and go into private rooms for the purpose of exchanging bodily fluids through copulation. Is that clear?"

"I don't respond to ultimatums," he huffed.

"That's fine," said Malloy. "Then chew on this. If you don't do as I ask, then certain parties, acting as private citizens concerned over a brothel in their neighborhood, will be out front of your home imploring your guests to think twice before entering, that the possibility of contracting syphilis and AIDS becomes more likely with each step toward your door."

"You wouldn't! My guests are to be left alone, not accosted by riffraff."

Malloy, grinning broadly, could almost see Vonderharr at the distal end of the phone, flipping his wig. He nodded at Betsy: you're up.

"Not riffraff," she corrected. "Didn't you hear? Concerned citizens who know how to make signs and fliers, how to persuade with well-chosen words. And if these concerned citizens are seen to be a nuisance, well then, so be it."

"Try it and I'll have you prosecuted," he promised.

Malloy could barely stifle his amusement. "Oh, we won't set foot on your lovely lawn. We'll keep to the street and sidewalks. If you'd like to send Freddie out with some Chianti Classico and appetizers, we probably wouldn't turn him away."

"Chianti Classico?" parroted Vonderhaar, voice dripping with scorn. "Is that what peons order in restaurants? And that's you, isn't it, Malloy? I had you pegged from the start, even before I saw you, just hearing your bourgeois voice over the intercom. Well congrats, my friend, you've sunk even deeper in the muck. As of now, you are not just a peon, but the anus of a peon. Goodbye!"

"That is one pissed-off person," said Betsy, putting the receiver back in its cradle.

"We definitely got a rise out of him," agreed Malloy. "Now we have to follow through and make good on our threat. How do you want to word the flier?"

"Not too wordy," answered Betsy. "Bold letters, pithy and to the point."

Trey Vonderhaar was, among other things, crafty. In the same vein, as described by admirers and detractors alike, he had been called scheming, cunning, clever, devious, even sneaky, but of all those modifiers, he liked crafty the best.

The word called to mind a fox, and its ability to outwit other forest animals and, of course, devour them. And crafty fellow that he was, he gave quick consideration to the problem at hand. Malloy and an unknown number of confederates planned to descend on his home and disrupt his soiree. That was unacceptable, but how to stop it? Time was short, leaving few options open.

He could hire some thugs to show up and drive them off, but he didn't know any thugs for hire. He could have Freddie go out there with a slop bucket, pretend to trip, and slosh liquid garbage all over them. Then they would have to go home and change their clothes. But that would put a stench over the entire area and his guests would be affected, too. The best solution, he decided, would be to have a police presence. The problem with that idea, though, was that the cops in St. Louis were so busy with real criminals that they would laugh themselves silly at the thought of staking out a residence where some ragtag protesters might show up and harass decent citizens. Still, it was the most viable option. He knew someone who might be able to make it happen.

It was past five and Mark Walter had almost certainly left for the day. You work at City Hall, you're out the door at 4:30, leaving the workaday grind behind until 9 AM the next day. Even in the mayor's office that was the rule, except, of course, if there was a crisis brewing and the mayor needed a freshly pressed suit for the television cameras. Then he might call on his aide, Mark Walter—errand boy and general factotum.

However, being the chief public servant's servant had its perks. Walter had connections throughout the miniature Machiavellian empire that City Hall represented. With a phone call or two, Walter could capture the ear of a certain person, perhaps an underling like himself, but set wheels in motion nonetheless.

Trey Vonderhaar had not heard of any crises brewing in the fair City of St. Louis this day, which meant that Mark Walter, at the present, was most likely occupying a barstool at The Peep Show over in Benton Park. He found the number in the phone book under "Bars / Taverns / Lounges" and gave it a try.

The bartender answered, "Peep Show, what'll I do you for?" Trey inquired if Mark Walter was there. Even with "My Sharona" filling in the background, he heard the bartender ask Mark if he was there. Bartender came back, "Who wants to know?" With an air of significance, Trey told him who. Seconds later, he heard the voice of his gregarious friend, "What's up, brother? You calling me here, at my favorite hideaway, it must be important. Hold on a moment, let me come around the bar so Mandrake here doesn't get his panties in a knot because I stretched out the phone cord."

Trey told him the situation, said it was dire, emphasized the need for intervention.

"What would you like me to do?" inquired Walter, ice tinkling as he spoke.

"You think you could rustle up a few boys in blue to swing by and check on things starting around eight?"

"I might could," he answered, "the Third District's a few blocks away. I could go over there in person, that's the best way—phone call, forget it. But there's one problem with that."

"You don't have any pull there?"

"Oh, be quiet. Mayor's Breakfast with Police Cadre—I know most of the higher-ups, including a couple watch captains. They love me over in the Third. No, my dear, the problem is it would take me away from my cocktails and the best bartender in the city, and I'm not finished here yet."

"Oh hell," said Trey, "I'll buy you all the cocktails you can drink. You'll be sweating liquor from your pores for a week. Whatever you want, just make this happen."

"Now that you mention it," coquettishly, "I want to meet that cute doctor friend of yours."

"Silber? He's up to his ears in social functions, Mister Man About Town. But sure, I can do that. Lunch next week, you and he and me. I'll leave after the appetizers come out, you two can be alone."

Mark Walter gushed, "That is so awesome. I can't wait. You're the best."

"This little job can't wait either," said Trey. "Could you see fit to get your tight ass over to the police station now? I'll never forget the favor."

"I'm already there," said Mark Walter. "Mandrake, please be a sweetie and chill my drink. I'll need it freshened when I get back."

Malloy was thinking they should have brought walkie-talkies, an operation like this called for ready communication. As it was, he was so distant from Betsy that if any shit went down he might not hear her calling for him. But he did not expect any trouble from a bunch of well-heeled wankers here to attend a fancy dinner. And besides, Betsy had some powerful pipes; her clarion voice had once flagged down a moving Bomb Pop truck on noisy Grand Avenue so she could get a Creamsicle. He looked at his watch with the light-up face: 7:50. Anytime now.

He peered through the binoculars and saw a couple guys stationed out front, on the sidewalk. Dressed in slacks and sport jackets, they looked to be passing time, waiting for something to occur, the same as he was. Valets, he guessed.

Nearby, on the opposite side of Missouri Avenue, facing Trey's house, Betsy waited in "Old Yeller," her Buick Apollo. The car being bright yellow with a bent antenna and a dented quarter-panel, she was about as inconspicuous as tin foil on a telephone pole. She had her fliers in a neat pile beside her, ready to hand out when the time came. The message was simple, yet compelling.

BE ADVISED! THESE PREMISES HAVE BEEN ASSOCIATED WITH AN OUTBREAK OF POTENTIALLY DEADLY DISEASE. PARTICIPATION OF ANY SPONSORED ACTIVITY WITHIN THIS RESIDENCE IS HIGHLY DISCOURAGED. LET THIS SERVE AS A WARNING: TURN AROUND, GO BACK HOME!

She was pleased with the composition; it had a sense of foreboding that would instill dread in the reader. She was sure that if she were going to a party at someone's house and a stranger walked up and handed her such a note, she would take it seriously, do an about-face and get the heck out of there. A car pulled up in front of the house. One of the valets approached, leaned over and spoke to the driver through an open window. He then pointed several spaces to the north, indicating where the car would go. Betsy heard the young man assure the driver that his vehicle would be safe.

She was out of her car and already walking across Missouri, her target already starting to walk toward the illumined house. She ignored the valets, and stood in the man's path as he approached. "Excuse me, sir. I don't think you want to go in there. This will explain." She held out the flier imploringly. "Please take this, and you'll see for yourself."

The man, a stock broker from the affluent suburb of Huntleigh Woods, took Betsy for some sort of deranged street person, and brushed her aside, saying, "Not now." He kept on walking toward the two frowning valets. But

Betsy was not so easily foiled. Moving fast, she caught up with the first guest as he strode purposefully along.

Half-skipping to keep up, she thrust her flier at him. "Just take this and read it, please!"

Abruptly, he snatched the flier, and without looking at the message, let it fall to the ground. He kept walking right into the arms of the two valets who flanked him protectively as they escorted him the rest of the way.

Betsy stood there crestfallen. Was every guest going to be this difficult? From the corner of her eye she saw someone else approaching, a policeman. The cop walked up, gave a slow shake of his head and a finger-wag. "Ma'am, you're under arrest," he said. "You'll need to come with me to the station."

She looked at the name plate on his blue uniform: MCBRIDE. White guy, late thirties, average appearance, sergeant stripes on his sleeve. "Officer Mc-Bride," she said calmly, rationally, "there's got to be a mistake. You saw me doing nothing illegal, I'm sure of that. Look, I'm on public property. This flier is a form of free speech. You can't be serious."

The cop chuckled slightly. "Do I look like I'm joking? You're coming with me to the station. I can cuff you right here, if you don't believe me."

"But what's the offense?"

"Solicitation," he pronounced.

"Get out of town!"

McBride gripped Betsy firmly around the bicep, and began leading her down the sidewalk. In the approaching distance, she saw the cruiser for the first time. She was in no hurry to get there and so she dragged her feet a little. Then she went limp, more or less, slumping toward the sidewalk. McBride grabbed her at the armpits, and began to lift her back up. Betsy reacted and screamed, "Malloy!"

"Damn it to hell, I think you pierced my friggin' eardrum," said Mc-Bride. Then he said, "I didn't want to have to do this, but you forced it." He unhooked the handcuffs from his utility belt, and put one cuff on her left wrist while the other went around the corrugated steel post of a nearby parking sign. "You can twiddle your thumbs for a few minutes," he told her. "I'll be right back."

Her accomplice came bursting out of the trees on the park side of the street, running like hell to save his damsel in distress. McBride, in response, held up his right arm, palm outstretched, like a traffic cop, which he had been in the old days. Seeing the universal stop-right-now gesture, Malloy skidded to a halt at the bottom of the embankment.

"Stay right there," said the cop, walking over to him.

"What's going on, officer?"

"I've got your friend in cuffs over there," he explained. "Except for dam-aged pride, she's all right. Now, as for you …"

"We're both with the health department, here's my ID." He reached for his back pocket.

"Leave your hands where they are," rumbled McBride. "You interrupt me again, I'll have your ass on a platter. I'll talk, you listen, clear?"

"Clear."

"I know who you are and I know what you're doing here. I can't say it's a bad idea either, because this is my beat and I know what goes on in there." He jerked his head in the direction of Trey's house. "Plato's Retreat, like in New York City, that's what we've got here in our own backyard, and I don't like it."

Malloy stared as McBride went on. "We're St. Louis, not New York, and we don't need this shit operating with impunity under our noses. If that was a common whorehouse, it've been shut down long ago. Instead, it's a rich fag with the brilliant idea of bringing a bunch of other rich fags together so they can shoot their wads fourteen ways from Sunday—Jesus, what a fucking world!

"So, yeah, I know that you and Missy over there are with the health department. I know you're here to stir up some shit, make a difference in your own small way, but guess what? *This* rich fag knows some people, he was able to pull some strings, so I get word from my watch captain to keep an eye on this place because a bunch of 'anarchists' have decided to target this residence tonight."

"Anarchists?" echoed Malloy, grinning at the thought.

"Yeah, anarchists. You don't like that? How about shit-disturbers, that's what you are. Or, do you see yourself more in the vein of Henry David Thoreau, practicing civil disobedience? You seem surprised. You shouldn't be. I went to college, I took American Literature, I know a lot of things the average cop doesn't know."

He paused to size up the man standing before him. "Another thing I know? You're under a restraining order to keep clear of Herr Vonderhaar over there, five hundred feet I believe, and right now you're in violation of that order. If I were you I'd turn around and go back up that hill and make yourself scarce. Kill an hour and then come down to the station—Third District lock-up, 12th and Lynch—and collect your friend. She thinks she's under arrest, but I won't book her. Now, go."

"Great plan," offered Malloy. "Thanks a lot, sarge." He turned to leave, chugging back up the embankment.

"Malloy," the cop called after him.

He turned, ready for more grief. "Yeah?"

"One Mick to another: you'd do well to keep your nose out of this. Leave it to the police, we'll find some way to settle his hash."

FORTY-FOUR

TREY VONDERHAAR WAS ALREADY on his second mimosa when Brock Silber walked up, pulled out a chair, and sat down in a huff. No "Sorry, I'm late," just a look of petulance. Silber's condition made Trey think of a cartoon character with a dark cloud squiggled over his head.

Silber looked at Trey's mimosa covetously. "I really need a drink," he said.

"Take mine," said Trey, passing the frosty goblet, "it's delicious."

"A genuine act of kindness," said Silber. "Thank you! There's so little kindness in the world, you know. It's quite the opposite."

This luncheon was supposed to be part business, the two of them discussing better ways to exploit certain wealthy patrons of their respective circles, but Trey could see that was going to have to wait. "Tell me what happened," he said earnestly.

Silber rolled his eyes dramatically to indicate that what had happened was almost too much to bear, and that talking about it would be difficult. He took a deep breath and perorated. "That buffoon from the health department ambushed me just now as I was leaving the office. It's the second time he's come looking for me, wanting to tell me how to run my business. The first time I blew him off, but this time he had me out in the open."

The doctor took a long sigh of exasperation. "He's accusing me of providing inadequate treatment and failing to report cases of communicable disease. I stood my ground, though, and told this nitwit that any treatment ordered by me was well-researched and within current guidelines. As far as reporting, it's my professional responsibility to protect my clients from intrusion in their lives by obnoxious people such as yourself—that's what I said, it just came out. And then, and then! he shoved a piece of paper in my face, said it was a copy of the law that mandates reporting. He said the next case of syphilis that came to his attention, if that person had ties to someone seen in my office and it wasn't reported that he was going straight to the health commissioner and ask that my license be suspended. That is some nerve!"

This story caught Trey's attention for two reasons: Any mention of Malloy raised his hackles, and secondly, he had often wondered about the quality of Silber's medical practice.

Some of Silber's patients were referrals from him, casualties on the littered field of same-sex encounters, and there had been comments from these referrals that filtered back about Silber not seeming to know what he was doing, Silber being unsure of his diagnoses—same thing—Silber stopping mid-exam to take personal phone calls, and, in a couple instances, perhaps more than a couple, the once-trusting person having to seek out another physician because Silber had failed to cure whatever it was they had. Trey liked Silber well enough, he ran in the right circles, he was on everyone's A-list, but if he, Trey, were ever to get sick he would not make a beeline for Silber's shingle.

"Malloy is a wart that won't go away," said Trey.

"A big, ugly wart," agreed Silber. "I'll never forget that hideous display in Robusto's, the man standing at our table, taking you to task as if he owned you. And now, questioning my expertise, acting as though my degree in medicine meant nothing." Silber hailed a passing waiter, and ordered a double Stoli with cranberry juice and a sprig of mint. They were in Panache, a new restaurant from the renowned chef Dieter Wolbeck, who had recently struck out on his own.

Trey reached for his former mimosa. "You know, I have a restraining order against him, he can't come near me under threat of arrest. You could do the same thing. I'll give you Frank Dunaway's number, he'll make it happen."

"I don't know," said Silber. "In your case it was a personal attack, but with me it's all business. He's not harassing me as a person, but as a doctor who he thinks he needs to get in line. It'd be nice to have something to ward him off, but I'm afraid that if we were to go to a judge and make our case then all the messy details of why he's bothering me would have to come out, and I just don't need that right now."

"Understood, but just so you know, and this is between us, Shaun

Malloy, public nuisance, has had his moment of anguish."

"Really? Do tell."

Trey leaned in to Silber and spoke *sotto voce*. "Without him knowing it, I arranged for him to attend a party at which he was drugged and sexually humiliated."

"Oh, that's rich!" said the doctor.

"Not rape in the sense of forcible entry," Trey emphasized, "that would be criminal. But a sloppy blowjob in front of an enthusiastic audience. Malloy awoke to find a leech on his prick, a long-haired leech named Drew—a twisted mind, that one. You should've seen the look on Malloy's face when he realized the knob-gobbler was a man."

"You were there?"

"No, I have it on video! It's priceless."

"May I see it sometime? It'll help the next time he comes by. I could needle him with it and maybe he'd leave me alone."

"I don't care if you watch it," said Trey, "and I don't care if you use it against him, fine by me. Just don't let on that I was behind it. He likely already suspects as much, but if he hears it directly he might go ballistic, and forget about the restraining order."

Silber put his little finger to his lips, smacked it, and held it aloft. "Pinky swear," he said. "Now let's eat."

"My thoughts exactly, I'm famished. Oh, by the way, I've invited another person here today. Mark Walter, aide to the mayor, quite the gadabout. You'll like him, he's fairly entertaining."

"I know who he is," said Silber, "a bigger lush than both of us put together."

"Yeah, but he can't hold it as well," snickered Trey.

The doctor's expressive brown eyes narrowed with suspicion. "You didn't invite him to try to hook us up, did you?"

"That wasn't my intention, no, but if you like what you see, he's on board with it."

"And how do you know that?" wondered Silber.

"A little bird told me," said Trey.

"Really? And would this little bird hope to feather his nest with my affections?"

Trey, reddening, "Oh, come on!"

"With your knack for matchmaking, I wouldn't doubt it."

"Wouldn't dream of it, old egg, wouldn't dream of it."

FORTY-FIVE

FRIDAY MORNING just after eight, Malloy was at a red light at Grand and Chouteau, the buildings of Midtown within sight. His desk and off-kilter swivel chair at the health department were pining for him. His pouch was on the seat next to him, and he was flipping through the ERs to see who he might try later during his afternoon field time.

Of those he was tasked with getting into the clinic for an exam and/or treatment, you could pretty much break down into four basic categories: those who would willingly comply, those who would comply only after so much coercion, those who would fight him with all they had, and, finally, those who might comply if he knew where to find them. Aside from the cooperativeness of any given contact, there was also the time factor. Every name on every ER had a deadline, a set duration before the case was disposed one way or another, four to six weeks, depending on priority. Thank god for that, otherwise they'd be running some of these contacts forever. He made note of eight or nine individuals to go after this day—a mix of optimistic, pessimistic, and coming down to the wire.

The radio was on KMOX and the national news had wrapped up, followed by commercials for a roofing company, "For a hole in your roof or a whole new roof "—nice jingle—and a car dealership, "Remember, if it isn't right, I'll make it right"—great pledge, if kept—and now the local news came on. KMOX was the voice of the beloved Cardinals, home games broadcast via 50,000 watts to literally millions of fans in Missouri and several neighboring states, and accordingly the station gave more than ample coverage to the team's exploits.

At the moment, a very enthused sports guy was recapping the game against the rival Chicago Cubs from the night before. The Cubs had a one-run lead for several innings and then Tommy Herr had doubled in the sixth. The catcher, Darrell Porter, a guy who never saw a fastball or a change-up he didn't like, drove in both Herr and Lonnie Smith with a homer. In the ninth, Willie McGee, newcomer and shortstop extraordinaire, knocked another homer, driving in Ozzie Smith. The broadcast segued to a sound bite of Jack Buck's jubilant summation: "Go crazy, folks, go crazy!" The Cubbies went down five-one.

With only a few games left, the Cards were 90-65 on the season and it looked as though they were heading to the playoffs. They played the Cubs again today, first pitch 1:10.

The light turned green and Malloy hit the pedal. A day game, he thought, how convenient. He had business with a certain mascot who would most definitely be present. It was just a matter of getting to him in front of thousands of rabid fans and informing him that he was a contact to GC.

It really galled him that the Cardinals' management covered for this goofball, wouldn't lift a finger to help get a message to him, wouldn't even reveal his identity, as if he were some spoiled rock star. At the next red light, the redundant Forest Park Parkway, Malloy flipped through his ERs once more and found the one for Fredbird. Along the margin, he had penciled in a note to self: The bigger the bird, the harder the fall.

He got through the morning with his usual pluck, first checking in with all sections of the clinic to see what was up. The patient load was average, the waiting room more like a library than a zoo. The clinicians were in good spirits, the female nurses and phlebotomists in the break room before the patient onslaught, comparing notes on their troublesome men. Wassermann, fussing with his test tubes and culture media and gram stains, took Malloy aside to listen to a poem he'd composed: To A *Gonococcus Dying Young*.

"You like it?" he asked, hopefully. "You probably know what it's based on."

"It's Sonny Corleone's last words before they cut him into Swiss cheese," guessed Malloy.

"No, it's an homage to the A.E. Housman poem, *To An Athlete Dying Young*. 'The time you won your town the race, we chaired you through the marketplace.'"

"I knew that," said Malloy. "Me and A.E. go way back."

"Malloy?"

"Yeah, Mike."

"I think you're wanted in the epi room."

Four hours and six GC interviews later, he was heading for the parking lot. It was a beautiful summer day, brimming with promise. Timba sat in a lawn chair outside his matchbox shack reading a Jim Thompson pulp,

The Killer Inside Me. "This guy's the real deal," Timba told Malloy. "He is to crime fiction what Ali is to boxing." Malloy asked to see it. He studied the cover, a montage of what he supposed was the killer in poses both menacing and brooding. At lower left was the bloody corpse of one of his victims. Set off from the illustration was a quote pulled from the lurid text within: "You see?—I had to destroy them."

"He had to kill them?" asked Malloy. "Couldn't he just cuff them upside the head. Taking a life, that's pretty drastic."

"No, man. He *had* to kill them because he's a sick fuck and he's a deputy sheriff in a small town. He can get away with it. You want to borrow it when I'm done?"

"I still haven't read the other one you gave me."

"You need to read more, Shaun. It'll relax you, take your mind off all those big bad problems."

"Time is the problem, there's not enough of it to go around. Reading is a luxury I don't often have."

"That's what Hemingway said, too."

"That reading is a luxury? Why would a writer say that?"

"No, he said that time is what we have the least of."

He paid the $14 at the gate and was given a ticket in the nosebleed section. But that wasn't where he was going to stay. His plan was to sight Fredbird somewhere in the stands, get to him, and get his attention. He climbed up the bleachers, found his seat, and got a $5 beer from a vendor. Tipped the man a buck. He took out a pocket notebook and jotted his expenses: $20 so far here in the stadium and $10 for the parking garage. A day at the ballpark probably wouldn't qualify on his monthly expense report, but he'd try anyway.

The stands were a sea of red which roared and swelled when the Cardinals came on the field. The announcer said the attendance today was 53,670, thanks in great part to Girl Scout Day at the Ballpark. Malloy looked around and sure enough there was a gaggle of them right down below, prepubescent girls in uniform with patch-bedecked sashes, flanked by some comely moms. These den leaders occupied the seats next to the aisles, the better to manage the nearly continuous potty breaks that would arise. The scouts themselves were giddy to say the least, squealing and jumping up and down and spilling popcorn as the Redbirds were introduced. Cheerleaders in training.

It was the top of the second inning and still no sign of The Bird. Malloy started to worry that he'd called in sick or got hit by a truck on the way in. And if this was the case, did a mascot have an understudy? There would be no way to know; the costume was a cloak of anonymity.

All around, people were going nuts. Every pitch, every swing of the bat, every throw to first, safe or out, brought exaggerated reaction; to Malloy, a social anthropologist by training, this heightened response was an interesting example of crowd mentality; every "ooh!" and "ahh!" building on each other in a crescendo of frenzied emotion until the whole place was ready to explode. That he was prone to analyzing the actions of rabid baseball fans did not mean he was critical of them; if anything, he was jealous.

In his home town, depending on where your family's loyalties lay, you might have grown up a Cubs fan, a White Sox fan, or even a Detroit Tigers fan. He, himself, liked the Tigers back when Al Kaline, Hank Aguirre, and Norm Cash ran the show. Thinking on it, Malloy realized that fandom was strictly a matter of geography and cultural familiarity. A mid-northern Indiana city such as Kokomo would relate more to sports teams based in the Rust Belt rather than in the Corn Belt. To a Hoosier like himself, St. Louis was a "Southern city," evidenced by sweltering summers and the tendency of certain locals to say "y'all." It was also a city where your baseball team was picked for you. Here, every man, woman, and child was born a Cardinals fan; it was their birthright.

Now it was the bottom of the third, the Redbirds were at bat, and there was a commotion over near the third base line. Aha! In the stands, riling up the crowd to an even greater frenzy, the familiar figure of Fredbird was getting up close and personal with the fans. Malloy rose from his seat and hastened to the scene far below. But when he tried to enter the section, he was stopped by an usher who asked to see his ticket.

"I'm sorry, I can't let you in," declared the small, earnest black man as old as God. "You're in the bleachers, up there." He pointed to a cloud.

Without missing a beat, Malloy said, "Yeah, I know where I am, but my dad's down there, a season ticket-holder, and I've got to tell him something important."

"Can it wait until the seventh-inning stretch?"

"No, it cannot. His sister, my aunt, has had a coronary. He'll want to be at the hospital."

The usher looked him up and down. He'd heard every fib in the book, people hoping to scam him to get closer to the game. "Against my own better judgment," he told him, "I'll assume you're on the level. Don't even think to bullshit me, you hear?"

"Thanks, man." Malloy started down the steps, his mission closer to becoming reality.

The usher called after him, "Five minutes, no longer!"

He got down there and Fredbird was pulling some guy's leg, tugging on it, twisting away, like maybe it would actually come off. What a weird job, thought Malloy. He got to a cross aisle and moved along the railing.

Closer, closer. Now Fredbird was in the midst of a Girl Scout troop, and he had some scout's head completely engulfed by his big yellow beak. Her arms were flailing and legs kicking. Hard to say if she was panicked or if that was her way of going with it. Fredbird made a show of opening and closing the beak like he was eating her head.

That didn't last long. Fredbird released the girl, and began doing a chicken dance, pumping his legs and flapping his "wings" to thundering cheers and applause. Malloy walked up and tapped him on the shoulder. Fredbird ignored him. Malloy tapped him harder, this time holding an unsealed envelope with a note inside.

"Siddown!" came the chorus. It was very uncool to mess with Fredbird.

When, at last, Fredbird regarded him, Malloy thrust the envelope at him. He took it in his claw, and did an impression of mock astonishment. Raucous laughter. Malloy cupped both hands around his mouth, shouted in his ear, "I've been trying to reach you about a public health matter. You need to read this letter. Put it in your pocket—do you have a pocket?"

He pointed to his ear or something approximating an ear, and wagged his big goofy head side-to-side: What say? Pantomime, of course.

"Public health!" Malloy shouted louder than before.

"Siddown!" Now hands were reaching out to yank him away.

Real birds don't have shoulders, but this one shrugged his as he handed the envelope to a random Girl Scout who was sitting idly nearby, enjoying her grape Slushie. She opened it as Fredbird moved on down the row, that stupid grin permanently fixed on his avian face.

Ten-year-old Allison Mottert was an exceptionally bright bulb and she was quite curious as to what Fredbird had given her. Deftly, she removed the letter from the envelope, being careful not to tear anything as she intended to place this keepsake in her special scrapbook. With her best friend, Bridget, looking over her shoulder, Allison unfolded the note. The first thing she saw was the letterhead that read CITY OF ST. LOUIS DIVISION OF HEALTH: PREVENTION AND CONTROL CENTER. "Uh oh," Allison said. Then she read aloud the contents of the typewritten letter:

"Dear Fred Bird, I have been trying to reach you for some time to inform you that you have been exposed to a communicable disease that could result in serious consequences, if left untreated ..."

Allison turned to Bridget and crinkled her nose. "Gross!"

"That's so tacky," said Bridget.

Allison continued, "Please call me ASAP to arrange for a free and confidential check-up at our modern clinic. Thank you in advance for your cooperation. Shaun Malloy, Investigator." Allison held the letter out with thumb and forefinger like you'd hold a dead mouse by its tail just before dropping it in the trash. "Ewww!" she exclaimed.

"Let me see that," said their den mother, who also happened to be Allison's mom.

Malloy was too far away to retrieve his carefully crafted letter. Watching the Girl Scouts toy with it, he wondered if he had made a mistake going about it this way. That was right before he saw the skeptical usher and a burly security guard coming for him.

FORTY-SIX

MALLOY GOT UP for good around five, made some instant Folgers, splashed his face with water from the tap, and sat at the kitchen table thinking. It had been a night of tossing and turning, a fitful six hours of discomfort and vexation. The beers and Buffalo wings he'd so lustily consumed at Harpo's likely had something to do with his current shitty condition, but there was something else as well. A gnawing feeling that something wasn't right throughout his entire system.

He hadn't felt his usual robust self lately. It took effort to climb the flight of stairs leading to his apartment, and there was wheezing involved. Afternoons, he found himself fatigued and he was tempted to go home and lay down. There was muscle tension, joint pain, and a general feeling of malaise. He could easily believe he was coming down with AIDS—

"coming down with" sounded like nothing worse than a cold!—but he wasn't ready to believe that just yet.

It could be allergies. Ever since he was a kid, he'd suffered terribly from late summer to early fall, ragweed and goldenrod, his eyes so crusted with matter upon waking that they were glued shut. "I'm blind," he would call out, and his mom would put a warm, wet washcloth to his face so he could see again. And this could be nothing more than allergies, he told himself, because some of his current symptoms were allergy-type symptoms and, besides, moving to a new climate as he had could change things quite a bit; new allergens, new antibodies, symptoms altered from what he was used to.

Time would tell if this was a seasonal thing, but if it wasn't and it turned out to be something else, something pernicious and unrecoverable, well, he knew what he would do. He would go after Trey Vonderhaar and his toady Freddie and even that prick Drew Conger and bust their asses good.

The stairs at work were equally arduous as those at home so Malloy took the elevator. "Hold that door," he called, and from within an arm reached out to stop the door from closing. The arm belonged to Prudence Calder, the health commissioner, a person that Malloy knew only in passing. He had seen her several times in the clinic, usually talking to Joe about something, and he thought she carried herself well. She was an MD, he knew, and he was curious whether she had ever practiced hands-on medicine or if she'd gravitated to public health early on, making her bones running a departmental division like Mohammed Shafi ran the clinical section of the VD division.

It was just the two of them. She said hello and he returned the salutation. She followed that with, "Don't you work on the second floor, an investigator?" He affirmed. She then asked how things were going. Was she just making chit-chit, not really wanting any detailed answer beyond some trite remark? He looked in her keen blue eyes and decided she really wanted to know. "Things are less than great," he informed. "First, there's so much VD out there and so few investigators to tackle it that we feel we're barely making a dent. You can feel the frustration in the epi room."

"Welcome to public health," fraternally. "What else?"

The elevator stopped at two, and the door opened. He looked at her and she looked at him. "Your call," she said.

"It'll wait," he answered. The door closed and cables hummed again. "Of course, recalcitrants are always a problem, but you would expect that with street people and low-income groups. People who would no sooner listen to common sense words from a health officer than they would stop running when a cop says Halt! It turns out that with the poor and disenfranchised, non-compliance with authority, no matter how well-meaning that authority may be, stems from an anticipation of the high they're going to experience when they've told the guy from the VD clinic to buzz off. In their world, devoid of meaningful accomplishment, it's a feeling of empowerment, however brief.

"But you wouldn't expect serious problems from a group of well-educated, professional people. At least that was my assumption once upon a time. The obstinance in the well-educated, who should know better, comes from a different place, a deep-seated arrogance that says, Who the hell are you to tell me what to do? They're up there, and we're down here—they want to make sure you know that. That's my theory anyway."

"It's an earful," Prudence Calder remarked, "and well considered. You came up with this on your own?"

"A degree in social anthropology probably helped."

"I should've guessed. I have fond memories of my anthropology class." She paused momentarily, caught up in a reminiscence, then she got back on track. "And these advantaged people causing you problems, they have names you can share? I may know them."

The elevator door opened. "Eighth floor, my stop," she said. "Care to continue this conversation in my office?"

He liked Dr. Calder's office. The little sofa was comfy, and she had a splendid view overlooking Powell Symphony Hall and, beyond that, North Grand in all its faded glory. She also had some quaint knick-knacks, like a collection of vintage eye-droppers and some ancient tapeworms in laboratory bottles, pickled in formaldehyde. A decree from her late, late predecessor, Health Commissioner Charles Banting, listing measures to be enacted during the St. Louis Cholera Epidemic of 1866 hung over her desk. Rendered portraits of Louis Pasteur, William Osler, Paul Ehrlich, and William John de Hunte Lyster were framed nearby—doctors all, and giants of public health. Her version of rock stars, he thought.

Best of all was the dialogue between them—incisive, thoughtful, forthright. He told of the Man 2 Man quandary, though he left out certain details such as being on the receiving end of a court order served in the clinic. Although, gossip being the primary currency in this building, he guessed she might already know that. When he broached the problem of Dr. Brock Silber, her eyes lit up, causing him to wonder. As much as he hated to, he cut it short. It was Monday morning and that meant Chalk Talk in the conference room downstairs. She said she would look into these issues and get back to him. They shook hands and he left feeling as though he had just had a meaningful talk with a true colleague.

Schuler presented the case of a young woman at Washington University. Student by day, enterprising hooker at night. She advertised herself as a masseuse in the back pages of a local free tabloid. Schuler had circled her ad with a Sharpie and passed it around as an indictment. "You do so much for others," it read, "now it's your turn! Sexy, voluptuous, gorgeous face. My sensual hands will bring you to unmatched levels of excitement as I stroke every inch. Available evenings and weekends. Outcalls only."

"It's a living," Arnold shrugged, passing the paper to Betsy.

"It's a living with a serious occupational hazard," added Schuler. "She turned up with a hot case of the clap, and she's probably infected scores of guys."

"Maybe she doesn't let them screw her," said Martha, "maybe she just gets them off with her hands or mouth."

"That's another occupational hazard," said Schuler. "Being alone with strange men who have no qualms about using force. In our interview she said how she noticed during one 'massage' that the client had a drip. She asked him about it and he said it was just semen, pre-ejaculate. She said it didn't look right and she wouldn't do him even with a rubber. That was when he forced himself on her."

"She go to the police?" asked Joe.

Schuler wagged his head no. "She didn't want the hassle. Said she'd be more selective in the future."

"How can she do that?" wondered Betsy. "She can't know what kind of jerk she's dealing with until she gets in the room with him face to face."

"Good point," said Malloy. "But here's an idea. She could initiate a selection process. Before saying yes to a john—I mean, client—she could ask for a photo, three references, and an essay titled 'What Sensual Stroking Means to Me.'"

Joe broke in. "Okay, bullshit aside. We're way off point now. What we care about is clamping down the lid on this Pandora's box. How many findable names did you get, Leo?"

"As you can imagine with a hooker, real names don't get exchanged. But she did go to their homes in many cases and the rest she met at hotels. We did a ride-along on Saturday and she pointed out five places where she remembers going. Two of them are apartment buildings and she wasn't sure of the unit. Not only that, she gets them mixed up, can't remember exactly which guy lived in which place. So if she does give a description, it may or may not be the guy who actually lives in that particular house or apartment. So, that's the problem. We've got a few good locations, but the contact within those walls—sketchy, for sure. I mean, the best I can do is knock on their door and ask if they've entertained a pretty woman named Delilah in the last few weeks."

"Delilah?"

"Her hooker name," Schuler told Arnold. "She got it from the Bible."

"Jesus H. Christ," spat Joe, "a Bible-toting pro. You'd think Mary Magdalene would be a better fit."

"Mary Magdalene reformed as a slut and became a saint," said Betsy, "but Delilah was the supreme temptress. She betrayed Samson, who loved her, and she did it for money. So, really, Delilah is the right name."

"Okay," groused Joe, "we're off-point again, and it's my fault for encouraging this Bible study. Leo, do your best with this thing, and stay on it. She's got contacts her own age, college kids, find out who they are."

"Will do," said Schuler.

"I bet I know what her major is," said Tut.

"What in the Sam Hill are you talking about?" Joe, flummoxed.

"Delilah, I bet you her major in school is Interpersonal Relations. Heh, heh!"

"That would almost be funny in a room full of retards," said Joe.

"Developmentally disabled, Joe," corrected Betsy, mildly. "'Retard' is on the way out, it's considered derogatory."

"What, to other retards? Whatever." Joe glanced at Tutweiler slumped in his chair and once again was reminded how much he looked like the cartoon character Baby Huey. "Derald, you're so chipper today. Why don't you go next. What's on your scope?"

Tut spoke without rising. "Aw, you guys don't want to hear my case, it's pretty bad."

Karl, silent until now, said to Joe, "I was going to tell you about this, but there wasn't time on Friday. It happened at the end of the day."

"What happened?" Joe fixing Tut with a look of disdain already.

Tut gulped and began, "Oh, I got a call from the clinic. They'd just diagnosed and treated a case of primary. I went and got him, put him in the interview room, but I forgot my pencil. You can't do an interview without a pencil, right? So I went to the epi room to get it, and when I came back he was gone."

"Tell me you found him wandering around the halls," said Joe.

"No such luck," interjected Karl, "he absconded. We checked the address the guy gave on his intake and Derald and I drove there, over on Finney near Spring, and it was a bad address. Now we're trying to track him down by his name, but that may be fake as well."

Joe was not placated by these feeble attempts to right a grievous wrong. He bore the entire weight of his considerable scorn down on Tut. "How could you let this happen?"

"I guess I suck," said Tut.

"You guess? I'd say it's a goddamn certainty! Shitfire, how am I gonna explain this to Montecalvo?" John Montecalvo was Joe's boss, a GS-18 in the state capital, Jefferson City. Joe was pissed, no doubt about it, and the others cowered in fear or at least braced themselves, expecting him to explode any second. But he surprised them, saying to Tut evenly, "I'll see you in my office after this."

Tut, treading on extremely thin ice, ventured, "Are you going to fire me?"

Joe pursed his lips, and said, "Not here in front of everyone."

"You may as well," said Tut, resignedly. "Sooner than later, it doesn't matter. I don't think I'm cut out for this work anyway. Too much pressure. You won't mind if I start to clean out my desk now?" He rose and started for the door.

"Wait!" said Malloy. "You can't fire him."

"Why not? He's a screw up, a constant screw up, and it's long overdue."

"Yeah," said Betsy, "but he's our screw up. Without Tut, morale will be like a flat tire."

The others said as much, too. They wanted Joe to give Derald Tutweiler another chance.

"Nope," said Joe. "I won't tolerate ineptitude. Insubordination, maybe, depending on my mood that day. But not ineptitude. Tell your excuses to the other poor saps in the unemployment line."

At that moment, the door burst open and Judy Parker, one of the nurse practitioners, barged in. "We've got an emergency in the clinic," she said, out of breath from hustling her 250-pound frame down the hall. "Anaphylactic reaction, he's wrecking the place!"

By the time they reached the clinic most of the damage was already done. The entire clinic staff was gathered three deep just outside of an examining room door. Inside, a patient named Charles Meriwether was putting on a one-man show, bludgeoning everything in sight with a three-foot metal stool. It was the textbook definition of a man gone berserk. Several of the clinicians were calling out to Meriwether, telling him to calm down, that he was having a severe reaction to the penicillin they'd given him. If he would only stop swinging that stool and throwing things, they could get him the medicine he needed and it would all be over.

Meriwether's glazed eyes and monomania with property destruction should have told them that he wasn't listening to anything they said. He had lost his sense of reason approximately five minutes after being injected with penicillin G as treatment for the gonorrhea that had brought him to the clinic.

The clinic staff was quite dutiful in trying to prevent these episodes. Like every patient under care, Meriwether had been explicitly asked about any previous reaction to medication, and Meriwether answered "No, never." But Meriwether had forgotten that long ago, at the age of fourteen, he had been treated with injectable penicillin for a festering infection on his leg, at which time his body produced antibodies against it. Those antibodies, still vigilant after so much time, were now locked in mortal battle with the penicillin/allergen which it saw as the enemy.

Crash! Meriwether brought the stool down on a glass shelf, sending blood-filled test tubes into space. The adrenaline coursing through his bloodstream made him do it. But now it appeared as though he was winding down. His breathing had grown laborious and he actually released his weapon, the stool falling to the floor with a clatter. He backed up to a corner. His eyes rolled, fixed on the ceiling, and he started to swoon. The clinicians saw their chance.

They swarmed the exam room, began to close in on him. Meriwether might have qualified as an animal at bay, except that he was unaware of them. "Hold on, brother," said Mohammed Shafi in a soothing voice, "we're going to take care of you. You'll be all right. We just need to get you on the table." He looked to the others standing by, gave an order: "I need at least three people to move him on this table so I can give him the epinephrine. Gently, move him gently. If he starts to bite or turn violent again, throw a sheet over him. Got it?"

Malloy, Arnold, and Mike Wassermann did the transfer; Meriwether had turned to a sack of grain. Now that he was horizontal on the exam table, Shafi wasted no time in readying the antidote. "Turn his head in case he vomits, and hold him tight," said the doctor. "Here we go." Shafi plunged a needle into one thigh and pressed the plunger down. Epinephrine made its way into Meriwether's bloodstream and began to tell the antibodies, "Battle's over, back to your stations." Shafi repeated the action with another dose in the same thigh.

As if on cue, two paramedics from the St. Louis Fire Department walked in. Shafi gave them a quick rundown as they intubated Meriwether and strapped him to a gurney. The room had cleared out and most of the staff had gone back to what they'd been doing before all the commotion. Some had taken the opportunity for a smoke out on the fire escape.

"Just another day in the clinic," said Mike Wassermann, wryly.

"You can't buy this kind of entertainment," added Arnold.

"At least it got us out of Chalk Talk," said Malloy, watching the paramedics wheel the gurney down the hall toward the elevator. "Going after Tut, singling him out, that's not right."

"Joe's always had a hard-on for Tut," said Arnold.

Schuler, standing nearby, overheard. "Hey, I like Tut as a person—we all do—but c'mon, you've got to admit he hasn't carried his weight for a long time."

"I heard that," said Tut, lumbering up.

Giving Schuler a start. "Oh, shit, I'm sorry."

"Hey, I can't be pissed at someone for telling the truth, can I?" The others saw that Tut was amused by Schuler's discomfort.

"Good old Tut," said Arnold, giving him a squeeze on the shoulder. "What'll you do now? I hear there's an opening for a burger flipper over at Wendy's."

"Hilarious," said Tut. "Know what? This is my golden opportunity. I'm gonna follow a dream I've had for years now. After this, my days are mine. I've decided to become a WWF wrestler."

"No shit!" from Wassermann. "Like Hulk Hogan or the Junkyard Dog?"

"Yeah, Ric Flair, Jake the Snake, the Von Erichs—those guys are awesome. But I'm more into costumes, the crazier the better. Think Legion of Doom, and you'll know where I'm at."

Said Malloy, "We'll see you in the ring, man, throwing guys around like firewood. Can't wait."

"Me neither. It's a brand new chapter in my oddball life. Gotta go, that junk in my desk can wait. Great workin' with you." He started off, but then stopped and turned. "Tell you one thing, though. Joe's had a hard-on for lots of people, not just me. I mean, look at the turnover."

FORTY-SEVEN

TREY VONDERHAAR found himself in the condiment aisle studying mustards. He counted thirty-nine varieties not including Durkee's, which may or may not be a mustard. Up ahead, he saw a familiar figure down on his haunches, stocking shelves. Upon hearing his name, Hal rose and gave a friendly greeting, asking how he might help.

Straub's on North Kingshighway was that kind of place, a gourmet grocery with eager-to-please employees who would not only direct you to the portobello mushrooms but deliver a soliloquy on the virtues of said fungi. Their produce was always shined, if it could be shined, and spotless; their delicatessen had the final say in defining "savory," featuring the best chicken salad in town and no less than eight different soups each day. Their butcher shop offered only the best cuts of meat and seafood, readily snapped up by the discriminating patrons living in million-dollar homes on the private streets across Kingshighway and in the luxury suites of the Chase Park Plaza next door. Everything from artichokes to Chilean sea bass to tins of Bremner Wafers was displayed tastefully, tantalizingly, not one item out of place. It was a pleasure to spend extravagantly there, buying things you didn't even know you wanted, for to be seen shopping at Straub's was almost the equivalent of being seen at a table in Robusto's on a Friday night.

Trey told Hal that he was looking for something that would make a great steak taste even better. Barbecuing? asked Hal. Trey had never thought to get an outdoor grill; it seemed like so much bother. Eduardo would probably like his steaks grilled, but who would do the honors? He couldn't see himself in an apron, a picture of a pig on the front, holding a long wooden-handled fork to spear some charred meat. Ugh. Did Freddie know how to barbecue?

"Well, I hadn't planned on it," he told Hal. "I was going to broil the steak in the oven. That's what I've done in the past."

"I see," said Hal with a hint of disappointment. "Well, we've probably got every sauce, glaze, marinade, and seasoning ever made in the civilized world." Hal took a container off the shelf; it read Snider's Prime Rib and Roast. "This is one of the old standbys, just add a little garlic and oil. In my opinion, you don't want much. I like to let the beef do the talking, not the seasoning."

Trey wondered if the beef reference was a double entendre; probably not, but since he and Hal had some history—he'd been shopping here for years—he decided to reveal his purpose in asking. "I've got a friend coming from Brazil and I want to treat him to something nice. At least one fantastic meal at home, and after that it'll be restaurants and steak houses. The best ones St. Louis has to offer."

"He must be a good friend to merit that kind of treatment."

"He is," said Trey, confidentially, "he's my special friend."

"Special friends are nice," said Hal with a knowing wink.

Malloy reached for the phone on the wall in the kitchen. "Hold on, I'm chewing," he said, and put the phone down. To the mystery caller, it sounded like "*Hode awn om choon.*" Malloy chewed faster and washed down the Braunschweiger sandwich with a big gulp of milk.

"Okay, I'm here," he told the receiver.

"You sure?" said Teri Kincaid.

"Oh, yeah. I came home to change clothes and have a little snack before going out for libation."

"Where you heading?"

"McDowell's I suppose. You want to join me?"

"Can't," she said, "I've got a date, believe it or not, a pipe-fitter with biceps like a tree trunk."

"A pipe-fitter, huh? Any chance he'll be fitting his pipe tonight?"

"Ha. You should leave comedy to people who are actually funny. No, the reason why I called, you remember we talked about that job in Lafayette

Square, the one involving a certain mansion on the corner?"

"Yeah?"

"Well, if you're good to go, I am, too."

"I didn't forget. It's an option I'm weighing. But why are you champing at the bit?"

"I'm bored," she said like she was really bored, "it's that simple. Work has fallen off, I'm in the doldrums. Perps are still getting arrested, but they must be going somewhere else for their bonds. I need something to take my mind off the overdue rent on this office."

"The last woman who tried to help me straighten out the owner of that home got arrested as a prostitute."

"So I heard. That's fucked up, but it won't happen to me. Or to you, because we won't get caught. I'm that good."

"It's good that you're willing, but listen. I spoke with the health commissioner about Vonderhaar, what he's doing and what we can do about it. She's giving it thought, so we should wait and see what she comes up with."

"I see," she said. "But in the meantime it wouldn't hurt to stake the place out. We'd have to do that anyway, note their routine. That's standard operating. So you see, we don't have to act now, just prepare to act."

"You're the only one I know who enjoys sitting in a car for hours on end."

"*Amat victoria curam.*"

"I know! 'Victory equals' … mm, something. Ah, it's been ten years since I sat in Mr. Crossett's Latin class."

"Victory loves preparation. Don't you agree?"

FORTY-EIGHT

"Don't you have any Stones or Doors or even The Who? There's nothing in this box except shitkicker music."

Teri gave a look that told him he was a fool. "Shitkicker's another name for cowboy boots—you know that? And to you cowboy boots mean backwoods music. Is that it? I didn't take you for such an elitist. If you had spent any time in some of the better clubs, you'd know that country music is hot these days. It's got a nice twang to it, which gives it a country sound, granted. But it's also part rock and bluegrass. Try it, you'll like it."

"But they're still singing about the same old stuff. His pickup broke down, the bank's about to foreclose on the trailer, his woman left him and he can't get drunk enough to forget her."

"You're back in the woebegone days of Hank Williams and Eddy Arnold," she said, putting the binoculars to her peepers. "This stuff's different, way more upbeat."

"Here's Alabama, we'll go with that." He popped the 8-track in the tape deck on the dash. Nothing. "I think it needs some juice," he muttered.

"Yeah, right," distractedly. She put down her binoculars and turned the key. They were parked on Lafayette this time, facing west toward Missouri Avenue and zeroed in on the front of the house. Beside them, the spreading branches of a gigantic pin oak draped over the fence and the sidewalk, forming a leafy umbrella and partly obscuring Teri's red F-150. They were engaged in seeing, but determined not to be seen.

This was day two. They were staking out the house in two-hour increments, spanning an agreed-upon total of twelve hours. Today was three to five, yesterday had been one to three, and tomorrow would be five to seven. And so it went. Malloy found two-hour stints hard to take. He didn't have the temperament to be stationary for long. Without Teri's company, he'd have lost his mind.

There was a gas station a few blocks over on Jefferson and, if nature called, they wouldn't be gone long, five minutes tops.

When they completed the circuit on day six, they would start over from the beginning, do another twelve hours if necessary, to see if there were any consistencies to what they had seen previously. So far, they hadn't seen much coming or going; a few delivery trucks, the letter-carrier around noon, Freddie watering shrubs in the yard. No sign of Trey Vonderhaar, but the window of watchfulness had not been very lengthy. They were just getting started.

"The music's okay," declared Malloy, "not too whiny, but that's a stupid name for a band. What if every state had a band named after it? 'Let's give a big round of applause to North Dakota!' Give me a break. There's a jillion cool band names just waiting to be picked. Why go with something so mundane?"

"Some states make better band names than others. What's your idea of a cool band name?"

"Talking Heads, of course. They were a band without a name and one day they're watching TV with the sound off, the news or some talk show, and David Byrne says, 'What do you see, exactly? Break it down.' Heads talking, nothing else. Talking Heads, I love it."

"I like the name Nitty Gritty Dirt Band," she said. "It's so ... earthy."

"Add water, you've got The Mud Band."

"Here we go," said Teri evenly. "Look what just came out."

Malloy leaned forward, squinted. "The man himself and his canine companion, the leg humper."

"Out for a walk," she guessed, "and it's a big park."

Malloy checked his watch. "Three twenty. Makes sense. He's a trader, and the market just closed. This could be a routine."

"Let's hope they head clockwise or else we're made."

"They are, they're heading away from us. Do we follow or what?"

"No, we move out of position, on that side street over there. If he passes this way going back, he won't see us. We'll time how long he's gone."

"There's a sidewalk around the park, but, inside the park, paths going every which way. There's a big field not far from here where dogs like to romp, meet other dogs, fall in love, whatever. Maybe they're going there."

Malloy sensed movement. In the rear view he saw the white-and-blue cruiser approaching slowly, sort of sneaking up on them. It stopped just parallel to the pickup. Malloy waved, and the cop acknowledged. McBride put the cruiser in park, got out, circled the vehicle, his expression quizzical. "Afternoon," he said, edging up to Teri's window, "nice day, huh?"

He's being coy, Malloy thought, but I'll go with it. "Afternoon sergeant. On patrol?"

"There's a brilliant guess." He stepped forward, close enough to look into the cab. Teri had already concealed the binoculars. "At it again, are we? Who's your accomplice this time?"

"Theresa Kincaid, officer. Pleased to meet you."

"Ms. Kincaid—may I call you Ms?—are you aware that Mr. Malloy here is under a restraining order to say away from Mr. Vonderhaar over there?"

"Yes I am, officer."

"Good," said McBride. "The rule is five hundred feet. Closer than that he's in violation, and I take him in. Do you feel as though you're outside the zone of protection?"

"I can't say, because I don't know where the center of this circumference is."

"You want to play dumb? Okay." McBride extended his arm and, like Horace Greeley, pointed west. "That house there on the corner is point zero.

The petitioner's residence."

"Oh, that. I'd say we're probably seven hundred feet from that," she told him.

McBride appeared to be taking measurements in his head. "I'm not good at distances," he admitted, "but one thing I do know: you're pushing it, Malloy. You're pushing the terms of the court order and you're pushing me. What did I tell you when we last parted?"

"Let the police handle it, you'll find some way to cook his goose."

"Settle his hash is what I said. Look, you may be legit right now, sitting here all innocent, but your agenda smells funky. You're up to something, and I don't like it." He gave them his "just try me" look and returned to his idling cruiser. "Oh," he called with a crisp snap of his fingers, "the reason I stopped to begin with? This is angled parking here, right front wheel to the curb. You're parallel parked."

After McBride left Teri moved the pickup to a side street across the way. At 4:02, they saw Trey Vonderhaar and Roscoe walking along the path just inside the perimeter of the park, lagging behind other dog walkers. At precisely 4:06 they saw them cross the threshold of Trey's castle and go inside.

FORTY-NINE

It was a little before nine on a Thursday and Joe Sargent was at his desk going through mail and memos that had accumulated. He had his coffee and his chocolate-covered peanuts. He had the radio on low volume so that only he could hear, tuned to his favorite oldies station. He had his reading glasses, his pencil sharpened in case he needed to jot something down. He was the epitome of a highly efficient upper-level bureaucrat.

There were the usual solicitations from various businesses and services that wanted a piece of the pie. A paper supply company, not the one they already used, hoping to insert their product line into the clinic's prodigious consumption of paper. Wastebasket. An application for an American Express card, telling him he was "already approved." Wastebasket. A personalized letter from a salesman with Office Solutions, wanting to drop by and discuss the purchase of some tables and chairs. Wastebasket. A new catalog from a scientific instrument company; he looked at that for a while, bookmarked a couple pages.

Here was a handwritten letter from a past patient addressed to "Person

In Charge." That would be me, Joe mused. With several comical misspellings, it told how this person had come to the clinic reluctantly and only because she could not afford "a real doctor." But once here she was made to feel at ease and was even impressed with the quality of care she received. The man who examined her—that would be one of the two physician's assistants—had a "special tinder touch in the you-no-where area." She was now a fan of the city VD clinic, recommending it to her friends. And "you kin bet" the next time she caught "something nasty" she would be sure to return.

He put that letter into a certain file marked COMPLIMENTS. He would have to remember to show these letters to John Montecalvo during their next quarterly meeting; unsolicited endorsements such as these would be another feather in his cap.

Now Joe was getting to the bottom of the pile. Here was an inter-office folder, an oversized manila envelope that had made the rounds through various departments over many months. The face of it had rows of rectangular boxes. The instructions at the top read: CROSS OUT PREVIOUS NAME ONCE RECEIVED. USE ALL SPACES. The box above his name showed that the folder had come from the office of the health commissioner. Joe felt a tinge of alarm. He didn't often hear from Prudence Calder and, when he did, it was usually her making some "helpful suggestion" in the way he ran his section.

He unwound the red string that held the flap down and looked inside. There was a single sheet of paper, light rose-colored stock, with Calder's letterhead. Cautiously, he plucked it out and read.

To: Joseph Sargent, Chief of Epidemiology
In re: Bordello in Lafayette Square / Uncooperative M.D.
Date: 22 September 1982

Dear Joe,
Having spoken with your investigator, Shaun Malloy, certain troubling issues have come to my attention. After looking into these matters, it is my assessment that these issues do indeed pose a threat to public health and may be acted on, directly or indirectly, by health department personnel.

The first problem being the above-referenced "bordello," which is not a bordello per se but may as well be, since its apparent purpose is to bring random men together under one roof for carnal activity. Your investigator further informs that several syphilis cases seen in your clinic claimed to have likely been exposed through encounters at sex parties at this residence. Moreover, some of these individuals have developed AIDS, which is very disturbing. While sex between consenting adults is certainly no crime, the promise of sex in exchange for money is. The health department, acting in concert with the police, could put a stop to this activity if only we could show that the person behind this "private club" was, in reality, a procurer.

In short, I have put in a request to speak with Chief Kinealy about this messy situation to explore what, if anything, might be done. I am currently researching what measures other cities have taken when faced with similar problems and I hope to bring some good ideas to this meeting.

As for the other problem, that of private physician Brock Silber consistently failing to provide adequate treatment for cases of communicable disease, primarily syphilis, and failing to report those new cases of syphilis stemming from his office, I will pay a visit to Dr. Silber and set him straight.

Please give my warm regards to your staff and tell them that their hard work does not go unnoticed. Were that they all as conscientious as Mr. Malloy.

Very Truly Yours,
Prudence Calder, M.D.

As Joe read this letter he wanted to scream. At least that would vent the constricting tension he now felt. That name, so casually mentioned at the beginning and end of the letter, as if they were colleagues. Fuck that! A flyspeck GS-9 had gone over his head and spoken to the health commissioner directly. Betrayal. Disloyalty. Sabotage.

Feeling the bile rise in his throat, he grit his teeth until they hurt. If he could have seen himself just then, he would have seen the sight of a man on the brink of spontaneous combustion.

Joe ripped the letter to shreds, then rose from his chair and made a beeline for the epi room. The room was empty save for Martha at her desk shoveling food into her mouth from a large bowl. It looked like chili mac, unheated, probably right from the can. A late breakfast or early lunch. She was a big woman and needed lots of food to get through the day.

Joe suddenly appearing at her desk looking like a lunatic scared the shit out of her. He demanded to know where Malloy was. She was in the midst of chewing and couldn't speak properly. She held up a finger to indicate she needed a moment.

Joe shook his jowls and scowled. He didn't have a moment. "Where the fuck is he?" he barked.

Martha dabbed her mouth with a napkin and pointed toward the door and the hallway beyond. She pantomimed someone writing on paper.

"The interview room? He's doing an interview?"

She nodded vigorously. Seconds later, she'd finished chewing. Tongue working, she called after Joe's fleeting behind, "You don't have to curse!"

Joe thrust open the door of Interview Room 1, and turned up Arnold and some mousy-looking white girl in the middle of what looked like an emotional give-and-take. He banged the door shut, and went to Room 2. It was unoccupied. That left Room 3, and he felt an intense, sick thrill knowing that Malloy had to be in there.

He banged open the door and, yes! Malloy and some young black guy were at the table talking. There was an open notebook and a perforated strand of prophylactics on the table top. They both jumped back in their chairs at Joe's forceful entry, unexpected and bizarre. The patient's eyes grew wide and fearful. Malloy quickly got on his feet and said, "Joe!"

"Don't you fucking 'Joe' me, you backstabber! Who are *you* to talk to the health commissioner about clinic business? Just who the fuck do you think you are, her trusted confidant? I'll have your ass for this."

Malloy spoke to Joe's deeply flushed mug. "Joe, it's not like that. It was just casual conversation in the elevator."

"Bullshit!" snapped Joe. "I know meddling when I see it. You had no right, no right … *ack ack!*" Joe began shaking his left wrist like he was in a washroom flinging off excess water. With his right hand he grabbed his chest and squeezed. Eyes bulging, mouth gaping, he looked at them with stunned surprise. As he began to wobble then list to one side, Malloy tried to guide him to the chair. But Joe's massive sagging frame was too much to handle; he missed the chair altogether and hit the floor, conking his head.

The patient, Cortez Jones, did not want any part of this. Crazy white people really spooked him. He looked to Malloy, said, "This some bad shit, man. I'm outta here."

Malloy assessed Joe, laying face up, eyes rolled back. His tremulous kisser looked like that of a carp out of water, gasping for air. Malloy quickly decided that he was a bit rusty on his mouth-to-mouth resuscitation. He grabbed the departing Jones by the jacket sleeve. "You stay here, I'll run to the clinic for help. Give me one minute."

Cortez Jones said, "Get some other nigger, I got a bus to catch."

FIFTY

MALLOY FINISHED with the caller on line twenty-nine, a man who wanted to know if you could get "gongarea" from eating off someone else's plate, and he picked up blinking line twenty-seven, a caller waiting for him specifically.

"You got time to visit the park this afternoon?" Teri wondered.

"Talking in code," he said. "I like that, makes me feel like a real spy."

"You don't know who might be listening."

"The powers that be? I can see why they might want to tap into this line. It's a source of endless amusement. Lots of yuks. And no, sorry. I can't come out and play, not till five."

"You'll recall a certain activity with a little dog. We need to see if that's a constant. Tell you what, I'm in the neighborhood. I'll do the honors, get back to you later when you're done there."

Malloy looked at his watch: 2:35. "Yeah, go ahead. That'd be good to know in case we decide it's a go."

"In case?"

"You're really gung-ho on this thing, huh?"

He heard her sigh. "I told you, I'm bored. And from what you told me, this thing we're going to do could bring down this guy's bad act like a house of cards. Plus, I have a new set of tools I want to try, know what I mean?"

"If anyone *is* listening in on this, their ears just pricked up. Okay, you do your thing and I'll wait to hear from you. Later."

"Alligator."

Great, he thought, now I'm committed to a burglary. A little voice, but a very dangerous voice, whispered counsel: *But it was your idea to begin with.*

A bigger voice countered, Yeah, but it was just that: an idea. It seemed good at the time, get Trey's membership list and use it against him. Now that it could actually happen, I'm scared. I can't get arrested over this. There's no happy hour in prison.

The little voice—his conscience?—said, *You need to stop thinking about your miserable self and look at the Big Picture. If your plan works, and it will, you will have made this city safer from the scourge knocking at the gates. If even one person is prevented from getting AIDS, it will be worth the risk.*

Malloy's big voice—his sense of self-preservation?—wasn't buying it. I don't think I have the balls to break into someone's house.

The little voice scoffed. *Aren't you the same person who's stood up to half a dozen vicious pimps and who-knows-how-many jealous boyfriends who were trying to keep you from "messing with their bitches"? That Bruce Lee wannabe, you took his nunchuks and sent him home, remember? If you don't have a pair, I don't know who does.*

Yeah, but that's in the line of duty, we're taught to expect trouble.

I'm losing patience here. Listen up, chum. That sort of courage comes from your own well of fortitude and resolve. In your case, the waters in that well are plentiful and guess what? It doesn't matter whether you draw from that well to accomplish something in the line of duty, as you put it, or something lawless, a bit of skullduggery, that courage is there for you when you need it.

Okay, said the big voice, I can see you've thought this out and have zero reservations. I don't know if you're foolhardy, reckless or merely bent on derailing my career, but promise me one thing.

What's that?

When we're in prison and the days are long, the nights even longer, and we know we'll never be the same again, just don't come crying to me.

A little before five, he returned from an interview and there was a note on his desk: "Call Teri at work 231-4508 Important".

He dialed, she answered. "It looks like a regular thing," she said, excited-ly, "at least during the week. Him and the dog out the door at three twenty-four this time, around the park, the dog stopping to sniff every tree and bush, back at the house at four oh-three. But then he left shortly afterward in his car. So, thirty-nine minutes, give or take. I think it's doable."

"You're crazy," he told her. "I'll be stressed out to the max."

"I told you, I'm good. We're in, we're out. That thing we're looking for? He doesn't see it as something worth stealing, it's not going to be concealed or locked up in a safe. It's probably in plain sight on his desk. You don't have to worry, okay?"

"I'll worry just the same, thank you."

"There is one thing, though."

"Here it comes."

"If we're going to do this right, we're going to need a lookout."

FIFTY-ONE

TREY BOUGHT TWO Orange Juliuses in the airport. Eduardo would see it as a sign of welcome, for it was their wont to sit in the outdoor cafes in Rio and sip such refreshment. But that was six years ago and a continent away.

Now, here they were again, about to reunite. Continue their relationship. Would it be like picking up where they left off, a seamless transition? Or would it take some getting used to, time and distance having estranged them even a tiny bit? They had spoken by phone and written letters; Eduardo never mentioned anyone else. But there had to have been others. Eduardo was too handsome, too virile, too devil-may-care for there not to have been anyone else.

That was all right, though. He was realistic enough to accept the idea of the man he loved in someone else's arms, but only when Trey himself was out of the picture. *O que os olhos não vêem, o coração não sente*—what the eye does not see, the heart does not feel. Trey, on the other hand, had no interest in anyone else whatsoever. Eduardo was the be-all and end-all.

Eduardo's flight had gone from Rio de Janeiro to Miami, with a two-hour layover, and then direct to St. Louis. He had been en route for twelve hours, and now the TWA wide-body jetliner, with its familiar white-and-red colors was taxiing up to the gate. Trey stood at the window looking down on the scene; men wearing Day-Glo orange vests and noise-muffling earphones, guiding the pilot with come-on hand signals. More men in matching vests, standing by with chocks draped round their necks, ready to secure the wheels once the Boeing 767 came to a halt. Still others, standing further back with a huge baggage cart, ready to rush up and offload suitcases as the 221 passengers disembarked. There, the plane had docked, the accordion-like Jetway extending out from the gate to the door of the 767. It wouldn't be long now.

"*Olá* my friend! You are looking wonderful. It is so nice to see you!"

He was all perfect white teeth and a self-amused grin. Eduardo looked better than Trey had ever seen him, if that was possible. A warm glow seemed to emanate from him. He took his friend in a cheek-to-cheek hug, affectionate pats on the back. "Here, I got you something." He handed him the clear plastic cup with a straw sticking out of the lid.

Eduardo took the smoothie and tested it, cocking his head and giving it obvious thought. "Not bad, *Senhor* Trey," he pronounced, "but I would have expected something with a little more kick. Not some frou-frou drink. How you like that? I just learned it on the trip here. The guy from Miami sitting next to me called my pina colada a 'frou-frou drink.' I say, 'What is that?' He say, 'It's a ladies' drink, something that *almost* gets you where you want to be.' I say, 'Where do I want to be?' He say, 'Between my legs, sucking on the big daddy.' Is that funny or what?"

"Did you do it?"

"Do it?"

"Make his wish come true."

"Well, yes, my friend," Eduardo gave a cavalier wink, "you know me. I don't mind telling you that when the passengers were asleep and the stewardesses were in the cabin helping themselves to cocktails, I believe I made something come—ha, ha! And when I was done with him he took a turn with me. Is only fair, eh?"

A wave of sadness passed over Trey. This was not going like he thought. "Let's head down to the baggage carousel," he said, and turned to go.

FIFTY-TWO

MALLOY RAPPED on Tut's door for the third time. It was 9:30 on a Wednesday. He had to be home. It wasn't like he had a job to go to. Besides, his Chrysler was parked out front. Malloy looked around, took in the shabby houses, the small front yards that had everything growing in them except grass. There were people waiting at a bus stop on the corner, four of them, three black. There was a time, so Malloy had heard, when all of the Southside was white, just as most of the Northside was black, the line of demarcation being right around Delmar, give or take a few blocks. Now, large sections of the Southside were black, especially those areas crisscrossed by the state streets.

Tut lived in a two-family at 3346A Arkansas, the "A" indicating an upstairs apartment. This screwy way of identifying dwelling units had baffled him plenty of times in the past. The doors were evenly spaced on the porch—either two or four, depending—and if there were no letters on or near the doors themselves you didn't know which was the downstairs apartment and which was the upstairs apartment.

If the door had a window not obscured by blinds or drapes you could look inside. If you saw steps, you knew that was the A unit. But quite often he had to knock at every door to the building because it wasn't clear which was which, and that put him at a disadvantage; when the occupant did come to the door, he couldn't know if this was the guy he was looking to bring into the clinic, or his neighbor. To ascertain identity, he had to ask true-or-false questions. Unclear addresses were just one more item in the long list of things that stymied the public health officer.

Maybe Tut was a sound sleeper. That would explain it. He rapped again, harder this time. Then he heard the sound of someone coming down the steps. "Hold your horses, I'm coming," said an exasperated Tut to whoever was there beating on his door. Tut got to the landing, looked through the small square door window and said, "I'll be!" Yanking the door open, Tut called Malloy a sight for sore eyes and pumped his hand spiritedly.

"Sorry it took so long to come down," he said, "you caught me taking a dump."

"That's a visual I don't need," said Malloy. "What's with the get-up?"

"You like it? It's my Masked Marauder costume. For the ring. It's like what the Mexican wrestlers wear. I sent away for the mask, the tights I bought at Woolworth's."

"In the plus size section, I suppose."

"Yeah, how'd you know? So, what do you think?"

"It's you, man. And if you decide to give up wrestling, you can go into bank robbing. It's strange to see the eyes and the lips and nothing else."

"It's meant to put fear in the hearts of my opponents, though I don't have any yet. I have to get a manager first, and I'm working on that. But I don't wear the mask too much 'cause it's rubber and it sweats in there. Fact, I think I'll take it off now." He removed the mask with slight difficulty and stood there with wet hair, tufts pointing in every direction. "So, what's going on? Like, why are you here? Gotta be a reason. You didn't just drop by to see how I'm doing, did you?"

"I've got a proposal. Let's go up to your place."

"A business proposal? Does it pay?"

"Yeah, probably. Let's go upstairs and I'll tell you about it."

"I'm always up for a proposal," he said. "But my place is kind of messy right now, the cleaning lady took sick and canceled on me."

"I'll pretend it's spic n' span."

"When I say messy, I mean deplorable."

"I can overlook it. Let's go."

"Okay, you had breakfast? You like Cap'n Crunch?"

"Sure, Tut, who doesn't?"

FIFTY-THREE

FOR THE SEVEN-HUNDREDTH time Brock Silber wished that Stephen Lipkin was still with him. His former assistant could draw blood as easily as write his own name. The highly proficient Lipkin certainly wouldn't have made a mess of it like he was doing now, spent needles and bloody gauze pads strewn about the exam table. It was embarrassing.

"Do you take me for a pin cushion?" asked the patient with heavy sarcasm.

Good, thought Silber, he sees the humor in this.

Silber kept tapping the man's upper forearm as he spoke. "You have, to use layman's terms, rolling veins. When the needle pushes against the vein, it moves. That's why I'm having a hard time sticking it in."

"I can relate to that," said the man, bare legs draped over the side of the table. "That's what brought me here, 'sticking it in.' Except the orifice I stuck it into happened to be contaminated. My misfortune."

Conrad Hirsch was a referral from Trey Vonderhaar, another victim of the ongoing saturnalia that wealthy, educated, seemingly sensible men such as Hirsch paid for in more ways than one. Hirsch had come to him with a cornucopia of symptoms—lesions on the genitals, red-brown spots on his torso, swollen lymph glands in the armpits. When asked, he complained of recent weight loss and unexplained fatigue, nausea, periodic diarrhea. In summation, Conrad Hirsch looked like hell, and Silber was pretty sure he had something horrible, but what?

Syphilis was one guess, that's what most of the other referrals had shown to have. And how did you test for syphilis? By taking a blood sample and sending it to a lab. A fairly simple task that was proving to be beyond his reach.

"Okay, let's go back to this other arm," said the doctor. "That vein seems promising." Again, he tied off the bicep with a rubber tourniquet, swabbed the crook of the elbow with an alcohol prep pad, took a fresh needle from the box, attached it to the syringe, and popped off the protective cap. He studied the terrain he was about to puncture, hoping for something he could easily tap into. There, the slight outline of a blood vessel presented itself. Silber teased the vein with one hand, stretching the skin below it, the better to get a clear shot. With the other hand, he guided the bevel to the vein at a twenty-degree angle and broke the skin. Unfortunately, the bevel was turned the wrong way, and blood came oozing out. Not copiously, but enough to nearly make him swoon.

"I'm leaking!" cried Conrad Hirsch. "Do something, damn it!"

Because Hirsch had reactively jerked at the first sight of blood, Silber let go of the syringe. Both the needle and syringe were now stuck in Hirsch's arm without support; it was gouging a bigger hole in his flesh. Silber, mortified by his error, acted swiftly. He grabbed the syringe by the barrel and yanked. The syringe broke free, but the needle stayed. He went for the needle, grasped it firmly and pulled, but the thing got away from him. He fumbled with it; instead of letting it fall to the floor, he played hot potato with it for a moment until it stuck in the palm of his right hand.

"Ouch!" he said, pulling it out.

"Ouch yourself," said Conrad Hirsch, glumly. "Thanks a lot."

Silber took off his exam glove and looked at the wound, no more than a needle stick, a small drop of blood showing in the area just south of the thumb. It wasn't the first time for him. He went to the sink and began to scrub with iodine solution. Preoccupied with his own injury, he barely noticed that his patient was getting dressed.

"That's it for me, doc. You tried. Not very well, but you tried. I'm going somewhere else. I hope there's no bill for this, that would really add insult to injury."

"No, of course," said Silber, at the sink, his back to the speaker. "No bill, that's understood. I apologize. But please, could you not mention this to anyone? That would be so kind of you."

"We'll see. Can I get a Band-Aid for this arm?"

FIFTY-FOUR

"Is this where the buttfuckers live?"

"Yeah, Tut," said Malloy, "if that's how you want to put it. Here in Lafayette Square, where maybe half the residents are gay, they're simply called neighbors."

Tut harrumphed. "You can call a pig a kitten and it's still a pig. But that's the place, huh? It sure is big. I've seen boarding houses smaller 'n that, and you say just one guy lives there? Lucky bastard."

Teri turned sideways in order to see Tut, who was taking up most of the backseat. "One guy in the main house, and another in the carriage house behind. The guy in the carriage house, we don't know his schedule or movements. He could be there or he could be out. His car's not there, anyway. We don't think he's in the main house very often."

"He's not the one we're going to rob," said Tut.

"You're very astute," said Malloy, "but robbery is not the term we want to use. Criminals rob people, and we're not criminals. We're after some documents with information that will allow us to warn people to stay away from here, and when we're done with them we'll put them back."

"We're actually doing this guy a favor," said Teri. "He's so caught up in making a buck that he doesn't see that he's hurting people."

"He needs to be reined in," added Malloy, who still needed a little more convincing.

It was close to three on an overcast Wednesday. They were in Malloy's Datsun, parked on the same side street across from the park and within sight of Trey Vonderhaar's home. When they were finished, Malloy and Teri would go their way and Tut would go his, hoofing it to the nearest bus stop.

Teri had met Tut only an hour ago. Shortly after being introduced, Teri had whispered to Malloy, "Good pick, Clyde." Malloy understood her meaning: that Tut was dense yet fearless, and the thought of being involved in a broad daylight burglary wouldn't faze him.

Malloy, on the other hand, was very fazed. All day long he had serious misgivings about the whole thing and he resolved not to go through with it as he gassed up the car. *Nope, won't do it*, as he went to the bank to get some cash. *Un uh, don't think so*, as he went to pick up Teri at her office and then on to fetch Tut. *Idiot! Back out now*, as they drove to the 7-Eleven so Tut could have his Slurpee. *No way, turn around*, as they passed in to Lafayette Square and got in position. Even now, there was a queasy ball of dread in his gut. Maybe it would go away when they moved into action.

"It's after three," said Teri, "let's go over this once more. When we see him come out with the dog and he's out of sight, we move in. Shaun and I will get out, you jump in the driver's seat. We go to the rear entrance, I'll beat the lock and we're in."

She studied Tut, engrossed in his Slurpee, for signs of comprehension. "Meanwhile you've turned around and parked on the corner there where you have a view of the entire house, front and side. You see anyone coming and it looks like they're going in the house, you honk twice—not short little beeps but prolonged blasts. You'll know what Vonderhaar looks like because you'll see him leaving, plus he'll be with a dog. But Freddie might come along, he's got a key. Or someone else, who knows? The main thing is be watchful, don't take your eyes off the house. No watching squirrels in the park, no fiddling with the radio. We'll need about thirty-five minutes or less. You can concentrate that long, right?"

"Yeah, no problem," assured Tut. "Um, can I get paid now in case you guys get caught and wind up in jail?"

"I love it how he instills confidence in our work. Pay the man."

Malloy took out his wallet, handed Tut a crisp bill.

Tut snapped it a few times. "Oooh, I like that. Hey there, Ben, long time, no see. You know, guys, this is fun. So far, anyway. Maybe we could do this again."

"God, I hope not," said Malloy.

"There he is," announced Teri. "A man of habit." It was 3:17 by the clock.

They waited less than a minute, coast clear, and drove to the entrance of the driveway as it wound behind the house and ended at Freddie's place. The two in front got out and Tut moved into the driver's seat. "Fingers crossed," said Teri, giving Tut a pat on the shoulder. "See you in two shakes."

They started up the driveway as Tut swung the car around. "Slow down," she told Malloy. "Act natural, make like you've every reason to be here. We're old friends coming to call."

"My heart's in my mouth," he said, slowing just a bit. "This is going to be the longest half-hour of my life. Just setting foot on his property I've already broken the court order."

"I've got news for you, Shaun. B and E trumps an order of protection, but forget that. You need to stop worrying. *Please* stop, because you won't be able to concentrate once we're inside poking around and then what use will you be?"

Then they were standing before a sturdy wooden door with a little mullioned window at eye level. It was not Teri's habit to carry a purse; she was a chain wallet kind of gal. But today she had a purse and she reached inside and took out a slim leather case. She opened it and Malloy saw a fine array of lock picks, each in its own little pocket. Teri studied the keyhole beside the door handle. She chose a pick. She had Malloy stand close behind her to obscure her from the eyes of any passersby. It was a half-ass concealment.

The tool in question looked a little like a dentist's pick. She hunkered down a little and went to work, probing the lock, ears keening for certain subtle sounds. To a passerby it may have looked as though she were trying to find the right key. With the passing of each excruciating second, Malloy began hoping for failure because then they could call it off and say they tried. Then, with a vehement under-the-breath curse, she stood up, and regarded her accomplice.

"Not one word," she said. Calmly, she took the leather case, replacing the one pick and taking another. She went back to the lock, this time on one knee. A jiggle here, a toggle there, precise calculated movements. The lock clicked. She turned the knob and they were in.

They stood in a mud porch. There were coats hanging on a wall and a bunch of garden tools resting in one corner. Teri looked at her watch. "Four minutes gone. Let's whisper just in case, okay? You smell that?"

"Something baking," he whispered.

"Yeah, smells good. Let's go."

They went up some steps and down a hallway and found themselves in a large parlor that looked out onto the street and the park beyond. They moved to the picture window and saw Tut parked near the corner, facing them. Malloy waved and got nothing in return.

"Nothing in here that looks like an office," she said, softly. "There's three floors, we'll take them systematically, one by one, starting here. You go that way, I'll go this way. Quick, but thorough, and leave things in their place. No luck, we meet back here, try the next floor."

"Okay," he whispered and padded off toward a door that led to an adjoining room. It was a kitchen, a spacious well-equipped kitchen that a chef would covet. There, in the middle, was an island with a marble counter top and a guy busily chopping celery. He looked up as Malloy's jaw dropped.

"Oh, you scared me!" he said, placing a hand over his heart, showing off a gold Piaget. "I did not hear you come in. You must be a friend of Trey's. He is out with Roscoe, but you are welcome to wait."

The guy had a heavy Latino accent and he looked like Guillermo Vilas, the tennis pro, so Malloy assumed he was not a local. Not that it really mattered, it was just one of many bits of information Malloy was processing before he chose to reply. He could go along with it, pretend he was invited, but where would that lead? The whole thing was blown, he'd better get the hell out before Guillermo here caught on. Seconds passed, it was getting awkward. He had to say something, so he did. In American Sign Language or some facsimile thereof.

He pointed at his lips and shook his head in the negative.

"Oh, I see!" said the man. "You are *mudo*, not a speaker. That must be difficult. Unfortunately, I do not speak the sign language. There may be a notebook around here. You can write, can't you?"

Malloy shrugged and held out both arms, palms up. This charade was already starting to stink.

"You don't know if you can write? That is odd. Well, okay, my name is Eduardo and I'm ..."

"Who are you talking to?" said Teri, one foot in the kitchen. Seeing the two of them, she stopped in mid-stride. "Uh oh."

"Bad luck or bad timing," said Malloy, miraculously cured of mutism.

"Oh, so you can talk!" exclaimed Eduardo. "Now I think you are here for no good."

Teri leveled an intimidating stare at the man. "Shut up, you. Let me think." She lowered her head and pinched the spot between her eyes. Pinched it good. "Okay," she said, "first things first." She moved to the island and snatched up the chopping knife from where it lay. "Just so you don't get any stupid ideas," she said."

"His name is Eduardo," said Malloy.

"Eduardo, huh? Well, Eduardo, we don't have a lot of time here so maybe you could answer a few questions without a fuss. Comprende?" He nodded yes, and Teri went on. "Just what is your role here? Are you hired help, a houseboy or a cook? Or are you a guest?"

Eduardo laughed sharply. "I assure you I am not the hired help. Quite the opposite, I have more money than you will see in your lifetimes."

"Look at his eyes," said Teri, "pupils like marbles. He's wired on something."

"This is true," said Eduardo, helpfully. "Would you care for a toot? It is over there by the stove. Help yourself. Trey does not do the cocaine and I prefer companionship when I do it."

"Do you believe this guy?" said Teri, shaking her head in dismay. "Okay, so you're a guest, a friend of Trey's. That's good, because you can tell us where's his office, his work place."

"Why do you want to know that?" he grinned. "You want to steal his gold pencil sharpener?"

Teri got in his face. "Look, you, we're not shitting around! Where is it?"

Eduardo regarded the knife she still held, the blade pointing at his navel. "On the top floor, of course, his royal chamber. What do I care if you go up there? Go, it's a nice view. I'll be here, making my tuna salad."

Teri turned to Malloy. "I'm going to stay with Eddie here, see how he makes tuna salad. You're going up to get the prize. Quickly."

Launching himself off the newel post, Malloy bounded up the stairs, patting the railing as he went. Other than a door marked Water Closet, Trey's office was the only room on the floor. Since it was directly below the gabled roof, it was a perfect compact space for one person. There were charts and graphs and notebooks everywhere, a large file cabinet against one wall beneath a Warhol print, a Campbell's soup can signed by Andy himself. "Where can you be?" he said to the client list in hiding. "I bet I can turn you up in less than two minutes." He checked his watch: "Go."

He started with the handsome desk that faced the only window. It was not too cluttered. He himself kept plenty of files and records and he was pretty sure he was looking for any of the following: folders in a vertical file, a Rolodex, a three-by-five card storage box, or even the proverbial Little Black Book. Nothing like that on the desk itself. He went to the horizontal drawer under the desk top. Lots of interesting things here that he would've liked to really gone through, but no time. He moved to the large, deep drawer on the side of the desk, pulled that out. Vertical files, a slew of them, contents identified by their tabs: MERC TRADES '81, HOLD POSITIONS, SHORTS FOR CONSIDERATION and so forth. He riffled through it twice; it was all stock market-related.

He looked to the file cabinet. "You're in there, I can feel it. Just please, don't be locked."

He walked over, Warhol's soup can gazing down on him. He pressed the release-tab near the top, pulled …"Fuck!" He bounded down the stairs, swung on the newel post, and headed for the kitchen. Teri was standing at the island, the knife in her hand pointed at Eduardo. It was like he hadn't left. "File cabinet, top floor," catching his breath. "Take your tool kit, I'll stay here."

"Gotcha." She passed him the knife and beat feet upstairs. Once again, it was him and the house guest. Eduardo fixed him with an expression somewhere between amusement and scorn. "Am I your prisoner?" he asked.

"No! Well, yeah, sort of, but just for a little while. Where you from?"

"Rio de Janeiro, a lovely place, where pointing knives at people is considered—how you say?—bad form."

Malloy didn't feel right pointing a knife at the guy anyway. He set it down, but kept his hand close by. Eduardo seemed civil enough, but it might be an act. "You like to cook?"

"Oh, yes. It is my passion. The kitchen is my playground. You smell those cookies baking? Coconut macaroon—mmm! They are nearly done."

"I like oatmeal cookies."

"This does not surprise me," declared Eduardo airily. "The humble oat is a basic grain, grown throughout the world. It is favored by both horses and a large unwashed class of people."

"What is it with you? Did you take a class: the Art of the Put-Down? Well, doesn't bother me. I am working class, and proud of it. My dad was a stone mason and my mom was a picture framer. Thing is, I went to college where my parents didn't. Found that I love to learn. Then, found my calling."

"As a burglar?"

"Nah, this is just a sideline. I'm actually a secret agent, an American version of James Bond."

"Forgive me if I don't believe you," said Eduardo. "You lack the savoir faire for such a profession."

"There you go again. Haughty—are you familiar with that term? That's you, man. But I have to hand it to you. Your arrows are slung with subtlety and finesse. We in this country could learn a lot from you. Our insults tend to be coarse and vulgar, calling each other asshole and dipshit and cocksucker. We lack imagination in the name-calling department."

"Cocksucker is an insult? You Americans are odd, and, as a whole, quite primitive, but there are enough shining lights to make me want to visit."

Suddenly, they heard the sound of footsteps coming closer. Not Teri's footsteps either. Eduardo looked to Malloy and smiled. Malloy felt his entire body tense up. He heard a clock ticking somewhere that he hadn't heard before.

Into the kitchen strode Tut, a chagrined look on his mug. "Hey, sorry about this, but I really gotta use the can. Where is it?"

"Damn it, Tut, you can't leave your post!"

"Who's this guy?"

"Never mind, take your piss and get back out there."

"Piss? Nah, it's number two. Big time," he grimaced.

Malloy turned to Eduardo. "Is that a bathroom, over there in the corner?"

Eduardo gave a gracious wave of his hand. "Be my guest."

"Thanks, whatever your name is," said Tut, heading off.

Malloy looked at his watch. The time made him nervous. Again, the misgivings. Earlier, when common sense spoke to him, why hadn't he done the right thing and bowed out? Now he imagined himself being led away in handcuffs.

"Maybe your friend would like some cocaine," said Eduardo. "It is primo, my own select stock."

"We don't want any cocaine," Malloy told him, "we just want to get going."

As if on cue, Teri came in. "Got it," she said, patting her purse. "Let's take care of Eddie here and get gone."

"Take care of me?" Eduardo repeated.

"We leave," said Teri, "and the first thing you do is call the cops. Not gonna happen. We'll tie you up and you sit tight 'til we're good and gone. By then, your friend will come back, untie you. It's the best I can offer."

"But I can get out of any bonds. I am like the Great Houdini in that way."

Wordlessly, she walked over to the far side of the room, where a phone sat on a small table. She unplugged the phone jack and jerked the remaining cord out of the wall. There was about four feet to work with. She went back to Eduardo. "Turn around," she ordered. He turned around. Behind his back, she bound his hands at the wrists.

"Not too tight," he protested.

"What's wrong Houdini? Afraid your powers won't work this time?" Just then, the sound of a toilet flushing. Wide-eyed, she appealed to Malloy. "What's going on?"

"I was about to tell you ..."

"Mr. Tut making the number two," said Eduardo, grinning broadly.

"You're fucking kidding, right? Tut's here and this joker knows his name?"

"It's fucked up," agreed Malloy, exasperated. "Nature calls at the most inopportune moments."

"Five minutes I'm gone, and the whole plan just falls apart." Tut came out of the john, shirt untucked. He waved at them sheepishly. "Hey, guys. You got what you need? We ready to split?"

"Ta da!" said Eduardo, holding out both hands for them to see. One hand still had the cord tied to it. "I told you," he crowed.

Teri went over, put her hands on her hips, spoke to him sternly. "Listen up good, Eddie. We're not doing this, okay? There's no time to shit around. We need you to stay tied up so we can go, get away from here. Will you cooperate?"

"I'll think about it."

"How about ten minutes, that's not very long."

"I cannot promise anything."

"Can we trust you not to run out and call the police, at least not immediately?"

"I think not," he said. "Maybe you should tie me up again."

"I'll keep him company for a while," offered Tut. "You guys go."

Teri shook her head. "No, too risky. The home owner's due back any moment."

Tut giggled. "You called the guy a homo," he told her.

"I did not."

"Yeah, you did. You said 'homo-ner.' That's funny."

"God," Teri moaned, "I wish I'd brought my handcuffs."

"No, really," he insisted. "You tie him up again. I'll stand guard for ten minutes, then I'll go out the way I came in. Meet you later at the secret hideout."

"What in hell're you talking about?" wondered Malloy.

"You know"—wink, wink—"the secret hideout."

"Uh, sure, good plan. What do you think, Bonnie. Can we take a chance on this desperado here watching the captive for a mere ten minutes while we make our escape?"

"I don't know, Clyde, but we don't have many other options."

"Good," said Malloy, "at least something is decided. Tie him up again, cut off his circulation if you have to, and let's book."

FIFTY-FIVE

"Why are you laughing?" Tut asked. People laughing to themselves like that bothered him. If there was something funny going on, he wanted to be let in on it. Plus, Eduardo was acting very different now that the others had left. He was tied up good, and it probably hurt some, his hands trussed behind his back, so that may have made him cranky. But there was a nastiness about him that hadn't been there before.

"You tied my hands, but you did not tie my feet," he answered midchuckle.

"So what?"

"You did not know that for the last three years I study jiu-jitsu under Rodrigo Gracie."

"Is he the guy where you come from? I'm trying to be a pro wrestler. Like Hulk Hogan, you've heard of him? Anyway, I'm looking for a manager and since martial arts is kind of a cousin to wrestling, maybe your teacher, this Rodrigo guy, knows somebody I could contact. What do you think?"

"This is what I think." He rose from the chair, took one step toward Tut and brought his right foot, shoe attached, hard upside Tut's left temple. The blow sent him staggering backwards. Eduardo hop-skipped across the tiled floor, tried to kick Tut in the head again but caught his shoulder instead.

"You'll have to do better'n that," said Tut to his newfound opponent. "You're dealing with a pro wrestler here."

Eduardo gave a nasty laugh. "All four of your limbs are no match for my two feet, you big ape."

"Try it again," said Tut, putting his arms out in grappling fashion, hands ready to grab, fingers fanned out and curved like claws. He was ready.

Eduardo faked a kick to the head then did a quick hop, changing to the other foot, and landed a solid blow to Tut's kneecap. Tut bellowed in pain, but remained on his feet. He advanced on Eduardo, hoping to grab something. If he could just get an arm or a leg, then he would be in business.

"Com'ere, you!"

Eduardo obliged by moving in for a high-placed kick to the trachea. Tut, breathless, was able to grab Eduardo's foot before it got away. He meant to say "Gotcha now!" but it came out as an unintelligible gurgle. He had a tight grip on the foot, but he wanted the man's head for a chokehold. He'd been practicing his chokehold on a willing neighbor. Tut, in turn, let the neighbor show him his model train set. Retching and swallowing hard from the last kick, he started up Eduardo's pant leg, drawing him within reach. Eduardo wasn't grinning now. Hands unavailable and with only one leg on the floor, he was at severe disadvantage. Tut now had his foot in a vice-grip under his armpit and was reaching for his belt.

Eduardo, balancing on the one foot, said, "My cookies!"

"*Uchh?*" said Tut.

"My cookies in the oven, they're burning! We have to take them out."

"*Ach ew yarrgh.*"

"Coconut macaroons, I'll give you some."

"Macaroon?" from Tut, puzzled. He was getting his words back.

Eduardo could feel the hold on him slackening. With a strong jerk of his captive leg, he broke free. He backed up a few steps, did a couple lifts on the balls of his feet to bring the blood back. He then closed the gap between him and Tut, who stood amazed at this turnaround. Quick as a blink, Eduardo delivered a finishing blow to Tut's noggin.

"Close your mouth, you look like an *imbecil*," said Eduardo. Instead of closing his mouth, he moved it around to make sure his jaw still worked. It sure felt out of set. Tut found himself tied to a chair, unable to move. The memory of this current predicament was somewhat patchy, Tut having been in and out of consciousness. Eduardo had kicked his ass and gotten loose, that was obvious. Then, from what he saw, his assailant had found some clothesline, and now he was bound fast like a fly in a spider web. But most unnerving, he was in his underwear. He could see his clothes in a pile over near the dishwasher.

"What shall we do with you?" asked Eduardo coyly. "A common criminal here in my kitchen. A person who, were he not presently helpless, might want to harm me, might want to steal from this beautiful home. A person who has no respect for others or their possessions. We must do something, so, tell me: what shall we do with you?"

"You're asking me?"

"I am not asking the chair."

"You could untie me, let me get dressed."

"I do not think so."

"Then can I have a cookie?"

"Yes, good idea! They are fresh from the oven. I'll get them, stay right there."

Tut didn't like the guy's manner, polite yet sinister. He wasn't as thick as people thought; he was pretty sure this Eduardo had something nasty in mind. He couldn't budge his arms or legs, all he could do was to scooch his chair around. And he in his underwear, why? Looking down, he saw his choice from this morning: grungy-looking briefs with a tear in the front, a worn-out pair he had meant to pitch several times in the past. Tighty whities. He'd worn them yesterday and maybe the day before. If he had known he'd be exposed like this, he'd have put on a clean pair.

Eduardo returned with a tray of cookies and a spatula. He held the tray with an oven mitt.

"They look good," said Tut, "but I can't reach. My hands."

"No problem, my friend. I will feed you. Here you go." There were three rows of coconut macaroons, all looking scorched, quite burnt. Eduardo slid the spatula beneath one; holding it with the oven mitt, he brought it to Tut's lips.

"Yow!" cried Tut, ejecting the blistering morsel with his tongue.

"Be careful," warned Eduardo, "they are very hot. Have another." He forced a second cookie into Tut's open maw. Tut shook his head violently. Then, more of the same, hot cookie burning the inside of his mouth, the oven mitt smothering, muffling his cries. As fast as he could shake his head, trying to thwart the onslaught, Eduardo was applying more. And not only to his face, but now his torso.

Eduardo stepped back to look at his work. "You are a mess, my friend. You really should clean up after yourself." He looked to the cookie tray and frowned. "But look, we are near the end. There's only a few left." He reached down and pulled the band of Tut's briefs way out, dropping the remaining cookies into the pouch. He released the band and it snapped back.

"You bastard!" cried Tut, squirming in his chair. He was crying, his tears mixing in with cookie crumbs, for never in his entire life had someone been so patently mean to him.

"Thank you so much for this delicious opportunity," said Eduardo, taking a little bow. "But wait, there is more!"

He came back with another tray, a small silver salver with two lines of white powder, a tightly-rolled twenty, and a small box of Diamond toothpicks, durable and pointy. "Cocaine, Mr. Tut. You like it? I like it. We do it together, a nice toot, and maybe I let you go."

Tut gave a small cry of desperation. "I don't do drugs, mister. But if you got a beer."

Eduardo laughed derisively. "You don't do drugs? What kind of criminal are you? This is the best coke in Rio, and I brought it through your customs, no problem, because they are old fools. You do not want to accept my invitation, then I will do your line as well as mine. And after that, my friend, I will pierce your nipples. How you like that?"

It was the most intense pain he'd ever endured, and he nearly passed out twice during the ordeal. At first, he'd tried to reason with Eduardo, but his tormentor kept insisting that pierced nipples would be a novel look for him as a pro wrestler. Between sobs, Tut explained he already had a theme. He was the Masked Marauder.

"I think that name is taken," said Eduardo, pinching a nipple between thumb and forefinger and stretching it out from his chest. "You can put some brass rings in these holes I am making, maybe a gold chain to connect them, and call yourself Ringo. I do not think you will be confused with the other Ringo."

"I don't want brass rings in my chest," Tut mewled.

"But it will give the other wrestlers something to grab onto," he smirked, flicking his tongue over his lips as he drove a toothpick through the dense flesh of the nipple itself.

"Oh, that hurts! *Please* stop."

"What, you are afraid of a little pain? I do not think you will make a very good wrestler. Think of me as your trainer."

"I think of you as a mean person," Tut whimpered, "someone I don't like. You won't even stop when I ask you to stop."

"Ha, ha!" Eduardo, gleefully, admiring his handiwork on Tut's chest. "You are killing me, you know that?"

When craven pleading didn't work, he threatened. "You just wait, you wait until Malloy hears about this, he'll make you pay."

They both heard a sound of a door shutting, someone coming. Tut prayed it was Shaun and Teri coming back for him. But they used the back door, and that sounded like the front door. Eduardo excused himself and left the kitchen.

"Hello there," said Trey, doffing his jacket. "The cookies smell wonderful!

You were just mixing the batch when I left."

"Yes, that's right," answered Eduardo, bending down and giving Roscoe a scratch behind the ears, "and you took longer than normal on your walk."

"I did, and that's because I ran into an old friend also walking his dog, a Doberman, and we threw sticks for the dogs and we talked ourselves silly. We had some catching up to do. But I'm back now, so let's have those cookies—coconut macaroons, can't wait. And I'll open a bottle of Dom Perignon. You think it's too early for Dom?"

"The cookies are ruined," Eduardo said matter of factly. "A lot has happened here while you've been gone. You want to see? Follow me."

"This is bad," said Trey, "unbelievably bad. And you say they were in my office?"

Eduardo nodded. "The woman held me at knife point while the man went up and looked around. He came back empty-handed and they switched roles. She went up to your office. While she was away, this *primitivo* appeared. Apparently, he'd been outside watching things, but then he had to poop." The Brazilian turned to Tut, still trussed in his chair, and said amusedly, "What a crew you have! A woman who can't tie a knot, a man who can't find the prize, and a fool who doesn't have sense to use the toilet before a job. You know how long you would last in Rio? Fifteen seconds, my friend, and then the police would throw you in a black van with no windows, and you would never be heard from again. Ho, I can see it easily."

Tut stared back wide-eyed and open-mouthed. Merciful Jesus, now there were two of them. What next? If only he could reach his hands, he could chew his nails.

"Tell my friend here what you told me just a moment ago, someone will make me pay."

Tut said nothing. Eduardo kicked him in the shin. "*Ooh hoo hoo!*" cried Tut.

"Do you have to do that?" questioned Trey. "He looks bad enough as it is."

"His pain is my pleasure," said Eduardo. "Again, Mr. Tut. Who did you say would make me pay for hurting you? Or shall I go for the other leg?"

"Malloy, I said Malloy will make you pay. And he will, if you don't let me go!"

"And who is this Malloy to you?" pressed Eduardo, raising his foot for another kick.

"Never mind," said Trey, waving him off. "I already know Malloy, and I know what he was doing here. I don't even need to go to my office to see what's missing. It can be only one thing." He paused, pondered the situation. "Without it, I'll be inconvenienced, but I can recreate it over time. Still ... in the wrong hands, it could mean trouble."

"Then, the solution is simple," said Eduardo. "Call the police. How you say, press charges. The phone here is not working, they ripped the cord out. Go in the other room, make the call. Tell them we have captured one already."

Trey looked at Eduardo in a new light. He was as much of a problem as these health department wackos. And was he really that naive? "Tell me you're joking, please tell me, because what I see in my kitchen is a man tied to a chair who has obviously been tortured. He has burns on his face and his nipples have been pierced with ... what is that, toothpicks? He is leaking blood, and what I think is urine, on my nice floor. The fact that he's in his underwear and his clothes are nearby suggests that you've undressed him and may have sexually assaulted him." Trey pursed his lips and came to an understanding within himself. "You've really outdone yourself, haven't you? And now that I look at you closer, I see that you've got white powder beneath your nostrils, spread across your upper lip. Nice look. You may want to lick that off before the police arrive ... well, maybe we should just hold off on calling the police, eh?"

Eduardo frowned puzzlement. Never in their shared history had Trey said an unkind word to him, and now he chose to upbraid. "He broke into your home, I subdued him. He is a criminal. If I want to have a little fun with this criminal, who should care?"

"I think it's called violating his civil rights. We can't torture people in this country. We're trying to get away from the mindset of the Spanish Inquisition. The police would come, see what has happened and they would arrest both you *and* I."

"Phhh," Eduardo, disgusted. "The Trey I knew once upon a time would not simply let it go."

"And the Eduardo I once knew would not have acted as a sadist. Look, I'm not letting it go. I just want to deal with it in my own way. No police."

"Ah, I see," said Eduardo. "Very smart. You know certain people who can get things done for a price. People who know how to keep secrets."

Hearing this, Tut gulped. They were discussing hiring a hit man right in front of him. That meant he was done for—didn't it?

"I'll take care of it," asserted Trey, "leave it at that. Now, to clean up the mess at hand. You called him by name, what was that?"

"Tut, like King Tut," answered Eduardo, gamely. "Maybe he is descended from royalty—ha ha!"

Trey leaned over and spoke to him on his own level. "Tut, you've been through hell, I can see that. My friend here got carried away and I apologize for him."

"*Que merda!*" Eduardo, seething.

Trey ignored the interruption. "I'm afraid that's all the apology you'll get. After all, you're a burglar, amateurish at best. But time heals all wounds, so I hear, and you'll be all right in a day or so." He paused for effect. "So, here's my question: Do you think you could just walk away from here and try to put this unpleasant experience behind you?"

Tut arched his eyebrows approvingly, bobbed his head up and down.

"And not talk about what happened?"

Again, the bobble-head gesture.

"Get his wallet, please."

"You are asking me to go through the filthy rags he calls clothing?"

"Yes, you removed them, didn't you? I'm asking you nicely, and I did say please."

Grudgingly, Eduardo brought him the wallet. Trey found the license and held it up. "Here's the deal, Derald Tutweiler of 3346 Arkansas Street Apartment A. We untie you, remove those grisly things from your chest -ouch!- get you cleaned up and dressed. You go back to wherever you came from and never speak a word of this to anyone. If you do talk, I will know, and that will be very unfortunate for you when certain individuals come to your door. You do not want to meet these people, they are not civilized like we are. They are brutes for whom cruelty has no meaning."

Tut's eyes brightened. "Like the Legion of Doom?"

Trey thought he was talking about a Roman legion, some legendary fighting outfit celebrated in the history books. "Yes, like them," said Trey, "only worse."

"Yikes!" said Tut.

"You like my deal so far? A pretty good deal, isn't it? Well, I'm going to add a bonus to the deal. I am going to offer compensation for your suffering."

Eduardo bristled. "I cannot stand it! You give this *pilantra* anything, I'm leaving."

"A token payment will seal the deal," said Trey, patiently. "You're a businessman, you understand." Then to Tut, "Is there something you've been wanting that perhaps you could not afford?"

"They got these really cool Mexican wrestling masks in the Lucha Libre catalog. There's one like the Blue Demon wears."

"And what is the price on this item?"

"It was thirty-five dollars."

Trey pulled out his wallet, opened it. "Then why don't you get two."

He turned to his lover and started to say something, but Eduardo was gone.

FIFTY-SIX

"THINK OF ALL the time and effort that went into getting this thing," said Malloy.

"It tried to be a professional operation," said Teri, sipping a screwdriver with not enough ice, "but there were unforeseen snags. As often happens," she added.

Malloy, ruefully, "There was no way to know some guy would be in there baking cookies. Where did he come from?"

"Doesn't matter, it's done." Tapping the ledger with a ruby-red fingernail, she said, "Tell you what, though. Whatever's in here, we'd better act fast before the APB goes out and we find ourselves looking over our shoulders."

"You're saying we could be in big trouble. What number public enemy will we be? Do we make the Top Ten? In the back of my head, I've always thought I might go out in a gun battle with the cops."

"Better off watching that happening to someone else on the big screen. But yeah, home invasion is definitely frowned on by law enforcement." She shrugged, bit a thumbnail. "Hey, I don't know if we're busted or not. This Vonderhaar character will have a good enough description from his pal to know it was you, especially when he sees what's missing. And then they've got Tut's name, well, nickname. Ball's in his court, that's for sure. He wants to make a report, he can, and we're fucked. We'll know by the end of the day, tomorrow at latest."

He saw serious concern on her face, and realized that post-burglary their moods were opposite what they had been earlier. He was jubilant, close to elated, while she was dour at best. "Sorry I got you into this," he offered.

"Did I put up one little argument? 'Oh no, Shaun, I couldn't do anything like that. That's just asking for trouble.' Did I get pissy like that?"

"No."

"Then shut up, and let's crack this thing."

They were in a dive bar on Gravois, about a mile from the scene of the crime. A jar of pickled hard-boiled eggs on the bar, a video poker game in the corner, the décor mid-60s Budweiser thanks to the local distributor. When they walked in, there were five guys sitting at the bar, schooners and shots, regaling one another with hard-bitten tales of Ain't Life a Bitch?

They ordered drinks and moved to a back booth, the purloined item resting on the table between them. It was a ledger like an old time business would have for bookkeeping, ideal for handwritten entries with blue-and-red rule lines. The covers of this book, woven cloth bound to thick board, were meant to hold the pages intact in the event of a nuclear blast. There were a couple black geometric shapes to break the otherwise monochromatic field of pale green. It was hefty, too, measuring maybe fourteen by ten, with 500 pages to fill. Inside the cover, the very first page announced the manufacturer: the National Blank Book Company of Holyoke, Mass.

Instead of a Little Black Book, they had come away with a big green ledger.

Malloy scooched in beside Teri. The open tome took up much of the center of the booth. There were no tabs to mark off sections, so he began turning pages. All headings and entries were written in small precise letters, very legible and neat. The first entry dated to mid-October, 1977, and a quick fan of the pages going forward showed the last entry recorded on page 246, a week ago. The back of the book, starting at page 400, held a record of Man 2 Man parties to include date, number of attendees, what was served, and who stayed the night. At the far right of this section was a column of figures with dollar signs. Trey's bank account, no doubt. With each dated entry, the amount increased substantially.

Back to the beginning, flipping pages in great curiosity. The headings at the top of the columns read from left to right: MEMBER – SPONSOR – CONTACT INFO – DUES PAID / DATE – AGE / STATUS – PREFERENCES

– SPECIAL REQUIREMENTS – RATING. The pedigree on each member took up two open pages side by side.

"What do you think that means, 'Rating'?" wondered Teri.

"Table manners," said Malloy. "Trey's big on etiquette."

"C'mon. It's probably sexual performance. Maybe he has them fill out three-by-five cards before they leave: 'Please rate your partner—or partners—in the gratification department. One is lousy, I'd rather fuck a goat. Ten is can I take him home?'" She laughed at this and drained her glass.

Malloy laughed, too, glad to see her mood lighten. "Maybe you're right, because the numbers mean something. This guy got a seven, this one got a six, this one got eight-point-five. Know what? It might be penis size. He's measuring their dicks!"

"But look over here," she pointed, "a two—there goes that theory. I've seen a few johnsons in my day and they're all bigger than two inches. More like the size of a zucchini."

He looked at her whimsically. "Lucky you, and the pointy, green vegetable you're with. But I've gotta set you straight. These numbers, you're thinking *erect* johnson, which is understandable considering that you're seeing the thing when its owner is aroused. Maybe these are limp-dick measurements."

"Those really exist?"

"Never mind," he said. "What we want here is member info. Names, addresses, phone numbers, stuff we can use." He flipped forward, arriving at October 1980. "Two years back," he said, "let's start here, see what we can find." They went down the columns and none of the names were familiar. Only a few of them had addresses listed. But all of the names had phone numbers, and two-thirds of those phone numbers had out-of-town area codes.

His Jameson rocks was empty, too, so he went to the bar for refills. When he came back, Teri was smiling broadly. "Pay dirt," she said. "You'll like this." She took her drink, frowned, "Where's my lime?"

"Damn! I'll go get it."

"It can wait." She put a hand on his arm. "Sit down. This name," she pointed to a particular entry mid-page, "take note. This guy I know, and he owes me."

Malloy looked at the name. Peter Shipley. "That's good, will he help us?"

"He sure ought to. I bonded his son for aggravated assault and when he ran I caught him and turned him in."

"That sounds par for the course. Why would this guy be in your debt?"

"Because when I found Steven, he was in a dope den over on Manchester with a needle in his arm, unconscious, cold, barely a heartbeat. If I hadn't carried him to my car and sped to the ER right then, Peter Shipley would be out one wayward son."

Malloy held up his glass. "To wayward sons," he said.

Teri's limeless glass clinked his. "Goop," she said.

He was taken aback. "Sorry, I'll go ask for another one."

"Not the drink, silly. Peter Shipley is president of the Goop Waterless Hand Cleaner Company."

FIFTY-SEVEN

RIGHT AFTER showing a dazed and unsteady Tut the back door, Trey Vonderhaar went to his room on the second floor, the room he had been sharing with Eduardo for the last three days. Eduardo was not there, but there was a note on the bed.

> I take a stroll through your city and intend to stop at every inviting bar or club along the way. Maybe there I will find someone who will appreciate my ways and not scold me like a child. Do not expect me back soon, and please do not come looking for me.

"Damn," muttered Trey to the note, "and I was hoping to kiss and make up."

Trey quickly assessed the situation. Despite the warning, maybe he should go after him. Eduardo didn't know the city. He could head in the wrong direction and meet with serious peril in the form of 9mm-toting muggers or bellicose rednecks or gangs of teenagers who would mock his foreign accent. It was probably better to let him go, Trey decided, after all. As referenced in the note, Eduardo was behaving like a child. Let his hot Latin temper cool down, he'll come back and we'll patch things up in no time. Trey imagined the two of them, jovial as two monks in a wine cellar, laughing at the crazy events over a sumptuous breakfast.

Eduardo is Eduardo, he will always land buttered-side up. Right now, there were things to attend to.

First, he went to the third floor, his office, and he looked in the file cabinet, which was part way open. He'd guessed right: the ledger was gone. It wasn't a random guess, either. The ledger had to be the only thing Malloy was after. He was going to use the membership, so diligently recorded, to somehow attack the private club he had built. Man 2 Man had faced other challenges—that bout of bad clams back in '79, five members hospitalized, good grief!—and survived. He was not going to let this pipsqueak Malloy best him.

He went to his desk, took out the phone book, picked up the phone and dialed. A voice at the other end said, "Peep Show, home of the never-ending happy hour."

"Is Mark Walter there?" Raucous sounds in the background.

"If it's after five, he's here," rejoined the bartender. "For you," he heard the bartender say, slightly irritated. "Come around the bar, I don't want my cord all stretched out."

"Yo!" said Walter into the phone. "This is?"

"Trey Vonderhaar, none other. I need to talk a minute. Another favor."

"Come on down, we'll talk in person."

"Can't, I have an emergency on my hands. I need to find someone who will take care of a thorny matter for me. It may involve violence and illegal activity. I can pay handsomely."

"You're calling me for this? Like I'm some kind of Don Vito Corleone? Like I could just look in my Rolodex under 'thugs', make a phone call, and your problems are solved?"

"That's the idea, Mark. You know everyone from every walk of life, from crooked aldermen to sheriff deputies to bottom-feeding opportunists. I need a dependable bottom feeder to do my bidding."

"I filled that last request for you, and the return favor of a lunch with that cute doctor didn't go so well."

"Really? I didn't know that."

"The vain prick dominated the conversation with talk of some fundraiser he was organizing—some trendy disease that runs in Jewish families, like I give a shit. The guy is so full of himself, I lost interest."

"Sorry about that. But I'll make this worth your while," he pressed. "How about an invitation to my next soiree?"

Abruptly, the bartender broke in. "Hey, Chatty Kathy! This ain't no public phone. Cut it short, my mom's supposed to call."

"Oh, shut up and pour me another martini," said Mark Walter. Then, back to Trey, "That might be interesting, a gay new world to explore. And if I like my trial experience, I get a full membership?"

"Uh, sure, why not? Now, give it up, the answer to my problem, before the bartender cuts us off."

"Local 659, ask for Mal."

Organized labor had never been one of Trey's areas of interest. "What is that, some union hall?"

"It's not an art gallery."

"Just Mal, no last name?"

"For a bright boy," he clucked, "you can be thick at times. Mal's all you need—or want. He does odd jobs for the Teamsters. Call now, he might still be there." Click went the phone.

FIFTY-EIGHT

MALLOY AND TERI left the bar with a decent buzz. The Datsun was parked on a side street beneath a stately sycamore. The leaves hadn't turned their fall colors yet. Any time now. It was clear and sunny, a perfect seventy-seven degrees. Indian summer was Malloy's favorite time of year. There was a song by the band Poco about this special time. Walking to the car, it played in his head: "Indian summer is on the way / it's cool at night, and hot all the day ..."

They were joking around as they got in the car. Thoughts of repercussion from their earlier misadventure had been erased by the booze, and they were back to their old selves. Malloy put the ledger on the floor in the back, among some magazines. He turned the ignition key. Backing up to pull out, he damn near crunched bumpers with the idling pickup parked on his ass.

Gravois is a major thoroughfare in the heart of the city. It runs at a southeastern diagonal going into downtown and along the way it changes names to 12th Street then Tucker Boulevard then North Florissant as it shoots out of downtown on another diagonal heading. There are four lanes, two in each direction, and for most of its length the posted speed limit is thirty-five.

Malloy got to the stop sign, his blinker signaling a left turn. He was taking Teri back to her office downtown. The traffic between medium and heavy, getting on rush hour. Suddenly, they were hit from behind with enough force to knock Teri's go-cup out of her hands.

Before Malloy could say "What the fuck!" it happened again. He looked in the rear view and saw the grill of a big white pickup, way too fucking close. He swore, put the Datsun in park and started to get out of the car. But just as he set foot on the asphalt, the Datsun began to move. In park or in neutral, it made no difference to the brawny Dodge Ram. The Datsun and everything in it was being pushed into the intersection.

Foot by foot, the truck plowed the little car into approaching traffic. Teri had the presence of mind to pull up the emergency brake and that might have worked, except that Malloy had driven off too many times with the thing on and the cable was busted. Not only was the car in park, but Malloy had the brake pedal mashed down all the way, alternately pressing and pumping, and *still* they were in motion. The Dodge Ram plowed on, making a godawful cacophony—gears grinding to ruination, tires squealing, metal crunching. Teri, failing to appreciate Malloy's maneuvers, punched him in the shoulder and screamed, "Idiot! Put it in drive and go!"

It was a good idea, but park was all he had. The gear box was scrap metal. Now horns were blaring and cars were swerving around them. The Dodge Ram backed off a few feet, then slammed forward, and the front quarter panel on Malloy's side was clipped by an oncoming Impala. A heart-stopping *whoom*, and they were sent spinning. He heard Teri scream, "I don't wanna die!"

The Datsun did a 180 and came to rest facing the Dodge Ram just as it turned to meld into traffic. The driver shouted something from his open window, but Malloy was too shaken up to comprehend. Then the driver gave the finger, and that Malloy caught. The guy's face, though. He recognized that beefy mug, but the name wasn't there. As the pickup finished its turn, he saw the Jesus fish on the back bumper and it came to him: Chris Dickerson, the renegade forklift driver.

Pandemonium reigned around them. Cars braking, the sound of another crash. They were still in the way, perpendicular to oncoming traffic. He reached for Teri, picking glass from the windshield out of her hair, asked if she was all right. She said something like "errr" in reply. He put his hand on hers and said, "We're getting out of here now! If you can't walk, I'll come around and get you." Then, everything seemed to be in slow motion, the seconds like the last drops of molasses dripping from a jar. He brought his hand back and went to open the car door when a black Corvette came out of nowhere, slaloming around cars both moving and stopped, and T-boned the Datsun just behind where Teri sat.

The paramedics had to use the Jaws of Life. When they weren't working on her, starting an IV or taking her vital signs, he was with her. Talking, reassuring, stroking her forearm. She was conscious and alert the entire time, but scared and really shaken up. Not at all liking the idea of being pinned in a wrecked Datsun. The crumpled floorboard clamped her right foot tight as a vise, and the passenger-side door wouldn't budge, either. The Jaws of Life, which looked something like a robotic crocodile snout, had already gotten a toehold on the banged-up door, and little by little was separating it from its hinges. *Crack!* The door popped off and fell to the pavement with a clatter. Now, Teri was fully accessible and the paramedic leaned in and checked her top to bottom. That was the thing about paramedics: one minute they're operating heavy machinery, the next minute they're Florence Nightingale.

Malloy was fine, but when he admitted to slight tingling in his hands they made him wear a foam neck brace. Finally, they had Teri out of the car and put her on a gurney. Malloy walked alongside as they wheeled her to the big red box of an EMS truck. They collapsed the struts of the gurney and carefully began to load her into the back. "You'll be all right," he told her with a wink, "just don't do any calisthenics for a while."

She managed a smile. "I'm sorry I called you an idiot."

"I've been called worse, and can't deny any of it."

"Go on, your turn," said the medic with captain's bars. "I'll help you in."

"I'm going, too?"

"Definitely," said the captain. "An accident like that? You're lucky as hell you walked away."

"My car." said Malloy.

"There's a tow truck en route."

He thought for a second. "Fine, just give me a moment. There's something I need to get out of there."

He didn't leave the ER at Alexian Brothers until nine that evening. Upon arrival, Teri had immediately been taken to an examining room, and that was the last he saw of her. No time to even say ciao. Meanwhile, he was consigned to a Naugahyde chair in a drab waiting room with a dozen gloomy-looking individuals for company. He took off his neck brace and gave it to an old woman to use as a pillow.

"There's some serious cases ahead of you," the charge nurse told him whenever he inquired, "you'll just have to be patient."

"That's the problem," he protested. "I'm a patient when I shouldn't be. How about this? I release you of all responsibility. Whatever happens to me, not your problem. So can I leave now?"

"Sit back down," she insisted. "Read your book."

He looked at the ledger clutched in his hand, firmly held to his side. "It's not that kind of book," he corrected. "Not the kind with an absorbing plot and characters in deep shit that you'd want to read and get into."

"Whatever," she said, and walked off.

He knew the nurse was already upset with him because he had signed in as Crabby Appleton, and she had called him on it. "I watched cartoons as a girl," she ragged, "I know who that is. Tom Terrific's grouchy neighbor. 'Rotten to the core.' Why you want to spoil my sign-in sheet with that nonsense? Now put down your real name, and get with the program."

He walked back to his chair, but a black man with malevolent eyes had claimed it so he went to a corner and leaned against the wall. Idly, he opened the ledger and began flipping through it.

Each name, he understood, had a story to it. Each name had hopes, dreams, aspirations. Each name was an entry in a grim lottery to win the same fate as Ren Peters and Douglas March. He'd been wrong about the nature of his "book." It did have a plot, a tragic one, and there were plenty of characters in very deep shit.

FIFTY-NINE

THE NEXT DAY was about as busy as it got at the city STD clinic. Maybe it was the post-season play and the Cardinals' march toward the pennant, but something in the air was prompting people to fuck like bunnies and spread gonorrhea like it was going out of style. Thing is, it never went out of style. That was impossible as long as men were horny and women were willing. Protection? Why bother, it might spoil the mood. And if you did catch a case, there was always the clinic. It's a busy place, so expect to wait. But, hey, it's free.

Things were different, too, with Joe out on permanent extended leave and Karl in charge. The investigators no longer cringed when the boss walked into the epi room, not knowing who would bear wrath on this particular day. The female investigators no longer felt like pieces of meat, being patently ogled at their desks, clasping their V-necked blouses at the top in a delicate attempt at modesty. Once again, personal tokens—posters, hand-printed words of wisdom, pictures drawn by kids—bloomed on the walls, the place starting to look more like a dorm room and less like a nose-to-the-grindstone bureaucrat's office. It was a shame that Tut wasn't here to experience it all.

A replacement for the banished Tut was still in the works, so they were a man short. On a busy day like this, that meant everyone had to hustle just a little more, abbreviate interviews, not spend so much time on the phone cajoling contacts to come in and be checked out, take one less smoke break on the fire escape.

Malloy's pouch was chock-full of ERs. He had let things slide while staking out Trey's house, time away from grass-roots epidemiology, but as of today he was back to working his contacts with renewed fervor.

This morning, for instance. Up at 6:15, hit the head, make a cup of Folgers instant, and then start calling. He didn't care who he woke up at this hour. If he waited until he got to the clinic, they might have left already. Or at least the responsible members of the household would be gone—the mothers, usually, who were the breadwinners of the family. He would catch them early as they readied for work and in couched words, easily deciphered, let them know that their sons and daughters had been exposed to venereal disease and it was up to them, the mothers, to see that their lustful offspring got their butts into the clinic. This approach of appealing vicariously to the mothers or the aunts or the grandmothers worked tolerably well, had maybe a thirty percent success rate. In the black households anyway, the women were the ones who carried the big stick.

He did seven interviews this morning, up until 12:30 when his field time began. In the next three hours, he was hoping to round up just as many contacts, some of them real prizes, sought after for weeks, and ferry them into the clinic if he had to.

He was motivated, and he had a new old car to work with. Thank Timba for that. When he heard Malloy's plight, the heart-of-gold parking lot attendant had given him a loaner from the lot. That was this morning, early. He led Malloy to the back row and there, blocked in by other cars, was a lime-green Ford Maverick, abandoned for all intents.

"It's been three weeks," said Timba, working his mouth around as if to spit. "I don't think he's coming back. You may as well take it. If he does come back, he won't want it, not after he sees the total I've worked up. Daily fees plus storage plus interest over time. It's more than this ugly duck is worth."

Malloy opened the driver door, peered in. There was a fold-out umbrella on the seat, some candy wrappers on the floor beside a *People* magazine with Carly Simon on the cover. The fabric on the headrest behind the wheel was darkened, slick with something. Malloy put his finger to it.

"Vaseline?" he wondered.

"Probably Afro Sheen," said Timba. "It's pretty grody, I know, but at least it's made by decent hard-working Americans, not like that rice burner you drove. Plus, it's got gas. Lucky you." He handed him the keys, on a keyring with a bottle opener and a pen knife. "I'll move these other cars, be just a second." He paused. "Hey, I've gotta tell you, I've always liked that word you used."

"Which one? So many roll off my silver tongue."

"Totaled, man. You said your car was totaled. That's cool, it conjures up some hairy images."

Malloy just stood there looking at Timba, his open face expecting some sort of reply. "Oh, you should've been there," he said, throwing his backpack in the Maverick and climbing in after it.

Early afternoon was a good time to roust contacts. Many of them had no jobs and would be up late roaming the streets, sitting on porches, partying. They crawled in bed well past midnight, slept late, and by the time they were moving around again the sun was past its zenith. A bowl of cereal, a shower, watch the tube, make some calls to the rest of the posse, line up the evening's action, and get ready to do it again. So, the one-to-three window tended to yield results. The guys, if he did find them at home, were fairly reasonable, with no one else to impress and not yet coked up on something that caused belligerence.

Up north, he found several of them home and was able to extract promises to visit the clinic very soon, like today. One young man seemed as though he wanted to get the matter taken care of right then, but he had no ride and no money for the bus. "You see that?" said Malloy, pointing to the Maverick at the curb. "Let's go."

They drove down Grand, the towering spire of St. Al's "The Rock Church" looming, when the contact, Frederick Bobo, said, "Man, you must be doin' pretty well, be able to afford a car like this."

"Oh, yeah," said Malloy, "public health pays pretty good, right up there with washing windows."

Frederick Bobo considered this. "This car treat you good, right? You ought to treat it good."

"Meaning what?" said Malloy.

"Hubcaps, man. You missin' three outta four. My buddy, Derrick, he sells hubcaps. You want to swing by there real quick?"

After he dropped off Frederick Bobo, making sure he really went in, Malloy turned his attention to the Southside. There were several possibilities there, including certain stubborn individuals who needed some serious motivating. First, he had an errand. He drove the Maverick up the long gradual incline that ranges from Lindell to Chouteau, engine chugging resistance, then, over the hill, he more or less coasted down to Arsenal. There, near the corner, a storefront, the gas-filled tube in the window glowing red and green. KOPY KAT, read the sign.

There were four self-service copiers, three of them taken. He set his backpack on the work table nearby, pulled out the ledger. The pages extended beyond the borders of the glass copy area. He hit a button that selected the tray with the largest size paper, and tried a sample copy. The copier hummed and spat out a sheet. Damn, it didn't pick up all of it. Malloy turned the ledger perpendicular and tried again. This time was better except that some of the characters were cut out at the far right. He adjusted the ledger several times more and, no matter what, something got left out. Finally, he settled on one not-so-bad option and decided that he would fill in any missing information by hand. That would take some time. Rousting contacts would just have to wait.

SIXTY

THE DOOR to Room 643 was half-open. He looked in, saw an empty bed, sheets all mussed up. Maybe he had the wrong room, maybe the blue hair at the information desk had mumbled some other room number. He stepped in, took a better look. There was a partition between two beds. She was on the other side. Of course. He went around the heavy curtain, expecting to see her propped up, watching a game show on the TV that he now heard. Instead, there was the sheet-covered form of a woman, Caucasian, middle-aged, long scraggly hair, mouth open, drool pooling on the pillow.

Then, he heard the powerful whoosh of a hospital toilet flushing. A door opened fast, as if kicked, and Teri emerged in a wheelchair. "There you are!" he said.

"Back at you." She gave a wan smile that spoke of tribulation. "You ever try to use the john from a wheelchair? It might not be so damned difficult if they'd think to hang monkey bars over the toilet. Geez!"

An extension jutted out from the wheelchair, a kind of plank with a foot rest at the end; Teri's elevated right leg occupied it. "I thought they gave out bedpans ... so you don't have to get up."

"Screw that. I'll get up if I want. I've even been down the hall, to the nurse's station, shoot the breeze with them. They're quite the comedians, you get to know them. Tie the back of my gown, will you?"

He moved behind her. "You like a bow on it?"

"I was hoping for a clove hitch."

"Back to your old sarcasm, that's good."

"You're taking a long time to tie that knot. Are you looking down my gown, you pervert? If so, you'll see the nice job they did on my ribcage."

He moved around to face her. "You broke a few, huh?"

"Broke a few, cracked a few more. They've got me all trussed up. Now I know what those Victorian women went through with the corsets and all. What's bad about it, broken ribs, is you're taking short breaths and then that catches up to where you need a deep breath. To even it out, I guess, but it's the deep breath that's a killer. Real agony."

"Sorry to hear it," he offered. "But you're on the mend, it's getting better, right?"

"Not that I can tell," she said, "but it's only been a little more than twenty-four hours. And my foot, you ask? Some of the little bones are broken and that'll take time, but no surgery. I'll have to use crutches for a few weeks. The good news is they're saying I can leave in a couple days. I'll be on bed rest at home. You can drop by and be my mixologist."

"Teri, I'm really sorry I got you into this."

"Don't start that again," she chided, rocking her wheelchair back and forth. "You want to see me do a wheelie?"

When he was done laughing, he told her, "You're the best, I'm so glad we're friends."

"Ditto, kiddo," she said, brushing away a long strand of brown hair, "and what do friends do for each other?"

"Uh, buy drinks, tell jokes, other benevolent stuff."

She gave a dismissive snort, then clutched her side, wincing. "They also move the ball forward by making phone calls to a certain party whose name was in that book. You know who I mean."

"Peter Shipley. You called Peter Shipley? How?"

"There's a phone at the nurse's station. A phone book, too. It wasn't hard to do. He's agreed to meet us at the diner down the street from my place. I'm to call when they release me."

"He'll do it, then? You talked him into helping us bring down Trey?"

"He doesn't know what it's about. I told him it was something important and that I needed his help, but the particulars best discussed face to face."

"That's great news, we're back on track. Now, let me tell you what I did before coming here."

He helped her on the bed and then took the wheelchair, rocking the wheels as he talked. It was almost impossible not to play with the thing. He told her how he'd copied the ledger, made two sets despite the mounting cost, kept one set for himself and the other he delivered to his contact at the *Globe-Democrat*. This contact, an investigative reporter named Urban Lehrer, was out on assignment but he'd left the copies with another reporter, a woman who had a desk near Lehrer's. He watched the reporter put the copies in a manila envelope and write Lehrer's name on it. Lehrer, he told Teri, would be happy to get the contents because he was working on a lengthy feature on AIDS in the city and he already knew that Vonderhaar's sex club was a part of the problem. If he could get to some of the members on the list, and if they were inclined to tattle, it might even make the lead in his forthcoming story.

"What about the other set of copies?" she asked.

"In my car. Oh, I have another car already. A Ford Maverick, three missing hubcaps and the color of baby poop. A real chick magnet."

"What are you going to do with the original, the actual ledger? It's evidence and we're not out of the bushes yet."

This gave him pause. He rocked to and fro a few times before answering. "You're right. It makes me nervous having it. It has the feel of contraband. I'll find a way to return it, maybe put it on his doorstep in the middle of night."

"Yeah, good plan. Don't mail it or UPS it. If we do get found out, that might add to the charges." Then he began to tell her how he called the beat cop, McBride and told him how the accident was no accident. Told him how this Chris Dickerson had it in for him, blamed him for having lost his job, lost his girlfriend, and now he was an outlaw cruising the streets in his deathmobile.

When McBride had asked why Dickerson, Malloy explained that he'd needed to put extra pressure on Dickerson to get checked out for VD by speaking to his boss. In check, rather than make the right move, Dickerson had left the board altogether and lost it. Plates? No, but he has a Jesus fish on his back bumper, and the front one'll have my Datsun on it. McBride had only sighed heavily over the phone, and said he might be able to muster up a vehicular assault.

Malloy looked to Teri, propped up with pillows, sipping through a straw from a half-gallon jug of water with measurements on the side. This was the first she'd heard of the full explanation of why they were targeted. "And that's where it stands now," he said. "Guess I'll go make the report. Anything to put that crazy asshole out of circulation."

"It's ironic," she commented.

"What?" he puzzled.

"Come here and I'll tell you." A stage whisper: "We're not alone, remember?" She jerked her head toward the curtain.

He stood, went to her side. She cupped a hand over his ear, said softly, "We're worried about getting arrested for home invasion—at least I am—and you're doing your bit to see that some other fool gets arrested. I think we should leave the cops out of it, for now at least."

He nodded assent. "Yeah, all right, but I'll be wary of any pickup trucks that come my way." He rose, returned to standing position, told her,

"And now I've got to go, your warm breath on my ear is giving me thoughts. I'll be back tomorrow. You need anything?"

"A radio," she said. "The Cards are red hot right now."

He didn't feel like going straight home, so he went to McDowell's and sat at the bar for two hours. At nine, an Irish band took the stage and played their hearts out. A guitar, a fiddle, a button accordion. He'd seen them before. They didn't do "Danny Boy" or any cry-in-your-beer folksy stuff. They did what they called Celtic rock, catchy riffs that spoke to your soul, and, for the while, the music and the Guinness took Malloy's mind off his troubles.

He got to his place around 10:30, walked up the steps, saw his door ajar. Cautiously cracking the door some more, he reached in and switched on the light. The entire apartment had been ransacked.

SIXTY-ONE

THE NEXT MORNING, Malloy sat at his desk, talking to Arnold about a disturbing case. A young girl, positive for the clap, had named her uncle as a contact. The girl was fourteen, the uncle thirty-six. The debate was over whether to call the Division of Family Services or the police. Arnold said it probably didn't matter who got the initial call, that the matter would spill over to the other agency eventually. Malloy felt the overworked social workers at the DFS would take too long with their investigation while the police would act more decisively.

"What's the cut-off age for consensual sex anyway?" wondered Arnold. "When you're no longer considered jailbait." They weren't up on their knowledge of sex crime statutes; it could be fourteen or fifteen or even sixteen.

"Maybe she's legal at fourteen," shrugged Malloy, "but it's her uncle. That's incest. That's still a crime, isn't it?"

"Not in Arkansas," deadpanned Arnold as Danielle's voice came over the intercom.

"Shaun, a call on twenty-six for you."

He picked up. "Malloy here."

"How you doin', buddy?" The voice of an older man, gruff, deceptively amiable. "You got a minute, we can talk?" Not waiting for a reply, he went on. "I represent an individual who says you have something of his, something he wants back immediately. You know what I'm talking about, don't you?"

"It sounds like rectal warts," said Malloy, winking at Arnold. "How long have you had these symptoms? I see, that's a shame. Have you tried taking a sitz bath?"

Momentary silence. "A comedian, huh? I like comedians. Maybe when we meet up you can tell me some funny jokes … *as I break your fucking legs.*" He paused, made a sound that could have been a burp. "You saw what I did to your place last night. You don't turn over that book today, I'll do the same to you." A menacing chuckle. "Topsy-turvy, that how you like it?"

"No, we don't recommend sandpaper for treatment of such delicate tissue. Why don't you come in and one of our capable clinicians will have a look. Tell me your name, and I'll see that you don't have to wait long."

"The name's Mal, as in malicious," rumbled the voice, "and you think I'm some crank caller, you're making a big mistake. I'm serious as a heart attack, and I'm way out of your league. Now, do you give me the book without a fuss, or do I wipe up the floor with you and take it anyway?"

"That's a hard choice," answered Malloy, waving bye to Arnold as he left the room. "Can I have a day or so to decide?"

"Fuck you, prick. Decide now."

He could feel the guy's ire coming through the lines, trying to throttle him. "Oh, all right," grudgingly, "have it your way. You know the newsstand two blocks down from the health department, across from Garavelli's? There's a guy there, Darius, looks like he just got off three weeks of KP. I'll leave it with him. In a brown paper bag with your name on it. Give me fifteen minutes, it'll be there. Happy now?"

"Well, I'm a little disappointed that I don't get to try out my new brass knuckles. But yeah, I'm real happy so long as you do it. And Malloy?"

"What is it, Mal?"

"I know what you look like, but not the other way around. I see you out and about, I'll introduce myself. Maybe you'll have a joke for me." The phone clicked on evil laughter.

Trey Vonderhaar also had an eventful morning. He was coming out of the kitchen with a plate of bagels, cream cheese and lox, when he heard the sound of someone clumping up the front steps. LaWanda, the rotund letter carrier, came into view. Not that Trey cared whether she was white and svelte or fat and black, so long as she delivered his mail without a problem. And to her credit, she was always cheerful. He set the plate down, went to the door.

"Morning, Mr. Vonderhaar," she beamed. "How we doin' today?"

"Just fine, LaWanda," taking the day's mail from her outstretched hand. "Oh, a letter. Handwritten, how nice. So often it's all junk mail, but anytime there's a letter it's a small thrill."

LaWanda chuckled good-naturedly, "You got that right, Mr. Vonderhaar. A letter from a friend can really make your day. Y'all take care now."

He watched her descend the steps. Back inside, he looked at the letter again. It was slightly mysterious. The envelope was a shortened version of the standard business envelopes he preferred. The handwriting was anything but calligraphic, a chicken scratch at best. The return address in the upper left corner bore the name of a street he had never heard of, but the zip code he recognized as an area north of downtown.

Also unusual, the sender had written his name as Bryson Vonderhaar III, Esq. There were but two possibilities for the honorific. "Esquire" at the end of a name was used to denote a lawyer, which he was not; it was also used as a term of endearment, usually when referencing a boy.

He took his mid-morning snack to the breakfast nook, then went to the half moon-shaped service opening connecting the kitchen to the dining room and found a letter opener. He would never open a letter by hand; ragged tears in paper disturbed him. Slitting the top of the envelope, he took out the letter, unfolded it, and laid it on the table. Smoothing it out, he made a mental snapshot of what he had. The body was short, one long paragraph; he would get to that in a minute. The greeting was "Dear Trey." The complimentary close and attendant signature read "Kind Regards, Your Friend, Arthur Tottingham."

That explained the Esquire. He returned to the body, reading it through cursorily, and then again, quite carefully.

I hope this letter finds you well. I am definitely not well. I have spent the last two months in this hospice, drinking dandelion tea and fighting nausea. For the record, I could have had the most up-to-date care that money can buy, but I chose this humble way station, close to the ghetto, because compassion abides here. At this point, compassion and kindness are worth more to me than any trifling commodity, for I am in the growing ranks of victims claimed by AIDS. It is sad beyond words the way it wastes your body, saps your strength, and erases any lust for life. I can barely move the pen across this paper! A few of the boys from the Gateway Men's Chorus came to visit. They sang show tunes for me. That was precious, although it's difficult to show enthusiasm when you feel like yesterday's leftovers. I know the word is out about my condition, people probably already talking about me in past tense. I can go anytime and I think I've made my peace with everyone I care for, everyone but you. I'm going to make this short and sweet, Trey, as I know you are not one to take criticism well. While I love you not only for who you are but also as the son of a dear friend, I must say that you've taken the wrong path. The clique you preside over is detrimental to the well being of its trusting members. I, for one, caught this disease while in your home, and I have passed it along to at least one other person who is no longer with us. The sex on those evenings was greatly anticipated and, as it played out, intoxicating. But in the end, the price was far too dear. Were it not for you as ringmaster of this carnal circus, I might still have a life ahead of me. But hindsight be damned, what's happened has happened. You did nothing sinful. You followed your business instincts, you played the entrepreneur, and you had great success with it. <u>Had</u>. Nature spoiled that success by introducing a deadly virus into the blood and semen of otherwise healthy men and now the outlook is grim. Trey, it's time to accept that it's over. You've had your fun. Cease operation of Man 2 Man, no more parties, refund monies if you must. Do it for all gay men, do it for a clear conscience, do it for me.

Well. That was a kick in the pants, a dying man asking him to fold his tent. If Art wasn't a friend, he might say, "What cheek!" He did understand, though, and it was unfortunate, Art's predicament, but no amount of sentimental attachment to a friend of his father's was going to convince him to stop Man 2 Man. However, and it was a big however, a thought that had been percolating in his brain as of late, was that he was tiring of it all. Not the trips to the bank, of course—he loved amassing wealth more than ever!—but the planning involved. Lining up all the help, selecting the menu, gathering the provisions from cigars to wines to chocolates, orchestrating the cooks in the kitchen, seeing that each course was done on time. Freddie did some of that, naturally, but he had to oversee Freddie.

And then there was the more arduous task of matchmaking. How little they appreciated the nuances of bringing together two unique human beings for sexual gratification. Birds of a feather or complete opposites? There was no formula, and in fact it was hit or miss, some fellow storming out of the room saying, "I want someone else, he's too rough!" No, matchmaking was both an art and a learned skill. If only it was as easy as pairing the evening's entree to a certain wine.

He took a bite of bagel, appreciating the rich, orange color of the lox set against the white cream cheese. Hmm. Maybe it was time to wind the thing down, take a long vacation, get lost in a good novel, lie on his back and watch clouds. Maybe Eduardo would come along, if they could ever patch things up. He failed to understand the nature of his lover's current pique. That he chided him for torturing that troglodyte in the kitchen? Still angry over that? Get over it. Come back, we'll laugh about it. He didn't remember Eduardo being this touchy, but then he didn't remember Eduardo with a coke spoon up his nose either.

He considered Eduardo's qualities, one by one, assigning values. Looks: still there, the most handsome man he'd ever been with. Intelligence: lackluster, merely average, probably never really tried in school. Sex appeal: top drawer, just thinking about Eduardo gave him an erection. Ambition: none, unless you call trying every vodka flavor under the sun ambitious. Depth of character: shallow as a kiddie pool. Ability to care for others: only when it suited his selfish purpose. Loyalty and fidelity: pathetically lacking. He'd walked out two days earlier and not even a phone call since, almost certainly partying his brains out with some libertines he'd met in the clubs—he would be such a hit!—sleeping in strange beds, carrying this estrangement way too far.

He was hurt by it, hurt and ashamed that he'd let this once-adored man take advantage of him. Still, he wished that Eduardo would walk through the door and fill the room with that radiant smile. What he would give for only that!

He puttered around downstairs for a while, changed the filing system in his bookshelf from alphabetical to topic, dusted the windowsills, and straightened a few pictures on the walls. He found himself pacing, lacking a clear plan for the day. This was antithetical to his nature; he always planned his activities out, made a to-do list first thing every morning. Then, the sound of footsteps on the porch. He wasn't expecting company.

The door opened before he could open it himself. Only Freddie and Eduardo had the key, and Freddie was a hundred miles away at a blues festival in Columbia. Eduardo entered, followed by two more, a man and a woman. Trey stood on the Persian Qum area carpet, arms akimbo, waiting, hoping for an explanation.

"Hello, my friend!" said Eduardo, beaming. He held the key out and looked at it in mock surprise, turning down his mouth theatrically. "The key you gave, it works!" He turned to the others, half in, half out, and said, "Come in, come in. Shut the door. Don't let the flies in—ha ha!"

That Trey was cheerless, and, in fact, gave the appearance of an Easter Island stone head, had no effect on Eduardo. "Are you working?" he asked. "Did we interrupt? I am sorry if we came at a bad time."

Seconds ticked by. The man and woman grew uncomfortable at the silence, began to shift in place. Trey took his arms off his hips and folded them across his chest. "Why are you here, Eduardo?" Evenly, but no mistaking the provocation.

"Oh," said Eduardo, seeming surprised at the question, "we are here because I wanted to show my new friends your beautiful home. And I wanted to get some things from my room—our room. But first, I must introduce." He stepped aside to give a better view. "This is Rocky and this wonderful creature is Kristi. I met them in a club on your Mississippi River, a place called Land … Land something."

"The Landing," offered Kristi, smartly, as if called on in a third grade classroom. Trey looked her over. Long ago, his mother had once referred to his father's secretary as voluptuous, said it none too flatteringly. He remembered going to the Webster's at first chance to look that up. "Sensual in appearance; conducive to or arising from sensuous or sensual gratification," the entry read. Kristi was voluptuousness amplified—not that he was going to get a rise from it.

"We've been up all night," Eduardo put in. "Do you have any of that excellent coffee available?"

"The coffee's all gone," said Trey, pursing his lips in what he hoped was a disapproving gesture. "That's rich," he added. "You're all fagged out from a night of partying and you want my coffee as a morning pick up. There's a 7-Eleven down the street."

They were still gathered just inside the door. Kristi gave Eduardo an affectionate squeeze, said to Trey, "That's an unfortunate choice of words,

Eddie is anything but a fag."

Trey looked at Eduardo, said, "Who is this woman?"

Eduardo laughed gaily, said admiringly, "She is the best dancer in the Western Hemisphere. She is at once a muse and a nymphomaniac, a rare combination."

"But she's not so bright, is she? Doesn't know the difference between being fagged out and being a fag. Here, let me edify you, Kristi"—acidly—"being fagged out means one is exhausted from some form of recreation, say, dancing or fucking. Whereas the derogatory term 'fag' denotes a man who is attracted to other men. As longtime lovers, 'Eddie' and I fit this description, although we would never describe ourselves as fags. But you, on the other hand, are someone who is commonly called a fag hag."

"Uncalled for," shot Kristi, "and factually incorrect. Fag hags only hang out with gay men, they love their wit and style. They don't go to bed with them."

"Is this a play?" asked Rocky.

Trey, startled by the impertinence of the remark, "What?"

"I saw this play, *A Doll's House*, and some of the dialogue going on here reminds me of that play. It was a good play, made you think. I'm working on a screenplay."

"That's great," said Trey. "Listen, would you two mind stepping back outside while Eduardo and I talk among ourselves?"

"No, no, my friend, whatever you have to say you can say openly. We are like a team. You don't break up the team."

Trey felt his heart in his throat. This was not at all the way he hoped to greet Eduardo on his return. The diorama of their life together, happy in this cozy Victorian house, was disintegrating before his eyes. "*We* are the team, you and I," he told Eduardo.

"This is true," said Eduardo, "but, as you know, teams have substitute players. Are you sure you don't have some coffee around? I will be glad to make it."

"If you're trying to hurt me, you're doing a good job."

"Your problem is that you are stuck on one person—me. You should open your mind to new possibilities." Turning to Kristi, "Each person is a new adventure, a land to be explored."

"That is so beautiful," pronounced Kristi.

"I wish I had a tape recorder," said Rocky.

"I was faithful," Trey faltered, knowing love would not prevail. "I waited for you a long, long time."

Eduardo pretended to be taken aback. "Faithful, what is that?"

"It's having the self-discipline to refrain from dipping your thing into some tuna twat!"

"She has a more sensual mouth, and," he whispered as an aside, "she has a pierced clitoris."

"That's it! Out the door, all of you. Now! Go!" Trey was shaking, rage and heartbreak tearing him up.

Kristi shot him a gloating look and took Eduardo by the hand. "Come on," she said, "I know a dynamite coffeehouse."

He watched them through the window. Down the steps, talking excitedly, laughing at what had just happened. Laughing at his expense. He saw them get into a red Toyota, the woman behind the wheel, and drive off. Simultaneously, a blue Buick LeSabre drove up and parked in the Toyota's vacated spot. It was a big boat, a convertible with the top down, despite the still-crisp air of late morning. The door opened, and a large man got out, a brown package in his hand. Trey watched him ascend the steps to his door, slowly, hitching one leg noticeably, a half-smoked cigarette dangling from his lips. The guy looked like Ernest Borgnine on a bad day.

"I thought you were going to call before you came," said Trey, attempting composure.

"I didn't have a quarter," wheezed the visitor, catching his breath after the climb. "You gonna let me in?"

He looked to the brown package, his spirits lifted a bit. "You got it, huh?"

"Damn right, I got it," he said, brushing past Trey. "And it's better you give me my money here inside 'stead of out there with everyone watching."

Trey peered up and down the empty street, then shut the door. "Of course. Um, may I see it first?"

"Sure, Bud." Mal opened the wrapping, the brown paper rustling, and handed the ledger to Trey.

"There you go, goods returned. Happy ending."

Trey caressed the volume, stroked its hubbed spine, ran his fingers over the familiar cover. Much of his life for the past five years was in the pages of this book. "Did you have to hurt him to get it?" he asked, hoping.

Mal shook his fat head in the negative, made furrows above his heavy black brows. "Nah, but I'd have liked to. You got my dough?"

"Five hundred, as agreed on, yes. Will you take a check?"

Then and there, the man seemed to emit a black aura. Trey felt a glimmer of worry, he and this fellow alone together. "Better make it six big ones, bonus pay. I sprained my pinkie tossing the guy's apartment. And hell no, I won't take a check. You want this on record? That's what a check is. Cash is king, no tracing it to anything in particular."

"Sorry," said Trey. "I didn't know how it worked. But, you see, that's why I asked that you call first, so I could be ready with the payment. It's not like I have five hundred, uh, six hundred laying around."

"Maybe you should check the cookie jar," said Mal, snatching the ledger out of Trey's hands.

"Okay, okay," Trey muttered. "Wait here, I'll be right back."

"Water," said Mal, and seeing Trey's blank look, he clarified. "I need a glass of water."

"Kitchen's that way," he pointed as he made toward the stairs.

In his office, he opened the wall safe with three practiced turns of the calibrated wheel. He took out the desired sum in fifties and hundreds, and dashed back down the stairs. He wanted this creep out of his house right now. When he walked into the kitchen, the fridge was open and Mal was at the counter making himself a sandwich.

Perturbed, "You got any French's mustard? All I can find is this Poop-on stuff."

Trey advanced cautiously. In the short time he'd been gone, Mal had made himself at home. Slices of Bavarian ham and smoked Gouda cheese lay on a cutting board, and his just-purchased loaf of pumpernickel had been ripped open. "No American mustard, sorry. Here, let me finish that for you." As Mal fingered the bills, his reward for being an unbearable asshole, Trey quickly assembled the sandwich. The ledger was no longer in Mal's grip; he had placed it on the counter, among the sandwich materials.

"If you don't have French's, I'll take some mayo," he directed. "Can't just eat it dry, right?"

It was all Trey could do to refrain from saying, "Persnickety, aren't we?" Trey got the Hellman's and spread it evenly on the top of the ham, careful not to go over the edges. Exactly the way he'd have done it, if the sandwich were for him. He cut it neatly in half, diagonally, and put it in a Baggie.

"There you go," said Trey. "Enjoy."

Mal took the bag, and frowned.

"Something else?" wondered Trey.

"Yeah," said Mal, "you got any dill pickle spears?"

As he had done with his previous unwelcome visitors, Trey stood at the window watching Mal depart, the impossibly huge car nearly colliding with a delivery truck as it pulled away. Good riddance!

Alone, finally, he moved to the sofa, made himself comfortable, and opened the OFFICIAL NOTES, RECORDS, AND ROSTER of the Man 2 Man Organization. He went through its pages, a walk down memory lane. He had used three colors of ink to differentiate the entries by category: black ball-point for names, addresses, phone numbers of members; blue ball-point for notes on sexual preferences and practices; and red ball-point for anything relating to membership dues—paid in full, paid for someone else, late fee assessed; bounced check made good, bounced check not made good / payment in arrears, and so forth. Each page contained some telling entry that made him smile.

But here, what was this? A note written by someone other than him, tainting the sanctity of his personal property. It read:

Trey, (I omit the Dear as in "Dear Trey," no love lost between us)

It's true, you're far more polished than I. And for all your sophistication I really hope you will have the common sense to take this entreaty (actually, a demand) seriously. To wit: AIDS is bigger than both of us. It is not going away. I (as public health officer) am seeing firsthand its devastation on human lives. You are enabling this, your very home is the nidus of the epidemic in this city. (Don't know that word, nidus? Look it up). Time to throw in the towel, cash in your chips, piss on the fire (and any other metaphors that may apply). In short, you're through. Maybe the thought of prison life appeals to you, mingling with shit-slurping pinheads, being reamed by scabrous donkey dicks or fucking hairy assholes day in, day out (it won't be your choice). But if not, you had better quit now.

Signed,

Your favorite peon.

Trey stared pensively at the note in his hands. One immediate thought filled his head. Other thoughts would come later, but the current, overarching thought had to do with writing style: too many parenthetical phrases.

SIXTY-TWO

PRUDENCE CALDER had no qualms about wielding power when the circumstances warranted it. Not that her reign as health commissioner would ever be described as phlegmatic, but there were times when conditions were ripe for taking swift and decisive action. One of those times was now.

The AIDS virus was no longer a smoldering ember, something that might be stamped out or at least contained. Over the past several months, it had become a blazing fire, claiming dozens of victims weekly—and that was only the number being reported. She and her staff had watched the situation unfold, going from tentative diagnoses made by puzzled physicians, to confident pronouncements as doctors became familiar with the most obvious signs and symptoms of the lethal disease. That diagnostic acumen for recognizing HIV/AIDS had improved was a direct outcome of a symposium she had organized for local physicians. For that gathering of scientific minds, she had recruited two stalwarts in their respective fields: Dr. Micah Fielding, of Johns Hopkins, who had scrutinized every aspect of the virus since it first became known; and Matthew Wicker, a San Francisco-based ER doc who had seen more men in the throes of full-blown AIDS than anyone in the country.

But any knowledge or wisdom that these dedicated men might pass on to their brethren in the medical field was merely striking at the branches of the problem. To get to the root, one had to backtrack to the source.

How the disease was passed on, simple: an exchange of bodily fluids, semen or blood or vaginal fluid, with one of the engaged parties infected. Sex, the most basic human urge, was the common vehicle to enable transmission of the virus. Where does this sex occur? In the privacy of one's own home. Nothing can be done about that, except to encourage the men to use condoms, and her staff was currently working on that.

Ah, but sex, fast and furtive, also occurs on the premises of gay bath houses and brothels as well as in the vehicles of men who pick up prostitutes who have no flophouse to take them to. And something could be done about that.

Calder personally phoned both the mayor and the chief of police, arranged a meeting in her office. Both men, Mayor Campau and Chief Kinealy, came knocking at the same time, just past one on a Thursday. She laid it out, the problem and the proposed solution, a crackdown of vice in St. Louis, particularly vice of a sexual nature.

"With all due respect," said Kinealy, "we're already doing that. We just arrested twelve johns and three hookers last week down around Belle Rive Park. It was on the news, one of the men was a Baptist preacher."

"That's only a dent," said Calder. "I'm telling you we've got to ramp it up. Not just sit there in a squad car waiting for money to be passed, but head it off at the pass. Stomp on them hard, let them know that illicit sex won't be tolerated in this city."

"Tough talk is just that," answered Kinealy. "We can go only so far before we're accused of violating civil rights."

"Why don't you pay a visit to the hospice over at St. Mary's, talk to the men whose lives have been cut short by AIDS. Tell them about your reluctance to stop this disease in its tracks."

"From what I know," offered Kinealy, "it's not going to be stopped. It's moving across the country like a banshee on the warpath." He shuddered at the thought.

"You may be right," said Calder. "But if it is unstoppable, for now anyway, at least we're going to give it an ass-kicking it won't forget. Now, besides cracking down hard on open prostitution including escort services, what I need is a closure of the two gay bath houses here along with any known brothel. And I mean boards on the doors and windows. Shuttered. Out of business for the duration. This has already been done in New York and San Francisco and Berkeley. We don't want to be behind the times, do we Donald?"

"That sounds too much like martial law. I'll need to talk to my legal department," the mayor told her.

"Huh! I would've thought you had more mettle. I can show you the statutes that cover closure of a business or residence that poses a threat to public health. The motive is there, and now we need the mechanism to make it happen. I'm talking about a contingent of maybe ten individuals. Police officers to keep things under control, someone from my staff to explain the action to the media or anyone else who legitimately inquires, legal counsel from your office, Donald, to keep the ACLU off our backs, and some strapping fellows from public works who can nail plywood to a building."

She looked at both men expectantly. The mayor and police chief looked at each other, one more doubtful than the other. After several long seconds, Kinealy shrugged and cocked an eyebrow. "What the hell," he said, "it's worth a try."

SIXTY-THREE

ONE OF THE ODDBALL outcomes of having his nest disturbed by that goon was a return to reading. In cleaning up, Malloy had found the *Amazing Stories* that Timba had given him. It looked to have been thrown with force, its cover torn away. He imagined Mal as an ogre, who upon finding a magazine with a lurid cover like that and a teaser to read a story about someone named Malloy—same name as the guy whose apartment he was wrecking—became enraged and took it out on the old pulp mag.

A good story was just what he needed right now, take his mind off the insanity buzzing around him. He was well into *You Can't Kill Mike Malloy* already, transported to New York City in the early 1930s, spending time in speakeasies with Mike and his pals.

But these pals were only pretend pals. They were heartless bastards who schemed to get Malloy to drink himself to death and then collect the payout on the life insurance policy in his name. In fact, his pals were so mindful of the perils facing the former fireman-turned-homeless-drunkard that they had three life insurance policies in his name. These pals had surnames such as Marino and Kriesberg and Pasqua, which explained, in the present-day Malloy's way of thinking, why they failed to understand that an Irishman's gut is lined with copper, and giving him drink after drink only burnishes the copper to a finer sheen.

Marino owned the speakeasy and gave Mike Malloy unlimited credit. Day after day, week after week, the group plied him with booze until he passed out. They hoped and prayed he wouldn't wake, but the next day, usually before noon, he'd be back for his drink. Standard eighty-proof spirits wouldn't do the trick and Malloy was drinking Marino out of business, so the pals got creative, adding lethal concoctions to his drinks. First, they tried antifreeze; Mike Malloy pronounced it "a bit sweet" and asked for more. When that didn't work, they tried turpentine, followed by horse liniment and finally rat poison. Still, Iron Mike Malloy lived.

They were a wicked bunch, these so-called pals, and they also poisoned his food, giving poor Mike Malloy raw oysters soaked in wood alcohol, and, on another desperate occasion, a sandwich of spoiled sardines mixed with carpet tacks.

For obvious reasons, they had to make Mike Malloy's death look accidental which explained why they didn't do him a favor and cut his throat. To Shaun Malloy, musing on it fifty years later, the solution was simple

and a lot less painful to Mike Malloy. You take him up to the roof of a tall
building. He's already drunk. You lead him to the edge of the rooftop, you
look down and say, "Hey Mike, isn't that Paddy McCarthy down there,
waving at us?" When Mike Malloy looks down, he gets a kick in the rear
and finds himself splat on the pavement. End of story.

But that ending would fall far short of the tension conveyed in this
story, sick as it was. Page after page contained passages and descriptions
of incredible cruelty. There wasn't even a plot to speak of, just a series of
ill-conceived and miserably botched attempts to take the life of another.
Vividly, he could see it played out. He was both sickened and fascinated by
the depravity of these would-be murderers as well as the oblivious nature
of the would-be victim. Did he not suspect that they were trying to do him
in? What a chump!

It was a Saturday morning. He decided to finish the piece, eager to be
appalled anew at still more sadistic acts perpetrated on this pathetic sot,
who may or may not be his distant cousin. The phone rang. It was Urban
Lehrer. "Hey, what're you doing?"

"Reading a story about a man who's hard to kill," answered Malloy.

"James Bond?"

"Not even close. What's up?"

"I got your file and read it through. Wow. There's some juicy stuff in
there. I'd like to use it in my story, but I need to know the provenance."

"What do you mean?"

"The provenance. Who it belongs to, where it was, how it came into your
possession. Whatever I write is going to be vetted and I have to validate my
source. Otherwise, I'm fabricating. Get it?"

"Oh ... um, well, that's a long story."

"I've got time," declared the reporter, "meet me at the Bluebird Cafe in a
half hour."

The Bluebird Cafe in Tower Grove South had a special going. Buy one
specialty omelet and get the second at half price. Why not? Malloy went
for the classic Denver omelet because it was all he knew, and Lehrer asked
for the spinach-and-feta treatment.

"Mediterranean," chimed the helpful waitress, all of nineteen.

"I hear it's a nice place," said Lehrer.

"You want a Mediterranean omelet—three eggs, spinach, feta, sun-dried tomatoes, and pesto. My favorite," she added.

Lehrer was thinking, Malloy could see it. "Can you leave out the yolks and just use the egg whites? Cholesterol, I've got issues."

"No problemo," said the waitress, scribbling on a pad. "We do that all the time."

"I'll take his yolks," said Malloy. "The doctor told me I don't have enough cholesterol in my diet."

"All right," said waitress, "the yolks on you."

"You set that up, didn't you," said Lehrer as the waitress disappeared. "Are you in league with her, thinking up clever comebacks to impress unwitting diners?"

"I'll tell you if you tell me when did problems become issues?"

"Good one," said Lehrer. "I've wondered about that myself."

Malloy clasped his hands, leaned forward in the booth. "Why replace a perfectly good word with another that's less precise? This guy has gambling issues, that guy has halitosis issues. The dog has flea issues. They're *problems*, man."

Lehrer nodded in appreciation. He brought out the manila envelope, laid it on the table, and tapped it significantly. "This file you gave me, looks like pages copied from a journal, does this have issues?"

"I'd say so," he whispered. "For one thing, it was stolen ... at great cost, I could add."

"That's wild," said Lehrer. "And I'll bet it came from that house in Lafayette Square, the rich guy who plans parties for fun and profit."

"You would be correct."

"What, you broke into his house? You hired someone? Where's the original?"

Malloy didn't care for the way this conversation was turning into an interrogation. "I can't see that it matters how it was done. What matters is that now we have a record of the scope of the activity. Names, contact information, payments, liner notes about fetishes, requests for hung schoolboys, a bloody good pounding, and a Marlboro Man." He studied Lehrer's brown eyes for signs of anything. "Not that fetishes and yearnings for kinky sex are shocking or horrible," he added, thinking to state his position for the record. "The old Shaun Malloy, the pre-investigator Malloy might've thought so—I've left that judgmental guy far behind—but it does speak to the larger question of irresponsible sex in the Age of AIDS, at least that's what I'm telling myself. Point is, we've got him where we want him. And yeah, the original has been returned."

"Maybe I can use it," said Lehrer, keeping a low tone, "probably. But let's back up a minute. You didn't tell me how you obtained it. I didn't hear that part. Okay? At some point my editor's going to see this, and he's going to ask 'Where'd you get this?' And I'm going to say that I got it from a friend. And my editor, who's suspicious by nature, is going to ask 'Where did your friend get it from?' And I'm going to say, 'I don't know, but he's reliable.' And that will probably be the end of it."

"Uh huh, that sounds good." He took a sip of coffee, and wondered aloud, "How do you see this being of use?"

"Okay," Lehrer ventured, "this Man 2 Man club is just part of the crazy quilt of AIDS in America, but it plays an important role in the spread of the disease. The reason being, that Vonderhaar is bringing in clients, members, whatever, from all over. Looking at the addresses on these pages, there are men coming here for an evening of debauchery from every major city.

"But it's the members who live in coastal cities that are the most troubling. There's a new study out that estimates the prevalence of human immunodeficiency virus among gay male residents of New York and San Francisco at five percent. Five percent, hmm. Doesn't seem like much, but that five percent is probably highly promiscuous and soon it becomes ten percent, twenty percent. Many don't realize they're infected. They went through the initial stages of the disease thinking it was a particularly bad flu, but now they're alright.

"The ones with money, the ones who hear about this sex club in St. Louis, decide to give it a try. Something novel for them. We're in the middle of the country, we're a stopover for a lot of flights elsewhere. It's convenient to spend twenty-four hours here. You take a taxi into the city, get a room, you and your virus, and get ready to party at Chateau Vonderhaar. The upshot is, he's introducing AIDS to the Midwest faster than it would otherwise have been introduced. He's accelerating the transmission."

"And for that," pronounced Malloy, "he's got to go."

"Yeah, no doubt. Now, the way I would use this," tapping the manila envelope again, "is to paint a picture of what I've just explained. But, in addition, I would call around, using the phone numbers provided here, to look for a couple things: Members who are unhappy with Vonderhaar and are willing to give the inside scoop on the club, go on record to say what it really is—a whorehouse for privileged, swinging gays. And maybe while I'm calling around, I'll run across someone who's actually infected and is willing to point the finger where the finger needs to be pointed. As mercenary as it sounds, that would be awesome."

Malloy nodded agreement. "I might be able to steer you toward someone local. But it just occurred to me that your calling around will get back to Trey. I wonder how he'll take that, you calling his members up, asking some very pointed questions. He's got this lawyer, a slickster named Dunaway."

"I'm going to have to approach Vonderhaar anyway," said Lehrer. "I'll want comment from his nibs. If he refuses to talk, then it's 'Vonderhaar declined to comment' in my story. At least I tried. As for the lawyer getting involved, maybe laying down the gauntlet with a TRO, we'll cross that bridge when we come to it."

The waitress appeared with plates of food. Lehrer removed the manila envelope from the table to make way. Seeing the omelets surrounded by hash browns, Malloy suddenly realized he was famished. He dug in, right along with Lehrer. They chewed in tandem for several minutes before Malloy decided to speak.

"There's a name in that ledger that I'd like you to leave alone, meaning don't call him. He's a local, the name is Peter Shipley."

Lehrer finished masticating and said, "Okay, but why not call Peter Shipley? The name has a nice ring to it, sounds like a movie star or an author."

"Because," said Malloy, "I've got designs on him."

SIXTY-FOUR

TREY WASN'T SURE what possessed him to get in his car and drive to the woolly part of the city where both mongrels and dark-skinned youth roam in packs. Where a BMW parked on the street may as well be a treasure chest brimming with booty, ripe for the taking. It wasn't as if Art Tottingham was his dear friend—he didn't have any dear friends. He was merely another member of the club, in good standing, who happened to be going through a bad patch, that is, dying. Perhaps he was sentimental after all; Art was the last link between him and his father—killed by a speeding taxi in Sao Paulo, an untimely death that served to open the floodgates of inheritance—maybe that was why he felt that he owed Art a goodbye.

On a street off Cass Avenue, set back in the shade of a stand of maples, he found the hospice. He parked the Beamer out front, took note of the Arch looming off in the distance, and paced the walkway to the entrance. The yard was more weeds than grass, but at least they were dandelions and clover flowers, the colors complementing nicely. Halfway to the door a plainly lettered sign was posted: BON VOYAGE RESIDENTIAL CARE. He kept walking. There was a rocker on the porch, and, in a cage suspended from a beam, a pair of finches chirped a greeting. The wooden door had a square window with a drawn curtain. Below the window someone had lettered a quote from Charles Dickens: "It is a far, far better thing that I do, than anything I have ever done; It is a far, far better rest that I go to, than I have ever known." There was no doorbell. He rapped on the door, waited a minute, then rapped again.

The curtain opened and a face peered out, filling the entire window like a framed portrait. The eyes blinked, the mouth worked itself like a cow chewing cud, and the door opened.

"Good morning," said a creature of indeterminate sex, "or is it afternoon? Time flies when you're having fun. How can I help you?"

It was the fat that masked the gender, layer upon layer, enough blubber to burn a score of oil lamps for a fortnight. The voice, too, was asexual, but pleasant enough. "I came by to see Art Tottingham," said Trey. "He sent me a letter from this address."

The face registered genuine alarm. "Oh dear! Please do come in, we can talk better."

The person stepped back, and opened the door fully. Trey entered, noting a strong antiseptic smell. He stood in the foyer, wondering what next.

"First, thank you for stopping by. We're so out of the way here, it's like the world has forgotten us." Extending a hand, "My name is Alan, and I'm the caregiver here." He gave a weary sigh, "Right now the only caregiver. And you?"

Trey took the hand, pumped it, and gave his name. Glancing over Alan's shoulder, he saw a sort of day room, some chairs, tables with jigsaw puzzles in progress, a TV screen flickering.

"About Arthur," said Alan, sadly. "I'm afraid he's no longer with us. He passed, let's see, was it four or five days ago? It was a Thursday, I know, because there was trash pick up that day. I'm so sorry to tell you this. He was a beautiful soul, never a complaint. Altruistic, too. He donated his body to

Saint Louis University, his alma mater. It was a very noble gesture, I told him so. I said, 'Art, some young medical student is going to look at you, laying there on a slab, and not see a random cadaver but a magnificent human being.'"

And when he was alive, Trey thought, Art would have made a pass at that young medical student. "Well, that's that," he conceded, glancing at the door. "Thank you kindly for anything you did for him. He was a good man, and he'll be missed."

"There'll never be another one like him," said Alan, cracking a smile, "but I say that about all my boys!"

"How many are there?" he wondered.

"Right now, four, with another arrival sometime tomorrow. Would you like a tour?"

"No, but thanks anyway."

Alan took him by the arm, and steered him down the hall. "As long as you're here," he urged, "may as well see the place. I'm quite proud of it. I got it at auction at the courthouse, back taxes, forty-two hundred. Another eight grand to make repairs and spruce the place up, and what do you know—it's livable."

"Just you doing this?" asked Trey, shuffling along, curiosity aroused.

"Myself and Walter. Walter was my lover, the dearest man alive. He left his wife for me, and we lived blissfully for many years until he got sick. He lingered a long time, and I was grateful for every day. Toward the end, before he became comatose, he looked at me and said, 'Alan, we were fortunate to have a nice home where I could go in peace and comfort. Not everyone is blessed like us. I want you to do something, something big and brave. I want you to take my savings and start a hospice, specifically for those men who have gotten this miserable disease and who have no good place to go. And please'—he said this quite emphatically—'I want it to be a home, a loving environment where human kindness shines like a beacon.'" He paused, wistfully, "I only wish that Walter could have seen the first resident come through the door."

They came to a half-open door in the hallway. "Okay, this first room, this is Curt, our longest resident. Curt was a florist, he did wonderful arrangements for many important functions. The Mayor's Ball at Mardi Gras, Fair Saint Louis. Isn't that right, Curt? Curt? Ah, he's asleep. Let him have his beauty rest, let's move on."

A half hour later, he had met the other occupants, spoken with them, small talk, felt their despair. He'd seen their modest rooms, the clothing hung in closets that they'd stopped wearing in favor of pajamas. He'd seen their personal belongings, pictures of loved ones, get-well cards, prayer cards, and even some childhood memories; one fellow had brought his collection of toy robots. There were ointments and pills and inhalers and tissues on the stands beside their beds, and with these props he saw the tender ministrations made by Alan:

"Have you had long enough on that side? May I turn you over?"

"May I put some Vaseline on that?"

"No, I don't think three Excedrin is too many. Here, let me get you a fresh glass of water."

He'd seen enough.

They were back in the foyer, Alan saying goodbye, by now gushing all over his guest, glad to have had the company. Trey said, "Funny, I just happen to have my checkbook with me."

Alan, affably, "Ha-ha funny? Or funny in a coincidental way?"

"Fortunate," replied Trey, "because after what I've seen here I feel like helping out, and since I've got more money than time, well ..." He took his checkbook from the inside pocket of his sport jacket, took a pen from his pants pocket, went to a small table near the door, bent over. Scribble, scribble. "Bon Voyage Rest Home?" he queried.

"Residential Care, Bon Voyage Residential Care," corrected Alan, hearing a small familiar sound as the check tore away from its pad.

If Alan had a discernible jawline it would have dropped. Instead, his ample jowls quivered in amazement. "Incredible! Too much! Are you sure?"

"I'm sure," said Trey, amused.

"Oh, thank you, thank you. I knew you were an angel when I saw you at the door. Do you know how much good works five thousand dollars can buy? How many situations, lives at the end of their tether, it can make more bearable?"

"I'll get you more later," Trey said.

SIXTY-FIVE

PETER SHIPLEY'S PROBLEM was that he just didn't see himself doing the perp walk for solicitation. As the owner of a large business, the Goop

Waterless Hand Cleaner Company, he had to think of his employees, all seventy-four of them. If he were to be arrested for patronizing a house of prostitution—even though the house in question wasn't really that, come on now!—it would cast shame on him which in turn would affect sales which would mean a loss of revenue leading to the reluctant discharge of certain faithful employees.

No, that wouldn't do. And even though he was more or less out of the closet, he still had a family to think about. Two children, a drug-addicted, headbanger son, a daughter in art school, and a long-suffering wife who only stayed with him because she had a thing going with the mailman, a quickie twice a week on the living room carpet. Family, he mused, the tie that binds until it cuts off your circulation. Though they saw him as little more than a fat wallet, doling out greenbacks to fulfill their various material desires, he wouldn't want to make them pariahs by association.

"You could put a grocery bag over your head, then you'd be anonymous," said Malloy. "I've seen that done."

"How would I see where I'm going with a bag over my head?" he wondered.

"We cut holes in the bag for you to see out of," said Malloy, helpfully.

"Look," said Teri, "I don't think there's going to be any perp walk or any TV cameras to record it. It's just a simple bust, one of many on any given night."

"I'm almost a public figure," said Shipley. "And besides, your plan is really iffy. What makes you think this exchange of money will be seen as dirty?"

A critical look fell over Teri's face, lacerated but healing; it was mostly her plan. "It'll work," she promised, "if you'll do what we say. You pull up in a taxi, go up to the house, ask them to break a hundred so you can pay the driver. You hand over the money, the cops swarm, you're taken to the station. Upon questioning, you admit it was payment for sex."

"And the cops just *happen* to be on the scene? Yeah, right."

"My cousin is a city cop who just got transferred to the Third District. He's looking to make a name for himself. He's already agreed to be there if I tell him when."

Shipley shook his head as if trying to dislodge a cumbersome thought. "Lord knows I'm no fan of Trey Vonderhaar, the pretentious prig." Looking at Teri now, "And if it weren't for you, Steven would be in Bellefontaine Cemetery right now. I owe you, I do, and I'd like to help. But goddamnit, you're asking too much."

That discouraging remark quieted them for a minute. The server happened by and refilled their cups. Shipley asked for a side order of toast with jam. Teri, still smarting from her injuries, shifted uncomfortably in her seat. Coffee was it for her. Malloy asked for a bowl of porridge.

The matronly server huffed, "Whadya think this is, the three bears' house? You mean oatmeal, don'tcha? Or is it grits? Either one, we got."

They were in the Gateway Diner on Olive and 18th, near Union Station. Peter Shipley had made good on his promise to hear them out. He had arrived before them, secured a booth, and waited. And he had been fascinated by the place with its counter stools taken up by what he assumed were street people, the cook in plain sight working over a griddle the size of a coffee table, the smell of grease permeating everything. He'd have to take the clothes he had on to the cleaners. When Teri and her friend came in, he could see that they had been through the wringer, especially Teri, all banged up and on crutches. He genuinely liked Teri, and he was hoping like hell he wouldn't have to disappoint her.

Shipley, stirring creamer into his coffee, looked to Malloy. "And why can't you do it?"

"Because I'm not a member of the club," he told Shipley, "and because Trey has a restraining order out on me. Two pretty good reasons."

"All right," said Shipley, "you can't do it and I won't do it. How about a proxy?"

"I like it," said Teri. "Who do you have in mind?"

Shipley let the idea sink in for a moment. "There's a young man I know, Josh Winger, he's polished, handsome, intelligent, and he'll do anything I ask. As I mentioned, Trey has a soiree coming up next week, his annual Halloween Hoopla. The tentative invitations have already been sent. I say 'tentative' because the way it's done, so many members RSVP and then Trey and his minion, Freddie, look at the mix of possible guests and decide who gets the final nod. The rejects get a call from Freddie, saying, 'Sorry, good man, maybe next time.' It's like waiting to learn if you've been cut from the football team."

"I'd like to see that football team," quipped Malloy. "'Coach, there's a run in my uniform!'"

Shipley decided that this friend of Teri's was a goofball. "Anyway, I sent in my RSVP. This particular party is a good one. He goes all out with the decorations, brings in actors to play Frankenstein and Dracula, things like that. What I'm thinking, whether I'm one of the 'chosen ones' or not, we could still play out the scene, Josh and I. We arrive by taxi, I send him up to flash the cash, make it obvious. He gets pinched, I make his bond, hire a lawyer to reduce the charge or make it go away altogether."

Teri looked at Malloy who was looking at Shipley. She had always liked his profile, which recalled Robert Redford as Jay Gatsby. Malloy pivoted slightly, looked askance at Teri, her almond-shaped eyes meeting his. "Sounds like a plan to me," he said.

SIXTY-SIX

FREDDIE COULD HARDLY BELIEVE what he was hearing. Trey was going to step down as president and organizer of Man 2 Man. The club, a cash cow for both of them, was being put out to pasture.

"Just like that?" said Freddie, already thinking about what he would do next.

"That's right," answered Trey. "I feel like I'm stuck in a rut, and if I don't make a move now I might never get out. I'm tired of being a party planner, tired of opening my house to men I barely know—some of whom are very interesting, granted. But others ... let's just say if I met them outside this house I wouldn't give them the time of day."

"Well, it was a hell of a run," said Freddie, resignedly. "What will you do instead? Get more involved in trading?"

"These preserves are really excellent," said Trey, offhandedly. "A Swiss brand. I almost bought the plum variety, but went for the apricot and the boysenberry instead. Try some on your bagel."

"I think I will," said Freddie. "Boysenberry has always been my favorite."

Fastidiously, Trey put a schmear of cream cheese on an onion bagel and overlaid it with apricot preserves. "This looks almost too beautiful to eat," he said, taking a small bite. Freddie followed suit, but with boysenberry. When Trey finished chewing, he said, "When you hear what I'm going to do next, you will be astounded. Are you ready to be astounded?" Freddie pointed to his mouth, busy masticating. "I am going to Tasmania," Trey told him, "going by myself, an extended vacation, and, if I like it well enough, I just might stay."

Freddie stopped chewing, snapped his head back in a way that told Trey he was astounded at the news. "Wow!" approvingly. "That's really radical, Trey."

"It came to me only the other day," he confessed. "I knew I needed a change of scenery, and then I saw this show on Oceania, basically Australia and all the islands around it. So, Tasmania is an island state of the Commonwealth of Australia. Its population is mostly of British descent, which means they speak English, a big plus. There will be lots to do, plenty to explore. There are world-class museums, galleries, a symphony, yacht races. It's as cultured as anywhere else, but it's its own unique culture and I intend to delve into it."

He considered his bagel with its beautiful schmear. "In the cuisine column, there's vineyards, boutique cheeses, seafood galore. Looking to sample all of that! And there are rivers all over brimming with trout. That excites me, because I intend to take up fly fishing. Why not? Can you see me in waders, water rushing around my waist, casting out for the wily trout? It's fishing at its most sporting, a gentleman's pastime. I'll get outfitted once there."

Freddie had listened to Trey with rapt attention, not for the travel brochure pitch of Tasmania but because he was fixated on the dreadful possibility that he might have to vacate. He loved his carriage house; it was the envy of everyone who knew him. "I could run Man 2 Man for you while you're gone," he suggested. "That way there'd still be a cash flow and you could keep your options open. If we stopped it entirely, put out the word it was done, then it would be damned difficult to kick-start it up again."

But Trey seemed not to hear. "And possibly best of all," he reflected. "They don't play baseball, they play cricket. I am so weary of hearing everyone in this town talk baseball, a game for philistines."

"Trey."

Trey snapped back. "Yes, Freddie?"

"What about me?"

"Oh, you needn't worry. I'll need someone to watch the house, make sure it's kept up, bills paid and all that. You can move in here if you like, but if you're thinking of shacking up with someone—forget it. I don't want anyone else here, just yourself. Oh, and please know that someone will be keeping an eye on you. That's just good policy, you understand. I can give you living expenses, but you'll have to live more austerely than you're living now. If I decide to live there, I'll return to sell the place and then of course it's sayonara for you."

Freddie looked dolefully at the boysenberry-cream cheese bagel on his fine china plate. He didn't feel hungry anymore. "Then I guess I should call around and tell the guests that Halloween Hoopla is canceled."

Trey frowned. "No, silly. Halloween Hoopla is definitely on, one last blowout. After that, give myself a day to recover, get to the bank, pack my things. I'm booking my flight for three days after."

SIXTY-SEVEN

IT WASN'T EASY for an officer of the St. Louis Metropolitan Police Department to be gay. For some reason it didn't set well with the other officers, so Tom Moffitt kept his sexuality under wraps.

That way, when he walked into a gay bar while in uniform the assumption was line of duty, not trolling for prospects. And so it was, on a weather-perfect Thursday in October around six o'clock, Moffitt walked into the Peep Show for a little of both. Earlier that day, the bartender had called the Third District and told the desk sergeant that the bar's exterior had been vandalized, and that it was a hate crime to boot.

"Why do you say that?" the desk sergeant had asked.

"Because we're a gay bar," Mandrake replied.

The desk sergeant didn't like the tone he was hearing, the caller talking to him like he was stupid. "Yeah, so, what of it?"

"I'll tell you what of it. Some asshole spray-painted 'Fagbutt' in big black letters across the wall that faces the street."

There were close to twenty guys in the place, most of them at the bar, which was like the kitchen at a party—the central hub of merriment with the bartender as court jester. Immediately, they all noticed the uniformed cop in their midst, a big man with wavy red hair and freckles, leaning over the rail, looking to get the attention of the bartender. The idea of a man with a sidearm and other hardware attached to his utility belt didn't concern these besotted patrons in the least. There was something about this cop, his demeanor relaxed, even friendly, that put them at ease. He seemed like the kind of guy they could relate to.

Over the din and vocal stylings of the Culture Club on the jukebox—Boy George chanting "Karma Chameleon"—Officer Moffitt finally hailed the bartender. Moffitt explained why he was here, that he'd already inspected the crime scene, but that he'd like someone from the bar, that is, an employee of the bar to view the offending message.

Mandrake wiped his hands on the towel draped over his shoulder, and asked Moffitt if he wanted a drink first. Moffitt said he'd have a Coke when they came back in. Mandrake assumed that the cop didn't want a cocktail because he was on duty and had to keep up appearances, but in fact Moffitt never drank. As a youth, he had been a Turner, an enthusiastic proponent of physical culture, and that organization's motto had always stuck with him: *Mens sana in corpore sano*. In English, "A sound mind in a sound body."

"You see?" said Mandrake. "It's on the brick, and I'll have to pay to get it sand-blasted."

"What do you estimate that will cost?" Moffitt had his pocket notebook out, ready to write.

"I don't know," Mandrake replied, stroking his unshaven cheek. "I'd have to call around. My brother-in-law's a tuck-pointer, works with brick every day, maybe he's got some way to take it off. Why?"

"Seven-fifty," informed Moffitt. "That's the monetary line between misde-meanor vandalism and felony vandalism. Of course, it's a moot issue if we never catch the person who did this."

Mandrake frowned. "You mean the hater, don't you? Look at that scrawl, the letters angry, spiteful. This guy's agenda is no different than some skinhead who'd like to carve up Jews on their way to temple. It's just another glaring example of how they hate us and use every chance they get to victimize us. And yeah, it'll definitely cost more than seven-fifty to erase this filth."

"I'm not going to pretend indifference," said Officer Moffitt. "You prob-ably have good reason to believe you're being persecuted for your sexual preference, but don't you think maybe ..."

"Yeah?"

"That maybe you're reading too much into this. I mean, fagbutt is not such a horrible word. I've even heard it used endearingly, as in 'Come on, fagbutt, the party's waiting.' You have to admit it has comical connotations," he added.

Mandrake gave him a sideways look. "That's a peculiar approach coming from a cop," he said. He indicated the epithet on the wall with a sneer, "However you want to interpret it, that's your thing. I say it's a fuck-ing eyesore and I hope the prick who did it dies a thousand deaths. Now, let's go back in and I'll get you that Coke."

Mark Walter had seen the cop come in and then leave with Mandrake. He knew they wouldn't be gone long because when the cat left the bar, certain sneaky mice were known to help themselves. Now, they were coming in again and his heart fluttered. Not only did he have a thing for police officers—the cop in The Village People was his favorite—but he was a sucker for redheads. During their little trip outside doing whatever, Walter had relocated from the end of the bar, where he normally sat, to where the cop had been standing. Maybe he would stick around for a bit.

Sure enough, the cop went back to the same spot, giving Walter a close-up of his handsome profile. Feigning disinterest, he watched the cop take a soda from Mandrake, saw him taste it, tentatively at first, followed by several lusty gulps that made his Adam's apple bob. Watched him wipe his mouth with the back of his hand and turn, his back leaning against the bar itself, the better to survey the place. Walter knew this was his chance, and he felt fairly assured considering it was still early and he wasn't even one sheet to the wind. He took a breath, calmed his mind, and gave it a go.

"Do I come in here often?"

"Beg pardon?" said the cop, glancing down at the fellow in the rumpled sport jacket and loosened tie. Mark Walter repeated the line.

"Oh, I get it," he chuckled. "It's a take-off on the old come-on."

"That's funny by itself," said Mark Walter, turning on the charm. "A take-off on a come-on—what a weird language we have."

They made small talk, then medium-sized talk, and just when they were getting to the good part where Walter was about to cross that threshold into the possibility of some future rendezvous, Moffitt looked at his watch and said he had to go.

"Aw, really?" grumped Walter, wanting to let him know that he would miss his company but not wanting to sound like a sniveling paramour.

"Yeah, I'm on duty until eleven and there's a bust in another hour or so."

"Really? You have an appointment to bust someone? It's scheduled?"

"This one is," said the cop. "We're acting on a tip, there's going to be some illicit activity at a residence not too far from here."

"That sounds intriguing," said Mark Walter, quaffing the dregs of another White Russian. "Can I ask the nature of this illicit activity, or is that top secret?"

This produced an introspective smile, a feature that Mark Walter already admired. "It's nothing that's going to get me Officer of the Month," he told him, "it's just a brothel posing as a dinner party. We're going to nab one of the johns as he walks in."

Moffitt didn't see any reason to tell this virtual stranger at his side that the tip he and his fellow officers were acting on had come from his cousin Teri, and that, when he had passed on the information to his immediate supervisor, Sgt. McBride, the seasoned McBride was very much interested.

Mark Walter's intuition was not so muddled by alcohol that he failed to hear the alarm go off. "You'd better watch out for those she-devil hookers," said Walter, "they bite and scratch like cats."

"Oh, it's not she-devils," said Moffitt. "It's a bunch of gays and as far as I'm concerned we're doing the gay community a favor by putting the kibosh on this place, especially with this AIDS thing going around." Moffitt finished his second Coke, placed the glass on the bar. "Look, I've really got to go. Maybe catch you later, some other time."

As soon as Moffitt was out the door, Mark Walter went behind the bar and dialed a number he now knew by heart. Freddie answered, told him that Trey was too busy to come to the phone. Walter insisted, it was a dire emergency. Two minutes of holding was trying his patience. He shouted to Mandrake to make him another drink; Mandrake said all right, but quit tying up the phone. Finally, Trey came on the line.

"What is it?"

"You sound all put out, brother. Don't be, you'll thank me for this. I've got information that will save your ass tonight."

"God, I don't need anymore fires to stamp out."

"This could be a bonfire if you don't pay attention. First, you're having a soiree this evening and where's my invitation? That was part of our deal last time, you were going to invite me."

"Sorry, I forgot."

"Screw you, I don't believe that. Second, and this is where you get serious with the payback, someone is out to crash your party in a big way. What's it worth to you to learn the particulars?"

SIXTY-EIGHT

THE LACLEDE CAB pulled up to the curb and sat there idling for the longest. The driver, a Pakistani immigrant named Mustafa Farsheed, played radio station roulette as the two men in back jabbered away. Meanwhile, other cars came along. Some parked unassisted, and some pulled up next to the idling taxi and waited for valet service.

The idea of providing valet service was actually ludicrous because there was plenty of available parking all around the Vonderhaar residence. It wasn't like the cars were being taken to a secure lot or garage somewhere to wait out the evening; they were merely driven across the street or a few doors down. All for effect. And from a pedestrian's point of view, at least, this event *was* all about appearances, from the hustling valets to the red carpet lining the steps to the cute cut-outs of spooks and witches spotlighted on the lawn.

Mustafa Farsheed turned to the passengers in his back seat and said, "Shall I wait for you or is this the end of the line?"

Peter Shipley looked to his date and said, "What the devil is he saying?"

Farsheed understood this remark and he was hurt by it. He'd been taking English classes at the International Institute for six months now, and he thought he had it nailed. But he shrugged, put aside his question and went back to the radio. He had settled on a classical station, which now played Ravel's *Bolero*.

"Any time you're ready," said Shipley.

"There's a word for this," said Josh Winger. "Entrapment."

"Don't tell me you're having second thoughts," said Shipley, squeezing his hand affectionately.

"Oh, no, I'm in all the way. You know I'd lay down in front of a truck for you. I just wanted you to know that I know what it's called, this thing we're doing."

"Fine," said Shipley, "I'm glad you're up on your vocabulary. Now, go up there and do your thing, put on a real show."

But young Winger was hesitant. "You said the police would be here. I don't see any police. Shouldn't we wait until they show up?"

"Turn around, casually, like you're checking out the street light. You see that black Pontiac at the corner, parked at an angle, facing this way? There's two guys in front, I think that's them."

"Oh, an undercover operation—cool! It's like we're in a movie. Peter, you come up with some wild stunts. Thanks for including me in your plans." Winger leaned into his part-time lover and gave Shipley a wet smack on the lips. "Okay, show time," he said, and opened the door.

"That's got to be him," said McBride, indicating a lone figure ascending the steps. "Looks like was just burped out of a prep school somewhere. Let's move up."

Moffitt turned the ignition on the Pontiac Parisienne, a shiny two-door job that the department had impounded during a raid on a dope den. It didn't seem like the sort of car that dopeheads would drive; it had zero pizzazz. Earlier, McBride had remarked that if there was a catalog for un-marked police cars, this would be on page one. The Parisienne crossed over Missouri Avenue and parked in front of the house, within striking distance.

Not a bad dresser," said Moffitt, admiring the wardrobe from behind the wheel—khaki slacks, pink Izod polo shirt, blue blazer and two-tone bucks. "Classic."

"Shit," said McBride, eyeballing the cab Winger had gotten out of, "an orange jumpsuit with DOC on the back is classic in its own way, too."

As Winger reached the porch, Moffitt cut the engine. The officers got out and walked around to the front of the car. Winger rang the bell, stepped back from the door.

Inside, Freddie was introducing the first guests and ushering them into the parlor for cocktails. Trey, in the dining room, was making last-minute substitutions to the seating arrangements, moving dinnerware around, checking for spots on the china. "Go see who that is," he called to Freddie, putting out the snack bowls, peanuts here, pretzels there. Freddie opened the door to find a jaunty young man standing at attention.

"Yes?"

The visitor cleared his throat, moved back a few paces to stand under the overhead light. "Hello," he said, "I'm here for the party. That's my taxi down there and I'm afraid I can't pay the driver. Would you possibly have change for a hundred dollar bill?" He took out a bill and dangled it in front of Freddie so there would be no mistaking his intentions.

But Freddie was ready for this. Chuckling, "You think I'd take the bait that easily? You're not as smart as you are handsome."

"What do you mean?" the visitor asked innocently.

Freddie glanced down the steps, saw a pair of uniforms looking up at him. He savored this moment, feeling quite empowered. If he went along with this idiotic ruse, the cops would rush up, and Trey's game would be over. He thought he'd like to see Trey squirm. After all the slings and arrows he'd endured, it might be worth it to take Mister High-and-Mighty down, even if he went down with him.

The bubble popped. It was enough just to imagine. "It doesn't matter," Freddie told him. "Now, take your money, do an about-face, and go back to your modeling agency."

This gave him pause, the arrangement was going awry. Holding the Franklin between thumb and forefinger, Winger displayed it conspicuously. "Here," he shouted, "take your money. Take it!"

"I can't fake it," boomed Freddie, getting into the act.

"Will you make the blowjob slow," Winger's clarion voice asked, "take your time?"

"My sister's a mime," bellowed Freddie.

"I hope this isn't illegal," said Winger, playing to the small audience down at street level.

"I don't own a beagle," Freddie countered loud and clear.

Winger became quite perplexed. "You're not doing this right," he said, in a normal conversational tone. "You have to take this money," he pleaded, "Peter will be upset if this doesn't work out."

"I've heard enough," said McBride to Moffitt. "Let's do it." Briskly, they climbed the steps.

Both Winger and Freddie saw them coming, two officers wearing baseball caps—not the ubiquitous Cardinal red, but a flat black with POLICE emblazoned on the front in yellow letters.

"Now you're in for it," said Josh Winger, rather snottily. Freddie, absorbed in watching the police draw closer and thinking a mile a minute, did not see Winger drop the bill at his feet.

Freddie greeted them before they reached the top step. "Hello, officers, I'm glad you're here. This man, a total stranger, came to the door and began making lewd comments, acting as though he's in a play. I tried to make him leave."

Moffitt looked from Freddie to Winger and back to Freddie. "We have a pretty good idea of what's going on, and it falls under vice crime. What's that at your feet?"

Freddie looked down, shook his head violently. "No way, I never took that. He tried to hand it to me, I refused."

"What was he trying to pay for?" asked McBride.

"Sex," answered Freddie. "A blowjob, he said, but that was totally out of the blue. All I did was answer the door and he starts propositioning me." Freddie shot a hateful look at Winger. "You fucking weirdo."

"Enough of that. What's the story?" McBride asked of Winger.

"I promised not to tell," he said, folding his arms across his chest.

"Nice shoes," commented Moffitt. "What's your size?"

"Ten and a half, why?"

"I think we've got a nice pair of prison shoes to fit you. Slip-ons, no messing with laces. You might want to get some deodorizer spray, though, 'cause they'll be hand-me-downs from other inmates."

Winger gulped, shrugged what-the-hell. "All right. I met this guy and his pal in a bar last week and they invited me over for some fun, but they said it would cost. So I finally show up, ready to party, and this guy acts like he doesn't know me."

"That's a lie!" spat Freddie. "He was put up to this by someone, someone who wants to ruin the party we're having. We had a phone call saying this would happen."

"Well, one of you is lying, that we know," said McBride.

The front door opened and Trey came out, introducing himself with great aplomb. He had their attention. "I can vouch for Freddie here, officers. We've never seen this man before, and we did get a call saying there would be some sort of sabotage. This is a private residence that hosts a private club which is meeting this evening. We've already begun. This man is not a member, so he's trespassing. I would appreciate it if you would arrest him"

"Oh, that's good," said McBride, facing him down, "you telling us our job. You just put yourself on my list. And I know all about your private club. Sex for money, same old formula that's been around since Jesus was a carpenter."

"You have no call to say that."

McBride walked into Trey, arms at his side but pushing him with his barrel chest; Third District cops took no guff whatsoever. "You wanna go to the wall?" he taunted.

Trey, courageous in the face of persecution, did not avert his gaze. "Homophobia rears its ugly head," he said to no one in particular.

McBride looked to Moffitt, gave a disgusted shake of his head, said, "Damn queers, always whining about something. Homophobia, give me a fucking break." He turned his attention back to Trey. "You wanna pretend that your hoity-toity club is any better than a common cathouse?" He bent down to pick up the fallen currency, then stuck it in Trey's face. "What the hell is this, huh?"

"That was supposed to be for my blowjob," said Winger. "I'm still waiting."

"That's ridiculous," said Freddie, appealing to the officers, "the going price is fifty bucks. You can see he's lying through his perfect white teeth."

"I've had it with you perverts," said McBride. "You're going to the station, *all* of you, and we're going to sort this thing out. Officer Moffitt, you will confiscate this hundred-dollar bill as evidence, and note the serial number."

Peter Shipley watched the five people descend the steps and noted that three had their hands cuffed in front. Josh had come through, and he would be rewarded—not so much with crass material possessions but with lavish attention from himself. If need be, he would give up time with his other young men to spend more time with Josh. For a while, anyway. "Time to leave," he told Mustafa Farsheed.

"What about your friend?" the cabbie asked.

"He's indisposed, so let's go."

"I am learning your language," said Mustafa, twisting around to address Shipley face to face, "and every new word is a gift. Please define 'indisposed.'"

"It means up shit creek. Now, let's go."

Just as Shipley's taxi pulled away, another one took its place. The door opened, a light went on, and a large, handsome black man got out. He paid the driver, then turned to watch the curious party filing down the steps. "Good evening," he said, congenially, as they began to parade past. But no salutation was returned; they were a grim bunch, indeed.

"Who are you?" asked Moffitt.

The newcomer, Trey's hand-picked entertainment for one particularly wealthy client who liked his meat dark, replied, "I'm Barry from Memphis. Is this the soiree?"

Out of sight, but within viewing distance, Shaun Malloy leaned against a cedar tree on a small hill overlooking the street. All the lights were on in

Trey's home, but the only people left inside were a cook, some servers, a guy in a Dracula costume, and the very first guests, all of whom now stood on the porch forlornly watching their host being led off to the pokey. He thought about the food that would probably go to waste now that the party was canceled. He wondered how fast word would get out that Trey didn't have his shit together and Man 2 Man was not to be relied on. He imagined the tight squeeze of three people in the back of a cop car.

Finally, he thought: maybe now this bullshit will come to an end.

SIXTY-NINE

"WOULDN'T YOU KNOW IT, the Hunt Club Ball just around the corner and I've got this … this stupid rash. It's hideous. How am I going to cover it up? I look like a leper, I can't be seen like this. Oh, dear!" Dr. Brock Silber muttered under his breath as he stood before the mirror in the examining room of his medical suite, probing one particularly nasty pustule on the side of his nose like a teenager picking at a pimple.

He spoke to himself because he was alone, but also because no one else wanted to hear his problems. This seemed by far to be the most serious of those.

The rash had started a few weeks back, first on his trunk and then inexorably, like some creeping crud, it began to spread to his upper chest and back, then his neck, and finally his face. Each day was a new low in self-esteem as the constellation of blemishes and blotches shifted locations and changed appearance. Some were flat, even appearing to be under the skin, and some were raised, having grown almost before his eyes until they looked like tiny volcanoes.

If that wasn't bad enough, he also had buboes in his armpits, angry lumps that sometimes throbbed, and he was feeling quite out of sorts. He needed a doctor, that he knew, but someone with more acumen than himself. And though he was a physician, he was subject to the same backward logic that cursed many of his patients; the notion that if you put off dealing with the problem it might just go away.

Of course he speculated on the cause of this affliction. The lesions did not itch so he ruled out contact dermatitis. He did experience nausea and diarrhea. Could it be some form of food poisoning? He went on a diet of whole grains and plain yogurt, but that didn't help. With the arrival of the buboes he knew it had to be an infection. He narrowed that down to two things: That needle stick he'd gotten while trying to draw blood from that patient with the rolling veins, or else some type of venereal disease.

The latter wouldn't surprise him, really. He was no fan of monogamy. His current stable of bed partners included two men and two women, a situation that required serious juggling to fit his schedule. And considering that each of them had their liaisons, well, maybe the odds had caught up to him. If so, he was in the same boat as all those unfortunates he'd been seeing in this very room: *Doctor, please do something, make me whole again!*

Who would diagnose him, and would that person report his condition to the health department? Would he then be hounded by some determined epidemiologist to explain his personal affairs? That's just what he needed— more meddling in his business from the so-called powers that be.

He took another look at the pustule on his nose, ready to erupt, and winced.

The Hunt Club Ball at Bridlespur was the social event of the year. The genteel private club set in tony West County had been founded by brewer-sportsman August A. Busch, Sr. during Prohibition. Since then, housing had filled in the adjoining lands, communities formed, and the remaining foxes had vacated for wilder territory.

Still, there was a years-long waiting list to join. In the tenor of the times, the club had softened its membership policies regarding race and religion but still discriminated on the very selective criteria of bloodline, legacy, character, and accomplishment. Since he, Brock Silber, did not possess any of those qualities, he was unable to join. Instead, he was going as the date of one Belinda Carpenter, a socialite from a privileged family who was not yet among his stable of lovers and probably never would be unless he could clear up his complexion.

His jodhpur boots were buffed and polished. Would he ever get to wear them?

Then his receptionist was at the door, knocking politely though the door was open. Silber turned, saw she was flustered. "Yes, Charlotte, what is it?"

"A visitor, sir."

"No appointment, no visit," snapped the doctor.

"I tried to tell her as much, sir, but she insisted. She said ..."

Suddenly, the gatekeeper was brushed aside and there was another presence in the room, a formidable one. "I said I'm going to speak to you in person no matter what it takes," declared the woman, silver-haired, intelligent face, professionally dressed. "By way of introduction, I'm the health commissioner, Dr. Prudence Calder, and we need to talk."

"I don't care who you are," said Silber, indignantly, "You can't just come barging in here."

"I just did, and you're going to listen to what I have to tell you."

"But ..."

"Shut up, and listen! My investigator came here to speak with you about your outdated treatment regimen for STDs, specifically gonorrhea and syphilis. He also meant to address your lack of reporting these cases to the health department, as required by Missouri statute. But he never got a chance to do that because you rebuffed him, playing some silly game, and left him waiting. After that, his supervisor came calling and you did the same to him. Well, you're not going to brush me off so easily."

It was a mouthful, delivered with verve and velocity; she paused for breath.

"I know you're aware of these shortcomings, because we've sent you letters stating the problem and expressing concern—you do read your mail, I hope. So, the question is, why in hell aren't you doing what you're supposed to be doing? It's not that damned difficult. Communicable disease? You fill out a short form, two minutes of your time, you send it in. Treatment of that disease? You read up on the current guidelines, you stock the medicines, you use them correctly. What's so hard about that?"

He looked to Charlotte, standing there mouth agape. "You can go now, thank you," he told her.

Silber regarded Calder warily. He decided to level with her. "Look, I don't have a good excuse except that I'm pretty distracted these days. Maybe that stuff is easy to do for some doctors, but for me it's hard. I don't even know how to spell gonorrhea." He thought that might crack a smile on her stern face, but no. "I had an assistant who was on top of things," he added, regretfully, "but after he left it all went downhill."

She fixed him with a look of scorn. "I hope like hell you're not looking for sympathy. I've got the same degree as you. I once had a practice, and I can testify that being a physician is more than 'Tell me your symptoms and I'll give you some meds.' No, it's keeping abreast of the technology and following through after your initial diagnosis. It's thinking about if this person is a danger to themselves or to others. And, as corny as it sounds, it's not forgetting your Hippocratic oath."

"You're right," he conceded, thinking that mollifying her would make her go away, "I promise you that I'll try harder. I'll get Charlotte to remind me to fill out those forms. Okay?"

The health commissioner's fierce blue eyes rolled in their sockets. "Nice try. You almost sound genuinely contrite. It's too late to 'try harder,' because, despite the fraternal warnings, you've continued on the same negligent path. Therefore, I have documented your transgressions, those I know about, and reported you to the Missouri Medical Board. The ball's in their court now, and I'm sure you'll be hearing from them very soon."

"That wasn't necessary. We could've worked it out."

"My investigator tried to work it out with you and you made a fool of him! I did this for your own good, and if it means you lose your license, then so be it. We'll all be on hand to help you find a new profession, one that doesn't involve taking responsibility over people's lives."

"You make it sound like I'm a quack or something."

"You said it, not me." She rolled her shoulders and straightened her skirt. "Thanks for your time, I'll be going now."

She had her hand on the doorknob when Silber called out. "Dr. Calder ... right? Hold on a second. Would you do me the kindest favor? Would you please look at this skin condition I have. It seems to be getting worse and I have no clue what to do about it."

SEVENTY

TREY VONDERHAAR consulted his Magic 8 Ball for the last time ever. Sitting at the kitchen island over coffee and scones, he asked of the novelty store oracle: "Are you certain this is a good idea?" He shook the black orb, turned it over, and waited for an answer to appear in the little window. When an answer came, it was slightly tilted and unreadable. He shook it again, and the message was clear: Stay here, don't go. Actually, it said THE OUTLOOK IS BLEAK.

"Oh, pooh!" said Trey, frowning mightily. "I'll go to Tasmania if I want, I don't need your advice anymore. I think I'll retire you." He went to a row of cabinets over the sink, and standing on his tiptoes, reached up to the top shelf and nudged the toy into a back corner among the cookbooks and scented candles. There. He was now master of his own destiny.

He went back to his light breakfast, back to reflecting over recent events and pending outcomes.

What a crazy ride these last ten days had been. Having his ledger stolen and then getting it back, Eduardo snubbing him for the low company of those awful people, the eye-opening visit to the hospice where Art Tottingham had breathed his last, getting raided by the police and taken into custody, his club now in a serious state of disrepair. Just one of those things was enough to ring the bell of trying times. But all of them happening as they did, bad luck upon bad luck, well, you'd think the gods had it in for him.

The one thing that really rubbed him, though, was the thought that Malloy would assume the closing of Man 2 Man was his doing. He would crow to his colleagues how he had single-handedly put an end to this Sodom and Gomorrah in their midst. His career would be furthered, his image enhanced, and it would be a farce.

He had no doubts that Malloy and his cohorts somehow instigated the bogus raid two evenings ago, but in fact that excuse for a police action served only to make his exit from the helm of the club that much easier. Did that mean he should be thankful to Malloy? Was Malloy in actuality his unwitting tool, ushering his way into a new chapter in the book of life?

And, really, he was not greatly inconvenienced that fateful evening. Just as he was about to be shoved into the police car, he'd shouted to Barry from Memphis, told him to call Dunaway and tell him to get to the Third District station pronto; luckily, Barry from Memphis was able to remember Dunaway's home number until he got to a phone. He and Freddie were there long enough to wipe the ink from their fingers by the time the lawyer showed up. He also had had the good sense not to say anything about what had transpired on the porch, which wasn't hard since he really didn't know any hard details.

Freddie was not so mute. He ranted at how it was a setup, he'd never seen the guy in his life, he never took the money, never agreed to anything, wouldn't blow the guy for a thousand bucks much less a hundred. Josh Winger, sitting in a beige metal folding chair a few desks over, awaiting his turn to tell all, beamed at the thought of what he'd done; Peter would be so pleased.

Dunaway's arrival was like the proverbial cavalry getting to the besieged settlers in the nick of time, dispatching the marauding Indians to the happy hunting ground. Only here, the Indians were the detectives, and, after a heated conference with Dunaway they reached a compromise. No charges pressed against the homeowner—no proof of complicity—but the servant, or whatever he may be, was good for solicitation. After Freddie was booked and moved to city jail downtown, he would be eligible for release on bond. Dunaway called George Bloch, his long-time bondsman, and told him where Freddie would be in the morning.

On the short trip back to Trey's house, Dunaway was already Mister Fix-it, saying how it was going to be a lot of work to straighten things out— he knew a public relations firm that would help—but that over time this mess would be forgotten and his home would once again be the destination for well-heeled, adventuresome men throughout the country.

"You can't keep a good club down," remarked the lawyer.

"Forget it," said Trey, staring out the window at the nightlife of Lafayette Square, one long block of bars and restaurants. "My heart's no longer in it. This was going to be the last soiree anyway."

"Oh, yeah? What do you have going?"

"I'm going to hitchhike across America."

"Like hell! That's not you. Come on, you, what's in store for the enterprising Trey Vonderhaar?"

It was past eleven and there were still a good number of people walking about, going from one charming establishment to another. He heard their banter, lilting in the night air. "You remember the old maps in the history books, the chapters on exploration? If the mapmakers didn't know what lay beyond this or that territory, they would write 'Terra Incognita.'"

"Yeah," said Dunaway, "like 'Unknown Land' or 'Where the Hell are We?'"

"Exactly," said Trey, "and that's where I'm going, to Terra Incognita, also known as Time for a Change. It'll take a couple days to prorate the membership fees and refund the monies, and then I'm up, up and away. And, you know, it feels right, this decision. It feels as though all is right with the world."

"It sounds intriguing," he said, "and though I hate to lose a good client, I'm glad for you. Just watch yourself out there. Like the song goes," breaking into a decent Cat Stevens, "Ooh, baby, baby, it's a wild world."

"That's right, Frank, wild and unpredictable, and I intend to delve into it. The new Trey Vonderhaar will be quite the adventurer."

They rode in silence for the remaining few blocks. Dunaway nosed the car into an open spot under a retro Victorian street lamp. Only the porch light shone from Trey's home; there was no one around. Trey thanked him, and said to send him the bill. Dunaway joked that he had aced the Billable Hours class in law school, and that if Trey ever needed a lawyer, no matter where he was, he would be there for him.

Trey began to get out, and hesitated. With one foot on the asphalt and the other still on the carpeted floorboard, he turned to Dunaway and said, "For last year's words belong to last year's language, and next year's words await another voice. And to make an end is to make a beginning."

The lawyer pondered the passage. "Who said that?" he wondered.

"A local boy made good," answered Trey, "name of T.S. Eliot."

SEVENTY-ONE

ROSCOE MUST HAVE SEEN a squirrel through the window of Wanderlust Travel, for he was jumping up and down like he had springs in his paws, panting and whining and scratching at the glass.

"He gets so excited," explained Trey. "Roscoe, stop that!"

"It's all right," said Adam Weissman, travel agent and longtime friend. "I don't think he can do any damage. He is excitable, though, like somebody wound him up too tight."

"That's putting it mildly," Trey chuckled. "And I'm glad it's all right, because he won't mind me anyway."

"At least you admit it. So, where were we? Oh, yes, the increased fare on such short lead time. If you could wait two weeks, I could save you a bundle. Do you have to go immediately?"

Trey was busy chewing on a fingernail. He stopped and examined his work. "Damned hangnail," he said. "Might you have a file?" As Adam searched through his desk drawer, Trey continued. "Yes, I do want to leave very soon, this week in fact. I'm afraid that if I tarry, I'll change my mind."

"I understand perfectly," declared Adam, handing him a disposable nail file. "I've used it once or twice, but it should do the trick. All right, that's settled then. I can get you in Hobart by the weekend, TWA all the way. It's a seventeen-hour flight with a stopover in Madrid. Would you like first class seating or coach?"

Trey took a bite of his red licorice, frowned at his friend, said, "Tell me you're kidding."

"I'm kidding! I know you well enough. Nothing but the best. Now, let's go through the checklist. Your passport is current? Good. Bags packed with the right clothing? Remember, we're going into winter, they're going into summer. Currency exchange, no sense in doing that here unless you want to."

"Once there, I'll find a bank I like and open an account."

"People are using credit cards more and more these days. It's getting so you don't even need cash. Oh, and the pooch, you've found someone to care for him?"

"I intend to take him along," said Trey.

"Oh, dear," said Adam. "Getting him on the plane is no problem, but once there, well, they have these ridiculous laws. He'll need to be quarantined for quite a while, something like two months, to make sure he isn't bringing any doggie diseases into the country. And the quarantine is at your expense." Adam saw the crestfallen look on Trey's face, and added, "Sorry."

"He's my pal," said Trey, looking at Roscoe, who had stopped bouncing and was now slobbering on the glass, "my best friend. There'll be separation anxiety."

"I know, I know," replied Adam, wringing his hands in empathy. "But you'd be surprised, give him a good environment with maybe another dog around—not a kennel, but a caring home—and he may be all right."

"I'm not talking about Roscoe," he told him. "It's me who'll have the separation anxiety."

Of the pending trip, they talked details and expectations for a few more minutes. Then they segued into personal matters.

Adam was well aware of Trey's lifestyle; many moons ago they had skinny-dipped at a friend's pool during a party and one thing led to another. That was their only close encounter, their little secret, and Adam remembered it fondly. As far as Adam knew, Trey himself was not particularly active in the sexual arena, but he had gone on to profit handsomely from the promiscuity that was rampant in America. His pedigree and attendant social skills made him a natural at matchmaking in the service of an apparently large contingent of men, mostly professionals, who yearned to get off in a cultured atmosphere. Yes, Trey had made a name for himself in St. Louis and beyond; he was considered a successful entrepreneur, a resource, shrewd and unrelenting in the pursuit of the almighty dollar. And now he was leaving it all behind.

The morning's *Globe* lay on his desk, front-fold up. Adam tapped the glaring headline for emphasis. "You're getting out just in time," he told him, "things are about to get hot." Trey leaned forward, glimpsed the headline: MAYOR, HEALTH DEPARTMENT JOIN FORCES IN SHUTTERING BATHHOUSES, SUSPECTED BROTHELS; MORE STRINGENT MEASURES PLANNED.

"The Club Baths gone," said Adam. "That's kind of a shame, but Destin's Sauna—good riddance. You ever been in that place? Talk about skanky! The walls breathed germs. Their so-called sauna was a cesspool. And the regulars in there, standing around, schlongs hanging out, waiting for a poke, you'd think you were on the set of *Night of the Living Dead*. I was there only once," he quickly added.

"Shh," said Trey, "I'm reading." He was already on the fourth paragraph, digesting the news about new policies enacted in the face of the AIDS contagion sweeping the country. Places that promoted or otherwise encouraged random, indiscriminate sex were on the list for closure until such time as the disease abated.

According to the story, under a new law passed this last week, AIDS-infected persons could be arrested and prosecuted for having said indiscriminate sex, or having concealed their HIV status. This law was prompted by a Southside drag queen, Benjamin "Shay" Dillon, who was responsible for passing his infection to three known individuals, and counting. And to deflect finger-pointing at the gay community, the police department was stepping up its clamp-down on prostitution, for women could pass the disease, same as men. The health commissioner, Dr. Prudence Calder, was quoted, saying, "In doing this, we are following the lead of other metro areas, particularly New York and San Francisco, where this disease has reached epidemic status. At the risk of being known as 'the sex police', we are doing what we can—what we must—to curtail the spread of this terrible disease. If citizens insist on indulging in unsafe and reckless sexual activity, at least we can make it difficult for them to do so."

The article jumped to page eight, and there was a teaser about an accompanying feature. Trey rustled the paper, turning the pages until another bold headline caught his eye: THE NEW EPIDEMIC: A SCOURGE FOR THE 80S. The byline read Urban Lehrer.

"Lawrence Beard was anticipating the night of his life," the lead went, "an evening of stimulating conversation, cocktails, fine dining, and, later, sex with a man he had just met. As a new member of this elite and private club, Beard had paid handsomely for this experience.

"Now, a year later, he's still paying—with his life. Lawrence Beard is among the growing population of The Good Shepherd Hospice on the terminal ward of St. Mary's Hospital, a facility filled with mostly gay men afflicted with HIV/AIDS."

Trey gulped as a sinking sensation enveloped him. Lawrence Beard was one of his members, a university professor who liked to walk on the wild side. He had attended a few soirees and then dropped off the radar. Invitations mailed to his house were not returned, but had brought no response either. Phone calls were not returned. Trey could only guess that he had taken a steady lover, or latched onto something else that took him away from the club he once so ardently embraced. Beard's name was in the ledger that Malloy had taken; Malloy must have shared the contents with this reporter, who had picked Beard from the roster and coaxed him to talk about the club. In a very public forum. Having one's affairs chronicled in the daily paper was mortifying, like strangers seeing your laundry.

Come to think of it, this Lehrer had left messages on his answering machine. He wanted a comment on certain allegations, preposterous assertions regarding his business. But he never responded, wouldn't dream of it, his business was none of this nosy reporter's business.

He read on, and it got worse. Lehrer had gotten to other members who had been willing to talk about the activities of the club, one claiming group sex was commonplace, giving the impression of a dozen randy participants, when, in fact, a threesome was about as far as it went. Another member, obviously disgruntled, referred to him by name, calling him "the Madam of Missouri Avenue, and nothing more than a common pimp." Common? He wondered if he could get Dunaway to sue for defamation. To hear Lehrer tell it, Man 2 Man was responsible for spreading sexually transmitted disease all over Christendom, its members susceptible to the wiles of the club's founder, the worst sort of charlatan.

"Here's your itinerary," said Adam, handing him a sheet with the travel agency's letterhead. "The longest leg of the flight is at night. If you're like me, you have trouble sleeping on a plane. If so, I've got some Sominex you can have."

"Did you read this part of the article?" Trey asked. Adam glanced down at the paper, spread open on Trey's lap. No, he hadn't gotten that far. "Well, don't. It's nothing but rubbish. I don't know how these reporters can live with themselves, fabricating lies the way they do."

"The standards have slipped," agreed Adam, "they'll print what they think they can get away with. You want some more coffee?"

Trey continued to read, and saw that he was not the only one skewered in this detestable article. Urban Lehrer's poison pen had now turned on Brock Silber. Building a case based on interviews with other private physicians, health officials, and former patients who supposedly had to seek medical attention elsewhere after seeing Silber, Lehrer accused the doctor of gross negligence in his methods, diagnostic technique, and subsequent treatment. This, at a time when sound medical practice was needed more than ever.

A former patient with a major grudge claimed that he "felt like a guinea pig," after Silber had prescribed "a bizarre regimen of apothecaries that only a bearded alchemist would have approved of." A fellow physician, who asked not to be named, said it was "almost common knowledge" in the gay community that if you went to Silber for a problem you had better get "a second look from a doctor who knows his stuff."

And to hammer one more nail in the coffin of Silber's career, Lehrer told how the doctor was currently under scrutiny by the state medical board, with allegations of malpractice brought by none other than the office of the St. Louis Health Commissioner. Poor Brock, thought Trey, he's all but washed up.

He was closing the spread when something in the Law & Order section grabbed his attention, a small item: BRAZILIAN TOURIST ARRESTED FOR POSSESSION. A single paragraph told it all.

"A man on vacation from Rio de Janeiro was arrested Wednesday evening for assault and possession of seven grams of cocaine, after police were called to a domestic disturbance in the 4900-block of McPherson Avenue in the Central West End. When police arrived, Eduardo de Siqueira, 28, told them he was defending himself from an attack by the home owner, Kristi Taylor, 29. Upon further investigation, a residual amount of high-grade cocaine was found on a coffee table, and a subsequent search of de Siqueira's person yielded several packets of the drug. Taylor was taken to a hospital for treatment of a broken nose and torn ear, and de Siqueira was booked on felony charges."

It was so peculiar the way things turned.

A ray of sunshine broke through Trey's gloomy skies. Maybe there was justice in the world after all. Eduardo, with his glamor-puss, would be a big hit in prison, the pride of the cell block.

SEVENTY-TWO

It took until dinnertime to go through all the accounts, prorate the remaining sums, and send out refunds with a short note of explanation: "All good things must come to an end ..." He would go to the post office in the morning and, after that, the bank. Then he would say goodbye to St. Louis.

Trey kept a careful tally on his balance, although there was still quite a lot left in his account. Definitely no chance of overdrawing! He was running low on checks, however. Sitting at the desk in his office, gazing wistfully at the dog walkers in the park, he wrote one last check, to Bon Voyage Residential Care, for $20,000. He placed the check inside an envelope with a note: "Angels of mercy come in all shapes and sizes. Keep up your good work. This gift is in memory of Arthur Tottingham."

The next morning, at Boatmen's Bank, he had Freddie wait in the car. Will Langley, his personal banker, greeted him warmly, leading him into his corner office with the glass partitions. The banker in Langley was saddened to hear that one of his favorite clients was pulling out assets, but gladdened to hear that he was embarking on a new adventure.

"You're very brave to make a move like that," Langley said, "taking yourself away from familiar settings. Most people are content with the status quo, change is a hassle, something to be avoided. But here's the thing. If we don't change, we don't grow. And if we don't grow, we stagnate. Now, how would you like your money?"

He took $4,000 in travelers checks, and told Will Langley that, when he found a bank in Tasmania as trustworthy and attentive as Boatmen's, he would arrange a wire transfer for the rest. He could live comfortably for several years on the remaining balance in his account.

His flight was at noon, his bags were packed and in the car. He was eager to get to the airport. He left the bank, strode to his Beamer parked at the curb, and opened the passenger-side door. "Drive, Jeeves," he said to Freddie at the wheel.

The twenty-minute drive to Lambert was punctuated with animated conversation followed by periods of introspection, mostly on Trey's part.

Freddie was fine with the silence. It helped conceal his excitement that soon he would have the run of the big house.

Looking out the window at the factories and warehouses along I-70, Trey asked about the pending court appearance for solicitation, a charge that Freddie had referred to as "a boil on my ass."

"November tenth," answered Freddie, "one-thirty, Division 14. I got a letter in the mail."

"Frank will be there with you. Just be sure you do and say exactly what he tells you. He tells me the chances are excellent that he'll get the charges dismissed. Or else you'll get off with a nominal fine."

"I don't know about that," said Freddie, "what with all this new evangelism over prostitution. I'm about as far from a prostitute as you can be, but what if they want to make an example of me?"

"Frank won't let that happen," Trey told him, but he wasn't sure. He reached over, gave Freddie an affectionate squeeze at the nape of his neck. "It'll be all right," he assured, "no worries. If there's a fine, Frank will pay and I'll pay him back. He's on the job."

Trey held out a bag of red licorice, one stick extended. "No thanks," said Freddie, "it sticks to my teeth."

Instead, Trey took it. "This is one thing I'm really going to miss," he said.

"They'll have licorice in Tasmania, I'm sure."

"It won't be Switzer's."

At the passenger drop-off, they parked and Freddie offered to help him with his bags. "Let the Skycap do it," Trey said, indicating an old black man hovering nearby, awaiting a sign, "that's what they're here for." His last words to Freddie were, "Take care of yourself, old egg, and, even more importantly, take care of Roscoe."

Two days later, Freddie removed Roscoe's collar, and "accidentally" left the front door open. The dog bolted and never returned. He never did like that hyperactive animal.

SEVENTY-THREE

TERRY FALLON, the Casanova of St. Louis, was smoking in the stairwell when Malloy encountered him. "Hey, my man! Good to see you." He held out his hand for a soul shake.

Malloy was amused; no matter how many times the guy got the clap, he always seemed to be in an up mood. "Monday morning, bright and early. Had a good weekend, did you? I can see being a regular at a great old bar, but here? What if we just give you the penicillin and the works that go with it, so you can treat yourself at home?"

"But then I wouldn't get to see your shining Irish mug like I do." The singer leaned in closer, whispered conspiratorially. "Here's the thing, and I know a virile man like you can appreciate this: I'm a fool for the ladies, and because of my profession I meet a lot of ladies—beautiful, not-so-beautiful, but willing, even *eager* for love. I'm tellin' you, there are beaucoup lonely women out there. Who am I to deny them? Know what my daddy once told me? 'Son, you should try to make every woman feel like she's fuckable.' So that's what I'm doing, and if I happen to catch something along the way then that's the price I'm willing to pay."

"You're a cocksman, that's for sure."

Fallon laughed heartily. "No, I'm *the* cocksman. Get it right. Guess how many women I've had."

Counting lovers was something Malloy could relate to. "As many as are in a deck of cards, including the jokers."

"Way more'n that!"

Malloy thought hard. "Oodles," he said. "More vaginas than you can shake a stick at."

"Hah! You're in the neighborhood. Two hundred and twelve, last count. Whad'ya think of that?"

"I think you ought to save some for the rest of us. So, hey, let's get up there, the clinic's about to open."

Terry Fallon took one long drag and flicked the butt on the steps. Malloy ground it out with his heel. "You know what I was doing a minute ago? Singing. This stairwell is an echo chamber, the acoustics are awesome. You wanna hear me do 'Beast of Burden'?"

In the waiting room, Fallon took a seat with the other early birds, eager to be seen right away and get their cases cleared up. Malloy walked up to the reception window where Danielle manned her station. She glanced up from her crossword and gave a little wave.

"What's a four-letter word for social intercourse?" she asked.

"Does it start with an F?"

"I thought of that," she said, "but the second letter is A, not U."

"Then the answer is what we're doing now."

"Guessing at words?"

"No, dummy, we're talking, engaging in social intercourse."

"Oh, of course! So now I can tell people that we've had intercourse?"

"In public even. How's it going?"

"It's going to be a good day, it's already started off with a bang. Here, look at this." She thumbed through a small stack of intake forms, took one out. In the box that asked for REASON WHY YOU ARE HERE, the patient had written "sore penis and itchy tentacles." Malloy cracked a smile.

"They'll probably give him Gold Bond powder. If it works for jock itch, it'll work for itchy tentacles."

"Oh god," said Danielle, wiping away a tear, "the things that go on around here. You could write a book. Hey, why aren't you wearing red?"

"Because all my red things were stolen by elves?"

"Because the Cardinals are two games away from clinching the series. You're supposed to wear red to show team spirit. We live and breathe baseball in this town, remember?"

"Thanks for the reminder," he said. "I'm in the field this afternoon, I'll pick up something red, a T-shirt or a ball cap, don't want to stick out. And they're playing here tonight? Is it the Cubs, I hope?"

"Cubs suck! They can't even throw a guy out at first much less play in the World Series. You don't even know who they're playing, really? It's the Brewers, a team from another beer-soaked town up north. Do you even follow baseball? I don't know how they get their jollies where you come from, but here you're nothing if you're not a fan."

"A fair-weather fan, that should count for something. So I guess Fredbird will be there, too."

She looked at him dumbfounded. "Of course he'll be there, the game wouldn't be the same without him."

"I've been after Chicken Man forever. Contact to gonorrhea, the ER has gotten so stale it reeks."

"Oh, that's a riot! And you haven't been able to catch him? It's not like he can't be found."

"He can be found, but getting his attention is another story."

She leaned her head back and looked at the ceiling for a moment. "If I were you, I'd go down to stadium and catch him as he's going to his car.

After the game, you don't want to upset him before the game."

"Yeah, okay, but how do I know which car's his?"

"My girlfriend, Trina, knows him. I can't recall his name, Trent or Travis or something. But he's got vanity plates on a big ol' Buick that say F-BIRD."

"Great lead, I think I'll go for it."

"You can buy me a drink after work sometime, okay? But listen, when you do tell him the news try to convince him to come here for treatment, and then tell me when he's coming. I want to get his autograph."

In the epi room there was a game of catch with an official Cardinals baseball, red instead of the usual white. A souvenir, most likely, and all the investigators except Arnold on the phone were having fun tossing it around. The general mood was as light as helium. Schuler threw the baseball a little too hard at Martha, who didn't even try to catch it. The zinger hit her phone console, knocking the receiver off the cradle.

Martha put the receiver back, said to Schuler, "You always have to take it a little too far, don't you? You wouldn't have done that to Betsy or Malloy. No, you do it to the black woman."

So much for light moods.

Malloy took his place across from Arnold, moving his swivel chair up to the desk. Arnold acknowledged him with a nod. Whoever he was talking to was indignant about something, and Arnold was trying to talk sense. "James, all I can tell you is that the one person you named in the interview was not infected. That tells me that there's someone else, someone who is infected and who needs medical attention right now. Why don't you do the right thing and give me the name? … I didn't say it was a guy, are you saying it was a guy?" For the benefit of Malloy watching his performance, he raised his eyebrows Groucho-Marx style, and went on. "If it is a guy, that's all right. Straight sex, gay sex, we cater to all tastes here. Except bestiality, if you're into that I have to refer you to Animal Control."

Malloy was having a good laugh when the red light on his console began to blink. He pressed it and spoke his name to the caller. "Hey, it's Urban Lehrer. Did you see it, my story? It came out today. I couldn't have done it without you, man, especially the bit about Dr. Mengele over there in the West End. I wouldn't have gotten that on my own. And this thing has legs, man, I've already been contacted by *60 Minutes*. The reaction will be strong, I promise you that. Buy you a drink after work?"

At that moment, Karl walked in the room and told everyone to be ready for Chalk Talk in fifteen. Betsy tossed the baseball to him and Karl caught it with his left hand, his right occupied by a cup of coffee. "We're going to humiliate the Brewers," Karl pronounced, "and that's a fact. Those dogs'll be going home with their tails between their legs."

"That sounds good," Malloy told Lehrer. "Meet you at McDowell's a little after five."

It was a good Chalk Talk, one of the best ever, productive and illuminating, witty banter at every turn. Karl had brought the *Globe*, and they passed it around, voicing approval of the initiative taken by one of their own, Dr. Calder, and speculating how Lehrer's "tattletale" piece might improve their efforts to do epidemiology on traditional STDs and curb the spread of AIDS at the same time.

"If there's anyone out there even thinking of unprotected serial sex with a bunch of strangers," said Laird Cantwell, "this article may discourage that. If they were to read it in time."

Karl agreed. "It's as lurid as anything I've read in the *Enquirer*. I'm talking about the one guy's descriptions of the anal dildos they used in that private club. 'The Big Boy – seventeen inches of fun.' Yeah, we'll see how much fun it is to be in the ER with a torn bowel."

"'Excuse me, sir, is that a rubber fist in your rectum or are you just happy to see me?'"

Malloy turned on Schuler, gave him a look. "What the hell are you talking about?"

"It's the doctor in the ER talking to the guy with the torn bowel."

Malloy scoffed. "It doesn't make any sense the way you said it, *and* if you have to explain it then it's decidedly unfunny."

"Oh, now you're a judge at the comedy open-mic night?"

Karl broke in. "All right, that's enough. I think we can all agree that this reporter, in doing his homework and writing a bang-up story, did us and everyone else a service by shining a spotlight on this activity. I can't imagine Vonderhaar will keep going after this negative publicity. Now maybe, just maybe, we'll see a decline in case load among the gay population in the coming months. I'm talking syphilis, and though we don't keep tabs on AIDS cases and there's no reliable way to know, it's possible that the incidence of that disease may abate as well."

"Hear, hear," said Betsy, raising her coffee mug in a toast.

Arnold stood and went to the chalkboard. He flipped it over to reveal an intriguing clockwork, multiple sets of lines with arrows going in circuitous directions, connecting this circle to that circle. Artistically, Arnold had used different colored chalks to differentiate the contacts from the suspects from the associates. He cleared his throat and looked them over. "As you all know, success in our profession is measured in inches, not feet or yards. So," pausing for effect, "you might want to table that 'hear, hear,' until you've seen this new case I've uncovered."

It was a busy morning, Mondays usually were, and Malloy was glad when the clock struck 12:30 and his field time began. Before he even set foot on the parking lot, he saw Timba waiting for him. Once there, the burly jamoke tossed him his keys and motioned to the Maverick off by itself in a corner of the lot. Playfully, he elbowed Malloy in the ribs. "Much as I want your business, I gotta tell you, you're better off parking that thing on the street. No self-respecting car thief would want that beater."

"I would," said Malloy, "except the Refuse Department might mistake it for trash and haul it away. Hey, any news on that little job I gave you?"

"Oh, yeah, there's news. Good news. We took his keys and spanked his ass. He won't bother you no more."

"What! Really! You found him so soon?" Meaning Chris Dickerson.

The parking lot attendant gave a wicked smile. "You come to Timba with a problem, that problem is taken care of. I got guys all over town with feelers out. He wasn't hard to find. And when we did find him, we used his ass for batting practice. He'll never look at a Louisville Slugger the same way again. Oh, and he was quite surprised to hear that his broken bones were courtesy of one Shaun Malloy."

"Wow! You really fucked him up—that's fantastic, man! Wait 'til Teri hears about this."

"What goes around, comes around. Words to live by."

"Look, I told you I'd pay you. So, whatever you think is fair."

Timba looked hurt. "Friends don't accept payment from friends for doing favors. You wanna do something for me in return? Here, read this book. I just finished it, it kicks ass. This guy can write."

Malloy took the paperback, glanced at the title, *Somebody Owes Me Money* by Donald E. Westlake. The cover showed a hot blonde in a mini-dress, her fur coat opened to reveal long legs encased in above-the-calf black leather boots. She had one hand on her hip and was looking down at a yellow taxi driving through her spread legs. The blurb on the cover read "Even a New York Cabbie Can Get Taken for a Ride."

"She's got to be sixty feet tall for that taxi to go between her legs."

"Nah," said Timba, "that's just pulp fiction cover art. She's a regular-size chick, and that's not all that goes between her legs. Now go on with your bad self, get out there and round up those sexual suspects."

SEVENTY-FOUR

HE FOUND HIMSELF heading toward the Central West End, to an antique shop on McPherson Avenue, where he might find Stoney, a part-time employee named as a possible contact to a primary case of syphilis. The case belonged to Betsy, and because the OP was as sexually active as a sailor on liberty there were scads people involved. Toward the momentous goal of rapid epidemiology, Karl had asked him to help out. He parked in front of Toussaint's with its hodge-podge of "Daily Specials" displayed on the sidewalk out front.

Among the items in the antique store were an old school desk, a faux Tiffany lamp, a large bowl filled with old-time pool balls, and a Chuck-A-Luck wheel with depictions of dice that once spun round at some parish picnic. A bell rang as he walked in, announcing to the proprietor, lest he be in the back counting money, that a live one was present.

The place was empty, although he heard a radio coming from the back. An office? Someone would be out, give it time. He began looking around, thinking how antique shops were windows to the past. Look at this collection of lead toy soldiers, posed in action, toting guns, throwing grenades on the run. This one's wounded, got a bandage on his arm, but still he's in the fight. They were probably bought at a dime store by some kid who'd saved his nickels back when Hoover was president. He was imagining what these brave little men might have meant to that kid when he heard a voice behind him. "Are you a collector?"

Malloy turned and saw a bright-eyed fellow with a shock of wavy white hair, longish. His rimless spectacles gave him a look of erudition, if not sagacity.

"I'm an antiquarian at heart," Malloy answered, "but I don't have room in my life for many possessions. I do like to look, though."

"There's plenty to look at here, and every object has a story. What brings you in?"

He seemed like an okay guy. Malloy showed him his federal ID and explained his purpose, adding that Stoney wasn't necessarily exposed to a serious communicable disease, just that he wanted to speak with him.

"You can probably find him over in Maryland Plaza, at that doctor's office. The one who was lambasted in the paper today."

Malloy nodded. "Yeah, I read that. He'll have a hard time living that down. Why would Stoney be over there?"

"They're *all* over there," he said, theatrically, "protesting, demonstrating, making a scene. That story caused a hell of a ruckus among the gays in this neighborhood, of which there are many, and I guess they felt they had to do something to voice their displeasure. You'd think there was a sale on cock rings over at Hard Times, that's how quickly the word went out. I'd be there myself, but who'd mind the store?"

"It's not like you're overrun with customers," countered Malloy. "Close for an hour, why not? It's not every day you get a chance to be a part of spontaneous street theater."

The Maverick was already pointed toward Euclid Avenue, and once there he took a left. In the three blocks that led to Maryland Plaza where Silber's office was, he saw several groups of men walking along the sidewalk, some holding hands, all heading in the same direction. Maryland Plaza was thronged, excitement abounding, and he had to inch his way up toward the classical fountain at the hub of the scene. There were maybe 150 people milling about, chanting, waving banners, flashing signs. Some had fists in the air, their faces taut with anger, but most of them were having a good time, feeling good about being united for a cause that meant something to them.

Guys were walking in front of his car, and he had to stop repeatedly. One old queen holding a sign reading QUACK QUACK pounded on his hood, and told him to "park that piece of shit and join us." He did park, just past the fountain, on the wrong side of the street, but where he could take in the entire scene. There was a sizable contingent on the lawn before the clinic, shouting in unison something which made Malloy smile: "*Ho ho homosexual – sodomy laws are ineffectual!*"

A second agitated group were pounding at the door of the clinic, which was apparently locked. It reminded him of the scene from the original *Frankenstein* where the irate villagers try to storm the castle, wanting to wring the doctor's neck. And it was easy to gloat. He'd tried to get Silber to comply, but the man was too proud or too stubborn or too set in his ways, and now this public relations disaster. His career was definitely on the skids, and he had no one to blame but himself.

But Malloy was bigger than that; gloating was for lesser men. The feeling he had was more sad than anything else. He looked past the circus on the lawn, and there, over to the west toward Kingshighway was a small parking lot with a few cars. In one of these cars sat a woman looking directly at him, studying him from a distance. Through the open window, Dr. Prudence Calder waved and smiled slightly.

As all this was unfolding Dr. Brock Silber sat alone in the darkness of the Esquire Theater two miles away, watching Dustin Hoffman as an out-of-work actor named Michael Dorsey try to re-boot his career by cross-dressing for a part in a daytime soap. Hoffman got the part and his takes on the gender-bender predicaments that arose were so funny that Silber found himself laughing despite the fact that he had come here to escape the hordes and the terrible realization that everything he had once cared about had turned to shit. But maybe that had happened before today.

SEVENTY- FIVE

LEHRER HAD GOTTEN to McDowell's first, and was about to have his second Bushmill's. It was early and the bar was wide open. Malloy took the stool next to Lehrer. With a white bar towel on his shoulder, Lucky walked up and said hello to Malloy, who introduced him to Lehrer. Jameson's neat, he told him.

"You two going to war?" asked Lucky with a wink.

"Temporary truce," said Malloy, "we've run out of bullets."

"Drinking's more productive, anyway," offered Lucky.

"What's he talking about?" wondered Lehrer as Lucky turned to his bank of booze.

"By your choice of whiskey in an Irish bar, you're broadcasting your religion. Bushmill's is the choice of Protestants—Northern Ireland—while

Jameson's is the Catholic brand. It can be a sensitive matter, too. Around here, you always ask before you buy someone a shot of Irish whiskey, or you just might find yourself deposited on your ass."

"You mean arse, don't you? Well, thanks for the tip. I wasn't aware of that particular distinction, didn't know that the Troubles had wormed their way into the bars of St. Louis."

Malloy took his glass from Lucky, three fingers full. "Not just any bar," he said for Lucky to hear, "but the best bar in the whole goddamn city. *Sláinte.*" He downed the tawny ichor in one lethal gulp.

"Slanch-ya?" wondered Lehrer.

"Just drink," said Malloy.

They were quiet for a while, content to take in the ambiance. There were a lot of Irish bars in the city, but McDowell's was the only one that had Jameson's on tap. Malloy ordered a Guinness. Lehrer did the same, asking whether there was some political subtext with beer labels, too. Finally, Lehrer asked about the reaction of Malloy's coworkers to his article.

"It was a big hit," Malloy told him, "the topic of discussion at Chalk Talk this morning. That's our weekly meeting. From here on out, we figure Trey Vonderhaar and Man 2 Man will be spoken of in past tense, and the city will be that much safer. On behalf of the hard-working and intrepid investigators of the St. Louis STD clinic, I thank you from the bottom of my alcohol-pickled heart."

"The power of the pen, my friend. Silber's done for, too. There was a big demonstration at his clinic today, a couple hundred gays, up in arms over accusations that they had been victims of bad medicine. It made the five o'clock news."

"I was there," said Malloy. "They had some creative signs and banners. My favorite was the depiction of Silber as a witch doctor with a bone through his nose."

"As I was leaving, they were building a human pyramid on the lawn and chanting something about 'Physician Heal Thyself.'"

"It's a good day for public health," confirmed Malloy, licking away a foam mustache, "except that the hydra has many heads ..."

"And for each head cut off three more grow. So what are you saying?"

"I'm saying that today another investigator presented a case that's about as grisly as anything I've ever heard, and I've heard a lot. Did you know that sex trafficking is alive and well in St. Louis? There's a nest of predators out there, maybe a sizable group, and organized—pimps, pederasts, general lowlifes who have kidnapped or otherwise taken kids, some of them runaways and some as young as twelve, boys and girls. And they have enslaved these kids, and they are selling their bodies for sex. One turned up at City Number Two with a fresh case of syphilis, and, on further examination, turns out she has AIDS, too. She's fourteen and has been missing for five months. She's now in custody of the DFS, but this is just the start, you see? We're working with the police on this. It's going to get bad, real bad."

"God, that's fucking horrible!" said Lehrer, concern all over his face. "But still, keep me posted, will you? This sounds like Pulitzer material."

It was a short drive to Busch Stadium, but all the nearby lots were full so he had to park in a downtown garage and walk several blocks. Hell, he may as well have hoofed it from McDowell's, at least it would have sobered him up some. He had introduced Lehrer to the Irish car bomb—downfall of many a hearty Celt—and, of course he had to demonstrate the proper means of imbibing such a concoction. Over and over again.

His plan was to somehow find Fredbird's car among the thousands of cars parked in dozens of parking lots near the stadium, and then wait at the car for the joker to arrive sometime after the game. He would talk to Fredbird like he would talk to any other contact, coming off concerned over his health, not judgmental in the least, wanting only for him to conduct his busy life free of disease. No soft-soap celebrity treatment for the Bird, just the unadulterated dope, and if that didn't work, he had a health summons in his back pocket.

Never mind how he, dogged public health officer that he was, would be perceived by said Bird as a stalker or deranged fan, having staked out the guy's car and spouting blather about germs while obviously soused.

He'd listened to the game in the car. They were only in the third inning so he had time to canvass the lots. He made his way toward the stadium, illuminated as though by a million candles shining through mullioned windows. He figured Fredbird had a designated parking spot close to the employee's entrance, wherever that was. He started by circumnavigating the stadium, hearing fairly well what was happening within, the periodic roar of the crowd as some Cardinals player made a catch, or the pitcher threw a strike, or a runner tried to steal a base. Once again, he mused that if you could somehow bottle all that energy, all that passion, you'd really have something.

The honchos-only parking at the rear of the stadium had maybe thirty cars, but access was restricted by those interlocking barricades seen at parades. Plus, there was a security guard posted in the area; he was enjoying the fine evening, one leg resting on a rail, having a smoke. Malloy went through an opening in the barricade and headed straight for him, weaving like a ship without ballast, clocking plates along the way. The guard noticed him, an intruder, and brought his foot down from its position on the rail to the asphalt. "Help you?"

Malloy despised that phrase—phony baloney for "What the hell do you want?" He gave a friendly wave to put the guard at ease, and when he got near, "Bum a cigarette?"

"They're menthol," said the guard, a thirty-something white guy with a buzz cut.

"Fine with me," said Malloy, reaching out. "Thanks, man. You got a light?"

Now the guard acted like he was put out or something. "Geez, you want me to smoke it for you, too?"

"Ha, good one," said Malloy. The guard flipped his Ronson and Malloy leaned in toward the flame. He took a drag, didn't inhale but coughed anyway.

"Smoke much?" The guard waited for him to walk off; the public was not permitted to hang out here, and besides, the guy was half in the bag. After an awkward silence, Malloy came right out and asked. "So, you ever see a car around here with vanity plates that say F-BIRD?"

"That's an odd question," said the guard. "And would this plate belong to someone in the Cardinals organization?"

"Well, yeah," said Malloy. "First name Fred, wears a chicken suit."

"Does he run around in the bleachers like he's fucking nuts?"

"That's the guy," slurring, "where's he park his car?"

"Why do you want to know?"

"I told my kid I'd get a picture of his license plate. It's an oddball hobby, I know, but he's got quite a collection. "

"I got sad news for your kid. Fredbird doesn't drive, he got his license revoked," the guard lied just to screw with Malloy, who was getting on his nerves. He pointed to a tricked-out Schwinn manacled to a bike rack. "That's his ride over there."

"Aw, shit," exclaimed Malloy, "the little guy'll be so disappointed. Well, thanks again, and go Cards."

"Go Cards," parroted the security guard. He watched Malloy egress, wondering why he lingered in the vicinity of certain vehicles as he moved along, making anything but a beeline to the way out. At one point he circled a car, appearing as though he was checking something out. It was damned suspicious, whatever he was up to, and he was about to put an end to it when the guy changed course and walked out. Weird.

Across 7th Street, to the immediate west, there was a vast parking lot which contained about a jillion cars—a big number anyway, stretching as far as the eye could see. It was a pay-on-your-own lot, remember the number of your spot and place the bills in the corresponding slot of a large, gray, metal box near the street. He wondered if that box ever got robbed. You could take a welding torch to it, cut off its legs, and haul it away. He figured whoever was in charge probably came and emptied it every hour or so.

It wasn't like he could just spot the vehicle from afar—oh, there's a Buick, might be the one. Nor did he trust Danielle's word that it even was a Buick; she had gotten that from another woman who might not know the difference between a Buick and a Pontiac. That meant he had to walk past each and every car on the lot and eyeball the license plate, looking for one in particular.

He paced along the first row, not dawdling. Not every car was parked in the same direction, which caused an unexpected delay, for some of them didn't have front plates or, where a front Department of Revenue-issued plate might have been, there was some sort of souvenir plate—Meramec Caverns being the second-most popular after St. Louis Cardinals; for these he had to walk around the car. With every spot filled, he counted forty-two vehicles taking up the first row. He moved to the second row and worked his way back to the start. The second row had thirty-nine vehicles; no reason to keep track, but it was something to do.

Midway along the third row he saw it: the vanity plate on the prettiest goddamn car he'd ever seen. A cherry-red Buick Invicta convertible with headlights like goggles on a frog and fins that would make a shark run for cover. Early '60s model, he guessed, and it was restored, too. He looked inside—aw, an automatic. He looked at his watch: 9:10. The game started at 7:15, so they were probably in the seventh or eighth inning. There was still time. He scanned his surroundings. Across the street, down from the stadium, neon-lit letters beckoned, pulsing BUDWEISER ON TAP. Good enough for him. He made his way toward the bar.

He had one inside and got three to go. Missouri had this stupid law that three beers was the minimum for take-out, but at least that wasn't as bad as the law in Indiana, where all beer for take-out had to be sold warm. Whoever made up these quirky liquor laws had to have their heads up their asses, he decided.

The TV on the wall told him the Cards were winning at the top of the ninth. Darrell Porter was at bat. Malloy looked out the front window onto the street. He could practically see the car from the bar; it was beneath a metal-halide floodlight. He walked back over with the beers in a brown paper bag. A prolonged roar emanated from the stadium, 53,000 fans shouting their ecstasy. Had to be a win or an imminent win. If they took this one, and then the game tomorrow, that was it. They'd be the World Champions. Big fucking deal, he thought, it's just a stupid game. In terms of meaningful impact on society, it wasn't even in the same league as public health. *That* was a game worth playing.

Danielle was right; he wasn't a fan.

He leaned up against the Invicta and popped a beer. Between this one and the one he'd had at the bar he could feel the edge of his Guinness-and-Jameson drunk softening. The tinny headache had dissipated, his nervous system returning to mellow or at least not jagged. Across the street, the first wave of fans began spilling from the stadium, hooting and hollering in the night air. Soon, the spiraling walkways were choked with people, the anthill emptying rapidly. Then, the sound of ignitions switching on, plumes of exhaust rising here and there, and cars pulling out into the lanes between rows. He popped another beer and waited.

He imagined Fred Bird in the locker room, awash in champagne or whatever they did when they won a game. Maybe the champagne shower was just for winning the big finale. But he would be in there now, toweling off after a shower, combing his hair, putting on his street clothes. Hurry up, would you?

Out of nowhere, the name of the car crossed his mind. Invicta, that had some loaded connotations, eh? Recalling his Latin, he knew that Invicta was derived from *invictus*. Unconquered. It was also the title of a short Victorian poem that people in dire circumstances liked to quote, the part about being "master of my fate," anyway.

His own fate had been tinkered with countless times by countless people, and in turn, he, as public health officer, had altered the fates of myriad others. Because of his well-meaning intrusions, delivering bad news as he often did, there'd been hurtful words, thrown punches, parted couples. He saw fate as a handball, something in constant motion, bouncing off walls, never on the same course for long. He envisioned the handball courts in Forest Park. He saw the arm with the gloved hand swinging, he heard the ponging sound of the ball hitting the wall, steady, rhythmic. But which was he—the handball or the player?

Malloy saw a figure approaching and knew it had to be him. He was tall and gangly and he didn't so much walk as he loped. He quit leaning on the car and stood up, arms at his side, the distance between them closing with every second. The guy had his keys in his hand when he stopped a few feet in front of Malloy. The floodlight overhead cast harsh shadows on both their facial features. The man studied him for a few seconds, looked him full in the face, said, "What's up, Bud?"

"I've been waiting for you," offered Malloy.

"I can see that," he said, glancing at the crushed beer cans on the ground. "You mind telling me why?" The accent was a bit Southern. Kentucky? Tennessee?

"No, not at all. I'm a health officer with the STD clinic. Up on Grand, you ever been there? Here's my ID." He felt his back right pocket, but his ID wasn't there. Ditto the health summons. He turned out the pockets of his jacket, nothing. "I must've left it in the car," he said, "but it's true. I've been here before, couple times, trying to reach you, trying to tell you that you've been exposed to a case of gonorrhea. You're a hard one to get to, so I had to ambush you. Here. Tonight."

"Gonorrhea, that's bad, right? You get symptoms that tell you something's wrong."

"Not all guys get the obvious symptoms. You could be in that twenty percent that don't."

"This is nuts. Why should I believe some guy who smells like a brewery and looks like a bum who's pissed himself?"

"You can look in my eyes and see that I'm talking straight. This is what I do, track down people exposed to communicable disease, make sure they get examined, diagnosed, and properly treated. You're on my list."

"What if I do believe you? Who's the girl? Who's the rotten crotch?"

"I can't say. Confidentiality, sorry."

"Then screw you. I'm leaving." He opened his door and got in. Malloy followed and knocked at his window. He rolled it down. "Yeah?"

"I can't give you a name, but I could give you her profession. Then would you believe me and get yourself checked out?"

"Maybe."

"Come on, we're too big for kid games. I'm trying to help you here."

"All right, I'll do it."

"Are your fingers crossed?"

"No."

"Toes?"

"No! Goddamnit, who is she?"

"She's a cop, teaches at the academy."

"Oh ... yeah. That was a while ago. And she has it, huh?"

"Had it. She got treated, now it's your turn."

"Why in hell didn't I know about this earlier?"

"I told you, I tried. Your handlers at the front desk wouldn't make you available or pass a note along. She didn't know your name, I didn't know your name. You wear a costume out in public, you're fucking incognito."

"That's bullshit, she knows my name. We've been going out, on and off, for six months. Well, isn't *that* a kick in the ass?"

"All right, so now you know. And you'll keep your side of the bargain and come in the clinic tomorrow? Ask for me, Shaun Malloy, I'll usher you through. Deal?"

"I've got my own doctor, thank you. Do me a favor, step back from the car. There's a funky smell coming from you."

"I spilled some beer on my pants."

"No, it's something else, kind of gamey. Take a piece of advice from an old bird? Get to a shower, man. You smell like a wet animal."

"Better than a washed-up chicken. Isn't that what you are?"

"This chicken makes more money in a week than you'll see in a year."

"At least I'm not the laughing stock of St. Louis."

"That's the point, you idiot."

He began backing up, and Malloy backed up with him until he turned the wheels to head out. "If you don't do as you promised, your name is Fred Turd," he said, running his words together.

"Go to hell," replied the other, and spun out.

Malloy cupped his hands to his mouth, and shouted after the receding fins, "Remember, I've got your plates. I can find out where you live."

SEVENTY-SIX

TREY FELT A TAP on his shoulder and suddenly his meditation on the lovely cerulean sea below went poof.

"Would you happen to have a pen?" asked a thick Aussie accent, "the ink just ran out on mine."

He turned away from the small window, reached inside his sport coat, unclipped a ballpoint from his shirt pocket, said, "Here you go."

They were on a regional jet, two seats on each side of the aisle. The bearded fellow in cut-offs, hiking boots, and a Wallabies rugby shirt beside Trey took up all of his seat and then some. The man thanked him kindly, glanced at the writing on the pen barrel, read aloud: "Tony's – St. Louis, Missouri. Ah, St. Louis," he said, "home of the famous Clydesdales and Budweiser, the King of Beers. You can get that here, sure, but you might wanna switch to Fosters or Castlemaine Lager. When in Rome, you know."

Trey nodded agreeably, not divulging that the taste of beer disgusted him. He turned back to the window. It was a one-hour flight from Melbourne to Hobart, 500 kilometers, and they were flying low enough that Trey could make out certain features on the ocean, indistinct as they were. "Is that a ship down there?" he asked.

The strapping fellow leaned over in front of Trey to see, his full ebony beard right in Trey's face; it was braided below the chin and the tip tied off in a small, pink ribbon. He smelled like patchouli oil or some other exotic herb.

"No ship, a small island. It's where we keep the prisoners." He nudged Trey playfully, and leaned back to his seat. "What brings you to Tas, mate?"

"An extended vacation," he offered. "I saw this show on PBS, *Oceania: The Allure of Down Under*, and decided that a change of scenery would do me good. I'm going to get out of my box, try new things. I want to go trout fishing."

A big smile swept over his open face. "Oh, you couldn't have picked a better place, mate! The rivers of Tasmania are teeming with trout, every one just waiting to be hooked. You're talking fly fishing, right? Well, I've got just the place, a cabin on the Weld River up near Huonville—rocky shallows, deep pools, and rapids. It's Abo land, and some of the locals who've set themselves up as guides get three hundred a day for sharing what they know. I'll do it for a case of Foster's."

He wondered what an Abo was, put it aside, held out his hand, "Trey

Vonderhaar, pleased to meet you."

"Oh, damn. I thought it was Ralph Lauren, that's what it says on your carrying case," amused, nodding toward a canvas brief on the floor. He gave Trey's hand a firm squeeze. "Norm Claypool, mate, I'm a surveyor here in Tas. Friends call me Abbie."

"Abbie?"

"That's one of my nicknames. You know how it goes: Norman becomes Normal which becomes Abnormal which becomes Abbie."

"Perfectly rational," said Trey. "What're your other nicknames?"

"Oh, Chopper. Mongo. Just don't call me poofter unless you mean it." He laughed heartily.

"Poofter? I don't know that one."

"Poofter is a man who goes around locker rooms sniffing jockstraps," he winked. "A mite queer. You're not afraid of poofters, I hope."

Trey studied him intently, liking what he saw. He doubted the man had ever seen a dismal day. The hirsute, somewhat zany Abbie was nothing like Eduardo. And that was good, because if you've resolved to change your life you may as well start with a change of paramours. The looming question, thought Trey, do I want to go traipsing off into Abo land with Blackbeard the Pirate?

"Afraid? No. Intrigued, yes." He gave the surveyor his most charming smile, adding, "Whatever floats your boat, mate."

SEVENTY-SEVEN

THE BEST IDEA for clandestine sex was invented by the Scottish biographer, diarist, and notorious rake James Boswell, in eighteenth-century London. It is a prearranged meeting for that very purpose, a sexual liaison.

There is no pretense of fatuous flattery meant to lure the maiden to the boudoir. No, the looming act is a done deal conducted with perfect civility; two people agree, through some verbal or written dispatch, to meet for an amorous session. The meeting may be all over the calendar, every Wednesday morning or the third Friday of the month, but is usually routine and carries on as long as either party wishes. No doubt the practice has been around for centuries, but Boswell wrote about it in his memoir, *A London Journal*, published in 1762. He called the practice "assignation."

For much of his adult life, Shaun Malloy had been looking for convenient assignations. Married women were out. Back in third grade, Sister Thomasina told him and the other students at St. Cletus Grade School that it was a sin to covet your neighbor's spouse—good advice to this day, for married women sometimes have jealous husbands who own firearms. Malloy's assignations always involved single women, often professionals, who were too busy for a relationship. Yet, they enjoyed lovemaking, and if you met their criteria they would pencil you in their Day-Timer for an hour or two.

Lynette Hettenbach—Dr. Hettenbach—fit the bill perfectly, a tall brunette with flashing green eyes who looked great in black panties on Malloy's Murphy bed. Their assignation was an outcome of their first date, pizza and bocce on The Hill. It was she who boldly proposed it: Thursdays, six thirty, his place—she had a roomie—but they had to be done by eight because she didn't want to miss *Dallas*. For Malloy, this was a fantastic situation because, besides the good sex, she would bring appetizers for afterwards—cream cheese roll-ups in wafer-thin pastrami, anchovy olives, bacon-wrapped water chestnuts. One treat after another!

Her nude figure was there for the taking, full breasts gleaming with Mango Love Butter, the glistening snatch, and the long, creamy thighs. He was guiding his missile to the target, penetration imminent, when someone knocked.

He actually went to answer it; his mistake. It was Teri, with a dog on a leash. He asked her to come back later, like tomorrow. It had been nine days since the accident, and she had graduated from crutches to a gnarled wooden cane that looked like it had once belonged to an octogenarian Romanian peasant. She pushed him aside with the cane and told him to get over himself. The dog in tow, she limped over to the sofa and plopped down.

"Turning in early or going for the continental look?"

He smoothed a wrinkle on his white terrycloth bathrobe and chuckled. "It's a far cry from a satin smoking jacket, and it doesn't have a monogram. So, what's up?"

"We've got business." There was a sound in the hallway, and suddenly a naked woman appeared, facing them full frontal, one hand on her hip, glaring at them. Two seconds later, she went back in the bedroom and slammed the door behind her.

"New roommate?"

"We were playing Twister. Nice dog."

"It's yours. I got it for you at the pound. I think they were about to ax-fixiate—you know, gas the poor thing."

"I don't want a dog," said Malloy.

"Yes, you do. Look at him, he's adorable."

"Then you take him."

"Listen, Buster, I've been planning this for a while and today's the day. You need something to take your mind off VD. You're obsessed with it, it's borderline psychotic." He looked at the dog, short wiry fur, some kind of terrier. Somehow it looked familiar.

"Look at that face," urged Teri. "How can you resist?"

"Easy. A dog would complicate my life. They want in when they're out, and they want out when they're in. They have needs. I can barely take care of my own needs."

She tossed him something. He caught it, a stuffed squirrel. "That's his toy," she said, "and there's a bag of food in the truck. Don't make me beg, you big jerk. Just try it for a week, and if it doesn't work out then I'll take him back to the pound where they can kill him."

Until now, she had the dog restrained on a leash, but then she let him go. With some trepidation he approached Malloy, sniffed him tentatively, and with a chorus of pig-like grunts, began to hump his leg.

Then, he remembered.

LEXICON

OP	original patient
PMD	private medical doctor
ER	epidemiologic report
GC	gonorrhea
RE-I	re-interview of an OP
FTA	fluorescent treponemal antibody test
RPR	rapid plasma reagent – quick test for syphilis
CDC	Centers for Disease Control – Atlanta, Georgia

For their valuable reading of this manuscript, I would like to thank Tom Karsten, Dan Meins, and my wife, Mary. Thanks as well to Doug Leeker, Jack Hickok, Dr. Mary Case, Gene Mackey, Bill McClellan, and Rich Knaup. Special thanks to my editor, Michelle Donahue, who did a bang up job in removing the proverbial spinach from my teeth.

AUTHOR'S NOTE:

This book is a work of fiction. I could add the standard disclaimer that any resemblance to actual events or persons, living or dead, is entirely coincidental. But that is not entirely true. Fact is the story is loosely based on people and events from my own life. From 1978 to 1982, I was, like Shaun Malloy, a VD investigator with the Centers for Disease Control assigned to the Saint Louis City Health Department STD Clinic. Now that I've confessed that, let me say that *some* of the characters, incidents and dialogue are based in reality, having been recollected 35 years later and percolated through my imagination.

That five-year stint at the health department left a great impression on me regarding the damaging effects of venereal disease and the nearly impossible effort in trying to control it. It also made me aware of the "rich pageant" found on the streets in my adopted hometown of Saint Louis. I began this novel in the summer of 1983, and put it aside a few months later, the rigors of staff writer for a weekly entertainment tabloid taking up all my time. For three decades this book nagged to be finished, until finally, in late 2013, I began to write and ... well, here you have it.

WM. STAGE GETS PAID TO BE A NUISANCE, and he is good at it. A process server in St. Louis, bearing bad news to strangers—no wonder people shun him. Apart from this peculiar work, he has his own secret mission: To find his unknown biological family and have cocktails with them. His neurotic mother aids in the search, hoping to bolster her theory that the child she and her husband adopted has indeed become a sociopath. Meanwhile, Stage desperately seeks a woman with a "friendly womb". Why is he trying to reproduce like some rutting animal? It takes a series of painful and awakening life-lessons for him to find out.

"Stage weaves a journey filled with hilarious situations, tightly written with sharp one-liners."
— Jim Orso, *The St. Louis Beacon*

"... a poignant and illuminating work that walks a fine balance between side-splitting humour and philosophical seriousness."
— John Gillis, *The Inverness* [Nova Scotia] *Oran*

A PANHANDLER HAS A PLUM SITUATION in the city, until she takes in a stray dog. A process server is caught relieving himself in an alley, a seemingly mundane event that sets off a cascade of ever-worsening misfortunes. During their getaway, two bank robbers make a wrong turn and accidentally end up in St. Louis' Hibernian Parade—a serious problem since Black Irish are not welcome. These are some of the hapless characters in Not Waving, Drowning, Wm. Stage's new work containing eight short stories, all set in the St. Louis area. Drawn from people he has either known or observed, the characters in these stories ring true, evoking drollery, pathos, and wonder.

"Stage's stories are about real people who face up to life like the rest of us. No bullshit, no pretense, just the guts of what makes life work for the fringe players in this old river town."
    — Steve Means, *St. Louis Journalism Review*

"Stage has developed a prose style that is quite his own, and really can carry a story convincingly."
    — Chris King, *St. Louis Magazine*